Ali McNamara attributes her overactive imagination to one thing – being an only child. Time spent dreaming up adventures when she was young has left her with a head constantly bursting with stories waiting to be told. When stories she wrote for fun on Ronan Keating's website became so popular they were sold as a fundraising project for his cancer awareness charity, Ali realised that not only was writing something she enjoyed doing, but something others enjoyed reading too. Ali lives in Cambridgeshire with her family and two Labradors. When she isn't writing, she likes to travel, read and people-watch, more often than not accompanied by a good cup of coffee. Her dogs and a love of exercise keep her sane!

To find out more about Ali visit her website at
www.alimcnamara.co.uk
or follow her on Twitter: @AliMcNamara

Praise for *From Notting Hill With Love ... Actually*:

'Perfectly plotted, gorgeously romantic, has some great gags and leaves you with that lovely gooey feeling you get at the end of a good Hollywood rom com'
Lucy-Anne Holmes, author of *The (Im)Perfect Girlfriend*

The Summer of
Serendipity

Ali McNamara

sphere

SPHERE

First published in Great Britain in 2017 by Sphere

1 3 5 7 9 10 8 6 4 2

A CIP catalogue record for this book
is available from the British Library.

ISBN 978-0-7515-6620-8

Typeset in Caslon by M Rules
Printed and bound in Great Britain by
Clays Ltd, St Ives plc

Papers used by Sphere are from well-managed forests
and other responsible sources.

Sphere
An imprint of
Little, Brown Book Group
Carmelite House
50 Victoria Embankment
London EC4Y 0DZ

An Hachette UK Company

www.hachette.co.uk
www.littlebrown.co.uk

The Summer of Serendipity

Dear Readers,

Another book! And my second to be set on the west coast of Ireland.

I've had an idea for a book about a property seeker for some time, but until I went on a research trip to the Lakes of Killarney in County Kerry, and was totally inspired by both the scenery and the people I met there, it had never totally come together as a full story.

Many of the places and tales in this book are inspired by real places and genuine Irish legends, (there's a full list below if you're interested to know more about any of them.)

Lots of you have asked me so many times to write more about the Island of Tara, so you can find out what happened to Darcy, Dermot and the others from *Breakfast at Darcy's*. So I hope this new book, although not a sequel, will give you a taste of what's been going on since we were last there. And if you've not already read *Breakfast at Darcy's* perhaps it will persuade you to give it a try!

But before I go I need to thank a few people without whom the stories and ideas that swirl around in my mind would never make it into a book for you lovely readers to enjoy!

My wonderful agent, Hannah Ferguson, and everyone at the Hardman & Swainson literary agency.

My fab editor, Maddie West, and the whole team at Sphere and Little, Brown.

My brilliant family: my husband, Jim, and children, Rosie and Tom.

And of course my dogs, Oscar and Sherlock, who give me so much inspiration for all my canine characters!

Also thank you to CLIC Sargent auction winner, Kim Fenwick, for bidding to be in this book and providing me with such a wonderful name for Kiki!

Thanks to all these places for the inspiration:

- The fictional town of Ballykiltara is inspired by the very touristy, but very friendly town of Killarney in the west of Ireland. You can walk around the Killarney National Park and see stags and deer — just like Ren does. Or visit the lakes and take a mystical boat trip . . .
- The Stag Hotel was very much based on the Killarney Park Hotel; a beautiful place to stay with wonderful staff.
- Rafferty Castle, Sheehy Abbey and Rafferty Island were inspired by Ross Castle by

Lough Leane (The lake of learning is a real place!) and Innisfallen Island with its seventh-century monastery. A magical place if ever I've been to one!

I got the idea for the Annals of Tara and the Book of Tara from the real Annals of Innisfallen and the Book of Kells. You can see the Book of Kells in Trinity Library, Dublin.

I couldn't have written about Mac's riding stables and the horses there unless I'd taken a visit to the Killarney riding stables. My invigorating pony trek was one the highlights of my visit.

And the white stag? Look it up on the internet, it makes for interesting reading ...

Until the next time,
Ali xx

'Until one has loved an animal, a part of one's soul remains unawakened'

—ANATOLE FRANCE

One

'La, lala, la, la, la, la, laa!' my passenger sings happily as we drive in our hire car from the airport to our destination. 'Come on, Ren, join in, we're on our holibobs, ain't we? A bit of Kylie never hurt anyone. Well maybe Jason Donovan, but that's another story.'

I glance quickly across at her before putting the little Fiat into fourth gear. I've only driven it a few miles, and already I know it's going to give me trouble. Why didn't I invest in a better car, instead of trying to do things on the cheap, as always? But I don't know how long we're going to be here, and I don't want to go over the budget we've been given. The hotel we're heading towards is expensive enough as it is.

'I keep telling you, this is not a holiday, this is a business trip.'

'Yeah, yeah,' Kiki says, waving her hand dismissively at me. 'Whatever. I know we have stuff to do while we're here. But we've never been to Ireland, have we? It's new, it's exciting!'

I continue to concentrate on the road in front of me. Even though it's showing on our satnav as a main road, it's bumpy and bendy and I'm driving a strange car I haven't had time to get used to, in a country I don't know. I need to focus, not get into a discussion with my assistant about the merits of treating our trip in a professional manner.

Not that it would make the slightest difference. Kiki is her own woman – yes, that's a good way to describe her. To the casual observer – and a lot of people do observe her, especially men – she comes across as petite, pretty and perhaps a bit kooky, but her blonde bubbly exterior houses a razor-sharp mind. Kiki's organisational skills have made her indispensable to me and my hectic schedule.

'How far until we get to the hotel?' I ask her as we stop at some traffic lights and wait for an elderly woman to cross.

Kiki glances at the satnav. 'It says ten minutes.'

'Good. I could do with a rest.'

Our journey from Stansted Airport in Essex to Kerry Airport in the west of Ireland wasn't without incident. We'd been slightly delayed getting through security, after Kiki got stopped because the airport scanning machine beeped as she walked through it. The delay wasn't caused by the search so much as Kiki's insistence on flirting with a male security officer the whole time his female colleague was frisking her. While she slipped back into her dainty ballerina pumps, fluttering her eyelashes and practically arranging a first date with the security officer, I was getting all hot and bothered trying to shove my size eight feet back into my clumpy boots.

'There's a time and a place,' I'd muttered to her afterwards as we made our way through to the airport shops.

'For ...?' she'd enquired, pressing her button nose up against the window of Ted Baker.

'For flirting. And airport security is not it!'

'Oh, Ren, you're hilarious sometimes. The guy was cute.'

'The guy was married. Didn't you see his ring?'

To her credit, Kiki had looked genuinely horrified. 'Ooh no, I didn't, I was too busy looking into his gorgeous blue eyes.' Then she gave a shrug, adding, 'Ah well, you win some, you lose some!' before skipping happily into a Sunglasses Hut to begin trying on frames.

Kiki removes her new sunglasses and squints at the satnav. 'You need to go left in about a mile,' she says, looking back at the road.

'Yeah, I saw the sign,' I reply, 'which is more than you'll be doing, if you don't wear your specs.'

Though she can't see a thing without them, Kiki never wears her prescription glasses except in the office, where I'm the only one who'll see her. She prefers to sport designer sunglasses, like her latest purchase, which she insists on wearing even though the Irish skies above us are cloudy and grey.

We turn down a narrow road bordered with evergreen hedges on either side, and continue on our way.

'The hotel looked pretty cool on the Internet,' Kiki says, looking out of her window. 'I hope you like it.'

'I'm sure I will. You rarely let me down when it comes to hotels.'

Kiki's a whizz when it comes to booking hotels. Whatever budget we're given, she always comes up trumps – whether it be a Premier Inn that's had great reviews, or a sumptuous five-star hotel with all the facilities you could wish for, Kiki invariably finds the perfect place for us.

'It has wonderful reviews on Trip Advisor, people couldn't fault it, and that almost never happens.'

'Sounds good. I'm looking forward to seeing it.'

'We're booked in for five nights, but the receptionist I spoke to said they would be able to extend it if we needed to. She said to let her know if we thought we might want to stay for longer. How long do you think we'll need?'

I shrug as we pass by a field full of sheep grazing on the lush grass. 'You know as well as I do that we might find what we're looking for on the first day we're here, or it could take a week or more if it's complicated.'

'Hmm …' Kiki sits back in her seat and folds her arms. 'I know you like to get things done and dusted as quickly as possible, but I wouldn't mind staying for a bit longer. I've never been to Ireland and it would be good to see some of it while we're here.'

'I'm sure we'll see plenty. It almost never happens that we stumble upon the right place immediately. That's why people pay us to search for them.'

'Yes, but I know you, Ren – you excel at this. You'll probably find the house before we even get to the hotel!'

I turn and smile at her. Kiki may be young, but she really is the best assistant I've ever had. What's more, we've become good friends in the year I've known her.

'Look,' I say kindly, 'even if I do find something straight away, how about we stay on a few extra nights so you can see the area? You deserve a break.'

Kiki fist-pumps the air. 'Get in there!' she exclaims. 'Look,' she says, suddenly peering out of the front window, 'we've arrived!'

We drive past a sign that says:

BALLYKILTARA

CÉAD MÍLE FÁILTE

'What does that mean?' Kiki asks. 'Seed mill fail-tee?'

'No idea, it must be Gaelic.'

'I'll ask when we get to the hotel,' she says, keenly observing our new surroundings as we pass through the town. 'This is so cool. Look at all the Irish pubs selling Guinness.'

'I expect they sell more than that,' I say, smiling. 'Have you ever had Guinness, Kiki? It's foul-tasting stuff.'

'Nope, but I'm going to try it while I'm here.'

'Good luck with that. Now *where* is this hotel?'

Our satnav has helpfully taken us into the centre of the small town of Ballykiltara, but is refusing to find our hotel. Eventually, I pull over and Kiki hurries out to ask one of the locals the way. Except it proves difficult to find anyone local on the street, so she ends up accosting a pair of American tourists, who luckily for us are staying at our hotel and are able to give us directions.

It's a relief when we pull up on a long gravel drive in front of a large, sprawling country house hotel and immediately a young man rushes out to greet us.

'Welcome to The Stag,' he says in a broad Irish accent as I wind down the window. 'Can I help you with your bags?'

'Yes, that would be lovely,' I say, smiling at him.

'Now, let me take your keys – I'll park your car and bring your bags in to you in a few moments.'

I'm impressed. The hotel looked pleasant enough from the outside, but for some reason I hadn't expected this sort of service, usually only found at five-star establishments.

'Thank you ...' I glance at his name badge, '... Eddie,' I say, climbing out of the car and handing him the keys.

'Just head up there to reception,' he says, pointing up some steps, 'and Orla will be pleased to assist you.'

'Thank you.' Kiki and I grab our handbags from the back seat, and leaving our car in Eddie's capable hands, head up the cream stone steps to reception.

'I like Eddie,' Kiki giggles as we reach the large glass door at the top and it opens automatically for us. 'He's a cutie.'

I roll my eyes at her and then smile warmly at the receptionist watching us enter through the doors.

'Welcome to The Stag Hotel,' Orla says in a soft Irish accent. 'Do you have reservations?'

'Yes,' Kiki says, taking over her organisational role. 'In the name of Parker – Serendipity Parker.'

'What a wonderful name,' Orla says as she scans the screen in front of her.

'Thank you, but I prefer Ren,' I tell her, glancing at Kiki. I'd told her many a time to book things with my shortened name. But Kiki thought Serendipity was a wonderful name, and delighted in using it when she could. 'It's easier.'

'Sure,' Orla says, glancing up at me with the look of one who has seen many an unusual name in her time. 'Now, we have you down for one deluxe twin room for five nights, with the possibility of extending your stay. Is that correct?'

'Yes, that's perfect.'

When Kiki had first come to work for me we'd always booked separate rooms on our business trips. But we found we always ended up spending all our time in one room – discussing – or, as Kiki liked to call it, gossiping about – the day's events. So in the end we decided to use the money we saved by booking one room to go for an upgrade instead.

'Grand. If I can take a swipe of a credit card?' Orla asks.

Kiki pulls our company card from her purse.

Orla glances at it before putting it into the machine. 'Is your stay for business or pleasure?' she asks without it seeming an intrusive question.

'Pleasure,' I say at the same time as Kiki says, 'Business.'

'Bit of both,' I hurriedly say when Orla looks intrigued.

'A good mix.' She smiles as she hands me two key cards wrapped in a small paper wallet. 'Your room is on the third floor – number seventy-eight. Now, would you like someone to show you up there?'

'Thank you, but we'll be fine.'

'Eddie will be up presently with your bags, and if there's anything further I can assist you with, don't hesitate to contact me.' She points towards the lobby. 'The lift is through there, on the right.'

'Thanks,' I say, thinking to myself what lovely staff this hotel has. Kiki has done exceedingly well this time.

We head through a chic yet cosy lobby with plush red velvet sofas set in front of a big cheery, log-burning fire that's lit, even though this is early May. I can imagine guests snuggled round the fire in the winter months, drinking brandy and talking about the day's events.

The small lift comes almost immediately, and we step inside.

'You insisted to me this was a business trip when we were in the car,' Kiki complains as soon as the lift doors shut. 'And there's you saying we're here for pleasure!'

'It is business. But we don't want everyone knowing why

7

we're here, do we? You know how it is: people in these types of communities tend to close ranks and become very tight-lipped if they think strangers are going to try and take something that's theirs.'

'But we're not trying to take something. We're trying to find something – a house for our client, Mr Dempsey.'

'Yes, but not every house I find is for sale, is it? Sometimes, the current owner has to be persuaded to sell.'

'Usually with money,' Kiki sighs as we exit the lift and look for our room. 'I love this job, you know that, Ren,' she whispers as we walk along the stylishly decorated corridor. 'Best thing I've ever done. But it saddens me that everything is always about money in the end. Where are people's morals, their disciples?'

I try not to laugh. Kiki was being her usual earnest self; it was one of the things I liked about her. But she was also prone to muddling her words, and would often ask the daftest of questions, that made sense to Kiki, but seemed hilarious to the rest of us.

'You mean their *principles*,' I correct her gently as we arrive at our room. I pause before entering. 'As it happens, I agree with you. I wish people would follow their heart instead of looking to make a quick profit. But, sadly, money talks, and that money not only pays our wages, it will help us find Mr Dempsey the perfect house with the perfect Irish views.'

Kiki nods as I run one of the key cards through the scanner. Then as we open the door we both gasp at the exquisite room laid out before us.

'Well, if this is money talking, then I'm all for it on this occasion!' Kiki announces before launching herself across the room on to one of the sumptuous double beds.

And as I look around the spotless room at the ornate gilt-framed mirrors and luxurious coordinating gilt and purple décor, I have to agree with her: this is a special room. But, not for the first time since we've arrived here, a strange feeling in the pit of my stomach tells me the room's not the only thing that's going to be special about this trip.

Two

As soon as we've unpacked, we head out into the town of
Ballykiltara for some basic supplies like water, and the Diet
Pepsi Kiki can't live without. As we walk through the centre
of town we pass many pubs, some with traditional names like
Molly Malone's and Fitzgerald's, and some slightly odder,
like The Raven's Knowledge. The one thing they all have in
common is signboards advertising live Irish music and traditional pints of Guinness. The shopfronts between the many
pubs are occupied by gift shops selling any item you could
ever possibly want with a shamrock, a sheep or sometimes both
embellished upon them. At last, hidden away amongst all this,
we find a small food store selling basic necessities.

'This place is soo cute!' Kiki declares as we head back
towards the hotel, having decided that on our first night in a
strange town a meal in the hotel bar will be our best bet. 'I
love it!'

'You love every new place we visit,' I tell her, enjoying Kiki's characteristic display of enthusiasm.

'I know, but this place feels special, doesn't it? It's enchanted – or even magical!'

I look around me as we enter the hotel grounds. 'Yes, I suppose it does have a certain charm. But I think magical is a bit strong.'

'Oh, puddings!' Kiki declares. 'I won't stand for your dourness today, Ren Parker. I like Ballykissangel, and I won't hear you say otherwise!'

'Ballykiltara,' I correct her. '*Ballykissangel* was a TV programme set in Ireland, about an English priest.'

Kiki thinks about this, 'Oh yes, you're right – that guy from *DCI Banks* was in it, wasn't he? He was in that one set in Africa too.'

'That was called *Wild at Heart*, and the actor's name is Stephen Tomkinson.'

'He's the chappie! We should get you on a pub quiz team, Ren, you're brilliant at common knowledge.'

'General knowledge.'

'Yes, that too.'

'Good evening, ladies.' Eddie pops up from behind a bush with some garden shears clutched in his hands.

'Hello, Eddie!' Kiki sings, waving at him. 'Isn't it a beautiful evening!'

Eddie looks up at the now darkening skies. 'It is indeed, if you like to get wet. There will be rain within the hour if I'm not mistaken.'

Kiki looks up. 'Oh, really? What a shame.'

'No, miss, we like it round here – overnight, at least, so it doesn't affect the tourists like. We're not called the Emerald Isle for nothing.'

'Oh, I thought you were called that because lots of emeralds had been found here over the years.'

Eddie looks at Kiki to see if she's joking, but quickly realises she's not.

'Excuse my learned friend here,' I say, leading Kiki in the direction of reception. 'She's the one who's a bit green.' I wink at Eddie, and he nods knowingly back.

'Why *is* it called the Emerald Isle then?' Kiki whispers furiously as we enter the hotel.

'Because of all the grass,' I whisper back, smiling sweetly at a new receptionist – a man this time – who's standing at the desk watching us with interest.

'*Drugs?*' Kiki asks, a horrified expression crossing her face.

'No, you fool. *Grass*, the sort that grows in the ground!'

Kiki looks relieved. 'Well, that makes sense,' she says matter-of-factly, immediately dismissing her faux pas. 'Now, shall I take these things up to our room while you get us a table in the bar? I'll try that Guinness, since you're buying.'

I watch her for a moment as she heads towards the lift.

I look at the receptionist again, and notice for the first time he's not wearing a uniform like the other staff I've seen about the hotel so far. Instead he wears black jeans and a casual red checked shirt as he stands behind the desk, an amused expression on his face.

'You're eating in our bar tonight?' he asks professionally, instead of the actual question he likely wanted an answer to: *Who is your crazy friend?*

'Yes please, if that's OK?'

'Sure, go on in. We're not too busy this evening. Midweek tends to be pretty quiet; we get much busier over the weekend.'

I pause for a moment, fascinated by his accent. It definitely has an Irish ring to it, but it's different to Orla and Eddie's, or even the lady that served us in the shop just now. It's ... Oh, I can't think what it is at the moment, but I will.

'We have a fancier restaurant too, if that's the type of thing you're after?' he continues. I look for his name tag – all the other staff seem to wear one, but this guy doesn't. The only thing covering his well-developed chest is his shirt. I realise I'm gazing a little too long at it and I look up swiftly. 'But between you and I,' he leans in towards me as if he's sharing a secret, 'you'll get more craic in the bar.'

'Sure ...' I murmur, captivated momentarily by his bright green eyes that twinkle like emeralds under the bright reception lights. 'I mean, yes, thank you, we want a bit of crack.'

An impish grin breaks out across his face; it's a perfect match for his mischievous eyes.

Oh Lord! I hurriedly try and recover my composure. 'Sorry, I didn't mean— I know what you meant when you said craic – a good time, right? We definitely want a good time.'

'Don't we all?' he winks, but he's more cheeky Irish chappie than leery lech when he does.

I give in and smile. 'I'm making a bit of an idiot of myself, aren't I?' I hold out my hand formally. 'Ren Parker.'

He takes my hand over the desk with a firm grip, and shakes it solidly. I'm secretly pleased. I make it my policy never to trust anyone with a weak, limp handshake.

'Pleased to meet you, Ren. Finn Cassidy, at your service. I'm the manager of the hotel.'

'Ah, I wondered why you weren't in the same uniform as the others.'

He grins. 'They keep trying – but I just keep resisting. Can't be flapping around like a trussed up penguin now, can I?'

13

I smile as another man arrives behind the desk, looking very penguin-like in a black three-piece suit with a crisp white shirt.

'Donal,' Finn announces, 'meet our new guest, Ren Parker.'

'Welcome to The Stag,' Donal says, giving the tiniest of bows. 'I'm guest services manager here, so anything you need or want during your stay, I'm the man to see.'

'Thank you, Donal. I'll be sure to do that.'

'Now, where are you eating tonight?' Donal enquires. 'I can recommend some wonderful restaurants in the town.'

'Oh, we're eating here tonight. In the bar,' I explain.

'Ah well, that's a good choice too. I don't know if Finn told you, but we have a beautiful restaurant in addition to our bar. It looks out over the hills, and one of the lakes. It's a gorgeous view, so it is.'

'He did, thank you. But your bar will be fine. My friend wants to try her first pint of Guinness tonight – I doubt that will fit too well in your restaurant.'

'Ah, a pint of the black stuff, another good choice.' Donal folds his hands in front of him and rests them on his stomach approvingly. 'And will you be joining her?'

I screw up my face. 'Sadly no, it's not one of my favourite drinks.'

'Have you ever had it in Ireland before?' Finn asks. 'There's a huge difference in the taste here. I don't know why, when it's exported all around the world. But you can't beat a pint on home soil.'

'No, I haven't, this is my first time in Ireland.'

Orla joins us at reception. She smiles at me.

'Thanks for covering, Finn,' she says. 'Sarah's kicking off in the kitchen – something about the wrong meat being delivered.

14

She nearly swung for Eddie with a meat cleaver. I think you'd better go and sort it out.'

Finn sighs, and gives me an apologetic smile. 'The joys of being in charge!' he says ruefully. 'Head through to the bar, Ren,' he gestures towards the entrance. 'I'll come and pour you that Guinness in a moment, if you're game?'

I nod, grateful to be allowed to escape. I'm heading through the foyer in the direction of the bar when Kiki steps out of the lift.

'Aren't you even in there yet?' she asks, falling into step beside me. I notice she's changed her shoes from the trainers she went out in earlier to a pair of purple suede pixie boots. 'I thought you'd have got the first round in by now. What's been keeping you?'

I glance back towards the desk in time to see Finn striding towards a door marked *Private*.

'Oh, nothing much,' I reply as we enter the cosy bar with another log fire burning merrily away at one end. 'Nothing much at all ...'

Three

Finn is right – Guinness *is* better in Ireland.

As promised, when he's dealt with the crisis in the kitchen, he arrives behind the bar, and I see him actively seek me out as he scans the room. He smiles when his eyes rest upon me, and he holds up an empty pint-glass with the Guinness logo etched across the top.

I shrug and hold up my own almost empty wine glass.

'*Who* is that?' Kiki demands as she watches our silent exchange. 'He's a bit of all right!'

'That's Finn, he's the hotel manager,' I reply, ignoring her innuendo.

'*Nice* … but why isn't he wearing a uniform like the others?'

'I'm not sure. I think he likes to be his own man.'

'He sure is …' Kiki murmurs dreamily. 'Oh look, he's coming over.'

Finn crosses the bar to greet us. 'Just letting your pints of Guinness settle,' he says.

'Ooh, about time,' Kiki replies before I can speak. 'Ren says it's like drinking cat pee, but I can't wait to try it.'

Finn looks with amusement at Kiki while I squirm.

'I did not say that,' I tell him, feeling my cheeks redden. 'I don't care for it, that's all. I believe it might be an acquired taste.'

'Talking of acquired tastes,' Kiki says, leaping to her feet and holding her hand out to Finn. 'I'm Kiki. Kiki Fisher.'

'Welcome to The Stag Hotel, Kiki Fisher,' Finn says, taking her hand. 'I hope you're enjoying your stay so far?'

'It's ace, Finn. This is quite the hotel you have here.'

'Well, it's not exactly mine. I only manage it for the owners, the O'Connells. They own Tara, too – the island across the water. You might have seen it as you drove in?'

'I do remember seeing something out there,' I say, remembering. 'But I was concentrating pretty hard on the road; the car we've hired isn't the best. They own an island, that's very cool.'

'Indeed it is.' He looks back at the bar. 'Right, let me get you those pints, they should have a nice, calm head on them by now.'

Kiki looks at me with delight as she sits down again. 'Just when I thought this hotel couldn't get any better – another hot Irishman appears!'

'Stop it now,' I tell her, a tad jealous of her self-confidence. 'He's probably married.'

'He doesn't have a ring.'

'A girlfriend then.'

Kiki looks across at Finn, who's carrying two full pints of Guinness over to our table.

17

'Only one way to find out,' she whispers, as Finn arrives and carefully places our glasses on two mats.

Before I have a chance to protest, she pats the velvet-covered stool next to her and says, 'Finn, why don't you join us for a bit? I'd love to hear all about what you get up to here at the hotel ... ' It's all I can do to stop myself rolling my eyes as she adds coyly, ' ... and in your spare time too.'

'Ah, I'd love to, ladies, but I have to go and check on some things back at reception,' he says in a regretful voice, but I suspect he's only being polite. 'Try your Guinness,' he says, gesturing to our glasses, 'I think you might like it.' He looks at me: 'I'll see you around – maybe tomorrow?'

'Yes, we're here for a few nights.'

'Good,' he says, giving us the briefest of farewell nods before making his way back through the bar and out the door.

'He fancies you,' Kiki says matter-of-factly as we watch him leave.

'*What?* Where on earth have you got that idea from?'

'I just know,' she says, lifting up her pint of Guinness and inspecting the white froth that rests on top of the rich black liquid below. 'Call it my fifth sense.'

'Sixth sense,' I correct. 'But we never even found out if he has a girlfriend or,' I add as another thought occurs, 'boyfriend ... '

Kiki, about to take a sip of her Guinness, splutters the froth over the side of her glass, so several tiny spots of white now decorate our table along with our unwrapped cutlery still waiting to be used, and the tiny posy of flowers that decorates every table in the bar.

'No,' she says firmly, recovering her composure while at the same time wiping a thin white line of Guinness from her top lip. 'Impossible.'

'Why is it?' I tease. I've had conversations like this with Kiki before. She's always adamant that a man she finds attractive can never be gay.

'He's far too macho, for one thing. Not that gay men can't be, of course – remember Lucien from the gym? He was ripped!' She shakes her head. 'But in this instance, definitely not.'

'Perhaps you mean masculine,' I ask, hiding a smile, 'rather than macho?'

'Nope, this time I actually do mean the word I've said. Finn is macho, like …' she struggles to find an analogy. 'Like, can't you imagine him outside in the fresh air, digging a field or something, looking like he did just now?'

I think about this while she continues:

'His strong muscular body, hot and sweaty as he toils under the midday sun …' She holds her hand up, anticipating my interruption. 'He stops for a moment,' she resumes, lost in her fantasy, 'and wipes the sweat from his brow, then he pushes his strong but sensitive fingers through his mane of jet-black hair, before eventually deciding it's too hot, and he simply must remove his red tartan shirt …'

I have to admit, Kiki got me going for a few seconds there. The image of Finn she'd conjured up wasn't an unpleasant one. She's right: he's the archetypal tall, dark and handsome Irish man. An Irish client once told me there are two types of Irishmen – tall and dark, or small and ginger, depending on what clan they'd descended from. I wasn't sure that was exactly true, but Finn definitely fitted into the first category.

'His shirt isn't tartan,' I correct her. 'The Americans would probably call it plaid, we just call it checked.'

'All that and you correct me about the pattern on his shirt!' Kiki asks, astonished. 'What about his hot, sweaty body?'

'Enough of this,' I tell her before she gets going again. 'We're here to work, remember, not make up stories—'

'Fantasies.' Kiki corrects me this time.

I eye her. 'Make *things* up about the hotel staff.'

'I don't want to make things up about all the staff, only Finn.'

'What about Eddie?' I ask. 'He's cute.'

Kiki considers this. 'Yeah, I suppose, if you like that type.' She lifts up her Guinness and takes a sip, and I watch as her face crumples. 'Ewww! What is this – toilet cleaner?' she asks, pulling a sour face.

'Told you,' I say, lifting my own glass. I hesitantly take a sip. But instead of the bitter, unpleasant flavour I'm expecting my taste buds to reject, they seem to positively rejoice at the nectar I'm dousing them with.

'Are you actually enjoying that?' Kiki asks, as I take another sip and a satisfied sigh escapes from my mouth.

'I actually am. Finn was right, it does taste different here. In fact it's rather nice.'

Kiki shakes her head. 'I think your judgement is being swayed by a pretty face. If Finn hadn't served us, you wouldn't have liked it anywhere near as much.'

I vehemently shake my head, and put my glass back down on the table.

'You know better than that,' I say in a stern voice. 'My judgement is never, ever swayed by a man. Not now. Not ever. Do I make myself clear?'

Kiki, knowing she's touched a sore spot, nods. 'Sorry.'

'It's fine.' I take another sip of my Guinness, and feel it soothe me. 'I'm sorry, Kiki,' I apologise, 'I shouldn't have snapped at you. Let's forget all about men for the moment, eh? We don't need them on this trip.'

Kiki half-heartedly nods in agreement.

'What we do need, however, is to do our jobs and find *the* perfect house with *the* best view for Mr Dempsey, and remember what we're really here for.'

Four

After breakfast the next morning – a delicious buffet of every breakfast item you could ever imagine – Kiki and I head out in our hire car in search of properties that might fit our client's idea of his dream holiday home.

I'd never set out to become a property seeker, far from it. As is often the way in life, I'd fallen into my line of work accidentally. It all started when a friend was struggling to find her perfect home. Fiona had complained to me over the phone several times that she couldn't find a house that had everything her family required in a property, and they were thinking of staying put rather than settle for second best. I had been horrified to hear this, partly because I felt sorry for them – they'd been trying to make the move back down south for over a year since Fiona's husband's company had relocated to London – but selfishly because I wanted Fiona, Simon and their two small children (my godchildren) to be closer to me.

So I'd made it my personal project to find them their ideal home. I'd needed something to take my mind off things – my own life had been pretty dismal back then – and searching for and then visiting properties before I passed them on to Fiona, seemed a kind of therapy.

After weeks of trawling estate agent's websites, checking out auctions and social media, I found them the house of their dreams. To my delight, they moved in a few months later. The buzz I got from their tangible relief and ensuing happiness in their new home was *the* best feeling, and gave me the boost I so desperately needed. Through word of mouth, other desperate couples began asking me to do something similar for them, and every success resulted in more people being sent in my direction, until eventually I decided to take the plunge, give up my job as a freelance journalist, and become a professional property seeker. I called my new company The Search for Serendipity, a play on my own name, and the happy accident it sometimes can be when you match a person to the house they've always longed for.

That was six years ago, and the company's still going strong. We've developed a nice little sideline as location scouts, with TV and film companies hiring us to find interiors where they can shoot scenes for films or television programmes. But most of our clients are individuals in search of residential homes, or luxury holiday homes – as in the case of the search that had brought us to Ireland.

The company is made up of me, Kiki and Doris, our receptionist, who deals with all the emails, phone calls and letters while we're out of the office on our searches. In the past, I've tried hiring other seekers when the volume of jobs coming into the office got too much for me to handle on my own, but I've yet to find anyone who shares the knack I seem to have for matching the perfect property with its ideal client. So these days we keep our business small, serving a select few clients at any one time. Of the many requests that come pouring into the office, I'm lucky enough to be able to pick the ones that appeal to me, the ones where I feel a certain empathy with the client, and turn the rest away.

'So, where are we starting this morning?' Kiki asks, unfolding a map and setting it on the dashboard in front of her.

I'm driving again today. I preferred it that way; I felt more in control. Plus, when we'd looked into insuring Kiki to drive the hire car too, we'd found it to be ridiculously expensive, because she was still under twenty-five.

'I thought we'd start with a drive around the Ring of Tara,' I tell her as I pull out of the hotel gates. 'I've already plotted it on the satnav.'

'Sounds good,' Kiki says, settling back into her seat. 'You've properties to visit on the way, I assume?'

While Kiki handles all the day-to-day organisation of the company, I like to do all the property hunting myself. I've always been *particular*, as Doris puts it – or *anal-retentive*, according to Kiki – when it comes to work. I prefer the term fastidious; I want everything done just right. And if I'm doing it myself, there's no danger of anyone letting me down.

'Of course I have properties,' I tell Kiki, 'on paper. I'm not sure any of them will be right for Mr Dempsey, but you never know until you see them for yourself, do you?'

'And you'll be keeping your eye on all the others we pass, eh?' Kiki says knowingly. 'Just in case … Gum?' She offers me a stick.

I shake my head. 'No thanks. You know on spec is how we find a lot of places – especially the expensive ones.'

'Yeah, like I said yesterday, money talks.' Kiki unwraps her stick of gum and pops it in her mouth.

We continue heading out of town and pick up one of the west coast of Ireland's biggest tourist trails: the Ring of Tara, a long circular route that we were promised would provide us with some fantastic scenery along the way.

'Can we have the radio on, Ren?' Kiki asks after we've been travelling about five minutes. 'It's awfully dull without it.'

'Gee, thanks!' I reply as I twist the knob on the dashboard. 'And I love your company too!'

'Ah, you know I don't mean anything by it,' Kiki says good-naturedly. 'I like my music, that's all.'

She fiddles with the tuning dial until she comes to a station she finds acceptable, and immediately the car is filled with the voice of Ed Sheeran.

I listen to Kiki sing along for a few moments, and I'm amused at her incorrect lyrics.

'I think you'll find that's *seventy* he's singing he'll love her to,' I tell her kindly, 'not seven*teen*.'

Kiki turns to look at me in astonishment. 'Do you know, I've always wondered why he sang that?' She nods her head approvingly. 'That song makes a lot more sense now.'

I shake my head and smile as I look out at the beautiful countryside we're driving through. Even though the roads are narrowing and becoming extremely twisty and turning as we begin to climb higher, I'm still managing to look out of my window occasionally at the scenery we pass and I'm beginning to understand why Mr Dempsey – or Ryan, as he insists I call him – is so keen for us to find him a holiday home here.

'Ah, Miss Parker,' he'd enthused when he first came to see us in the office, 'there's nothing like it in the world. From the rolling green hillsides with majestic mountains soaring up above them into the heavens, to the soft quiet valleys with their gentle streams trickling through their heart, the Kerry countryside has always been special, and will always mean home to me.'

I think about this now as I drive, and Kiki hums away to the radio. Home is a peculiar word, one which most people use to mean their current place of residence. But in the job I do, I find it's often used the way Ryan Dempsey used it – a place where that person felt contented; a place where they felt happy, safe and secure; a place they felt truly at peace with life.

I've never known anywhere like that. I've had homes in the sense of places I've lived in; flats, houses, the Victorian terrace in London I live in now. But the closest I've ever come to calling somewhere home in the sense Ryan meant . . . would have to be my parents' house in the remote part of Northumberland I grew up in. But even that wasn't home any more; not since Dad took early retirement and him and Mum decided to move to Spain. Northumberland, although beautiful, couldn't compete with the lure of guaranteed sunshine all year round.

Something about the Irish countryside I'm driving through now reminds me a little of Northumberland, and that thought makes me smile.

'What ya smiling about?' Kiki asks. 'Are you thinking about Finn?'

'I most certainly am not!' I say, shaking myself from my thoughts. 'Whatever gave you that idea?'

'Your smile. I don't see you smile like that too often. It was sort of warm and dreamy.'

'Well, I can assure you I was not thinking about our hotel manager.' I glance at a signpost as we pass, our first stop shouldn't be too far from here. 'I was thinking about the countryside here; how pretty it is.'

'Yeah, right.'

'I was. It reminds me of where I grew up.'

'Bambi Castle?'

'*Bamburgh*. And we didn't actually live in the castle, we lived not far from there.'

Kiki looks out of the window. 'I guess both places have lots of hills.'

'No, it's not that, it's . . . something else.' I can't quite put my finger on what that thing is, though. 'Oh, I think we've arrived at the first place.'

We stop in the middle of a village filled with whitewashed stone cottages, and I pull up in front of a post office, which because it's on the Ring of Tara also doubles as a gift shop.

'Right, we can walk from here,' I tell Kiki. 'Then I can explore some of the village along the way and see if it's suitable.'

We grab our bags, lock up the car, and set off in search of our first house.

As I had expected from my research on the area, the village is tiny. Aside from the post-office-cum-gift-shop, the only other public building is a pub.

First box ticked, I think silently as we head out of the village along a narrow road up a hill towards the first house I wanted to view; Ryan had requested a pub nearby.

'How far along here is it?' Kiki asks, squinting up at the sun which has decided to make a fleeting appearance through the many clouds filling the sky this morning.

'Not far; but it's going to be a bit remote – after all, that's what Mr Dempsey wants.'

A few minutes' walk along the tree-lined road, we spot a *For Sale* sign poking out of a high hedge.

'This must be it,' I say, hurrying along the road a bit further. I pause before I open the gate, and turn to look out in the direction the house faces. The information I'd been sent by the estate agent said the house had views over rolling green valleys, down towards a lake. But from where I'm standing, all I can see are tall, bushy trees. I look up towards the house; it's set high up on a steep slope, so maybe there are better views from the windows? At the very least, the upstairs ought to have a clear view.

I've been informed the house is currently uninhabited after the previous owner defaulted on their mortgage. This generally makes my job much easier, because in return for a quick sale it's often possible to negotiate a lower price for my client. It also means we can take a preliminary look around without having to explain ourselves to an estate agent or householder, so I open the gate and set off towards the house with Kiki in tow, eager to see what we might find.

'Nah,' I say, shaking my head after we've spent a few minutes in the derelict garden. 'It's not right. Even from the upstairs windows, you're not going to get a clear view down to that valley – and that's the main thing Ryan – I mean, Mr Dempsey – wants: a fabulous view, preferably with a lake.'

'You can call him Ryan,' Kiki says, pulling a pair of Ray Bans from her bag and putting them on. 'You don't have to be all official with me. But I agree: from the moment we got out of the car, this place didn't feel right to me.'

I smile. Even I can't tell that early whether a property is going to be right or not.

'Well, you were correct,' I tell her. 'Let's head back to the car: we've plenty of other places to be stopping at on the way.'

So we set off again, but it wasn't to be our lucky morning. On paper, the houses I'd picked out had promised so much, but each one turned out to be lacking – often in more than one respect. None offered the combination of amenities, views and local facilities that Ryan Dempsey was looking for. But I'm used to disappointments of this nature; sometimes it can take weeks to find the right property, and even then I can never be 100 per cent certain the client will agree.

Undaunted, we stop for lunch at a pub by a bubbling river, taking a seat outside at a wooden picnic table to make the most of the sun, now that the clouds have started to disperse around it.

'Not a great start, eh?' Kiki says after we've ordered our food from a jolly woman wearing a navy-and-white striped apron.

'No, but I never expect it to be. It's so rare we find something quickly.'

'And even if we do find something, you always spend ages checking all the others out anyway.'

'I like to cover all eventualities, in case we find something even better.'

Kiki looks around her at the other people having lunch. There are a couple of walkers taking a break from their travels through the Irish hills, but most of the tables appear to be occupied by holidaymakers in trainers, T-shirts and the occasional fleece top.

'Popular place, this,' Kiki says, turning back to me.

'Yes, the Ring of Tara is very popular with tourists. We've been lucky not to get caught behind any of the coaches that cruise around here every day.'

'I wonder why Ryan is so desperate to come and live here?'

I'm about to correct her – regardless of his invitation to address him as Ryan, he's a client and should therefore be Mr Dempsey – but I decide it's not worth it. 'Isn't it obvious, after what you've seen this morning? It's beautiful.'

'Yeah, I can see that, but it's so remote, isn't it? I mean, Ballykiltara doesn't seem too bad, but there aren't a lot of shops – and I don't mean tourist shops, I mean Top Shop, H&M, the occasional Ted Baker, that kind of thing.'

I smile at her across the table. 'Maybe there's no need for those types of outlets here. Maybe the locals have everything they want on their doorstep without the need for fashion boutiques.'

Kiki thinks about this. 'They probably do a lot of online shopping,' she says matter-of-factly.

'Now,' the lady in the apron is back. 'Your food won't be long, girls, but here's your drinks to be going on with.' She places two Diet Cokes on the table in front of us and smiles. 'On your holidays, are you?' she asks, then she sees my black leather notebook with some of my estate agent papers poking out of it. 'Oh, are you here looking for a house?' she asks, her eyes wide.

I hurriedly tuck the papers back into my book. 'Yes, sort of.'

'Ah, there's a lot of lovely houses around these parts that would suit the two of you. Property around here don't go for so much these days.' She looks between us and lowers her voice. 'Couple, are you?'

'No,' I say, at the same time as Kiki says, 'Yes.'

'Ah, don't be shy about it,' she tells me. 'We get all sorts around here, you know. Everybody's welcome in Kerry. Back with your food in a bit, dears.' And she winks as she heads off to serve another table.

'Why did you say we were a couple?' I hiss, picking up my drink.

'Because *you* said we had to remain undercover so as not to attract suspicion from the locals,' Kiki says, doing the same.

'I said we shouldn't tell anyone what we were doing, not that we had to be undercover!'

Kiki shrugs. 'Same thing. Besides, I think we'd make a great couple – if we were that way inclined.'

I shake my head dismissively at her.

'Oh, not good enough for you, am I? I see . . . like that, is it?' she pretends to huff.

'You love men far too much to even play-act at this,' I tell her, opening up my book to check where we're due to stop this afternoon. I've noted down addresses for a couple of properties that I have high hopes for.

'Yeah, I do, don't I?' Kiki concludes, sitting back and sipping at her Coke. 'It ain't ever going to happen, is it? Sorry, Ren, I'm a metrosexual woman through and through.'

'Heterosexual,' I correct her. 'And anyway, after this afternoon we might not have to worry about pretending to be anything we're not.' I tap the cover of my book. 'If one of these houses is the one, it will make life so much easier. It always does if the house we find is actually for sale.'

'And if it's not?'

'Then we'll cross that tricky little bridge when we come to it.'

Kiki grins. 'It's those tricky little bridges I enjoy crossing the most.'

I smile at her. Kiki might relish the challenge of persuading a home-owner to sell when they'd never even thought about it, but I didn't. I much preferred to find the perfect property in the simplest way I could. Crossing tricky bridges usually involved dealing with awkward people, and dealing with awkward people usually meant trouble. Especially for me.

Five

Our luck doesn't improve in the afternoon. The viewings go the same way as the ones this morning: each house is lacking some vital detail that would make it the one for Mr Dempsey. So we head back to the hotel to get freshened up after our long day exploring the Ring of Tara.

Even though I've been the one doing the driving, it's Kiki who's crashed out sound asleep on the bed when I emerge from the bathroom. Feeling much more awake than I had done when we arrived back at our room, I sit on my bed for a few minutes thumbing through the pages of houses we still have to view.

I knew when I accepted this job that it wasn't going to be easy. Ryan Dempsey had set out very precise criteria for his ideal holiday and future retirement home, and I had wondered from the start whether I was taking on an impossible task. But I like a challenge, and I'd never searched for a property in Ireland before. I'd once found someone a little flat in Dublin online, but this was my first time 'out in the field' in the heart of the Irish countryside.

Looking across at Kiki, still fast asleep, I begin to feel a little drowsy myself. The hotel room is warm and comfortable, but I know if I fall asleep now I'll find it hard to sleep tonight. Sleep and I have never been the best of friends, especially when I'm staying away from home – an occupational hazard in this job. So I decide to take a walk in the hotel grounds, reasoning that should keep me occupied and awake until Kiki's finished her nap. Then the two of us can head out into the town for the evening.

Reception is quiet as I arrive downstairs. I wave casually to Orla, standing behind the desk looking at her computer screen, then make my way outside and around the back of the hotel to the small garden we can see from our room.

The garden is pretty, and as I wander along gravel paths I find rose bushes, cheery beds of spring flowers, and magnolia trees in full bloom. When I reach the bottom, I notice a small wooden gate in the red-brick wall that surrounds the garden. There's no sign marking it as private, so I reach for the handle.

I swing open the gate to find a narrow path with high hedges either side. It leads away from the hotel, but more than that I can't tell, because the hedges block my view of what lies at the end of the path.

I pause to think for a moment. Kiki will likely be asleep for some time, so why not do a little exploring? My decision made, I close the gate behind me and begin to follow the path.

As I approach the end of the dusty track, I can see what looks like a farmyard in front of me. I'm about to step out from my enclosed walkway to investigate when a small red ball rolls past the entrance, followed by a large dog in hot pursuit. The dog leaps on the ball, picks it up and is about to make its way back towards its hidden owner, when it spots me. It immediately drops the ball and begins barking.

'Hey, fella,' I say, holding up my hand to try and calm it down. 'It's OK, I'm friendly, honestly.'

But the dog keeps barking.

'Fergus!' I hear a male voice shout. 'What are you ... oh, it's you,' the voice says, as a familiar face pokes around the end of the hedge. 'Fergus, stop it. Ren is friend not foe.' Finn comes into full view, and he reaches down to pat the now much friendlier-looking dog – probably some sort of cross-breed by the look of his shaggy, multicoloured coat.

'Sorry,' I apologise. 'I probably shouldn't even be here. But there wasn't a private sign on the gate back there.'

'No, yer all right, that gate is a shortcut to the stables.' He raises his arm, and I move forward so I can see what he's pointing to.

What I'd thought was a farmyard when I glimpsed it through the narrow opening is in fact a large square yard. Flanking the yard on three sides are rows of stable blocks, most of which are occupied by horses, who are all watching me with interest as I stare at them.

'Oh wow,' I say, as I look around. 'I didn't expect this.'

'No, not many of the hotel guests do. The main entrance is off the road, up there –' He points again. 'The one that runs into Ballykiltara.'

'And what sort of horses are they?' I ask, looking at the many heads peering over stable doors.

'Oh, the usual four-legged kind.'

I glance at Finn. He's watching me, obviously amused.

'Ha ha, very funny. I mean, are they race horses?'

35

He smiles again. 'No, they're only ponies. This is a riding stable, we take people out for treks – holidaymakers much of the time, but we have our regulars too.'

'You run this as well?' I ask, surprised he's involved in this as well as the hotel.

'No, Mac runs it – that's the owner – well, part-owner, since the O'Connells bought in to this too.'

I look at him for a few moments confused, then I remember: 'Oh, the owners of the hotel? And didn't you say they own the island too?'

'That's them – Dermot and Darcy. When they found out the stables were in trouble, they bought a share. That's sort of why we have the path through from the hotel, for guests that want to ride while they're here.'

'Sounds like a good idea. So what do *you* do here?'

'Ah, I pop in from time to time to see the horses – often when I'm supposed to be working.' He goes over to one of the stalls and runs his hand along the nose of a chestnut mare, who according to the plaque outside her box is called Trixie. 'The horses can be a darn sight nicer company than a lot of folk I know ...' To my relief, he winks. I smile in return. 'Do you ride?' he asks, taking a treat from his pocket and feeding it to Trixie on the flat of his hand.

I shake my head. 'Not in a long, long time. I did for a while, when I was a child, but I fell off and got scared.'

'Ah, that's a shame. You could have gone out while you were here.'

'Do you?'

'Sometimes,' he says, patting Trixie and walking back towards me. 'When I get the time.'

Fergus barks suddenly and I jump.

'Hush, Fergus, ya big eejit!' Finn calls, patting his leg so Fergus comes to him.

Fergus bounds over to me with his long pink tongue lolloping from the side of his mouth, and I jump again as something painful stirs deep within me.

Finn grabs Fergus's collar, obviously misinterpreting my jumpiness as fright. 'Sorry, I didn't realise you were afraid.'

'No, I'm not.' I try to explain: 'I'm a bit wary, that's all.' This isn't strictly true, but it's a darn sight easier than trying to explain the real reason I'm wary around animals.

'Calm down, Fergus,' Finn tells him. 'Shall I put him on a lead?' He looks around. 'I think there's one here somewhere . . .'

'No, it's fine. I'm fine.'

'Walk you back then?' Finn offers. 'I was about to head back to the hotel myself.'

'Sure,' I agree, pleased to have company.

Fergus races ahead of us down the path while Finn and I take our time following behind him. 'So what did you and your friend get up to today?' he asks as we stroll along.

'We took a drive around the Ring of Tara,' I tell him truthfully.

'Very touristy,' he replies, smiling.

Finn has the most amazing set of teeth. You would think he'd had them straightened, polished and bleached to within an inch of their life to make them whiter than white. Except it's hard to imagine Finn being that vain, so I have to assume he's been blessed with a perfect, natural smile to match the rest of his rather pleasing exterior.

'Yeah, well, when in Rome!'

'Most of the locals only drive that road when they absolutely have to. They'd never drive it for pleasure.'

'What would you suggest we do then?' I ask, slightly irked by his apparent snub.

'Go for a walk in the mountains, away from the gift shops and tearooms. Take a boat trip on one of the lakes. Go pony trekking on one of our four-legged friends back there. All much more enjoyable than sitting in a car or a bus all day, getting out where you're told to every few minutes.'

'You don't much like doing what you're told, do you?' I ask, wanting to get my own back. 'In fact, I'd go so far as to say you're a bit of a rebel.'

Finn's green eyes twinkle as he looks at me. 'How can you tell?'

'Oh, where do I begin?' I hold up my hand and pretend to count on my fingers. 'Let's start with your blatant disregard for hotel uniform, then there's your visits to the stables when you're supposed to be working, and ...'

'No, don't,' he says with a wave of his hand. 'I don't think my employers would be too happy if after one day a guest at the hotel knew all that about me. Even such a perceptive one as yourself.'

'Thanks.' I smile at him, and I'm surprised to find I'm secretly pleased he thinks this. 'So what are you up to tonight?' I ask, meaning at the hotel.

'Are you asking me out, Miss Parker?' Finn asks, pressing his hand to his chest dramatically. 'How very modern of you!'

'Oh, I ... I meant at the hotel,' I say, my face flushing red. 'I assumed you'd be on duty, like last night.'

'Ah ... of course you do.' He drops his head sadly, then looks up at me and winks. 'Yes, I knew you meant that, I was only teasing.'

'Good,' I nod hurriedly. 'I'm glad.'

Finn looks back out into the hotel garden. 'Actually, I'm not on duty this evening,' he says casually.

'Oh, do you have something nice planned? Sorry,' I swiftly apologise as Finn glances at me. 'Obviously, that's none of my business.'

'No, I don't,' Finn replies, equally fast. 'Do you?'

'My friend and I were going to go into town. Kiki is keen to hear some traditional Irish music.'

'Nice. Where are you going?'

We've reached the gate again, and Finn steps forward to open it for me.

'Thank you,' I say, passing through the brick archway back into the hotel garden. 'I'm not too sure yet. We thought we'd wander around until we find something we like the look of.'

'Can I recommend The Raven's Knowledge? Bit of an odd name, but both the food and the music are excellent.'

'Thanks, we'll look out for it.'

'And will you be partaking in another pint of Guinness tonight?' Finn asks, teasingly.

'I will, but I doubt Kiki will be joining me.'

Finn nods knowingly. 'I knew the moment I saw you you'd enjoy a pint of the black stuff.'

'How could you possibly know that?'

We've reached the door that leads into the hotel, and Finn pauses before opening it.

'It's the Celtic in you,' he says, without explaining further. He pulls the door open and waits for me to enter.

'What do you mean, the Celtic in me?' I demand, making no move to go through the door.

'Fiery temperament, have you?' Finn asks.

I shrug. 'Sometimes.'

'How red is that hair of yours naturally?'

'What do you mean?' I ask, reaching up and absent-mindedly touching my hair.

'Come on, Ren, that's not your natural colour now, is it?'

He was right. My natural colour was full-on ginger, but I regularly went to a hairdresser and had it toned down to a more manageable auburn.

'No, it's not. But what's that to do with anything?'

Finn wiggles his finger in front of my nose. 'And what about all these freckles here, and your whiter-than-white skin? It all adds up to you being Celtic in my eyes.'

I'm about to continue this conversation when Donal appears at the open door. 'Oh, Finn, it's you,' he says, sounding a tad annoyed. 'I thought the door had been left open by a guest. You know what a chill wind blows through here at this time of the year.'

'Yes, sorry, Donal.' Finn turns to me and rolls his eyes.

'Now that I've found you, Finn,' Donal begins, but then he notices me standing on the other side of the open door. 'Oh good afternoon, Miss Parker, I didn't see you there.'

'Hi again.'

'Your friend was down in reception looking for you,' Donal says. 'I had no idea you were out here in the gardens or I'd have sent her this way.'

'I was showing Ren the stables,' Finn says. 'She's thinking of going for a ride one day.'

I flash my eyes at him.

'Oh really?' Donal says. 'I can't say I understand the fascination with riding horses myself, but if that's what you enjoy then I'm sure Cormac will look after you well.'

'Cormac?'

'Mac is his nickname,' Finn explains. '*Everyone* calls him that.'

'Names were bestowed upon us to be used, Finn,' Donal insists. 'Not to be shortened.'

Finn shakes his head.

'I'd better be getting back inside to find Kiki,' I tell them both. 'She'll be wondering where I am.'

Donal does his trademark tiny bow, while Finn continues holding the door for me. 'Enjoy your night out,' he says as I pass him.

I turn towards his voice and find our faces are inches away from each other.

'Thank you, I will,' I whisper, and to my annoyance I'm sure I feel my legs wobble, before I hurry down the corridor to find Kiki.

Six

'So what were the two of you doing wandering hand in hand in the garden earlier?' Kiki asks as we walk along Ballykiltara's high street towards The Raven's Knowledge. 'I saw you through the window.'

'If you *were* looking out of the window, and not just surmising because I told you I bumped into Finn, then you'd know we were not wandering hand in hand, we were simply walking through the gardens together on our way back to the hotel.'

'Yeah, yeah,' Kiki says, nudging me. 'And the rest.'

I stop walking and grab her arm. 'Look, I know you like to romanticise everything and always see hearts and flowers everywhere, but like I told you before, I bumped into him at the stables and we walked back to the hotel together. *That. Is. It.*'

'*Touch-eey!*' Kiki says, looking down at my hand on her arm – which I quickly remove. 'We both know that means— OK,

42

OK,' she says as I glare at her. She pulls an imaginary zip across her lips. 'I won't mention Finn's name any more tonight.'

'Good.' I look up at the sign over the pub we're standing in front of. 'Oh, it looks like we've found it.'

The Raven's Knowledge, even with its slightly odd name, is what I imagine a typical Irish pub to be. Whether it's deliberately designed that way to please the tourists – and I'd say about 70 per cent of the people in here tonight are just that – or whether the dark oak panels, antique sporting prints, and carved wooden furniture are indeed genuine, is difficult to say, but what is definitely genuine from the moment we walk through the doors is the welcome we receive.

'Evening, ladies,' a small middle-aged barman greets us as we head over to the bar. 'What can I get you?'

'Hmm . . .' Kiki scans the assortment of alcohol behind the bar. 'Do you have any WKD?'

'No, I'm sorry we don't stock that.'

'Smirnoff Ice then?'

The barman looks behind him at the shelves.

'Sorry, no.'

'Kopparberg?'

'That's cider, yes?' the barman says hopefully.

'Yep. Do you have some?'

'No, we don't, but we do have Magners. It's an Irish cider,' he adds when Kiki doesn't immediately respond.

Kiki thinks about this. 'You know what, I think I'll have a vodka and orange.'

'Orange juice or Club Orange?'

'Do I have to be in the Club to drink it?'

'If you are, I'd better leave the vodka out, eh?' the barman jokes, and I smile.

43

'What does he mean, Ren?' Kiki asks, confused.

'She means orange juice,' I tell the barman.

He nods gratefully and turns to begin pouring the drink.

'Club Orange is a type of orange drink you only get in Ireland,' I explain for Kiki's benefit.

'Oh ... oh, now I get it!' Kiki says with relief as the penny drops.

The barman brings Kiki's drink over to us, then he looks with concern at me, probably wondering if my order will be as complicated.

'I'll have a—'

'She'll have a Guinness,' someone finishes off for me. 'And make it a pint too, Brendan.'

'Sure thing, Finn,' Brendan says, pulling a pint-glass from below the counter.

I turn to find Finn standing behind us, casually drinking from a glass.

'Finn!' Kiki calls out, then she slaps her hand over her mouth. 'Whoops, sorry!'

Finn, wearing jeans and a checked shirt similar to the ones we've seen him in at the hotel, looks puzzled.

'Ren said I wasn't allowed to mention your name this evening,' she blurts out without thinking, then looks between us. 'Ah, I've done it again, haven't I?' She grimaces as she grabs her vodka and orange from the bar. '*Awkward!*'

'Is that right, Ren?' Finn asks, looking to me for clarification.

'Er, yes, sort of ... ' I struggle for an answer. 'What I actually said was, it would be nice to talk to someone new tonight – we've only met people from the hotel so far, you see?'

Finn doesn't look entirely convinced, but does a good job of hiding it.

'Then I shall take my leave of you, ladies. I wouldn't want to cramp your style.' He turns and takes a few steps away from us.

'No … Finn,' I jump down from the bar stool I've been perched on and scamper in his direction. 'I'm sorry,' I say, catching up with him. 'I didn't mean to be rude. Kiki got the wrong end of the stick, that's all. She gets a bit confused sometimes.'

Finn turns and I'm relieved to see he's smiling.

'Let's put it down to the language barrier, eh?' he says, then looks over my shoulder at the bar, where Brendan has my drink waiting for me. 'Now, you'd better be collecting that pint of yours – there's letting it rest and there's wasting it!'

We spend the rest of the evening at the pub. I continue to drink Guinness and Kiki sticks to her vodka. Finn diligently sticks to soft drinks all night because he's on duty early tomorrow morning, but we have a lovely time either chatting amongst ourselves, or with locals who Finn introduces us to. We manage to order some pub food before the band comes on, which I'm grateful for. I'd been beginning to feel quite light-headed, drinking so much on an empty stomach, and the cheeseburger and chips Brendan brings to our table is just what's needed to soak up the alcohol. The Irish band that begins playing at around 9 p.m. is very well received, and Kiki and I try to sing along with everyone else in the bar. But after the crowd-pleasers 'Whiskey in the Jar' and 'Wild Rover', I'm a bit lost for the words, so I sit patting the table in time with the tune.

'Don't worry about it,' Finn says, leaning in towards me so I can hear him above the noise. 'Not many in here know all the words. I'm not even sure the band does half the time!'

The band is made up of a violinist, a keyboard player, a

guy playing the guitar, and a woman who plays various wind instruments and does all the percussion too. There's a lead singer – an elderly man with a beard who seems to slur many of the song's lyrics together to make them fit, or simply hums when he doesn't remember them. In between songs, when he's talking to the crowd, which has swollen greatly since the music began, I can barely make out a word he's saying.

'I thought it was only me,' I say, smiling gratefully at Finn.

'Nah.' He shakes his head. 'It's often like this. The more yer man there drinks, the worse it gets!' He winks and turns back to listen to the music.

I half watch him as the music drops down a gear and the band play an Irish love song – well, I think that's what it is; it's slower than much of their previous music, and their singer looks desolate as he wails his lament.

I've tried to find out a little about Finn tonight, but it's not easy. Finn seems happy to answer all our questions about Ballykiltara and the hotel, but when pressed for information about himself, he immediately becomes evasive and changes the subject.

I can't say I blame him; I'm guilty of the same thing. Most of the time I'm happy to chat to people about what I do for a living – unless I'm out in the field, searching; then I prefer to keep shtum until I've managed to find a house or a property to suit my client. But if anyone asks me to talk about myself, I clam up at once. Perhaps in Finn I've discovered a kindred spirit?

I shake my head. I must have had too much Guinness – kindred spirit, indeed! I've been spending far too much time with Kiki.

Talking of which, I look around the room to see where she's got to, and I spy her with a few other uninhibited souls dancing to the music. Well, when I say dancing, right now they're slowly rocking from side to side as they listen to the mournful ballad, but a few minutes ago they were all jigging across the pub's wooden floor arm in arm.

Finn turns back to me and wrinkles up his nose. 'Bit woeful this, eh?'

'It is a bit.'

He looks at my pint-glass. 'Another?' he offers.

'I think I'd better join you and have an orange juice this time,' I say. 'I have to drive again in the morning.'

'Where are you off to tomorrow?' Finn asks, picking up my glass and getting to his feet.

'Oh, just around,' I tell him. 'No particular plans.'

Finn seems to accept this relaxed idea easily, and heads over to the bar. 'Back in a minute,' he says, moving away from the table.

Within seconds Kiki appears at my side again, plonking herself down in Finn's vacated seat.

'*So?*' she asks breathlessly. 'How's it going?'

'How's what going?'

'You and Finn, of course!'

'Go back and play with your new friends,' I tell her. 'There's nothing to see here.'

Kiki puts on her frustrated face. 'You wanna try letting go, Ren. Have a little fun before it's too late.'

'What do you mean, before it's too late?'

'Well, you're hardly getting any younger, are you?'

'Wha . . .' I'm almost lost for words. 'I'm hardly ancient!'

'You're the wrong side of thirty – and that's getting on, in my book. Especially when it comes to matters of the heart, or should I say *the bedroom* . . .' She winks purposefully at me.

I put my fingers in my ears and close my eyes. 'I'm not listening to any more of your nonsense. Go away. La. La. La!' I sing.

I open my eyes to see what Kiki's reaction is, and I'm horrified to find Finn already back in his seat, and Kiki nowhere to be seen.

Finn observes me silently as I slowly remove my fingers from my ears, an amused expression on his face.

'It was Kiki,' I explain, my cheeks now flushed bright red, mostly from embarrassment, but partly from all the Guinness I've had this evening. 'She was annoying me.'

'I often feel like doing that in the hotel when things go wrong. Either that, or throwing myself down on the ground like a toddler, and having a full-blown tantrum, kicking and screaming on the floor until the problem goes away.'

I laugh at the mental image of Finn doing just that with Donal and Orla watching him.

'But I think I'd probably get fired if I did that, hmm?'

'I think you probably would.' I take my chance. 'How *did* you become the manager – and I quote the Internet here – of "Ballykiltara's premier four-star hotel"? It doesn't seem like your ideal job.'

'What do you think my ideal job would be then?' Finn asks, evading the question as usual.

'Not the manager of a hotel, that's for sure. It's manic, and busy, and stressful. Three words that don't spring to mind when I think of you.'

Finn considers this. 'It's always good to know people are thinking about you. Especially people as pretty as you.'

Can my face get any hotter? I wonder as my cheeks redden even further.

'You're very good at avoiding my questions, aren't you?'

I reply, taking a leaf out of his book and sidestepping his compliment.

'And you're very good at ignoring praise.'

I lift my glass of orange juice in a toast. 'Here's to being stubborn, uncooperative, and secretive!' I flash my eyes at him meaningfully.

Finn leans forward from where he's been relaxing back in his chair, and chinks his glass to mine. 'Secrets have a habit of catching up with all of us, Ren. If you want me to share mine, are you ready to share yours too?'

Seven

The next day dawns bright and sunny, which is in sharp contrast to how I'm feeling as I haul myself out of bed and into the bathroom for a shower.

Kiki is still fast asleep, and I wonder as I let warm water rain down on my face and body, if she will feel as rough as I do when she awakes.

I'm not used to drinking as much alcohol as I managed to put away last night – far from it. My usual limit is a few glasses of wine, and last night I must have drunk … I try to tot it up in my head … Oh my, I must have had at least four pints of Guinness before Finn bought me the orange juice, and we'd had that odd conversation about secrets. Then we'd been joined at our table by Eddie, who Kiki had discovered hiding on the other side of the pub, and had dragged over to join us. Finn then insisted we try some Jameson's Irish Whiskey to finish up the night, and I think I must've had two of those as well …

I groan in the shower. No wonder I feel so bad.

By the time I emerge from the cubicle I'm feeling a tad better. I dry myself and clean my teeth, then I venture into the bedroom and pull back the heavy curtains in the hope the bright sunlight will wake Kiki.

She doesn't stir, so I put the TV on, but hurriedly turn it down when the volume is too loud for my sore head. Then finally, when Kiki still hasn't woken, I go over to her bed and shake her.

'Kiki, time to wake up or we'll miss breakfast. They stop serving at ten.'

I don't think I can face breakfast after last night, but I know Kiki would never voluntarily miss a meal.

Kiki shoots up in her bed. 'Have I time for a shower?' she asks brightly.

'Er . . . yes, if you're quick.'

Kiki leaps from her bed and hurries across the room, but she pauses and turns back at the door. 'You OK, Ren?' she asks. 'You look a bit peaky.'

'I'm fine. How are you?'

'Fab. I had a great night's sleep.'

'No after-effects?'

Kiki thinks about this. 'How do you mean?'

'I mean the vast quantity of alcohol we drank.'

She shrugs. 'Nah, that's nothing. When I go out with my mates, that would just be an aperitif!' She grins at me and disappears into the bathroom, where I hear a medley of One Direction songs warbled for the next few minutes as she showers.

I must be getting old, I think as I continue getting dressed. If that amount of alcohol is an aperitif, I wouldn't want to go for a three-course dinner!

*

51

At breakfast the choice is as varied as yesterday, but I stick with plain toast and a pot of tea this morning. I don't think my stomach would be too happy with me downing smoked salmon and scrambled eggs. But Kiki has the works – cereal, a full Irish breakfast, and then croissants and jam to finish.

'How can you eat all that?' I ask, looking with disbelief at her plate.

'I'm hungry – aren't you? It must be all this fresh air we're having.'

'We spent most of yesterday in the car, and last night in a pub. Where are you getting all your *air* from?'

'So what are we doing today?' she asks, popping the last bit of croissant in her mouth.

'We have two properties to visit this morning, then this afternoon I thought we'd take a boat trip.'

Kiki's eyes light up. 'That sounds fun, and not at all like you, Ren. Where did you get that idea from?'

I decide it's best not to mention Finn. There was no sign of him this morning when we came down to breakfast; maybe he's in his office? He certainly wouldn't be lying in bed, sleeping off a hangover – something I wouldn't mind doing right now – because he was on soft drinks all night. I'm starting to wish I'd joined him.

'Touring the lakes is a popular thing to do here,' I tell her. 'I thought it would be nice.'

'Good morning, ladies,' Donal says, pausing by our table. 'And how are you both today?'

'Very well, thank you,' I fib.

'And did you find your Irish music last night?'

'We did, at The Raven's Knowledge.'

'Ah, yes, a few of the staff go there, I'm led to believe it's very good.'

'It's ace,' Kiki says. 'We danced and everything.'

Donal does his trademark nod, and I wonder if in his mind he's clicking his heels at the same time. 'And what will you be doing today, ladies? Remember, if you ever want to know anything about the area – I'm your man.'

'A boat trip around the lakes,' Kiki tells him.

Donal nods his approval. 'From Rafferty Castle?'

Kiki looks to me.

'Yes.'

'Excellent!' Donal looks approvingly at me. 'And you'll take the boat over to Sheehy Abbey?'

'Yes – if you think so?'

'I do. Those two places have some wonderful legends surrounding them. Would you like me to tell you some of the tales?' He looks around the breakfast room, but because we're late this morning it's quiet. 'I have a few moments.'

I'm about to politely decline and tell him we have to be getting on, when I hear Kiki pipe up: 'Yes please, Donal!'

Donal looks delighted. 'Let's see ... legend has it that Rafferty Mor, the original owner of the castle, still exists in a deep slumber under the waters of Lough Leane. Every seven years, on the first morning in May, he is said to arise from the water on a white horse and ride around the whole lake. Anyone catching a glimpse of him is said to be assured of good fortune for the rest of their lives.'

'What a shame we weren't here a few days earlier,' Kiki says, looking genuinely disappointed. 'We might have seen him.'

I sigh. 'Please continue, Donal.'

'Of course.' Donal nods. 'If you take the boat trip over the water to Rafferty Island, you will find the ruins of Sheehy Abbey, a monastery that's said to date from the early Christian period. Sheehy means mysterious or eerie, it's said to be where Irish monks wrote the Annals of Tara, an early history of Christian Ireland.'

Kiki listens amazed.

'Is that something like the Book of Kells?' I ask. 'Wasn't that done by monks too?'

'Yes and no; the Book of Kells is an illustrated manuscript depicting the four Gospels; it dates from around the sixth or seventh century. The Annals of Tara date from around the twelfth to fifteenth century.'

'Three hundred years?'

'It took them a long time.' Donal smiles. 'It's said that Irish kings came to Sheehy Abbey to be educated by the monks, which is why the lake surrounding the island is called Lough Leane, which means "Lake of Learning", and why the Annals of Tara were so called, because Tara is the hill in County Meath where the Irish kings were crowned.'

'Wow,' Kiki sighs. 'That's awesome.'

'Isn't the island the owners of the hotel have called Tara too? I'm sure Finn mentioned something about that?'

'Yes, that's right, it is,' Donal says. 'Its full name is Glentara. Many things around here have taken on the Tara name because it's synonymous with the high kings. Our own Ballykiltara being one of them.'

'Fascinating, Donal,' I tell him, meaning it. 'Thank you for sharing all that with us, it's much appreciated.'

'Anytime, miss. I have many, many stories to tell if you ever want to hear more. I've lived around here all my life. Now, I've taken up too much of your time already – I'd best go and see to some of our other guests. I do hope you enjoy your day.' He gives a nod and a smile, and quickly moves across the carpet, collecting a stray white cotton napkin on the way that a guest has allowed to slide to the floor.

'Who knew it was all so exciting!' Kiki says, looking at me in wonder. 'I told you this place was magical.'

'Celtic myths and legends are interesting, perhaps not magical though. More like stories that have been passed down through the generations. I could get you a book on them, if you want to read more?'

Kiki shakes her head as we stand up from the table. 'No, you're all right. If I want to know anything else, I'll ask Donal.'

'I think he'd like that.' I smile. 'He seems to thrive on giving the best customer service he can.'

'All the staff here are so nice,' Kiki says as we walk back through the foyer towards the lift. 'It was really cool spending time with Eddie and Finn last night.'

'Yes, they're quite an amusing pair.'

'Morning, ladies.' We turn to see Eddie carrying a bucket and mop. 'Are you well today?'

I'd thought at first Eddie was a porter, judging by the way he'd taken our bags from the car when we arrived, but he seems to do all sorts of odd jobs around the hotel, and is always popping up everywhere. Last night he'd described himself to us laughingly as a general dogsbody, but I suspect he's far more valuable to The Stag than that, and without him the place might crumble.

'Yes, thank you, Eddie!' Kiki sings. 'Are you?'

'I am indeed, miss,' he says. 'What's not to be happy about? It's a beautiful day, the sun is shining, and I have a half day later.'

Am I the only one who has a hangover?

55

'Call me, Kiki,' Kiki says, smiling coyly at him. 'I asked you to last night.'

'Ah well, it's different when I'm in the hotel,' Eddie says, looking a tad self-conscious. 'You're a guest.'

Kiki is about to protest when the lift pings and the doors open behind us.

'Got to go, see you later,' Kiki says, backing into the lift. She waves shyly at Eddie as the doors close and we rise up to our room.

I smile secretly to myself as we do. Kiki seems quite taken with Eddie after last night; perhaps if she has a love interest while we're here she'll stop trying to persuade me to have one too.

But in the time it takes the lift to carry us up two floors, I realise that the thought of that *not* happening makes me feel very sad indeed.

Eight

It takes us most of the morning to visit the last two properties I have listed, because they are both quite remote and we have to drive quite a while to reach them.

The first is not suitable at all; or rather, the house is almost perfect, but the views sadly are not. When we arrive at the second, we spend some time looking around the exterior while we wait for a local estate agent to come and open it up for us. From the outside, I'm convinced this house could be the one. The setting and views seem to be exactly what Ryan Dempsey wants. But when we finally venture inside, the agent informs me that there is no central heating, only open fires, with the option of installing an expensive boiler system – something they'd decided to leave out of their listing details. Ryan had said he didn't mind a few basic renovations to any property we might find, but I knew something as drastic as installing a full central heating system was going to make this house a total non-starter.

So as we drive away, feeling quite despondent that our first two days of searching haven't turned up anything positive, the prospect of an afternoon off is a very pleasant thought indeed.

We grab some lunch at a local pub, then set off in search of Rafferty Castle, which is not too far from Ballykiltara.

'This must be it!' Kiki shrieks as our little Fiat turns a corner and a tall imposing castle looms up in front of us. 'Quick, pull into the car park.'

'Calm down,' I tell her, indicating and turning into a small pull-off area with a few cars and a coach already parked in it. 'One, I can clearly see it's Rafferty Castle, and two, there was a sign on the road before we pulled in.'

Kiki, undaunted, shakes her head. 'It's big, isn't it?' she says, craning her neck out of the car window.

'Yes, it seems so. Shall we go and take a look?'

We climb out of the car, pulling our raincoats with us and stuffing them into our bags just in case. The earlier sunny weather has quickly become overcast and cloudy, and we don't want to get soaking wet if the rain decides to make an appearance while we're out in the middle of the lake on a boat.

The approach to Rafferty Castle is a short dusty track, at the end of which stand more of the horses and traps we've seen so many times already in Ballykiltara, accompanied by the elderly men who drive them. They stand waiting hopefully for a gullible tourist who wants to go for a short but no doubt expensive ride.

Kiki looks at me, but before she can speak I shake my head. 'No, we are not going for a ride on one of them. End of.'

Ignoring Kiki's sulky face, and the steady gaze of the men, I look at the ponies as we pass them. In contrast to the happy healthy horses I'd seen at the stables with Finn, these horses looked tired and a little sad, and I feel quite sorry for them.

I shake my head and tell myself: Stop it, Ren, they're probably perfectly happy with their lot. They have food and water, and they get regular exercise – what more could a horse want? But as hard as I try not to, whenever I see an animal that might be in distress, I can't help but want to rescue it. Old habits die hard . . .

Luckily for me, Kiki is already distracted from her longing for a horse-and-trap ride by the dramatic view that greets us as we cross a small bridge.

Rafferty Castle stands before us. It's a fairly unremarkable castle as castles go; my home county of Northumberland has more castles than you could ever want, from the enormously ornate to the small and unassuming, so I know a good castle when I see one. Rafferty seems to be more of a fortress, as far as I can see; a stronghold built to protect against marauding invaders, rather than a family home, as some castles are.

'You see those windows?' Kiki says, looking up at the mottled grey walls of the castle. 'The thin ones.'

'Yes,' I say, following her gaze.

'Did they make them that narrow to stop people falling out because there was no glass in the old days?'

I have to stifle a laugh.

'Er no, I think it was more likely to do with preventing the inhabitants from being killed by stray arrows that might have their name on them.'

'Yeah,' Kiki says, not sensing my amusement. 'You're probably right.' She spins around. 'Wow,' she exclaims as she sees the lake behind her. 'Look at that!'

I turn around to join her and am quite taken aback by what

59

I see. In front of the castle is a huge and very beautiful lake; a wide expanse of clear water protected either side by gentle mist-covered mountains. In the distance, I can see a few islands dotted about in the water, and I wonder which of them might be home to Sheehy Abbey. No wonder it's called that, if as Donal says, Sheehy means eerie or mystical. This place certainly has a touch of the magical about it.

'I'm almost glad the sun went in if this is what you see when it's misty,' Kiki says, mirroring my thoughts. 'It's beautiful. Magical even.' She glances in my direction when she says the word *magical* to gauge my reaction.

'On this occasion, I agree with you, Kiki. This place truly does deserve the use of that word.'

'Boat trip to see the islands?' an elderly man enquires as he wanders past us.

'Oh yes,' I reply, turning around. 'It was suggested to us that we should go over and visit the abbey?'

'Ah, a good choice,' he says with a toothy grin. 'I'll be happy to take you. My boat is over there.' He gestures to a large wooden boat, big enough to hold six to eight people.

Just then we hear shrieks and loud voices. I look back to the castle to see a large party of teenage visitors exiting through one of the doors. Oh lord, I mutter, please tell me they're not planning to visit this ancient place of learning and prayer. They'd ruin any sense of peace and tranquillity the Internet description of the island had promised.

'Shall we get going before anyone else decides they want to come over too?' our guide asks, seeing my horrified face. 'One of the other boatmen can take them yuns – you'll not get any peace and quiet with them about.'

'Oh yes, please,' I tell him gratefully.

Kiki and I climb into the boat and Jackie, as he insists we call him, expertly begins rowing out into the lake.

'You'd best put them there lifejackets on,' Jackie says as soon as the boat is out on the water. 'It's all health and safety,' he says to me as Kiki scrabbles about at the bottom of the boat, getting us each a bright orange jacket. 'We have to stick to their guidelines or the boat trips don't happen any more.'

'I bet it wasn't like that in the old days,' I ask, sensing this is probably where Jackie has always felt happiest.

'No, you'd be right there, miss. The old days were much easier, you just ferried folk around the loughs and they paid you what they thought best. Now it's all rules and regulations.'

'Oh sorry, I didn't ask how much the trip was going to be,' I apologise as I pull on my lifejacket.

'Ah, we'll sort something out when we get back,' he says with a smile so wide I can count all the gaps in his pearly white teeth. 'I don't know how long you'll want me for yet. The abbey is a wondrous sight 'n' all, but you'd be best fared seeing some of the other islands too, if you want the full lake experience, so to speak.'

'Yes, I'd like that,' I tell him. 'It's so beautiful here on the water.'

'Ah, this is only the beginning, miss. Only the beginning.'

I half watch our passing scenery, half watch Jackie as we continue our journey across the water. The scenery is stunning, there's no doubt about that, but I find Jackie equally beguiling. There's something about him I can't quite define – a *quality*, my American clients often call it when they're looking for homes. Yes, that's it, Jackie has a calm and gentle quality, but there's something about him that seems a little odd, murky even as he rows us across the lake. No, murky is the wrong word; eerie or even ethereal might be a better one. Perhaps it's all those years of going back and forth across this lake to Sheehy Abbey, but he seems somehow to blend into his surroundings.

'You girls on holiday, are you?' Jackie asks, continuing to row steadily across the water.

'Kind of,' I reply before Kiki can say yes or no.

Jackie nods, but doesn't question me any further. 'Well, it's a fine area to visit, whatever the reason you find yourself here.'

'Have you lived here long, Jackie?' Kiki asks. 'I bet you have.'

Jackie smiles. 'I have indeed, miss. Some would say far too long.'

'So you know all about the tales surrounding the lake? A guy at our hotel was telling us all about it this morning over breakfast.'

'Which hotel would that be then?'

'The Stag. Do you know it?' I ask.

'I do indeed. So your storyteller would likely be Donal then? Knows a lot about the area, does Donal. Did he tell you the story surrounding your hotel's name too?'

'No. Why, is there one?' I ask, wondering what Jackie might tell us.

'There is, but we're arriving at the island now. How about I tell you after your visit?'

'Yes, please,' Kiki says. Grabbing a rope, she leaps up on to a little wooden landing platform and expertly pulls the boat into dock. *Where did she learn how to do that?* I wonder.

'How long will you be wanting, here on the island?' Jackie asks as Kiki takes my hand and pulls me up next to her. 'About half an hour is enough for most folk. It's not that big.'

'Half an hour will be fine,' I tell him. 'You'll wait then?'

'Oh yes, I'll wait,' Jackie says, sitting back in his boat and closing his eyes. 'Been waiting most of my life, me.'

We leave Jackie and head up away from the landing platform on to the soft spongy ground of the island, and immediately we see the promised ruins of the abbey directly in front of us. With the crumbling abbey sitting majestically on top of it, this mysterious island in the middle of a lake looks like something from a fairy tale.

Jackie is right: the island is tiny, so it doesn't take us more than a few minutes to explore the ruins, then wander a little further until we reach the far side of the island. Other than the abbey and a few ancient trees that I expect have stood here almost as long as the abbey itself, there's not a lot else to see, so we head back to take another look at the ruins.

'It's so peaceful here,' I say as we explore. 'It's easy to imagine the monks coming here to teach the kings of Ireland in the past.'

Kiki has been unusually quiet since we arrived on the island. 'Can you feel it too then, Ren?' she asks.

'Feel what?'

'The energy here, it's amazing, so clean and ... ' she struggles for the word, 'holy.'

'Well, it would be holy if it was once an abbey, wouldn't it?' I smile.

'No, maybe holy isn't the right word ... perhaps spiritual is a better one?'

Kiki is right, I *can* feel something, standing here on this tiny island, but since I'm unsure what that something is, I'm not going to admit it, even to Kiki.

'Ooh, look,' Kiki says, spying another ruined building we

haven't spotted before. It's set slightly away from the others, further up the hill. 'I wonder what that once was?'

'It was probably a chapel,' I say as we climb the hill and find an engraved stone Celtic cross standing in the middle of what once would have been the stone floor of a tiny building. But unlike the cross, the stone floor has long gone, and the cross now stands slightly crookedly, surrounded by grass and weeds. 'That cross is like the high crosses you find in many areas that were once inhabited by Celts,' I tell Kiki. 'Unlike this one, they're usually pretty big though, some rise to over—'

But Kiki cuts me off. 'Look, Ren, people have left coins around the cross. Do you think we can make a wish?'

I've never been one for wishes. I believe everything that happens in life happens because you make it, not because some mystical force has decided you can have what it is you desire.

'If you want to,' I tell her, taking a step back.

'No, you have to do it too,' she insists, pulling me forward again. She scrabbles around in her bag and pulls out her purse. 'Here's a euro,' she says, handing me a coin. 'Do you think that will be OK?'

I don't have the heart to tell her that a chocolate coin would probably do as much good. So I merely nod.

'Right, I'll go first,' Kiki announces, a coin squeezed tightly in her hand. She closes her eyes for a few seconds, then she opens them again and leans forward to place her coin on top of the others. 'All done, you go now.'

'No point in me asking what you wished for, I suppose?' I say, reluctantly taking her place in front of the cross.

Kiki shakes her head. 'I'll tell you if it comes true!'

I stand in front of the cross, not thinking about what I want to wish for, but instead wondering how many other people have fallen for this trick that seems to spring up everywhere these days of leaving coins to make wishes. Since when have the fairies, or whatever other power was supposed to grant your wish, started charging for it?

But I don't want to disappoint Kiki – I know I'll get more grief if I don't do this than it would cost me to pretend that I have – so I close my eyes the way she did and think about where I'm going to look next for a house for Ryan Dempsey. We'll have to go out on the road again, and see if we can spot anything along the way. It's surprising how often that works; maybe it will this time too?

'It's a long wish you're making,' Kiki interrupts. 'It must be complicated!'

'All done,' I say, placing my coin on top of the others. 'Now, if we're all done here, shall we head back to the boat?'

'Yeah. As much as I've fallen in love with this island, I can't wait to hear what Jackie has to tell us next!'

Neither can I, I think as we wander back to the edge of the lake and our waiting boat. There's something about Jackie that intrigues me, and like so many other things in this part of Ireland, I can't be sure exactly what it is, but I'm keen to find out.

Nine

Jackie rows us from Rafferty Island, further out into the water on a tour of the neighbouring lakes. As we travel peacefully across the water, he points out places of interest and tells us stories of both the lakes and the surrounding area.

'So this hotel you're staying in – The Stag,' he says as we travel through a quiet tree-lined stretch of water and move on to the adjoining lake. 'Donal didn't tell you the story?'

I shake my head.

'You've noticed the sign above the outside of the hotel, though?' he asks.

I look at Kiki.

'It's a stag, isn't it?' she asks. 'Never looked that closely, have we, Ren?'

'Not really, no.'

'So you'll not have noticed the colour of the stag?' Jackie asks.

Kiki furrows her brow as she tries to recall.

'Hmm ... white, I think?'

'White is correct, young lady. Now, do either of you know what a white stag means?'

'It's albino?' I reply, hoping this to be right.

'Yes, some deer would be called this – that is, if their eyes were red as well as their coat being white. But I'm talking about white deer with a condition called Leucism. It's rare, so it is; it causes the deer's natural skin and hair colour to turn white, but they keep their dark eyes, making them different than the albino deer.'

Interesting though this is, I'm wondering where Jackie is going with it.

'A white stag is very unusual to behold,' Jackie continues, 'some would even say exceptional. There are reports of folk seeing white deer around these parts, but those are exceedingly rare. So many believe, when a white stag appears, it comes with a message.'

'What sort of a message?' Kiki asks in wonder.

Jackie smiles, obviously enjoying his willing audience. 'Well, the ancient Celts believed a white stag appeared when it brought a message from the other world. Usually when the person it showed itself to was transgressing a taboo, such as trespassing on hunting ground.'

Kiki's eyes are like saucers as she listens to Jackie. 'Have you ever seen one, Jackie?' she asks eagerly.

'Aye, yes. Many years ago now, though.'

'What were you doing?' I ask, wondering how much of this tale was for the tourists' amusement.

'Poaching,' Jackie says, looking shamefaced. 'Never seen one before, and never seen one since, mind. But it sure knocked some sense into me, seeing one that day.'

'Why?'

'I'd been a bad lad up until then,' he says, looking straight at me. 'Always on the wrong side of the law, I was. I won't go into details, but let's just say it wasn't pretty.'

'So what did you do?'

'Cleaned up my act. Got myself a proper job, working the land. It was hard, but it was good honest toil – which was exactly what I needed. Then when I got too old to be of use doing that, I got meself a boat, and I started doing trips for the tourists out here on the lakes, and here I still am, many, many years later.'

'So you have the white stag to thank for that?' I ask, playing along for Kiki's benefit. 'His message turned your life around?'

'It's not to be sniffed at, miss,' Jackie says, seeing straight through me. 'Anyone around here will tell you: if you ever see a white stag, take note. They only appear to those that need their help.' He eyes me meaningfully. 'Plus,' he adds, 'on a more practical note, if you do happen upon a white stag, don't go telling everyone. It's important to keep it very, very quiet. They're quite the prized possession for those that would want to mount their heads on a wall somewhere. I'm told they go for big bucks.'

'That's horrible!' Kiki says, pulling a face. 'Poor things.'

'Sadly, that is the world you inhabit today.' Jackie looks over towards me. 'Are you OK, miss?' he asks.

Even though I've been listening to everything Jackie has been telling us, we've now arrived on the next lake, another huge open expanse of water, and I've been distracted by something I spy across the still lake, nested up in the hills.

'Yes, I'm fine.' I turn quickly towards him. 'That house up

there,' I say, pointing. 'Where is it located? I mean, how would I get to it if I was in a car?'

Jackie looks up to where I'm pointing: a remote white house, almost hidden in the trees. 'Ah yes, I know it. That's The Welcome House,' he says calmly. 'It's on the old road that circles the lakes just outside Ballykiltara.'

'Is it?' I say, looking back up at the house, trying to get my bearings. 'I didn't think we'd come that far.'

'The lakes can be deceiving,' Jackie says mysteriously. 'They hold many secrets within them.'

'Why did you call it The Welcome House?' I ask, 'You must know it well if you know its name.'

'Everyone around here knows The Welcome House,' Jackie says knowingly.

'They do? Why?'

'It's part of the local history. You ask anyone and they'll have a tale to tell about that place.'

My brow furrows as I look questioningly at him.

'Ah now, you've heard enough of my tales for one day,' he says maddeningly. 'Perhaps it's time we turned back. I'll be quiet now so you can enjoy the peace and tranquillity of the lakes.' He pulls on the oars and expertly turns the boat around in the water, then to my frustration doesn't speak another word until we get back to the castle and disembark on to dry land.

'How much do we owe you?' I ask, keen to get away and investigate this house I'd spotted – it looked perfect, and must have sensational views across the lakes. This could be the one.

Jackie waves his hand at me.

'No, really. How much?'

'My job is to put people in the right frame of mind to see

69

what they need to see,' he says cryptically. 'I've done my job for today, miss. Now you go do yours.'

I look at him questioningly, hoping to prompt him into saying more, but he turns away.

How odd, I think as I join Kiki, who's a little way up the hill, taking photos of the lakes on her phone. *Ah well, never look a gift horse in the mouth.*

But not for the first time since we arrived here in Ballykiltara, something isn't sitting right with me about this, and I resolve to discover just what it is about this place we're in, that on one hand I didn't understand, but on the other feels so very familiar.

Ten

'It can't be much further,' I tell Kiki as I peer through the windscreen.

We're driving along the road that Jackie had informed us the house was on, I'm driving so slowly that I have to keep pulling over so cars can go around us, but I'm determined to find this house that from the lake had looked so perfect.

'Perhaps you can't see it from the road?' Kiki says practically. 'Perhaps it's set back off a long drive, hidden in all these trees.'

'Even if it is, there would have to be a driveway. What did Jackie call it – The Welcome House? It will probably have a nameplate.'

Kiki doesn't look so hopeful as we crawl along the road, getting ever closer to the outskirts of Ballykiltara. Even though this old, twisty, turny road had been tarmacked and painted with white lines, it's easy to imagine horses and carts trundling along it in years gone by.

I have to slow down to a complete standstill as a long line of ponies with young riders sitting confidently on top of them cross the road in front of us.

'This must be the front entrance to the stables,' I say absent-mindedly, thinking about Finn.

'What stables?' Kiki asks.

'The stables that sit at the back of the hotel. Oh, didn't I tell you about that? I bumped into Finn there . . . ' I have to think about when that was: ' . . . yesterday. It seems like we've been here longer, doesn't it?'

Kiki, ignoring my question, immediately jumps in: 'You bumped into Finn at a riding stables? Was he wearing tight breeches and carrying a whip?'

I shake my head. 'No, don't be daft. He was only there visiting.'

'Still, I wouldn't mind seeing him like that, would you?' she asks innocently.

I give her a warning look.

'*What?*' she asks, her eyes wide.

A horn beeps behind us, and I realise the ponies have now crossed safely. So I put the car into first gear and move off, quickly changing up to second. But I don't quite get into third before I whack on my indicator and swerve to the side of the road, causing even more honks of derision from the cars behind me.

But I don't care, because at last I've spotted it, raised up off the road on its own tiny hill – The Welcome House.

'What on earth are you doing?' Kiki asks, removing her hand from the dashboard where she'd had to thrust it to balance herself as I swerved from the road. 'Oh . . . ' she says, following my gaze. 'You think that's it?'

'I know it is,' I reply with confidence. From the lake, I'd taken note that the bright white house had a red-tiled roof, but that it had been patched up in places with grey tiles, giving it a patchwork appearance.

There's a small lay-by further up the road, so we drive towards it and park up safely. Then we climb out to investigate.

From the road, the house appears to be well looked after. There's a front garden leading up to it, which is on several levels because of the steep gradient. It doesn't have any flowers or lawn, but isn't filled with junk either, it's simply empty, but it looks like someone might have recently swept it clean. A winding path leads up through the layers to the house, so Kiki and I follow it. As we reach the top, we notice over the wooden front door, carved into a stone archway, are the words: An Fáilte Teach.

'I wonder what that means?' Kiki asks.

I look up at the words; something about them was familiar. 'Wasn't *Fáilte* what it said when we arrived in Ballykiltara? It must mean welcome in Gaelic.'

'And Teach must mean house!' Kiki says excitedly. 'That would make sense, if what Jackie said was right.'

'Yes … The Welcome House.' I'm still staring up at the words. They looked like they'd been carved up there a long time ago.

'Looks like someone is living here,' Kiki says, looking either side of the door. 'There's curtains at the windows.'

'Yes, I noticed that as we climbed up. Shame, I was hoping it might be empty. I'll knock and see what's what.'

This is one of the most precarious parts of my job, knocking at a door when a property is clearly not for sale. The reaction I get from the person who answers the door can range from intense outrage to extreme curiosity when I tell them what I do for a living and that I'm interested in possibly purchasing their home.

I take a deep breath and reach for a door knocker, but find there isn't one. I look either side of the door for a bell, but there's not one of those either. So I ball my hand into a fist and bang hard on the wooden door.

I notice Kiki has stood back. She too knows what sort of reaction we're liable to get from the person who comes to the door, and it looks as if she's preparing herself for a quick getaway.

I wait a few seconds, and when no one answers, I bang hard again.

But this time my banging seems to dislodge the door, and it swings open a little. I look back at Kiki and pull a face. This would not be a good start if someone came to the door now.

But no one does, so I reach forward and call through the narrow opening. 'Hello! Is anyone in?'

But there's no reply, so I put one foot in the doorway and ask the same question again. But still no one answers.

'What shall we do now?' Kiki asks. 'Come back another day?'

I should say yes, that's exactly what we'll do, but I don't. Something is pulling me into the house – not some strange supernatural force or anything weird like that, simply a feeling that we should go through this door.

'*Ren!*' I hear Kiki call from outside as I take another step into the hall. 'You can't go in there. What if the owner comes back, or there's someone in there asleep!'

I know she's right, but I can't help myself, I have to see what's inside. This could be the house, the perfect place for Ryan Dempsey to see out his retirement in.

I step further into the hallway and take a look around. The décor in the hall is quite plain – cream-coloured walls with no pictures or photos hanging on them to give me a clue to the age of the owner of this house. Nothing but a narrow wooden table with a Tiffany-style lamp sitting on it, so I inch forward a bit more.

'Ren!' I hear Kiki hiss from the doorway. 'What are you doing?'

'I'm only taking a quick look,' I say, glancing over my shoulder. 'I can't decide if this is the right house if I don't see inside it, can I?'

Without waiting for Kiki's reply, I head further along the hall towards one of several plain wooden doors to see if I can discover anything else about this house or its owner. I hear the front door gently close behind me and Kiki's footsteps along the tiled floor as I take hold of the first handle I come to. I turn to her and hold my finger to my lips.

She pretends to zip hers shut.

I gently turn the handle and push open the door and a large sitting room is revealed. There's no one in there, so I step inside to look around.

The sitting room, like the hall, is furnished quite basically. There's a multicoloured brocade sofa, and two mismatched armchairs, with a small coffee table standing in between them. Against one cream-coloured wall stands a tall, dark wood dresser with a few ornaments sitting on its shelves, and on another a large heavy bookcase filled with old books. There's no carpet, just a stripped wooden floor with a rug, and some thick velvet curtains at the window that sort of coordinate with the furniture. But what's most odd in this eclectic room is there are no gadgets of any kind, not even a TV, the only thing to watch in here would be an open fire when it was lit in the large fireplace.

'Bit dull, isn't it?' Kiki whispers, looking around.

'Maybe someone older owns it?' I say, hoping this isn't the case. In my experience, the older the resident, the more stubborn they are when it comes to moving.

'Well, whoever it is, they can't be here or they would surely have heard us by now. Oh!' Kiki suddenly gasps. 'You don't think . . . ?'

'I don't think what?'

She looks up to the ceiling. 'You don't think they're dead, do you, and they're lying up in their bed rotting away.'

'Kiki!' I shake my head. 'Don't be silly.'

'But you hear about these things, don't you – old people dying and no one finding their body until weeks or months afterwards. And this looks like an old person's house.'

'Let's go and look in one of the other rooms,' I say hurriedly, before my own mind begins to wander too far. 'And see what we find there.'

We leave the sitting room and head across the hall to find a kitchen behind the next door we open.

Again, the room is basic, with kitchen units circa 1980s, but it's clean and there are all the amenities you could need: a small cooker, a Belfast-style sink, and a fridge freezer.

I go over to the fridge freezer and open the door to the fridge.

'This is no time for a snack,' Kiki says. 'What if there's a dead body upstairs?'

'Well, if there is, they've been out to buy milk recently,' I say, lifting a plastic bottle from the fridge, 'judging by the sell-by date on this.' I put the milk back and inspect the other contents of the fridge. There's some cheese, butter, and a packet of ham, all basic but all edible. Then I close the fridge door, and open a bread bin that sits on the side; a fresh uncut loaf waits inside for someone to eat it.

'The inhabitant of this house is definitely alive,' I say to Kiki. 'They must be out, and didn't shut the door properly behind them.'

'All the more reason we shouldn't be here then,' Kiki says, looking nervously behind her.

'I need to see the back of the house. I've only seen the front so far, and I want to see what the view is like from upstairs.' I look at Kiki's anxious face. 'Why don't you stay down here and raise the alarm if anyone comes back home.'

'OK, but what shall I do if someone does? Do we need a special signal?'

'We're property hunters, not secret agents. Just call me if anyone looks like they're coming up the steps outside.'

'I'll call out "The Search for Serendipity",' Kiki says, starting to look like she might be enjoying this. 'It'll be our code.'

'If you like,' I say, walking back into the hall. 'Right, I'm going upstairs.'

Kiki looks anxious again.

'There are no dead bodies,' I reassure her. 'Only ours, if we get caught here. Now go and keep a lookout.'

I climb confidently up the wooden stairs, my exterior bravado hiding my trepidation well. There *is* something a bit strange about this house. Unlike Kiki, I don't think it's hiding any dead bodies, but it is hiding something, though I don't know what yet. All the rooms we've visited so far have been stark, there's no denying that. Whoever lives here prefers a minimal approach to home décor, that's for sure. But even though the rooms are plain, the house manages to retain a sense of homeliness, which is quite enchanting in its own way.

I reach the top of the stairs and off a T-shaped landing I have the choice of four rooms. The first door I try is a bathroom, which like the kitchen below is clean and equipped with all the basic necessities. I then enter a series of bedrooms, all of which contain basic furniture and beds that are fully made up. Oddly, even though all the rooms have soft furnishings, there are no personal effects anywhere; no clothes, photographs, trophies, anything that might give me a clue to the owner of this house.

But what I am pleased to find as I enter the rooms that face the back of the house is a view. The view I'd hoped for when we'd been out on the boat earlier, and most importantly a view that I knew Ryan Dempsey would love – a perfect panorama of lakes and mountains, seen through long French windows designed to exploit a flawless outlook. It is absolutely stunning.

After I've stood and gazed at the view myself for a few minutes, I head downstairs, and on my way back to Kiki I quickly open a couple more doors to discover an unused dining room, and a large but un-stocked larder. I close all the doors behind me and return to the sitting room, where I find Kiki furtively looking through the front window.

'All done?' she asks. 'There's been no movement out here, only passing traffic. But I really think we should go soon.'

I look around the sitting room again. The house is old, and needs a fair bit of refurbishment, but it's the sort of size Ryan wanted so he could have his grandchildren to stay occasionally. It appears to have all the necessary amenities – like running water and electricity, and it's in the area that Ryan had specified. This house ticks all the boxes, but the biggest tick of all has to be the stunning view that was top of his list. The

Welcome House has everything, including an atmosphere; no, it's more of a feeling, an emotion, a sentiment, that like its name makes you feel welcome, for all its sparseness.

But the house feels cold right now, and almost a little sad, like it needs someone new to come and live here.

'What are you thinking, Ren?' Kiki asks, still looking out of the window. 'You're very quiet. No dead bodies were there?' she jokes.

I shake my head. 'No, on the contrary, this house has everything *but* that. It has everything Ryan wants. This is it, Kiki, we've found our house. All we have to do now is find out who owns it.'

Eleven

We drive back to the hotel, excitedly discussing our next move.

I'd been quite glad that the owner of the house hadn't made an appearance while we were there. Now I had time to think about the best way of making them an offer on their home while causing as little offence as possible.

It isn't always problematic. Sometimes, unbeknown to me, the owner of a house is actually thinking of putting their home up for sale, and they're quite pleased when I turn up at their door and make them an offer they can't refuse.

'Evening, ladies,' Donal calls from the reception desk as we make our way into the hotel. 'How was your day?'

'Very nice thank you,' I tell him. 'Most productive.'

'Good. And did you go on your boat trip?'

'Oh yes,' Kiki pipes up. 'We had a lovely old guy who took us across to the abbey. He knew all sorts.'

'Excellent. Did you catch his name? I might know him.'

'Jackie,' Kiki says. 'He told us lots of stories and told Ren about The Welcome House.'

When Kiki says Jackie's name, Donal looks puzzled for a second, then his face changes to surprise when she mentions The Welcome House. 'Now why would you ladies be interested in that old place?' he asks.

I stare hard at Kiki.

'Just more of Jackie's tales,' Kiki covers well. 'He has so many, doesn't he?'

Donal looks suspiciously at us.

'Do you know the house then, Donal?' I ask. *Or more importantly, who owns it?*

'Sure now,' Donal appears to relax, 'everyone around here knows The Welcome House.'

'That's what Jackie said,' I begin, hoping to pump him for more information. But some new guests arrive through the double doors, and Kiki and I need to move aside as they approach the reception desk, to allow them to check in.

If anyone would know who owned that house, then it would surely be Donal. He seems to know everything about the local area. I decide I'll pop back later to have a chat with him.

'I wonder if Eddie might know who owns that house?' Kiki muses as we wait for the lift. 'I could ask him, if you like? Once I've changed and freshened up, obviously.'

'Obviously.' I smile at her.

'Well, you have to take your chances, Ren. Maybe you should ask Finn too? As manager of the hotel, he must know a fair bit about the local area.'

'You might be right,' I reply, thinking about Finn as we step inside the lift.

I notice Kiki smiling slyly, but on this occasion I choose to ignore her, I haven't the energy to complain. She isn't the only one who needs to freshen up, today has been rewarding, yet tiring and I'm longing for a shower and a rest before I do any more metaphorical digging about The Welcome House.

Kiki spends the next hour snoring loudly on her bed, while I lie on mine staring up at the ceiling trying not to think about The Welcome House, but finding myself doing just that. Afterwards, we freshen up, change and head downstairs to find food, and hopefully some answers.

Donal is not on reception any more, and someone we haven't met before is, so we decide to split up and go in search of Eddie and Finn respectively.

'I wonder if you could tell me where I might find Finn Cassidy?' I ask the new lady on reception while Kiki heads outside to look for Eddie.

The receptionist, who according to her name badge is called Moira, looks at me slightly oddly but is polite in her reply. 'Finn isn't on duty right now. Is there anything I can help you with?'

I'm about to decline, but then I think better of it.

'I don't suppose you know who owns that white house on the main road out of Ballykiltara, do you?' I ask. 'I believe it's known as The Welcome House?'

Again Moira looks at me slightly oddly.

'No, I don't,' she says. 'Why do you ask?'

'Oh no reason,' I say. 'It's quite pretty, that's all. Thanks for your help.' I smile and turn towards the door.

'You might find Finn at the stables,' Moira says suddenly, and I turn back. 'He spends quite a bit of time over there when he's not on duty. And quite a lot of time when he is.' She smiles knowingly.

'Thanks, Moira,' I say happily. 'I'll see if he's there now.'

I head back through the hotel and out the back door into the hotel garden. It's a lovely bright end to the day, and the evening sun's rays warm the terracotta bricks of the wall that runs around the perimeter of the garden. I find the gate easily, now I know where it is, and this time don't hesitate to go straight through, following the path towards the stables much more confidently than I had the last time I was here.

When I reach the opening and the stable courtyard, there is no one to be seen. No one except the horses, who eye me curiously, wondering who I am, and more likely if I have food for them.

I wander over towards their stalls, and dither uncertainly a few feet in front of a black-and-white horse, who according to his nameplate is called Alfie.

'Hello, Alfie,' I say quietly. 'I'm Ren.' I move a little closer to Alfie and reach my hand out slowly to stroke his nose in the same way I'd seen Finn do the other day with Trixie.

Alfie closes his eyes as I continue to stroke his nose. 'You like that, do you?' I ask. 'I'm afraid I don't have any treats on me, is that OK?'

Alfie opens one eye, and then closes it again, and as I continue to stroke him I'm not sure who is more comforted by this simple motion, Alfie or me.

'He'll let you do that all day,' I hear a familiar voice call and I turn to see Finn wearing his usual casual attire, but with the addition of long boots and a riding hat, striding confidently across the stable yard. He leads Trixie, his favoured light-brown mare from the other day, and is accompanied by Fergus, his mottled brown dog, who trots happily alongside them both, his tongue lolloping out of the side of his mouth.

'Have you been riding?' I stupidly ask.

'Did the outfit give me away?' he says, grinning.

While Fergus wanders amiably about the yard, I follow Finn as he leads Trixie back into her stall. Then I watch while he expertly removes her bridle and saddle, and silently begins grooming her.

'I'm surprised to find you here again,' I say to break the silence.

Finn glances at me, then continues with Trixie's grooming. 'I used to have horses, many moons ago,' he explains. 'So I like to spend time here when I can.'

'Where was that?' I ask, expecting him to give me his usual vague answer.

'Just outside of Dublin,' he says, running the brush over Trixie's neck. 'My parents kept horses on their land when I was young.'

This was more information than Finn had ever offered me before.

'You must have had a lot of land then?' I try, pushing him a bit further.

'We did that.' Finn looks wistfully at Trixie's mane for a moment. Then he quickly straightens himself up. 'But, like I said, that was many moons ago.' He gives Trixie a hearty pat. 'One of the stable girls will be around to feed and water you in a bit,' he tells her before producing a treat from his pocket, which Trixie nuzzles gratefully from the palm of his hand. Then he pats her again and leaves the stable, shutting the door firmly behind him.

'Were you wanting me for something?' he asks bluntly, looking straight at me.

I've been so mesmerised watching Finn deal with Trixie

that for a moment it had slipped my mind why I'd come here in the first place.

'Oh yes, I was wondering if you knew who owned the white house on the main road out of Ballykiltara?'

'You mean The Welcome House?' Finn asks, unbuckling his helmet.

'Yes, that's the one.'

'I don't think anyone does,' he says, to my surprise.

'How do you mean?'

Finn whistles Fergus and the big dog comes bounding over to him. Finn pats him as he arrives by his side and produces yet another treat from his other pocket, a dog one this time, which he feeds to Fergus.

'I mean what I said. No one knows who owns that house.'

'But it's not derelict. I saw it today; it's very well looked after. It's definitely lived in, there's food inside and everything . . .' My voice trails off while Finn looks at me with interest, his head cocked slightly to the side, a bit like Fergus.

'I mean . . .' I try and recover. 'It . . . it looks like there would be someone living there . . . from the outside.'

To my relief, Finn doesn't question me further about how I know there is food in the house's kitchen.

'Mac!' Finn calls across the yard. And I turn to see a man with greying hair pop his head out from one of the stalls. 'This lady here wants to know more about The Welcome House.'

'Does she now?' Mac says, the rest of his body following his head. Like Finn, Mac bolts the stable gate firmly behind him.

'Mac knows everything there is to know about this area,' Finn says as we watch Mac hobble his way across the courtyard towards us, using a knobbly old walking stick.

'More than Donal?' I ask.

'Oh Christ, yes, a *lot* more than Donal. Donal is like a walking guidebook. Mac is the real deal when it comes to local knowledge.'

'Now,' Mac says as he arrives in front of us. 'What would you like to know, lass?'

'Do you know who owns the house?' I ask.

Mac looks at Finn and raises his bushy eyebrows.

'I did tell her,' Finn says, shrugging. 'She won't believe me, though.'

'Young lady, no one knows who owns The Welcome House, that's part of its charm.'

'But how can no one own it? Is it rented from someone? A company, perhaps?'

The men exchange a knowing smile.

'What? What are you smiling about? It's a fair question, isn't it?'

'It is indeed,' Mac says, nodding. 'And one many people before you have asked. You're not alone in your wondering.'

I look between them; what is going on here?

Mac checks his watch. 'Is it too early?' he asks Finn. He raises his hand and gestures a drinking motion.

'It's never too early for you, Mac!' Finn replies. 'Shall we head back to the hotel bar and you can answer all Ren's many questions about the house?'

'Sounds like a plan to me! Let me finish up here and I'll be right over to join you.'

We watch Mac hobble away again.

'Lives for this place, does Mac,' Finn says, and he gestures for us to make our way back along the path to the hotel. 'Never seems to leave it, unless of course he has a date with a glass of the black stuff somewhere.' He calls Fergus, who immediately comes bounding over.

'You seem to spend a fair amount of time here too,' I tell him as we make our way along the path. I have to walk briskly to keep up with Finn's long bouncy strides. I want to ask more about the house as we walk, but there seems little point until pints of Guinness are poured. At least now I have hope of some answers.

'When I have spare time, I like to spend it at the stable, I can't deny that,' Finn says. 'I much prefer time spent in the great outdoors than stuck inside the hotel. But sadly it's the hotel that pays my bills.'

'The more I get to know you, the less likely it seems that hotel manager is the job for you,' I try, hoping to get the truth out of him this time.

'The more you get to know me, eh?' Finn smiles to himself then turns towards me. 'Sounds serious.'

'Stop avoiding my questions,' I reply, accustomed to this evasion technique of his now.

'I'm not. In a few minutes, I'm taking you to get all the answers you require from Mac, aren't I?'

I sigh and shake my head.

'Perhaps it should be me asking the questions?' he continues. 'Like why you're so interested in a house when you're here on holiday?'

'My turn to be evasive,' I call, skipping on ahead of him. I grab the handle of the gate and let myself through. 'Two can play at that game!' I tease, pausing in the archway.

'Ah, but the difference between the two of us is . . . I can live without the answers,' Finn says knowingly. 'Whereas I don't think you, Ren Parker, can.'

I'm about to defend myself when, instead of heading towards the back door of the hotel, Finn takes a detour to the left of the building.

'I need to pop Fergus back to my place – it's not looked on too favourably if I have him in the hotel.'

I'm about to offer to come with him when he says, 'I'll meet you in the bar in about ten minutes. My place is round the back of the hotel. I just need to get him settled and I'll be there.'

Secretive as ever, I think. 'Sure,' I say. 'See you in a bit.'

Finally, I'm sitting at a table, the same table Kiki and I had sat at the night we arrived in Ballykiltara, with Finn sitting on one side of me and Mac sitting opposite. I texted Kiki to see where she was, but so far I haven't had a reply. So it's just the boys and me. I've joined Mac in a Guinness, something that seems to impress him, but Finn is drinking orange juice again.

To my annoyance, all I've discovered so far is something I already knew, that Mac's full name is Cormac, and he's lived in Ballykiltara all his life.

'So,' I say, desperate to bring the conversation around to The Welcome House. 'You were going to tell me about this house, Mac?'

'Ah yes, lass, so I was. What is it you want to know again?'

'Well, to begin with, who owns it?'

'Ah now, that is a very tricky thing to explain, young lady.'

'Why is it?'

Mac puts down his pint-glass. 'Do you like stories?' he asks.

'I'm in Ireland, I'm getting pretty used to them by now. Why, though?'

Mac grins. 'Because if you want to know about The Welcome House, it's quite a long tale.'

'Go on then,' I say, taking a sip of my drink. 'I'm in no hurry.'

Mac glances at Finn before beginning. 'The Welcome House has stood in Ballykiltara for as long as anyone can remember. An Fáilte Teach, to give it its proper name, is a house with its doors always open. Open to passers-by in need of shelter or accommodation for one or a few nights, or to those that need protection or help. Its front door, they say, has never been locked or bolted.'

I look at Mac, trying to take all this in.

'But someone must own the house, surely? They must do.'

Mac shakes his head. 'The legend of The Welcome House is one that has been passed down through the generations. I don't know how long that house has been there, but it's always been the same: a house that welcomes and is open to anyone that needs it.'

I nod politely. This is getting a bit awkward; it's a lovely story Mac is telling me, but someone must own the place, and if Mac believes this legend that has sprung up around the house, then perhaps he isn't the best person to be asking.

'That story is lovely, Mac. But if you don't know who owns the house, then who looks after it? Even if the welcome story is true, the house is hardly derelict, is it? I mean, who puts food in the cupboards and the fridge?'

I notice Finn's eyebrows raise a little when I mention the inside of the house. Damn, I'm giving myself away again.

'Jackie told me about the food,' I improvise.

'Jackie?' Mac asks, his tone suddenly changing. He sits forward in his chair. 'Where did you meet this *Jackie*?'

'He took me and my friend out in his boat. We went over to Rafferty Island to see the abbey today.'

'Did he now?' Mac says, again in the same strange voice.

'And what did this Jackie look like, if you don't mind me asking.'

'Er … he was fairly old,' I say, trying to remember, 'but powerful. Yes, I remember thinking that someone who was as old as him shouldn't still have the strength to row a boat about on the lake like he did, but he did it with ease.'

Mac nods. 'What else?'

'He was really knowledgeable about the area and the lake. That's how I spotted the house, when we were out on the water, but when I asked Jackie about it he was evasive with his answers, a bit like you both were when I asked you at the stables earlier, so I didn't think that was anything odd.'

'White hair?' Mac asks.

'Yes, and a tattoo on his lower right arm of a—'

'Celtic cross?' Mac finishes for me.

'Yes, do you know him then?'

Mac picks up his Guinness again. He takes a long, slow sip. I glance at Finn, but he looks as mystified as I feel.

'Mac, who is this Jackie?' Finn asks. 'I don't think I've ever seen him around the area, but you seem to know him?'

Mac puts down his pint again. 'There have been sightings over the years of a man that goes by the description you just gave, Ren.'

'And … ?'

'Ghostly sightings.'

I can't help but laugh. 'Come on! You can't expect me to believe that Kiki and I were rowed across a lake by a ghost!'

'Jackie Byrne was an eighteenth-century ferryman who kept the town of Ballykiltara, on one side of the great lake, linked with the town of Ballybun on the other. The ferryboat was the quickest way to get from one side of the lake to the other.

90

Now we'd take motorised transport, but in those days the boat was the fastest direct route. Even horses took longer and were more expensive.'

'Go on, Mac,' Finn encourages.

'Jackie was a well-known local figure, a hero to many after he saved a child's life when she fell into the lake one afternoon while playing at the side of it. But even though the water was his life, it would be his death too. They say Jackie drowned one night while trying to ferry a son over from Ballykiltara to Ballybun to his elderly, dying mother. The son had bought medicine that could help his mother, but he needed to get it to her immediately. So even though the winds were fierce over the water that night, and a boat should never have attempted the crossing, that's just what Jackie did.'

'What happened?' I ask, now totally caught up in this tale.

'They never made it,' Mac says gravely. 'Both were drowned in the middle of the lake, never to be seen again. Jackie's boat was washed to shore the following morning – empty.

'However,' Mac continues before Finn or I can speak, 'that wasn't the last time Jackie was spotted on the lake. There have been sightings of him and his boat many times in the years since, usually in the early morning, or late evening, when a mist sits over the water. It's as if his spirit can't rest until he takes his boat on one last successful journey. But never,' he looks solemnly at me, 'never has anyone reported being taken out in his boat with him.'

Finn and Mac's eyes both fix on me.

'Stop it,' I tell them. 'There is no way that Kiki and I were rowed across a lake today by a ghost! This guy must look very similar to this other Jackie, that's all. He was definitely alive and breathing, I'm sure of it.'

'How much did he charge you for the trip?' Mac asks.

'He didn't; he waved me away when I tried to pay him.'

'Cash isn't any good to you in heaven,' Finn says. I glance at him and he winks at me.

'Mock all you like, young Finn,' Mac says. 'I tell nothing but the truth.'

'Look, I know you Irish like your myths and legends,' I tell Mac, 'and that's great – I get it. I'm quite interested in all that kind of stuff, as it goes. But you've sat here tonight and told me about a house that doesn't have an owner, and yet is filled with fresh food to welcome random guests, and about a ghostly ferryman who apparently rows people across a lake so his spirit can ascend to heaven. I know I'm English, but come on, you don't seriously expect me to believe all this, do you?'

Mac lifts his pint-glass and downs the dregs of his Guinness. 'Young lady,' he says, placing his glass firmly down on the table. 'You can believe what you like. I can only tell you what I know, and what I know is the truth.' He lifts his stick then uses it to ease himself up to a standing position. But before he leaves, he leans down again, resting his hand on the table. 'What I do know is,' he says quietly, 'if Jackie took you and your friend out to show you The Welcome House, then there's a very special reason for it, a very special one indeed. Now all *you* have to do is find out why.'

Twelve

'What on earth just went on here?' I ask Finn as we watch Mac walk out of the bar. 'Was he serious about all that stuff?'

'It's quite hard to believe, I agree, especially the part about the ghost. I'd never come across that tale, and I've heard a few since I've been here. But Mac's right about The Welcome House, it does welcome in passers-by and has for as long as anyone can remember. It's part of Ballykiltara's history.'

'But someone must put the stuff in there,' I insist. I feel like I'm labouring the point, but it's a fact: there has to be a person or persons who look after that house, and if they don't own it themselves, they must know who does.

Finn shrugs. 'It's a funny one, I'll give you that. I've often wondered about it myself. But the locals here simply accept it as read.'

'You don't count yourself as a local then?'

'No, not me, I've only lived here for a few years. I'm still seen as a newcomer. Another drink?'

I look at my glass. 'Sure, yes, why not? Thank you.'

Finn picks up my empty glass and heads to the bar. While he does, I check my phone. Ah, at last, a text from Kiki:

Don't worry about me, I'm with Eddie at the pub. Trying to get to the bottom of the mystery as well as a few glasses! See u later, K xx

I'm about to text her back, when I hesitate. I haven't found out that much yet; maybe Kiki can get a little further than I have.

Finn is still at the bar, waiting for my Guinness to settle, so I pick up the menu that sits on the table and realise in all the excitement tonight I haven't eaten yet. I probably shouldn't drink much more on an empty stomach, so I peruse the menu while I wait.

'Are you wanting to order some food?' Finn asks as he brings a pint of Guinness and a pint of Coke over to the table. 'I could probably do with some myself. It's been a fair while since lunch.'

'I was thinking about it,' I reply as he sits down again. I wish I'd asked for a soft drink now that Mac's gone and I'm the only one drinking; I don't want Finn to think I'm an alcoholic with all this Guinness. 'You'd be welcome to join me, if you're not busy?' I ask in a quiet voice, burying my head in the menu in my embarrassment.

'Nope, not busy at all,' he says calmly. 'I've had an afternoon off today. I don't normally spend it at the hotel, but since it's you ... ' he winks.

'I'll take that as a compliment,' I reply, blushing even more.

'You should. Now,' Finn says, picking up the menu, 'what are they serving up today?'

We order our food then settle back to wait for it.

'So,' Finn asks after a bit, 'I think it's time you came clean, Miss Parker.'

'About?'

'About your interest in the house. Your questions are much more passionate than those of our usual curious tourist.'

'You could be on to something there, Mr Cassidy. Tell you what, I'll answer your question on one condition: you promise to answer one of mine this time.'

'Sure,' Finn agrees, to my surprise. 'Not a problem. Only the one question, mind – you seem to have so many!'

'Goes with the name, doesn't it?' I smile. 'Parker?' I hint when Finn doesn't appear to get it. 'As in nosy parker?'

'Ah yes, of course, the *perfect* name for you! So, your turn first: why are you and your friend *really* here? I knew the day you walked into the hotel you weren't our usual type of holidaymakers.'

I take a deep breath. He's going to find out eventually.

'I'm a property seeker,' I tell him. 'My job is to find properties for clients who have specific requirements in a house or home.'

'A property seeker . . . ' Finn repeats, as if I've told him I'm a spy. 'I don't think I've ever heard of one of those before.'

'There aren't too many of us. I have my own company, and Kiki works with me.'

Finn nods, taking it all in. 'Cool. So you're over here seeking properties?'

'One property – a house for a client who wants to buy a retirement home here.'

'And let me guess: The Welcome House fits all his *requirements*?'

'We've been all over in the last couple of days, but I haven't been able to find anywhere else that's even close. They're always missing one thing. They have a view but not the right facilities, or they have all the facilities but no view. The Welcome House has everything I'm looking for; it's perfect.'

'Except for one thing.'

I look questioningly at Finn.

'An owner!' he replies. 'How can you buy a house for your client if you can't find a vendor to purchase it from?'

'And that is exactly why I need to find out who owns it. Someone must. Or if I can't find that out, I need to find out who looks after it. That would be a start, at least.'

'Well, I wish you luck with that. As far as I'm aware, no one knows who looks after the place. It's the biggest secret here in Ballykiltara.'

'Secrets are there to be revealed,' I say with meaning.

'Some secrets,' Finn says. 'Not all.'

'Talking of which, what's yours?' I ask, lifting my glass and taking a sip.

'My secret?' Finn asks, his bright green eyes wide with innocence.

'Yes, yours. You must have one – you're always so evasive when I speak to you.'

'Am I?'

'You are, and you know it. So now I've told you how I came to be here, how did you?'

'Come to be *here*?' Finn asks, pointing at the floor. 'In this very room?'

'Funny,' I say flatly. 'No, here in Ballykiltara and here at The Stag.'

'That's two questions. I only agreed to one.'

I sigh. 'OK ... here as manager of the hotel.'

Finn takes his time in answering. He drinks from his glass of Coke, looks around the bar, probably willing the food to arrive to get him out of having to give me an answer, but when it doesn't he leans in towards me conspiratorially.

'Dermot O'Connell asked me to do it,' he says. Then he leans back in his chair smugly, his arms folded.

'Oh no, you're not getting out of it that easily! Had you been a hotel manager before? How did you know Dermot? Did you apply for the job or were you head-hunted?'

'Whoa!' Finn holds his hand up to protect himself against my torrent of questions. 'What were you before you were a property seeker – military interrogation?'

'Look, you agreed to answer my question if I answered yours. Now you're being your usual obstinate self! I don't know why I bother.' I toss my head, still playing the game, and pretend to get up as if I'm about to leave, but Finn, to my surprise, grabs my hand.

'I'm sorry,' he apologises, looking up at me. 'Please stay.'

I look down at my hand, still gripped tightly in his, and then into his sorrowful eyes, and it's as I do I feel my hand fall to my side as he loosens his grip.

Finn looks somewhat shamefaced as I slowly sit down again opposite him, still a little dazed by his previous reaction.

'So, are you going to tell me or not?' I ask him when I've recovered my composure. 'It must be some secret if you work this hard at keeping it.'

'No. It's just, when you've built a wall up around you and

you find someone chipping at it, your natural response is to protect yourself.'

I know all about that.

'I understand,' I hear myself saying. 'Really I do.'

'Do you?' Finn asks warily. 'How?'

'This is supposed to be about you this time,' I remind him. 'Not me.'

'Sorry,' he says again. He takes a deep breath, and prepares to lower his own internal drawbridge. 'I got the job here because I met Dermot when I took a trip to Tara – his island. It was one of those bonding trips companies send you on – you know, outward bound, that kind of thing. We met and got on well, that's all there was to it.'

I suspected there was a tad more to it than that.

'And he offered you a job here?'

'No, not then – later.'

'So you worked in the hospitality industry?'

'Yeah, I knew a fair bit about it.'

'What happened later then, for you to want to come and work here?'

'Change of direction – that's all.'

'*Finn?*'

'What are you, part bloodhound? Once you get the scent of something you won't let go, will you?'

I silently watch him and wait for his answer.

'OK,' Finn says with a sigh, 'if I tell you the whole story, I get at least another three questions about you – deal?'

I think about this. Am I ready to answer the sort of questions I know Finn will ask? I'm about to answer him when our food arrives; one of the plates is covered with a silver cloche, the sort used for room service.

'Thank you,' I tell Ciaran, who I now recognise from behind the bar, as he puts a bowl of piping-hot vegetable lasagne in front of me.

'You're most welcome,' he says, smiling. He looks hesitantly at Finn as he rests his covered plate down on the table in front of him. 'Finn, I've brought yours to the table, but I've been asked by Sarah to see if you'll pop back to the kitchen to settle a dispute. I'm so sorry, I know you're off duty. But she says it won't take a minute.'

'That's what she always says!' Finn rolls his eyes. 'This is exactly why I don't spend time here on my days off. I'm sorry, Ren,' he says apologetically. 'I guess our Q&A will have to wait for a bit. You go ahead with your food – I'll be back as quickly as I can.'

'Sure, no worries. Go do your job.'

Ciaran leaves Finn's covered plate at the table, and then he and Finn hurry off to the kitchen. While I tuck into my food, I try and imagine what this Sarah looks like. She seems to be quite the tyrant in the hotel kitchen; she's certainly got everyone jumping, and probably tells them how high too.

As I wait for Finn to return, my mind returns to The Welcome House. Why did the only house in the area that fitted Ryan Dempsey's needs have to be one that was so tied up in local folklore?

Like I'd said to Mac, I was quite interested in that sort of thing, and I would never usually think about interfering in, or possibly destroying a tale like that. But I had a job to do, and a reputation to uphold. I couldn't possibly let anything or anyone prevent me from doing it, myth, legend or otherwise.

Thirteen

No sooner has Finn apologetically returned to our table than Kiki appears in the bar.

'Do you two want to be left alone?' she asks, eyeing the two plates of food – one full, as Finn tucks hungrily into his ale pie, and the other empty, except for a stray lettuce leaf from the lasagne's accompanying side salad.

'No, you're fine, sit down.' Finn waves her into the seat Mac had vacated earlier.

Great, now I'll never get Finn back on to our earlier topic. But on the plus side, I won't have to answer any of *his* questions either.

'Where's Eddie?' I ask, looking for him.

'He's on earlies tomorrow,' Kiki says, lifting my glass and wrinkling her nose up at the dregs of my Guinness. 'Had to get an early night. But I did find out some *stuff* ...' She taps the side of her nose and glances at Finn.

'Don't mind me,' Finn says, polishing off his plate of food. How can he have eaten that so fast? He's a big guy – he towers over Kiki, and he's a fair bit taller than my five-foot-nine frame – and he's broad with it, but still his plate had been loaded, and now it's empty, apart from some stray peas. 'I'm heading up to the bar now. Kiki, what ya having?'

Kiki thinks about it. 'Malibu and Coke,' she decides, fluttering her eyelashes at Finn. 'Thank you.'

'Ren, another Guinness?'

I look at my glass.

'No, I'll have an orange juice this time, thanks. But it's my round.' I grab my bag.

'Put that down,' Finn insists. 'What use is being the manager if you don't have a tab – and,' he adds grinning, 'a healthy discount!'

He heads back up to the bar.

'I like him!' Kiki announces, watching him go. 'So what's happening, Ren?'

'Well, I've found out some more about The Welcome House,' I begin.

'No, not about that – about you and Finn!'

'There's nothing *to* tell.'

'So why are you having dinner together?' Kiki points to the empty plates on the table.

'Technically, we didn't have dinner together ...' And I begin to explain as quickly as I can what had taken place this evening.

Finn comes back during my explanation.

'It's fine,' I tell Kiki when she flashes her eyes in warning at me. 'Finn knows what we do.'

'And I'm cool with it,' Finn says, lifting our drinks from a

101

tray and sitting down. 'But some around here might not be if they find out you're messing with The Welcome House. Best you keep it quiet.'

'We're not messing with it,' I insist. 'Well, we might be if we can find out who owns it. But that seems unlikely right now.'

'Don't speak so soon, my friend,' Kiki says, taking a long slow sip of her drink. She looks tantalisingly over the rim of her glass at us.

'What do you know?'

'Well,' Kiki says eagerly, 'when I asked Eddie about it, at first he said he knew nothing, all I got was the usual Blarney – see what I did there? Blarney?'

'Yeah,' I groan. 'I get it.'

'He told me all the same stuff you heard, Ren. Except for the ghost part – we really need to talk about that some more ...'

'Kiki,' I prompt, knowing she's liable to go way off topic, given the chance.

'OK, we'll do the ghost later. Oh, I didn't mean ...' she giggles, and looks shyly at Finn, who doesn't bat an eyelid.

Internally I roll my eyes. Kiki obviously enjoyed several Malibu and Cokes with Eddie before joining us.

'Kiki, the facts, please?' I ask as calmly as I can.

'Oh yes, sorry.' She clears her throat and composes herself. 'Right: Eddie. So, when I pushed him a bit harder about the house, he said he remembered cycling past there once in the early morning on his way into work – he lives with his mammy you know, isn't that sweet?'

I wait patiently.

'So anyway he was cycling past when he saw someone going into the house carrying a couple of Super-Valu bags. Is that like a supermarket here?' she asks Finn.

'It is, yes.'

'Ah, I didn't like to ask.'

'What happened then?' I prompt. 'Did Eddie see the person's face; did he recognise them?'

'Nah,' Kiki says, lifting her glass. She shrugs. 'Shame really.'

I look apologetically at Finn with a 'This is what I have to deal with' face. He smiles back.

'So all we know is that the owner or person that looks after The Welcome House shops at Super-Valu. Great.'

'It might not have been them,' Finn points out. 'It could have been someone passing through – one of The Welcome House's temporary guests.'

'Oh yeah, I didn't think of that.' Kiki sounds disappointed. 'But Eddie seemed pretty sure. I wonder why?'

'What time did he see them?' I ask. I look at Finn. 'What time does an early shift start here?'

'It varies. Eddie could have been biking past around six a.m., I guess. Possibly even earlier.'

'I'm pretty certain your local supermarket doesn't open before then, am I right?'

'Eight o'clock, if it's the one in Ballykiltara.'

'Then it's more than likely that the person Eddie saw going into the house was our mystery caretaker, right?'

The other two don't look quite as convinced as I sound.

'Perhaps you should talk to Eddie,' Finn says. 'He'll be about early tomorrow morning.'

'I'll certainly be doing that,' I tell him. 'I'll also be speaking to as many locals as I can tomorrow, and spending a fair bit of time on the Internet. Someone must know who owns that house. And I intend to find out who that person is.'

Fourteen

The next day I do exactly what I'd promised Finn I would.

After breakfast, I take my laptop and I sit in the comfortable foyer of the hotel on one of their red velvet sofas drinking coffee and searching every website I know for clues as to who might own The Welcome House. But the house proves as elusive as its owner.

Infuriatingly, I can find the history of virtually every other surrounding property. Although the house stands alone and doesn't have any immediate neighbours, I easily trace similar properties in the locality through sale sites and estate agents, but sadly not the one I'm interested in. The only mention of the house is on a random walker's blog. The walker talks in great detail about the time he got caught just outside Ballykiltara in a torrential storm and found shelter in a strange little house that offered hospitality and a much-needed roof over his head. The blog described how the walker had found a note telling him he was most welcome to stay as long as he needed to, and to help himself to anything he found in the fridge and kitchen cupboards. All it asked in return was that he left the house the way he'd found it, and if possible replenished any food he had used, or left some compensation for it.

I read the blog post through twice, in case I've missed anything, then I sit back in my seat and think.

There must be some way of finding out who owns this house. The Internet hadn't been any help, but *someone* in Ballykiltara must know. The question is, will they tell me? Mac had suggested the house had been like this for generations; it sounded as though it was a well-known local myth that people around here had grown up with. Why would any of the locals confide in me, a foreign tourist, the truth about their precious fable? They'd be suspicious. Chances were, they'd clam up immediately and tell others not to speak to me once it got out I was asking 'awkward' questions. I wouldn't stand a chance in a tight-knit community such as this.

Which is exactly why I'd sent Kiki out to speak to people.

Kiki has an innocent, open quality about her that makes people trust her immediately. I'd seen it many a time when we'd been in negotiations for a property. Whereas I brought a cool, calm, organised air to the proceedings, Kiki would be her usual exuberant, energetic self. People weren't threatened by her, and that in turn allowed them to be completely honest. Which is what I was hoping would happen this morning when she hit the streets of Ballykiltara.

I open up my laptop again and fire off a quick reply to an email Ryan Dempsey has sent me, assuring him things are going well in Ireland, and we're currently 'in negotiations' over a property that might be the perfect one for him, and promising

I'll keep him updated. As I close the lid, I spy Eddie hurrying across the foyer carrying a bucket and mop.

'Eddie!' I call, getting up and rushing over to him. 'Have you got a moment?'

Eddie looks flustered. 'Not right now, miss.' He lifts his mop. 'There's been a nasty spillage. One of the maids dropped a breakfast tray upstairs. Apparently, there's a sea of porridge running between rooms thirteen and fourteen.'

'Oh no! Well, you'd best go then. If you've time, can you pop back and see me afterwards though? I'd like to ask you a couple of questions, if you don't mind.'

'Sure. Just give me a few minutes.'

I watch him hurry away towards the staircase, carrying his bucket and mop.

At the moment, Eddie is my equivalent to a key witness in a murder inquiry. He's the only lead I have, and I need to bring him in for further questioning.

I notice Orla is watching me from reception, so I go over to her.

'Is everything all right, miss?' Orla asks as I approach.

'Yes, everything is fine, thank you,' I assure her.

'You wanted to speak with my brother?'

'I did? Oh, Eddie is your brother ... sorry, I didn't know.'

'Stepbrother, actually. But we're very close.'

'I only wanted to ask him a couple of questions. It can wait, though,' I lie, 'nothing urgent.'

'Anything I can help you with?' Orla asks brightly, in her super-helpful receptionist way.

I shake my head. 'I doubt it, not unless you know anything about that old house on the road out of Ballykiltara – The Welcome House, I believe it's called.'

Orla looks surprised at my question, then her usual calm placid expression returns to her face. 'I only know there's a fair bit of legend surrounding it. I think my father first told me the story when I was a girl. Not that long before he died, as a matter of fact.' Sorrow is now the emotion covering Orla's pretty face.

'I'm sorry to hear that,' I tell her. 'Yes, I've heard there are a lot of old tales surrounding the house. That's why I'm so interested in it. I'm writing a book, see,' I tell her in a flash of inspiration that makes me wonder why I didn't think of it sooner. 'I'm here doing research on Irish myths and legends, and this one is so interesting and different.'

'I didn't know you were a writer.' Orla suddenly looks interested. 'Have you had anything published?'

'Not an actual book as such, no,' I reply truthfully. 'I usually write features, quite often about property ...'

'Ah, I see.' Orla doesn't look quite as impressed now.

'But I'm hoping the book I'm researching will be picked up. I have a party who's keen to know how it's all going while I'm here.'

Orla nods.

'So, can you tell me anything about the house?' I ask. 'What did your father tell you?'

'Oh, I'm sorry. We have guests ...' Orla looks over my shoulder as some new guests dragging suitcases arrive through the main door.

'Welcome to The Stag,' she says brightly. 'I'm so sorry there was no one to take your bags for you. Our bellboy has temporarily been dispatched to another part of the hotel. Now, you're aware our check-in isn't until three p.m. ...'

I leave Orla and her guests at the reception desk and walk

back to my laptop to wait for Eddie. Maybe he can shed a little more light on that early morning mystery visitor …

'So, the only thing you can tell me about this guy is that he was tall, broad, and definitely male?' I ask Eddie again.

'Yeah, like I said, I didn't take much notice. I was late for work, so I was cycling quite fast. It wasn't until I got to work I thought properly about what I saw.'

'Sure, I understand.'

'I told Kiki everything I know last night.' Eddie looks down at his feet. 'Grand girl, she is.'

'She likes you,' I tell him, still thinking about the house and its early morning visitor.

'Nooo,' Eddie insists, looking down at the floor again. But his pale grey eyes glance up at me from under a pair of dark heavy brows. 'Does she?' he asks, looking pleased.

I smile. 'Yes, she does. I wish you all the luck in the world – if Kiki's set her sights on you, you'll need it!'

'Eddie, what are you doing here?' Finn calls across the foyer, 'You're supposed to be helping Sarah in the kitchen. That new fridge is being delivered today and she needs help moving the old one.'

'Surprised she can't move it on her own,' Eddie mutters. He winks at me, and hurries – the only speed Eddie seems to have – over towards Finn. 'Right on it, boss!' he salutes, and Finn shakes his head as Eddie speeds off in the direction of the kitchen.

'I thought you were supposed to be on holiday?' Finn asks, wandering over towards me, nodding at my laptop. 'You'll blow your cover.'

'I have a new cover now,' I explain, sitting down. 'I'm a writer, here doing research.'

'Oh?' Finn says. 'Let me guess, research into old houses with odd names and even odder backstories?'

'Something like that, yes.' I look at Finn as he sits down next to me. Today he's wearing blue jeans and a casual white shirt, and as he turns towards me his shirt opens just far enough for me to catch a glimpse of a fine smattering of dark hair scattered over what I knew would be a muscular chest. 'I had to think of something fast,' I tell him, looking away and developing a sudden interest in my empty coffee cup. 'I was asking Orla questions and she wondered why.'

'As will most people, when you start pressing them about this. A writer isn't a bad cover, I suppose.'

'Thanks.'

'Did you find out anything more from Eddie? I'm assuming you were grilling him?'

'I was not *grilling* him. I was simply attempting to clarify his information, that's all.'

'He looked pretty scared to me.'

'That's probably because I was telling him Kiki had the hots for him,' I say, ignoring Finn's usual teasing.

Finn's eyebrows raise. 'Oh, does she now?'

'Well, she likes him – a lot.'

'Does liking someone always mean you have the hots for them?' Finn asks, his serious expression fighting for supremacy with his mischievous eyes.

'Not always, I suppose . . .' I try to answer with an equally solemn voice, even though to my annoyance my heart is racing, making my voice quiver slightly as I speak.

'Only sometimes, eh?' Finn smiles again.

'Yes,' I whisper. 'Only sometimes.'

Finn and I are sitting very close to each other on the sofa, and as I find myself gazing into his handsome face, my eyes are drawn towards his with a magnetic force that scares, and yet excites me at the same time.

Finn leans in a little closer ...

'*Ren* ...' the voice sounds muffled, as if it's a long way away, it's so at odds with the moment I find myself in right now with Finn. I turn my head to the side to listen.

'Ren, are you there?' I hear again through my perfect bubble, and it's as I realise who the voice belongs to that I feel the bubble pop.

Finn and I sit bolt upright on the sofa as Kiki appears in front of the alcove my sofa is positioned in.

She looks between us with a delighted smile.

'What's wrong?' I ask, unnecessarily standing up to greet her.

'Nothing. Everything is absolutely wonderful! Well, it is from where I'm standing.' She winks at us both.

'So why were you calling me?' I ask, trying to ignore her even though I can feel my cheeks are flushed. 'It sounded important.'

'Oh that,' Kiki says, flopping down in the armchair opposite Finn, still grinning at him. 'I think I've found us another lead. And this time, it comes heaven sent ... '

Fifteen

'I'm not sure about this,' I whisper as we reach the top of a steep hill and approach an imposing church set a short way from the centre of Ballykiltara. 'Religion and me don't get on.'

'How can you not *get on* with religion?' Finn asks, amusement in his voice. 'Have you argued with it often?'

'No, I mean I don't like it. Especially – and I mean no offence when I say this, Finn – the *Catholic* religion.' I wrinkle my nose apologetically.

'Ah,' Finn says knowingly. 'Yes, that has had quite a bad press of late.'

'I mean, I don't want to single out Catholicism,' I say hurriedly, in case he takes offence. 'I just assume that's what this church will be. Because it's all religions I take issue with. They're so conformist, there's no room to question anything.'

'Like?' Finn asks, pausing as we reach a gate that acts as the entrance to the church.

'Like different beliefs, alternate ways to interpret what goes on when you die.'

'What do you think happens when you die then?' Finn asks, as if he genuinely wants to know.

I consider this for a moment. 'I think you go to a sort of halfway house to begin with. Somewhere you can watch over your loved ones for a while, and if you need to, try and put right your wrongs.'

'And after that?'

'When we've checked our loved ones are OK without us, and dealt with any unfinished business, we are reincarnated into someone or something new, and everything in our previous life is wiped from our memories.'

'Whoa, heavy,' Finn says, nodding. 'You've certainly thought about it.'

'Haven't you?'

He shrugs. 'Not really.'

'You're not religious? Worrying whether you'll be condemned to eternal damnation in hell for your sins?'

'Maybe I don't have any sins,' Finn says, trying to sound angelic. 'Can't you see my halo shining?' He glances up above him.

'Everyone has sins,' I tell him. 'It's only a question of how bad they are.'

'Ooh ... you've just become even more fascinating, Miss Parker.'

I roll my eyes. 'I highly doubt that. I'm very dull.' I look over the gate at the church and sigh. 'I guess we'd better get this over with.'

Kiki had told us about her tip to go and visit the local Catholic priest, Father Duffy. Apparently, she'd got into quite a long, in-depth conversation with a young guy in an alternative cloth-ing store, and he'd told her that Father Duffy would more than likely know about the house because 'he'd lived in Ballykiltara forever'. We'd then had a quick discussion about who would be best to go and see him, and it had been decided that Finn and I should go that afternoon. Kiki's excuse was she might say something 'unreligious', and she was probably right. I didn't know what this Father Duffy was like, but if he was anything like the Catholic priests I'd come across in the past, he wouldn't appreciate Kiki's ditziness. And I knew when Kiki was under pressure, it only got worse.

So Finn had agreed to go with me for moral support, plus we figured as a well-known local figure, his presence would help make my questions about the house seem less suspicious.

It was quite nice to have Finn on board with us; he seemed as keen as we were to solve this mystery. He said the house was something he'd always wondered about since he'd come to Ballykiltara, and he wanted to see if we could discover some proper answers.

And as we approach the church, where we've been told Father Duffy will be this afternoon preparing for evening Mass, that's what I'm hoping we'll be able to achieve.

Finn turns the big iron handle on one of the huge wooden double doors at the entrance to the church and it swings open. 'So far so good,' he says, opening the door just wide enough for us to go through.

Inside, we find ourselves in a small vestibule that leads into a surprisingly big and very ornate church.

'We could be getting married!' Finn says, holding out his arm as we walk along an intricately tiled floor towards the altar.

'Except we're going the wrong way up the aisle,' I point out, not taking him up on his offer. 'Unless you're my father in this scenario, in which case we're spot on.'

'Oh, have a bit of fun, Ren,' Finn says, walking backwards up the aisle in front of me. 'You only think you're dull. You don't have to act like it all the time!'

I know Finn is only teasing, but he's beginning to sound a lot like Kiki. I open my mouth to respond, but up ahead, hidden by Finn's tall frame, a voice calls out to us. 'Can I help you?'

Finn spins around and we see, waiting for us at the top of the aisle, a tall, jolly-looking man wearing a black clerical shirt with a white tab collar, black trousers, and smart black shoes.

'Blimey,' Finn hisses, looking upwards, 'I didn't mean it, about us getting married!'

'Father Duffy?' I ask, walking past Finn towards him.

'Yes, that's me. What can I do for you?'

Father Duffy is not what I was expecting at all. I'd anticipated a tubby, white-haired, miserly old priest in a black cassock and formal clothing, but he's a trim-looking middle-aged man, with a friendly smile and what I consider to be quite modern dress for a man of the cloth.

'Finn?' he says, as Finn catches up with me. 'We don't see you in here very often – what's the special occasion?'

I turn to Finn; he hadn't mentioned that he knew Father Duffy.

'Helping out a friend, Father,' Finn says, holding out his hand, which Father Duffy takes with a firm shake. 'We wondered if you had a few moments to answer some questions?'

Father Duffy takes us back to his cottage, which is right next to the church, where he then insists on putting the kettle on and making us tea.

'Now,' he says, smiling as he returns to the room to wait for the kettle to boil. He sits down on a chair opposite the sofa where Finn and I are sitting squashed next to each other. 'You want to know about The Welcome House, is that right?'

'How did you know that?' I ask in astonishment.

'Ballykiltara is a small town with a *lot* of people,' he says in a gentle voice. 'And people have a habit of talking – especially if there's something new happening, or someone is asking unusual questions.'

'I am interested to know more about the house – if you know anything, that is?'

'You're a writer, yes?' Father Duffy asks, looking at me with curiosity through gold-rimmed spectacles.

Oh Lord, I can't lie to a priest!

'No,' I admit, shamefaced. 'I'm not. I'm a property seeker.'

'Ah, a property seeker. Let me guess: the property you're seeking is our Welcome House?'

'Sort of . . . '

'And what about you, Finn? Are you seeking this house too?'

Finn shakes his head. 'No, I just want to know what it's all about, Father – the mystery, I mean.'

'Ah, the mystery, yes.' He stands up. 'That will be the kettle whistling already. Now, how do you take your tea?'

When Father Duffy is happy we have every refreshment we need, including an assortment of biscuits to go with our tea, he sits down. He then takes a sip of his own tea before he places his cup carefully back on its saucer.

'So, what is it you would like to know,' he asks. 'About the house?'

'Who owns it, for starters,' I ask, not messing about.

Father Duffy smiles. 'I'm sure you know the answer to that by now, Ren. The house belongs to the people who need it.'

'Yes, I know all that, and I think it's a lovely idea to have a house like that for people to stop off in. But someone must own the house. If they didn't, surely it would be a ruin by now, or have squatters or something?'

Father Duffy smiles. 'That would be the sad truth in most places, I'm afraid. But here we like to look after the needy.'

'Do you know who looks after the house then?' Finn asks now, while I take a frustrated sip of my tea. 'Someone must put the food and stuff in there – it doesn't just magic itself into the house.'

'Sadly, I do not. But even if I did, I wouldn't be able to tell you if it was told to me in confidence.'

'I understand,' Finn says.

'I don't!' I suddenly explode. 'Why all the secrecy? Why doesn't anyone know the answer to all this. Sorry,' I mutter, when I feel both Father Duffy and Finn's eyes upon me. 'I'm finding this extremely frustrating, that's all.'

'And understandably so,' Father Duffy says gently. 'Many have tried to find the answer to this mystery, and few have succeeded.'

'But some have?' I ask, picking up on his words.

'A few.'

'Who? Oh, let me guess: you're not at liberty to say.'

Father Duffy smiles. 'I can tell you something about the history of the house, though, if you're interested. Quite a lot, as a matter of fact. You never know – it might help you in your endeavours.'

'Yes, thank you, that would be grand, Father,' Finn says, glancing at me with a look that suggests he doesn't think it will be of any more help than I do, but we need to be polite.

'That would be lovely, Father. Thank you,' I say, finding my manners again. 'Please go ahead.'

Father Duffy tells us everything that Mac had, and although I'm grateful to him for taking the time to tell us all this, I can't help thinking my time might be better spent elsewhere trying to find out more about the house as it is now rather than the house as it was in the past.

'... so a house has stood on that site for as long as anyone can remember,' Father Duffy says, continuing his story. 'It's said that during every troubled time this country and this county have ever encountered, a Welcome House has stood on that site to help those in trouble or in need. I have records here at the church from centuries ago that refer to a Welcome House, through the Irish rebellion and the nine years war to the Cromwell conquests and the potato famine. I even have records that tell of people hiding out in the house in the two world wars. But a Welcome House has stood on that site for as long as our records go back, that's for sure.'

'I had no idea it went back that far,' Finn says, sounding surprised.

'Oh, I have my suspicions it goes back even further,' Father Duffy says. 'I think it might have been the monks that built the first house when the Vikings came over, to provide protection against the invading marauders.'

'But you're talking as far back as the eighth or ninth century?' I say, as amazed now as Finn had been.

'You know your history, young lady. That is correct. The Vikings were a threat to these shores from 795 onwards.'

'How did you know that about the Vikings?' Finn asks, looking impressed. 'I know a fair bit about Irish history, but I wouldn't have been able to tell you that.'

'Oh, I remember all sorts of rubbish,' I reply. 'I have a mind full of facts. Kiki is always making fun of me for it.' Then I realise what I've said. 'Oh, sorry – I didn't mean your story was rubbish, Father ... Your story was anything but that,' I insist.

Father Duffy holds up his hand. 'No offence taken, I assure you. You know, Finn,' he says, turning to him. 'This young lady would be quite the asset on the quiz team.'

Finn looks at me. 'You could be right, Father.'

'What quiz team?' I ask, looking between them both.

'Ballykiltara has a pub quiz every Tuesday evening,' Finn explains. 'Father Duffy here is in The Stag's team.'

'I couldn't pull together a church team,' Father Duffy says regretfully. 'Besides, everyone would think I had an unfair advantage.' He casts his eyes upwards. 'So Finn kindly lets me compete for his team.'

'We're not that good,' Finn says. 'Father Duffy is one of our better players.'

'Your words are too kind, Finn,' he smiles. 'We're two players short this week, because the Dooleys are away on holiday. You, my dear, could be our secret weapon.'

'Oh, I'm not sure I'll still be here on Tuesday,' I say, but then I remember the house and how far we still have to go in tracing its owner. Kiki and I had discussed the possibility of staying on longer ... 'But I might be able to stay on – that's if Finn can accommodate us for another few days. Our room might be booked?'

'I'm sure I can sort something out,' Finn says. 'If you're sure you want to stay, Ren? I can't have the local priest pressuring one of my guests into taking part in a quiz if they don't want to.'

'It's absolutely fine. I'd like to stay on in Ballykiltara for a while longer. There's many questions I'd still like answers to, about the house and . . . other things,' I imply, looking directly into his eyes like I had earlier.

Finn silently holds my gaze.

'It seems that you, Finn, are the answer to all this lady's problems,' I hear Father Duffy quietly say. 'How do you feel about that?'

'Grand,' Finn says, his eyes not moving a millimetre away from mine. 'Absolutely grand.'

Sixteen

The next day Kiki and I decide to visit The Welcome House again to see if we can find any clues to its mysterious owner hidden inside. As I drive along in the direction of the house, I think about Finn and my visit to see Father Duffy yesterday.

After I'd agreed to stay long enough in Ballykiltara to take part in the quiz on Tuesday night, we'd gone back to discussing the history of the house. Father Duffy hadn't disclosed any more information that would help us with our search, but he had told us more about the monks who came to Ireland to learn and to study, and he had also explained how Ballykiltara got its name.

'The place of the church on the hill,' I say out loud as we drive along.

'What?' Kiki asks, looking up from where she's filing one of her nails.

'That's what Ballykiltara means. Father Duffy told us last

night. Bally means place of, kil means church, and Tara is the ancient hill where the Irish high kings were crowned, so it has become a common name for a hill or elevated place.'

'Oh,' Kiki says, trying to sound interested. 'That's fascinating.'

'Well, I think it is.'

Kiki puts her nail file down. 'So it's called that because of the church you went to yesterday being up that big hill? I had to climb that yesterday when I was talking to people for you. Nearly did me in, it did.'

'Yeah, I suppose it is. It's possible the town was named that before the church was ever built, though. Often churches are built on places that are of religious significance for many centuries before a building is ever erected to commemorate it.'

'The encyclopaedia of Ren strikes again,' Kiki says, grinning. 'It's no wonder they want you on their quiz team. I'm not complaining, though, if it means we get to spend more time here.'

'You mean more time with Eddie,' I say, as we pull off into the same lay-by where we'd parked a couple of days ago. 'You were gone long enough last night.'

I'd spent most of yesterday evening alone, after Eddie had knocked at our door asking for Kiki. He'd then asked her in a very roundabout way if she'd like to go for a Chinese meal with him that night, which she'd accepted eagerly. After our visit to Father Duffy, Finn sadly had to go back to work, so I hadn't seen much of him for the rest of the day.

'About that,' Kiki says as we exit the car and head up on to the footpath that runs alongside the road, 'Did you tell Eddie I liked him?'

'I might have mentioned something,' I say, looking up at the house as we approach it. 'Why? You do, don't you?'

'Yes, but don't tell him that. You might scare him off!'

'If Eddie isn't scared off by now, he's a pretty sound bet.'

'I do like him,' Kiki says dreamily, following me up the windy path that leads up to the house. 'I'm glad you're letting us stay on a few days longer. Now I can get to know him better.'

I'd arranged with Finn to extend our stay by another few nights. In fact, Finn said we could have the room for as long as we wanted it. He'd seemed quite pleased when he had extended our stay on the hotel's computer, and I had to admit I felt the same. Ballykiltara was surprising me in ways I'd never expected it to, but I was enjoying those surprises as much as everyone else seemed to enjoy us being here.

Now all I need to do is get my house problems sorted so that I can relax and enjoy the rest of my time here in Ireland.

We've reached the top of the path and this time as we approach the house I find myself wondering if there's anyone staying here at the moment, and not if the owner might be in.

I push the front door and again it opens for us just like it had two days ago.

This time we don't hesitate on the doorstep; we walk confidently into the house. Now we know what this place is, the décor, which had seemed sparse before, seems appropriate for this peculiar, almost halfway house we find ourselves in.

'What are we looking for?' Kiki asks, following me as I walk through the hall towards the kitchen.

'Clues to either the owner or the caretaker of this place.'

'But it's empty, we saw that the other day. There are no personal effects here, nothing to tie the house to anyone.'

'There must be something!' I call as I disappear into the

kitchen. 'I've been in enough houses in my time to know there's always something.'

Kiki follows me into the kitchen and watches as I start opening drawers and cupboard doors in my hunt for a clue that might lead us to the owner.

'I feel like a detective in a TV show,' Kiki announces, as I rifle through a drawer filled with kitchen utensils. 'Trying to solve the mystery of The Welcome House.'

'You're more like my wise-cracking sidekick,' I tell her, closing the drawer and moving on to the next one. 'Making smart remarks while your boss does all the work!'

'OK, I'll look too,' Kiki concedes. She opens the fridge door and surveys the contents. 'Which one?' she asks, lifting a bottle of milk from the door.

'Which one what?'

'Which sidekick would I be?'

'Depends on who I am, I guess.' Nothing in this drawer, so I move on to the upper cupboards.

'This milk isn't too fresh,' Kiki says, putting the milk back in the door. 'It doesn't look like anyone's been here recently.' She closes the fridge door. 'I think you'd be . . . ' She watches me as she thinks.

'Sherlock Holmes?' I suggest. 'You could be Dr Watson.'

'I'm not being the Hobbit!' Kiki says in horror.

'*Sherlock* was a book before it was a TV show,' I remind her. 'I don't think there's anything in this kitchen. Let's try the sitting room. There might be something in that big dresser there.'

We head across the hall to the sitting room, and I begin searching through the huge wooden dresser while Kiki looks over the bookshelf.

'Miss Marple?' she asks, lifting a paperback book from one of the shelves.

'What?'

'Miss Marple,' she says, tapping the cover of the book. 'Agatha Christie? You could be her.'

'Hmm, thanks for that – I think. But she doesn't have a sidekick, does she?'

'True ... I'll keep thinking.'

'As long as you keep searching at the same time, that's fine. These drawers are empty, there's nothing in here. Anything on the bookshelves?'

Kiki shakes her head. 'Only a lot of old second-hand books, mostly novels by the look of it.'

'Upstairs then?'

We head up the stairs, Kiki suggesting possible detective duos as we go.

'... Cagney and Lacey,' she says as we reach the first bedroom.

'At least they're both women. I'm surprised you know them, bit old for you, aren't they?'

'There's a Sky channel that does re-runs of vintage detective shows,' she explains.

'I wondered where you were getting all your knowledge from. There's nothing in this room,' I say after I've had a quick look in the first bedroom, so we head across the landing to the second.

'You suggest one then,' Kiki says, opening a drawer in a small wooden bedside table.

'Why do we have to be like anyone else?' I close the doors to the wardrobe – nothing, only some empty hangers. 'Why can't we just be us?'

'Parker and Fisher.' Kiki wrinkles up her nose. 'We sound like a firm of estate agents, not a crime-fighting duo!'

'Much as I hate to admit it, we're closer to the first than the second. Especially since we're still no further forward in solving this mystery!'

We give up on the upstairs of the house when we've checked all the rooms, but not before I take another look from one of the windows to check if the view is everything I remember it to be.

And annoyingly it is. This is definitely the house for Ryan Dempsey, and I have to keep trying to at least give him a chance of owning it.

'Dempsey and Makepeace?' I suggest to Kiki as I descend the stairs to meet her.

'Hmm?' a distracted voice replies.

'Dempsey and Makepeace. I was thinking about Ryan Dempsey and it came to me. Perhaps you don't remember them, they ... What have you got there?' I ask as I see Kiki standing in the hall looking at something.

'I found it,' she says, holding up a brown leather-bound notebook. 'In here –' She points to the hall table next to her. 'It says it's a visitors' book. Can you believe we went all around the house and never looked here first? What are the chances?'

I hurry along the hall towards her and reach for the book, but Kiki protectively turns away. 'Ah, ah, I found it. I get to look inside first.'

She opens the front cover of the book. 'This looks like the letter that walker said he saw on that blog you found.' She reads from the page: '*Céad míle fáilte* – that means a hundred thousand welcomes,' she explains. 'Eddie told me.'

'Yes, I know. What else does it say?' I ask excitedly, trying to peer over her shoulder.

'*Céad míle fáilte. Welcome to Ballykiltara's very own Welcome House. Please feel free to stay here for as long as your need requires. A house has stood on this site for hundreds, possibly thousands of years, offering shelter and food to those that need it. Be assured, you didn't find The Welcome House, The Welcome House found you ...*'

She raises her eyebrows at me before continuing: '*It knew you needed help and made itself available to you. The house would be grateful when your stay is over if you could leave it in the same way you found it, and if possible replace any food or supplies you have used with new ones. But if you can't, please don't worry, The Welcome House will continue to provide for those in need, just as it has done for you. Go raibh maith agat. Thank you and enjoy your stay.*' Kiki hands the book to me. 'That's so cute, isn't it?' she says as I cast my eyes over the page and see lines of ornate handwriting. 'Don't you think, Ren?'

'It's odd, that's what I think. This talks about the house like it was real, like the house provides the food if the visitor doesn't.'

'Maybe it does?'

'Kiki,' I say firmly, 'don't you get drawn into all this nonsense too. There *is* a real-life person that looks after this house. There has to be. Don't forget that.'

I turn the next page of the visitors' book, and read the first entry. It's from about three years ago, there's a date, a man's name, and then a short account of why he found himself here – like the blogger, another lost walker. Then there's another entry underneath, a woman this time, who stayed at the house with her children, to escape her abusive husband. I show Kiki and again her eyebrows rise in surprise. We keep reading as the entries continue; there are notes from walkers and cyclists caught in dreadful weather conditions who stayed only one night at the house until they could be on their way again. Then there are entries from people who stayed here for longer, some like the woman and her children, caught in oppressive situations, and some from people simply down on their luck. But they all say the same thing: The Welcome House gave them shelter when no one else would.

I look at Kiki, we've both been reading the book open-mouthed for the last few minutes, astounded at the many diverse people who have found themselves here.

'I bet this isn't the only visitors' book either,' I say, tapping the cover, 'I bet there've been many more before this one, if the house has been going for as long as everyone says it has.'

'You're right; I bet they tell some tales too. Do you think they're here? Have we missed them? We've looked everywhere, though.'

'I don't think they can be. I expect whoever looks after this place has them hidden away somewhere.'

'Yes, I bet they do,' Kiki says, her eyes widening. 'If only we were real cops, then we could get a search warrant to check everyone's houses.'

'Yeah, if only. That would make life a lot easier right now.'

'You know, Ren, this book is pretty amazing,' Kiki says softly, taking the visitors' book from me. She runs her fingers gently over the leather cover before putting it back safely in the drawer. 'This whole house is pretty special too. I'm beginning to wonder if we should be messing with it.'

I don't want to admit it, but a similar thought has been niggling at me too – a tiny voice inside me that doesn't want to rock this particular boat. But a much louder one keeps shouting it down because it knows I have to do just that.

'We're not messing with it,' I try and justify, not only to Kiki

127

but to myself. 'We're simply investigating the possibilities, that's all.'

'The possibility that it might be sold and used as a holiday home? I don't think this house would want to be owned by one person – it's too much of a free spirit for that.'

'Perhaps that's exactly what it *would* like after having strangers living in it for so long. Maybe the house would like the security and comfort of having one familiar owner.'

'Oh, I hadn't thought of it like that,' Kiki says, nodding. 'Yes, I suppose you might be right.'

I hadn't thought of it either, until now.

But what if I'm correct? What if the house did want to be owned by a nice family, like a foster child that kept being passed from family to family; maybe it wanted to belong to one special person.

I shake my head. Even I'm being drawn into this madness now. This place we're standing in is simply a building, a house made of bricks and mortar. It doesn't care what happens to it, it doesn't care who owns it. It doesn't have feelings or a heart. It's just a house, plain and simple.

But as we make our way back down the hall and let ourselves out of the front door – leaving it as we found it, on the latch, for the next visitor – I can't shake the feeling that this house is anything but plain and simple. In fact, as we walk down the path towards our car, and I turn back for a moment to look at the house behind me, I can't shake the feeling that someone or something is watching us go.

Seventeen

We leave the house and drive back towards the hotel.

'You're quiet,' Kiki says as we pass the 'Welcome to Ballykiltara' sign that we'd passed the first time we'd driven into the town. 'What're ya thinking about?'

'Not much. The house really.'

'Gets you like that, doesn't it?' Kiki ponders. 'It's like a ... feeling? Yes, that's what it is: when you enter that house you can feel the presence of all the people that have stepped through that front door before you. It's not a creepy feeling, either; it feels warm and ... welcoming, like its name. In fact, is it just me, or did the house feel warmer today? The other day, it felt quite cold and chilly.'

She was right, I'd felt it too: both the warmth and the slightly odd feeling that the house seemed to generate. But I had to forget about all that and concentrate on what was important – my job.

'We could try to find another house for Ryan?' Kiki suggests after a few minutes of silence. 'Something similar, but not that house.'

'No,' I say, pulling up at a zebra crossing. I watch two mothers push prams across it while they chat to each other.

'Why? There must be loads of houses that would do.'

'Kiki,' I say, moving away again now the crossing is clear, 'we don't find houses for people that *will do*. We find *the perfect* house for them. So they can't imagine ever living anywhere else.'

Kiki sighs. 'I'm only suggesting that maybe, this once, another house could be found.'

'No,' I insist again. 'We will discover who owns this house, and then we'll do our best to encourage them to sell. Then, and only then, if they can't be convinced, will we look elsewhere.'

Kiki sighs again; only this time it's more of a huff. 'When did you become so stubborn?' she asks, folding her arms across her chest. 'You're like a dog we used to have when I was small. Bobby, he was called; lovely placid fella, but when he had a bone, he wouldn't let go of it until he'd ripped all the meat off, then he'd spend hours crunching down all the bone, until that had all gone too. You're like that, only with houses. You won't rest until the job is fully crunched down.'

I keep my eyes firmly on the road. Kiki's analogy isn't one I particularly appreciate.

'Although, sometimes that's a good thing in life,' Kiki continues in a gentler tone, 'being as tenacious and driven as you are gets results, that's for sure. But sometimes you need a little give and take. Oh, why are we pulling over?' she asks as I swerve to the side of the road. 'Have I said too much?'

I've been distracted from Kiki's words by something on the pavement next to us.

'See that dog over there?' I say, pointing to a large hairy dog poddling quite happily along the street. It stops to cock its leg on a litter bin. 'He belongs to Finn.'

'Is Finn with him?' Kiki asks, peering along the street.

'I don't think so.' I look in my rear-view mirrors in case we've missed him. 'I can't see him around, can you?'

'No,' Kiki shakes her head. 'Do you think he's allowed to be out roaming on his own?'

'Finn thinks the world of that dog, so I very much doubt it.'

'What should we do then? We can't let him run around on his own – he might get lost. Or worse, hit by a car.'

My stomach twists at the thought.

'I guess we should try and take him back to the hotel.' I look over at the tiny back seat. 'He might fit.'

'I'll go get him,' Kiki says, purposefully opening her door. 'You get ready to put him in the back. What's his name?'

'Fergus.'

While Kiki goes after Fergus, I climb out on to the pavement and pull Kiki's passenger seat forward. Fergus is quite a big dog, so there's no way we're going to get him in the boot; he'll have to go on the back seat. I wish I had Finn's mobile number so I could call him, but we never got as far as exchanging numbers. Maybe we never would; he was only our hotel manager, after all. Why would he want to give me his number?

I'm thinking how weird, and perhaps how sad it will be when we have to leave this funny little world we've found ourselves cosseted in over the last few days, when Kiki comes rushing back along the pavement.

'He won't come to me,' she exclaims breathlessly. 'He keeps

131

running away. He's too big to pull by his collar – believe me, I tried, but he only dug his heels in harder. Can you have a go, Ren?'

I hesitate. I try to steer well clear of dogs these days; it's easier that way. The thought of trying to cajóle a large hairy one into following me back to my tiny car isn't something I particularly relish.

I look down the street and see Fergus trotting happily across the road. A car has to brake sharply to avoid hitting him, and the driver beeps his horn in annoyance. As I feel the sound of the horn go right through me, something stirs deep inside.

'I'll be right back,' I tell Kiki as I sprint off up the road, and unlike Fergus use a zebra crossing to negotiate the always-busy traffic along Ballykiltara's high street.

'Fergus,' I call sternly as he pauses to sniff at a dustbin about to overflow with used chip papers. 'You wait right there.' As I walk towards him, I hold up my hand like a policeman stopping traffic.

Fergus looks up at the person calling his name, and for one moment I think he's going to trot off again, but he doesn't; he waits by the bin until I catch up with him, all the time watching me.

'Good boy,' I tell him as I reach his side. I squat down next to him. 'Now, Fergus,' I say, looking into his dark eyes. 'I need you to behave right now. This isn't easy for me, you know? So if you'll just come with me back to my car, we can return you safely to Finn.'

Fergus's ears twitch at the mention of Finn's name.

'Is that OK?' I ask him, instinctively reaching out my hand to pat him. But before my hand reaches his head, Fergus quickly turns and a big pink tongue licks my hand.

My heart swells, and I feel a tear spring into my eye.

'I'll take that as a yes,' I tell him. I pat his side, then I slip my hand through his collar and gently guide him towards the crossing. Once we've safely reached the other side of the road, I loosen my grip and allow him to trot obediently beside me as we make our way back to Kiki and the car.

'Wow, you're a dog whisperer,' Kiki says in awe, as we reach the little hire car again.

'I hardly think so,' I say as I encourage Fergus on to the back seat. Which I'm relieved to find he actually fits on. I go around to the driver's side of the car and climb in while Kiki does the same on her side.

'You obviously have a way with dogs though,' Kiki says, as we set off again. 'I saw you with him back there. Have you ever had a dog of your own?'

'Yes, a long time ago,' I reply, hoping she won't ask anything further. But that's not Kiki's style.

'Oh, what sort? You never said so before, and we've been to loads of houses with dogs. I thought you were afraid – you always seem to avoid them.'

I look in my rear-view mirror at Fergus panting happily on the back seat.

'We'll have to get this car cleaned now,' I say, avoiding Kiki's question. 'There'll be dog hairs all over that seat. The hire company will have a fit.'

'Eddie will help us,' Kiki says, her mind wandering in a direction it was always happy to go lately. 'He has all sorts of gadgets. He'll probably have an industrial-strength Hoover too.'

And with that we turn into the gates of The Stag, and I'm relieved I seem to have prevented Kiki asking me any further questions for the time being.

We find a space in the car park, then Kiki climbs out with Fergus while I lock up the car. 'Pop into the hotel and see if Finn is about, will you?' I ask Kiki. 'Otherwise I'll have to take Fergus around to his cottage.'

Kiki is about to head up the stone steps to reception when Eddie appears around the corner of the building, pushing a number of large suitcases on his big gold luggage trolley.

'Eddie!' Kiki shrieks with delight.

'Kiki, howaya?' he asks looking equally as delighted to see her, then he sees me standing by the car with Fergus. 'Is that Finn's dog ya have there?' he asks, puzzled.

'We found him running wild in the town centre,' Kiki explains. 'Ren was quite the hero getting him back here.'

'Is that so?' Eddie says calmly, but his eyes shine with amusement at Kiki's description.

'Is Finn around, Eddie?' I ask. 'I could do with getting Fergus back to him.'

Eddie leaves his trolley and wanders over to me, with Kiki not far behind him.

'Finn's gone to Limerick on business. He won't be back until later today. I'd offer to look after Fergus, but I'm pure swamped with bags right now – we've a conference on, see?'

'No, that's fine, Eddie, I wouldn't expect you to. We'll sort something out.'

'Look, I shouldn't be telling you this,' Eddie says, leaning in towards me. 'But Finn keeps a key to his front door under the horse statue in his front garden. Perhaps you could let Fergus back in that way until Finn gets home? That's just between you and me, mind?' He taps the side of his nose.

'Of course, you can trust me, Eddie. Thanks for that.'

'No worries, miss. Kiki, I'll see you later, yes?'

'Definitely,' Kiki says. 'Can't wait.' She blows him a kiss, and small pink spots appear on Eddie's pale cheeks as he scurries back to his luggage.

'Kiki, shall I meet you upstairs in a few minutes, after I've taken Fergus back to Finn's cottage?' I ask ruffling Fergus's head.

'How about down in the bar? I could do with a coffee.'

'Sure, then we can talk about what comes next for operation Welcome House.'

'If you want,' Kiki says, sounding less than enthused.

'I'll see you in a few minutes then. Come on, Fergus.'

It's supposed to be me leading Fergus as we walk together towards the back of the hotel where Finn had indicated his cottage was. But in fact it's Fergus who guides me confidently back to his home.

Finn's cottage stands alone at the end of a small driveway.

I would have described it as a bungalow with character rather than a cottage in the English sense of the word. But looking at its position, halfway between the hotel and the riding stables, I would guess it was the Irish equivalent of a tied cottage, when the hotel was once a large country house with the stables as part of the owner's land.

The cottage is surrounded by an unpainted wooden fence that runs around the outside of a tidy, but unremarkable garden. Fergus bounds over to the gate, and I expect him to sit and wait for me to open it for him, but instead he takes a run at it, and leaps easily over the top with a foot to spare.

'I'm beginning to see how you went AWOL today,' I tell him as I follow him through the gate into the garden. 'Now where do we find this key?'

135

I look around the garden and spy by the front doorstep a stone racehorse in full flight, mounted on top of a stone pillar. So I tip up the pillar, and sure enough, as Eddie had promised, I find a key.

While Fergus waits patiently next to me, I take the key and place it in the front door, then I turn it and the door swings open easily.

'Right, let's go find you some water,' I say as Fergus bounds into the house in front of me. 'I'm sure you'll show me the way.'

I follow Fergus through into a neat hall decorated in shades of cream, with a painting on one wall of the Ha'penny Bridge in Dublin. We then move through to a bright modern kitchen with white wooden kitchen units, a stainless steel sink, and a yellow Aga. Fergus waits impatiently by his water bowl, so I bend down and refill it, first moving a mug decorated with the Dublin flag from the bottom of the sink.

Then, while Fergus sloppily laps up his water, I look around to see if I can spot any food for him. Helpfully there's a large bag of dry dog food sitting on the kitchen worktop out of Fergus's reach – although after today's escapades, I'm pretty sure if Fergus wanted it, it would be his immediately.

I fill a silver bowl that sits next to the bag with plenty of food, then I put it down on the floor next to the water. Fergus wastes no time in burying his nose in the food, but instead of gulping it down immediately he looks up at me, an enquiring expression on his face.

'What? You don't like being watched when you eat?'

Fergus simply waits.

'OK, OK, I'll leave you then. Let me know when you're finished, won't you?' I say, grinning at him.

I wander back through the kitchen with the intention of

waiting for Fergus to eat his food, then hopefully I can settle him down on his dog bed, where I hope he will sleep until Finn gets home so that I can return to Kiki.

Other than the painting, there's not much to see in the cream-coloured hall, so I decide to wander a bit further, and I find myself in a cosy lounge, which like the other rooms I've visited so far has stripped wooden floorboards adding to the warm feel of the house. There's a flat-screen TV, a brown leather sofa with a blanket – also in Dublin colours – thrown casually across its back, and a matching comfy armchair that's obviously Finn's favourite because it faces the TV, and still retains the imprint from where he last sat in it. The afternoon sun streams through a large patio window, so I shield my eyes and head towards the window with the intention of drawing the curtains to prevent the sun from fading the leather sofa.

'Ah, this is how you got out, Fergus!' I exclaim, on finding the door slightly open behind the curtain. 'You must have wriggled through this gap!' I slide the door closed, and glance through the glass as I do. The view is uninspiring, just another small garden, tidy like its front counterpart, but bereft of any inspired planting. It's quite clear the owner of this house either doesn't like gardening, or more likely, knowing Finn, doesn't have the time to do it.

'There, that's better,' I say, drawing the curtains so they block out the sun. I turn back to face the room. I'm about to leave when I spy several framed photos sitting on a stripped pine chest of drawers, so naturally I have to go over and take a look.

The first photo I pick up is of a large group of people; they're standing in front of a huge building, which I assume must be a hotel, as the people are obviously a wedding party.

137

I look closely at the photo and spot Finn standing on the front row looking very smart in full morning dress; he holds a top hat under his arm, and I can't help but smirk at the thought of Finn having to wear 'official' wedding gear such as this. If this Finn was anything like the Finn I know now, he'd have absolutely hated it.

The other people in the photo aren't really of any interest. Finn clearly isn't the groom, but likely a best man or possibly an usher, considering his placing in the line-up. I'm surprised at the feeling I get on discovering this. Why should it matter to me whether Finn has been married before? But my insides tell me otherwise.

I'm about to put the photo back down on the table when I notice the similarity between Finn and a few of the people he's standing with, particularly an older man, also in morning dress. This must be a family wedding, I suddenly realise, and the man Finn is standing next to is definitely his father, accompanied possibly by his mother and likely his brother and his sister, as they appear to be the only ones who have Finn's colouring and the same cute dimple as he has on his chin.

Big family ... I muse, and by the look of the women's outfits and hats, a wealthy family too. I put the photo down and pick up another; this time it's a photo of Finn outside a stable, standing next to a pretty chestnut horse with its head hanging over a stable door. I look more closely and realise this is not the Ballykiltara stable; the wood making up the stable door is smoother and darker, for one thing, and this elegant shiny horse isn't the sort that takes visitors out on pony treks; it looks more accustomed to carrying a brightly clad jockey along a race track.

The horse's name is on a sign over the stable door: *Celtic Cassidy*.

Finn looks happier than I think I've ever seen him, as he smiles back at whoever is taking this photo. His smile not only reaches his eyes but floats all around him like a joyful halo.

I'm surprised to find the rest of the framed photos are either of horses, dogs or both. Other than the family group, there are no other humans. It's obvious what the two loves of Finn's life are, and it's as I think this that I hear one of them bark from the kitchen.

Fergus.

I'm about to go back to check on him when suddenly I hear the front door open. I freeze on the spot like a child playing musical statues. Then I look down at the photo still in my hand, and as quietly and carefully as I can I put it back down with the others. I'm about to move towards the hallway and explain myself when I hear Finn's voice, but he's not talking to me, he's talking to a mobile phone.

'Yes, Mam, I'm fine – really . . . Yes, I know what day it is, you've just reminded me, haven't you?' The front door closes and there's another pause in the conversation while Finn listens to his mother, and I hear Fergus trot through to the hall to greet him.

I hesitate. Should I make my presence known? Otherwise it will seem like I'm eavesdropping on Finn's conversation . . . but I don't want to surprise him too much when he's on the phone to his mother – who appears to be quite a formidable woman, judging by the wedding photo.

But my dilemma is quickly resolved when Finn comes wandering through to the sitting room, Fergus by his side.

To his credit, he doesn't jump too much on seeing me dithering next to his armchair, but the look on his face suggests a fair bit of shock.

'Mam, I need to go,' he says quickly into the phone. 'Yeah, like I said, I'm fine. You're the one making a big deal out of it ... Yes, I'll call you soon ... yes, I promise ... Love you too.'

Finn ends the call, puts the phone in his shirt pocket, then he turns his full attention to me.

I expect a flood of questions to spill forth from his mouth, but instead he simply raises his eyebrows questioningly, and waits for my explanation ...

Eighteen

'I ... I'm sorry,' I try to explain in a rush. 'I didn't mean to eavesdrop on your conversation.'

Finn still looks questioningly at me.

'And I didn't mean to look at your photos either.'

Finn looks across at the frames, then back to me.

'I didn't expect I'd still be here when you got back. I thought I'd be long gone.'

Finn pulls an even more quizzical expression, and for a moment we both stare silently at each other.

'Thank you for your many apologies,' he says eventually, to my relief. 'But what you haven't explained is what you're doing here inside my house in the first place?'

I breathe a sigh of relief. Finn hadn't sounded angry or cross, his voice had simply been calm, if a little confused.

'It was Fergus,' I explain. 'Kiki and I found him wandering about on the high street, so we brought him back to the hotel in our car, but Eddie said you were in Limerick and wouldn't be home until later, so I decided to bring him back here myself.'

'He's a terror for getting out of the house, is that one,' Finn says, still calm. 'It's not the first time.'

'You left the patio door open.' I gesture behind me. 'He must have slipped out that way.'

'More likely he's learnt how to undo the catch and slide it open with his nose.' Finn bends down to Fergus, who's watching our conversation with interest. 'You'll get yourself hit by a car one day if you keep taking yourself for a walk,' he tries to admonish, but Fergus just licks his face.

Finn sighs, then he pats Fergus and stands up again.

'Perhaps you should lock the doors?' I suggest. 'In case it happens again?'

'Probably wouldn't make a difference. He'd only learn how to turn the key. He's a smart cookie, this fella.' Finn ruffles his pal's head.

'Well, you need to find a way to stop him wandering in amongst traffic, that's for sure,' I say sharply.

Finn looks at me with amusement. 'Yes, miss.' He gives a quick salute.

'I'm serious. He ... he could cause an accident. People might get hurt. Fergus might get hurt ... ' My voice fades away.

Finn looks at me with concern this time.

'Sure, if it means that much to you, I'll be more careful next time I have to leave him. And there was me the other day thinking you didn't care all that much for our canine friends.'

'I never said that. You just assumed.'

'I did that.' Finn looks at me with an odd expression.

'Look, I'd better be going,' I say, moving towards Finn and the door. 'I'm glad we helped get him home OK.'

'Stay,' Finn says, more as a question than an instruction.

I pause by his side and look up into his eyes.

'I was about to make tea?' he offers as an incentive. 'If you'd like some, that is?'

We sit in Finn's lounge. Me at one end of the sofa, Finn at the other, both nursing mugs of tea, and Fergus curled up in the warm sun that streams through the gap in the curtains of the now re-opened patio doors.

'So, how's the search for the mystery owner coming along?' Finn asks, taking a sip from his mug. 'Are you any further to unravelling him yet?'

'Or her,' I add.

'I stand corrected; the owner could indeed be a woman. Actually, that would make a lot of sense.'

'Why would it?' I ask, then I realise where Finn is likely heading with this.

Finn looks uncomfortable and takes a large gulp of his tea this time, confirming my suspicions.

'Come on, spit it out,' I insist. 'You were going to say that it might be a woman because the person who looks after the house obviously cleans it and changes bed sheets and the like, weren't you?'

'No,' Finn shakes his head. 'I wasn't.'

'OK, what *were* you going to say then?' I demand.

'I was going to say it might be a woman because ... ' He plays for time by placing his tea carefully down on a coaster next to him. 'Ah, all right I give in,' he concedes. 'I *was* going to say that. But that doesn't make me a chauvinist, before you start.'

'I'm not starting. You're right, that place *is* obviously kept spotless, and in my experience that does point towards a female caretaker. A man would never take such pride in a house as this person obviously takes in The Welcome House.'

'Ahem.' Finn gestures around his lounge. 'Are you saying this is slovenly?'

'No, not at all – there are always exceptions to every rule. I'm just talking about past experience, that's all.'

'Lived with a lot of men, have you?' Finn asks, that twinkle in his eye again.

'That is none of your business,' I say in an overly haughty voice. 'I was referring to my experience of homes that have a single male owner.'

'Ah yes, I forgot you were the consummate property seeker . . . '

I can't help but smile. Finn has this lovely relaxed attitude to everything that makes it impossible to get annoyed with either him or yourself.

'Anyway, Eddie said the person he saw was, quote: "a fairly bulky fella". That doesn't usually suggest a woman.'

'Could be a very unfortunate one?'

'*Finn . . . *'

'OK, I'll stop!' He holds up his hands. 'So, if you've not got any further with this mystery, we'll have to talk about something else.' He pretends to think. 'How about your extensive list of male housemates?'

I raise my eyebrows at him.

'No? Hmm . . . '

'How about we talk about you?' I suggest. 'You still owe me an explanation from the other evening.'

Even though I know he knows exactly what I'm talking about, Finn feigns innocence. 'An explanation . . . About what?'

'You know what I'm talking about. Besides, you can't hide now that I know things about you.'

'Things? What things?'

I glance across at the photographs. 'Things like, you have a large family. You love horses as much as you love dogs. You're not only from Dublin, judging by your accent and the fact you told me your parents kept horses near there when you were young, but you obviously still love and likely miss the place, seeing as how there's so much Dublin memorabilia around this house.' I pause, waiting for his reaction.

'Anything else?' Finn says.

'Erm . . . ' I look at the photos again. 'Yes, you probably hated wearing that suit for the wedding as much as you hate wearing one for work.'

'Impressive,' he concedes eventually. 'Right on all counts.'

'So then?' I ask. 'What else is there? You're definitely hiding something else.'

'I'm hardly hiding all the things you just pointed out. If I was, do you think I'd have them dotted about my house?'

'Probably not.'

'There you go then.'

'There I go *what*?'

'They're not secrets, are they? I told you I wasn't hiding anything.' Finn calmly picks up his tea, which must be getting a bit cold by now, but he doesn't flinch as he takes a sip.

Aargh! He was doing it again – his well-practised avoidance technique. I thought I was good, but he's in another league.

'Today a special day, is it?' I ask, suddenly remembering the phone call.

'Not particularly, why?'

'Your mum seemed concerned about you on the phone.'

Finn's relaxed face tightens, just a tiny bit.

'Mums are like that, aren't they?' he answers casually.

'It's not your birthday, is it?' I ask, horrified it might be and I hadn't known. Although why I *should* know when a virtual stranger's special day was . . .

'No! Of course it isn't.'

'Your mum's then?'

He shakes his head.

'The anniversary of something?'

Finn turns to me. 'Sounds like that suppressed detective in you is rising to the surface again.' He tries to sound breezy, but there's a definite tension to his reply.

'It *is* an anniversary, isn't it?'

'Look, Ren, much as I'd like to stay and play Columbo with you all afternoon, I have to get back to the hotel.'

'Getting a bit close, am I?' I ask in the same light-hearted way Finn usually maintains during our conversations.

'No, I really do have to go. Dermot is popping over later from the island. His daughter is going to be working here for the summer – apparently, she doesn't want to work over on Tara this year. Stroppy teenager, if you ask me. However, I have to go along with what my boss wants, and if he wants his daughter to work at The Stag, then who am I to question him?' He stands up. 'So you will have to excuse me.'

I can take a hint. 'Sure, I understand. I'll go.' I stand up too. 'Thank you for the tea, I've enjoyed our chat. I'll see myself out.' I head towards the door in what I feel is a slightly awkward silence. Have I pushed Finn a bit too far? I didn't think I had . . .

'I'll maybe see you later, Ren,' I hear Finn call from the lounge as I'm about to open the front door. 'If you're around, that is?'

'Maybe,' I call as I let myself out, a relieved smile breaking out on my face.

And I continue to smile as I walk all the way back to the hotel and up to my room, forgetting all about the fact I'm supposed to be meeting Kiki in the bar, and by now she's likely to be high as a kite on caffeine, having waited for me to return from Finn's cottage.

Nineteen

'Where have you been?' a hyper-looking Kiki asks, as I make my way into the bar and find her sitting at a table with an empty cup and saucer in front of her.

'At Finn's,' I reply, sliding along the sofa next to her.

'All this time?' she exclaims in a voice loud enough for an elderly couple enjoying a pot of tea and some scones to look over in our direction.

'Shush,' I hush. 'No need to shout at me.'

'Sorry, I'm feeling a bit manic after all the coffee I've had while I've been waiting for you.'

'How much *have* you had?'

Kiki thinks, tapping her foot up and down while she does. 'Hmm … I started with a latte, thinking it would last long enough for you to get over to Finn's and back. Then when you didn't arrive, I felt bad just sitting here – Danny over there kept looking at me.'

I look over to the bar, the barman nods his head in our direction, so I smile.

'So then I ordered two cappuccinos, thinking you would have the other one, but when you didn't return I drank them as well.'

'Kiki!'

'Oh, it doesn't end there! I wasn't going to have any more, but that elderly couple ordered tea and they brought them two coffees by mistake, so they asked if I'd like them. I hadn't the heart to say no. So I had an espresso and I think it was an Americano?' She looks at the cup. 'I don't know, it was after that I started to feel a bit shaky.'

'I'm not surprised! I like my caffeine fix, but that's ridiculous.'

'So where *have* you been?' Kiki's knees bounce up and down as she taps her heels on the floor. 'You still haven't told me?'

I tell her all about what happened at Finn's cottage.

'That's it?' she asks when I've finished. 'I've digested a whole Costa Coffee store for it to end like that?'

'What did you expect?'

'A kiss.'

'What? Why would that happen?'

'Come on, Ren. You like Finn, I know you do.'

'Shush,' I whisper looking around in case any hotel staff are in earshot. 'Everyone doesn't need to know.'

'Ha!' she exclaims triumphantly. 'So you do! I knew it.'

I look around the bar again, playing for time. *How can I backtrack now?*

'Who's that?' I ask, my eyes resting on a large woman who has just appeared behind the bar. Instead of the usual Stag

149

uniform of a white shirt, black trousers and waistcoat, she's wearing what look like white chef's overalls, with a navy-and-white striped apron tied under her rather large bust. She towers over poor Danny, who looks petrified as he tries to answer her questions.

'Oh, that's Sarah,' Kiki says. 'She's one of the cooks here. Eddie and I saw her down the pub one night. Eddie says she can drink any man under the table, and her record in one night is nine pints of Guinness.'

'*Nine?*' I look back at Sarah. She's very tall for a woman; in fact, as she turns away from us, her interrogation of Danny complete, she could almost be a man as I watch her back view disappear through the staff entrance to the bar.

'Yeah, that's what Eddie says. She's been here for years – used to be the housekeeper, apparently, until they needed a cook, and then she took on that role. She's pretty good, but fierce too; Eddie is scared to death of her. Anyway, Ren, stop trying to change the subject – now what about Finn?'

'Hmm?' I ask, having genuinely forgotten about Kiki's cross-examination of me.

'*Finn*. You know the one: tall, brooding, totally gorgeous in every way?'

But I was still thinking about Sarah. I'd assumed after Eddie had given us a description of the person he saw going into The Welcome House that it must be a man we were looking for, but what if it wasn't? What if the person was a woman – a very tall, very broad woman, a woman much like Sarah? Finn had suggested it was more likely to be a woman caretaker, and although I hadn't liked his sexist suggestion, I had to admit he was right.

'Yes, I know Finn,' I reply distractedly. 'Kiki?' I ask, turning to her as a flash of inspiration sparks in my mind. 'Have you ever gone on a stake-out?'

Kiki's eyes light up. 'You mean like they do in cop shows? With doughnuts and coffee?'

'Perhaps not the coffee for you – I think you've had enough of that for one day. But we could maybe manage some doughnuts . . .'

Later that evening, Kiki and I head out towards our car through the hotel's reception.

'Off out, ladies?' Donal calls from behind the reception desk.

'Yes,' I reply quickly. I'd hoped we might be able to sneak out without anyone noticing us. We're hardly dressed for a night on the town. I'm in jeans, a hoody and my trainers, and Kiki, for reasons known only to her, is wearing a tartan onesie with a pair of tan UGG boots.

Donal doesn't seem to see anything odd about our appearance. 'Lovely evening for a stroll,' he says, looking at my trainers. Then he sees Kiki, 'and a . . . a . . .' he stutters, for once at a loss for something to say.

'Warmth,' Kiki says, pulling her zip a little higher. 'I'm wearing it to keep me warm.'

'We're going to star-gaze,' I improvise. 'Northumberland, where I come from in England, has what are called Dark Skies where you can see thousands and thousands of stars in night skies unpolluted by light. I was hoping we might see something similar here.'

'Yes, you can,' Donal says, to my surprise and relief. 'Kerry is an international Dark-Sky Reserve. It's forecast a clear night tonight, so you should be in luck. Do you know where you're going to view the skies?'

I knew as soon as I mentioned star-gazing he would ask me that. 'I have a few ideas, but I'm sure you will know much better than me, Donal.'

Donal reaches under the desk, and with a flourish produces a map which he proceeds to lay out in front of us, and spends the next few minutes instructing us on all the places we might try.

'Good evening,' I hear a familiar but strangely formal voice say, while our backs are turned and our heads are buried in the map.

I turn to see Finn approaching; he's with a tall, broad man I don't recognise, and a teenage girl.

'Hello,' I reply politely, smiling at him.

'Off out tonight, ladies?' Finn enquires in the same formal voice, and I realise that the man with him must be the owner of the hotel, Dermot, and the girl most likely Dermot's daughter.

'The ladies are going star-gazing,' Donal informs them from behind the desk. 'I'm advising them on where they might see the best constellations.'

'Star-gazing?' Finn's lips twitch, but he manages to keep up his managerial façade. 'I didn't know you were into astronomy, Miss Parker?'

'We're not really, we'd just like to view the dark skies, that's all. It's supposed to be quite magical.'

'It is indeed – magical,' Finn repeats, holding my gaze for a moment. 'I hope you get to see them, it's something you won't forget in a hurry if you do.' He smiles at me, then swiftly returns to manager mode. 'Now, may I introduce the owner of the hotel to you? This is Dermot O'Connell, and his daughter, Megan, who is coming to work here part-time.'

'Pleased to meet you,' a deep, slightly gruff English voice

says. He shakes my hand and then Kiki's. 'I hope you're enjoying your stay at The Stag?'

'Yes, we're having the best time!' Kiki replies before I can speak. 'I must say though, Dermot, you don't look much like the owner of a hotel.'

Dermot smiles. 'I'm pleased to hear it. Never set out to be one either, it just sort of happened.'

'Finn was telling me you own an island too,' I say. 'I think we saw it on our way in to Ballykiltara.'

'Well technically it's my wife, Darcy, that owns the island, but we manage it together.'

'How exciting!' Kiki says. 'Owning your own island.'

'Ah, it's a lot of hard work, but we enjoy it. Can't imagine living anywhere else now, can we, Megan?' he asks the sullen-looking girl next to him.

'I can,' she says, rolling her eyes. 'It's you and Darcy that love the place so much. That's why I want to work here for the summer and not be stranded over there, away from civilisation.'

'Please excuse my daughter,' Dermot says, sighing. 'Her mother's influence weighs heavy with her. Darcy is my second wife,' he explains.

'Don't worry, Mr O'Connell,' Donal pipes up. 'We'll look after Megan here at The Stag, won't we, Finn?'

'We will indeed,' Finn says. 'Now we won't hold you ladies up any further. I hope you have a wonderful evening and may the stars shine brightly for you.' He catches my eye briefly again. 'In the meantime, we will continue with Megan's tour.'

I smile at Dermot. 'Nice to meet you.'

'And you. Enjoy your stay, ladies.'

Finn leads the way and they depart towards the restaurant.

'Thank you for all your help, Donal,' I say quickly before he can get back to the map. 'I'm sure we'll find what we need now. I'll let you know tomorrow how we get on.'

I quickly escort Kiki out of the hotel and towards the car.

'Right, let's go,' I say, jumping into the driver's seat. 'We have work to do.'

'Yes, boss!' Kiki salutes as she slides into her seat next to me. 'And as Starsky and Butch would say, "Let's be careful out there!"'

'Kiki, you are wrong on so many levels,' I say, starting the engine and putting the car into gear. 'Firstly it's Starsky and Hutch, not Butch, and we are definitely not American TV cops – far from it. If you must make us out to be a crime-fighting duo, I was much happier when you were comparing us to British TV detectives with a little bit of class.' I pause for a moment at the hotel entrance and wait for a gap in the traffic so I can pull out on to the road. 'And secondly,' I say when we're safely out, 'that catchphrase is from *Hill Street Blues*, not *Starsky and Hutch*.'

'Hill Street what?' Kiki asks, opening her rucksack and pulling out a paper bag.

'Another American cop show. And you're also confusing your decades. *Starsky and Hutch* aired in the seventies, and *Hill Street Blues* the eighties.'

'How many encyclopaedias did you have to swallow to be this clever?' Kiki asks, lifting a sugary doughnut from her paper bag. 'I'll never be as clever as you because instead of knowledge I'm much happier swallowing this.' She takes a large bite of the doughnut, and jam begins to ooze from the bottom.

'Watch out! I could do without having to clean jam *and* dog hair from this car before we give it back.'

'Sorry,' Kiki says, grabbing a tissue from her bag. 'But they're just so yummy.'

'When I said you could bring doughnuts, I meant for the actual stakeout, not the journey to it!'

'Well, I can't go back now,' Kiki says, taking another bite. 'The doughnut's destiny is my tummy! Ooh, that rhymes,' she sings happily, 'Yummy and tummy! I'm a poet and I don't know it!'

I shake my head and concentrate on the road.

'That guy Dermot seemed nice,' Kiki ponders while she finishes her sugar fix.

'Yeah, I thought he'd be Irish though, not English. His name sounds Irish enough.'

'It's quite a romantic story. Eddie told me about it.'

'Do you and Eddie do anything but gossip?' I ask, smiling at her.

'Oh we *do*! You want me to tell you about that instead?' Kiki asks, knowing exactly what I'll say.

'*No.* I do not, thank you. The Dermot story will be fine until we reach The Welcome House.'

'OK then. Well, apparently this Darcy, Dermot's wife, inherited the island from a rich aunt, but it said in the terms of the will that she had to set up a little town or something on the island before she could get her hands on the rest of the aunt's money. That's when Dermot came in; he was one of the builders who was helping her renovate the place, and they fell in *love* . . . '

'Nice,' I say without feeling.

'Oh it *is*!' Kiki enthuses. 'It's a real love story. Dermot gave

155

up everything to come and live with Darcy on the island, and they've been there ever since. Come on, Ren, even you must be able to see the romance in that?'

'What do you mean, *even* me?'

'Well,' Kiki winds down the window and brushes the sugar from her hands. 'In matters of the heart, you're quite ... practical.'

'Practical?' I repeat. 'How does that work?'

'You should let your heart rule your head sometimes, instead of the other way around. Stop worrying about the consequences all the time and live in the moment.'

'I do ... occasionally.'

'How often is occasionally? Name one time you've let your gorgeous red hair down and gone for it?'

'I have done in the past, I'm a bit more cautious these days, that's all.'

'So what changed?' Kiki asks. 'I've asked you this before, Ren, but what changed to make you like this?'

'I think if we pull down this little road ... ' I say, indicating and turning down a narrow dirt track, 'we should be able to see the house quite clearly once I turn around and head back up to the top again. That tree should partly camouflage us, and stop anyone from seeing us watching.'

Out of the corner of my eye I see Kiki shake her head. But she's used to getting nothing back from me when she asks about my past.

I'd decided long ago to keep that part of my life buried. Burying it where it was inaccessible, even to me most of the time, meant I didn't have to deal with the feelings that thinking about it evoked. And as far as I was concerned, no one was ever going to make me dig it up again.

'Right, this will do us,' I say as I pull up again at the top of the dirt track, just far enough down so the car is partly hidden by a large tree. 'I have a good feeling about this, Kiki. Tonight might be the night we discover who it is that looks after this house – and if we're lucky, we might even find out who the mysterious owner is too.'

Twenty

'But I need to go, Ren!' Kiki insists, wriggling about in her seat.

'Didn't you go before we left?' I ask, sounding like a mother scolding a small child.

'Yes, but it's the pressure of *not* being able to go that's making me need to all the more!'

I sigh, 'Why don't you walk down the path behind the car and squat down there? I'm sure no one will see you. We've been here over an hour and we haven't seen another soul other than the traffic on the road in front of us.'

Kiki looks horrified. 'I can't go *outside*,' she whispers.

'But if you're desperate?'

'I've never been able to do that. It just won't come. Plus I'm wearing a onesie! That's a lot of undressing...'

I sigh again. 'OK, fine, you'll have to walk back to the hotel and go there, won't you?'

'But it will take me ages to get back there on foot. Can't I pop over to the house and go? We know it's open.'

'No, what if the caretaker comes?'

'What if they don't?'

'Sorry, Kiki, it's behind the car or the hotel. You choose.'

Kiki thinks about this. 'How about I see if Eddie can come and pick me up?' she suggests, lifting her phone. 'He's got a motorbike.'

'Yes, you've told me. But you can't tell him where you are or you'll give the game away. Start walking and then ring him. Say you got lost or something. He'll easily believe that now he knows you.'

Kiki gives me a withering look. 'Fine, I'll go then ... You're sure you won't change your mind and give me a lift back?' She looks pleadingly at me.

'No, we have to stake this place out. The fresh food in the kitchen must be replaced every couple of days, otherwise things like the bread would go stale. So even if I see nothing tonight, I'm going to be here every night until I do.'

'Oh goody,' Kiki says sourly, opening her door and climbing out. 'I'll make sure I buy some Pampers then.'

'That's not a bad idea!' I call as she closes the door.

Kiki waves dismissively as she walks away up the path and back on to the main pavement, then all too quickly she disappears from my sight.

It feels a bit eerie sitting here on my own in the car, and for a moment I begin to regret letting Kiki leave. But what was I supposed to do, she needed the loo and I needed to stay here on house watch. I don't know why, but I have a feeling tonight we're going to make real progress with this mystery.

I look up at the house. It stands high on a rocky outcrop, one side gazing out over the vast picturesque lakes of Ballykiltara, and the other looking majestically down at the constant stream of passing cars on the road below, which now it was getting later in the evening were beginning to thin somewhat.

'I bet you've seen some changes over the years,' I tell it. 'You probably remember horses and carts trundling along here at a much steadier pace than all this noisy traffic.'

The house as always is stoic in its silence.

'What is this hold you have over me?' I ask as I look up at its white exterior. 'You seem to have a hold over so many people in this town. What is your secret, my mysterious Welcome House, and when are you going to reveal it to me?'

I reach for one of Kiki's remaining doughnuts, and slowly devour it while I keep up my surveillance of the house.

But nothing happens. All that changes as the skies darken above me and the moon comes out from behind a cloud, is the traffic, which with each minute that passes seems to lessen more and more. I glance at my phone, but there's nothing new on the screen. I was hoping Kiki might have texted me to let me know she got back to the hotel all right. I didn't feel good about making her walk, but what else could I do? Hopefully her knight in shining armour, Sir Eddie, was able to pick her up and transport her to the nearest ladies.

I'm beginning to wish that I'd brought something highly caffeinated with me, to prevent my eyelids from doing what they wanted to do – which right now was shut tightly to allow my body and brain to drift off into a deep restful sleep – when I spot something over on the pavement next to the house.

I sit bolt upright and lift the pair of binoculars that I'd sent Kiki out to buy from one of the many shops on Ballykiltara high street. Kiki had returned with a pair that were Spider-Man

inspired – bright red and blue, with a spiderweb design embla-
zoned across them – which I'd scornfully told her to take
straight back to the shop, until Kiki had persuaded me to try
them out of the hotel window. To my surprise, I'd not only
been able to pick out the horses at the riding stable across the
hotel gardens, but also their stable nameplates too.

So, my spidey senses tingling, I lift the binoculars to my
eyes and focus them on the person who is walking towards the
house. I almost drop them again when I see who it is, and that
the person is waving at me.

Finn and Fergus cross the busy road and head towards the
car. Automatically I find myself dropping down in the front seat
so Finn doesn't see me, but stupidly I realise he already has,
so I sit back up again, trying to check my face in the dimmed
rear-view mirror as I arrange myself in my seat.

Casually I wind my window down as Finn approaches the
car. Even though he's not lit by street lights now, he is still
easily visible under a bright, almost full moon that glows in
the night sky above us.

'What ya doing?' he asks, leaning down so he can see me
properly through the open window.

'What do you think I'm doing, parked out here at this time
of night – learning how to Riverdance?'

I feel pleased with my witty retort, but Finn doesn't even
flinch. 'So you're not gazing at the stars then? Somehow I didn't
think you would be.'

I'm not sure how to take that comment, so I choose to ignore
it.

'I'm on surveillance.'

'So I see . . . ' Finn looks down at my hand, still clutching the
Spider-Man binoculars. 'Very professional.'

Hurriedly I put the binoculars down on the seat next to me, but they hit the bag of doughnuts, which I have to grab so they don't spill even more sugar on to the floor.

'Doughnuts too? Watch a lot of American cop shows, do you?'

'What do you want, Finn?' I sigh, reaching behind me to put both the binoculars and the doughnuts down on the back seat.

'I thought you might like some company?' Finn says, ruffling the top of Fergus's head. 'Fergus and I were out on our evening walk when we saw Kiki. She was sure in a hurry; she wouldn't even stop to talk to us, just called out something about you being alone up here. So I thought I'd better wander along and see what you were up to.' He looks back at the house. 'Have you seen anything yet?'

I shake my head. 'Nope, not a thing.'

'You're not the first to try this, you know – staking out the house. But no one has ever seen anything. It's like magic, how everything goes on up there.'

'No such thing,' I tell him.

'Not a believer eh?' Finn asks.

'In magic – no.'

'Makes sense.'

'I wish everyone would stop judging me!' I snap, suddenly feeling irritated. 'First it's Kiki, now you.'

'*Sor-ry!*' Finn says, backing away from the car. 'Come on, Fergus, we're obviously not welcome here.'

'No . . . no you are,' I insist, not wanting to be on my own out here any longer. 'Why don't you come and sit in the car until Kiki gets back?'

'Sure,' Finn shrugs and he and Fergus walk around to the passenger side. 'OK if he sits in the back?' Finn asks opening the door.

'Yes, it's not like he hasn't been in there before is it?'

Finn tilts the seat forward and Fergus jumps up on to the back seat, then Finn puts the seat forward again and sits down next to me.

'Your doughnuts!' he says, leaning over towards the back seat. But Fergus has already found them and is snuffling in the top of the bag.

'Oh let him have them,' I say shaking my head dismissively, 'There was only one left. But I will have the binoculars, if you can reach them.'

Finn retrieves the binoculars and we continue my vigil.

'Have you thought what you might do if you actually see someone going in there?' Finn asks, looking straight in front of him through the windscreen like I am.

'Confront them, obviously.'

'Really? Would that be the best thing to do?'

'Why wouldn't it? The quicker I find out who owns this place, the quicker I can try to arrange a sale for my client.'

'Yes, I know that. I'm sure you can't wait to get away from us all and return home to London.'

'No, I didn't mean—' I protest, but Finn continues.

'It's clear the person doesn't want to be discovered. They could be angry, even aggressive if you just bowl up and confront them. Perhaps it's a good thing I'm here.'

I take my eyes off the house for a moment so I can stare at Finn speechlessly.

'What?' he asks, turning to look at me.

'I do not need protecting by a man!' I tell him, my voice recovering from its shock. 'I can take care of myself thank you very much.'

Finn grins.

163

'I can! I've been doing it long enough ...' my voice trails off. Damn, what was it about being here in Ballykiltara? I was allowing my guard to drop far too often.

'Oh really?' Finn asks, his dark eyebrows rising high in his forehead.

'Yes, really,' I reply in a calmer tone, turning back to the windscreen.

There's silence in the car for a few moments, broken only by the gentle snores of Fergus, who inexplicably has managed to curl up and fall asleep on the tiny back seat of the car.

'So why has it been so long since you had a man in your life?' Finn asks eventually, breaking the silence. 'You might as well tell me. We could be here a long time, looking at nothing.'

'Is that any of your business?' I ask, still staring straight ahead.

'No, probably not; but I sort of thought we were becoming friends, that's all.'

Surprised, I turn to look at him. 'We are,' I reply carefully, as a lovely warm feeling spreads up from my tummy to my chest. 'I'd like to be your friend.'

Finn turns to look at me, his eyes scan my face as if he's searching for an answer to an invisible question.

'Are you allowed to befriend your guests though?' I ask, slightly unnerved by the intensity of his gaze. 'I thought that sort of thing would be frowned upon.'

'Befriending them is not a problem,' he says softly, his face moving closer to mine. 'However, doing anything more than that might be.'

'More?' I ask, knowing exactly what he means.

'Yes, more.' He leans in even closer to me, and I don't pull away. 'Something like *kissing* a guest would be frowned upon, for instance.'

'Would it?' I ask, my voice trembling.

'It would indeed,' he says, his face so close to mine that I can feel his warm breath tickling my lips. 'But then I've never been one to obey the rules, now have I?'

I smile and wait for Finn's lips to reach mine, the butterflies in my tummy eagerly anticipating how that would feel, as I allow my eyes to close.

But instead of Finn's lips gently resting themselves upon my own, they speak, jolting me from my dreamlike trance.

'Look!' he whispers, pointing through the windscreen towards the house. 'A torch.'

I turn to see what he's pointing to – a soft beam of light making its way up the windy path towards the front door.

'Can you see who's holding the torch?' I ask, immediately forgetting all about what's just happened inside the car, in favour of what's happening outside. I hoist my binoculars to my eyes, but it's too dark over by the house to see anything.

'No, the beam caught my eye as they turned into the gate.'

'What should we do?' I ask, suddenly scared of who the torchbearer might be.

'Do you want to go and see who it is?' Finn asks. 'I know you don't need protecting and all that. But I'll come with you for backup.'

'Yes, please,' I say, grateful now that he's here. Kiki would have been great, but Finn is tall and fit looking. He could be a huge asset if, like he'd suggested, the person in the house wasn't too happy at being discovered.

Leaving Fergus locked safely in the car, we make our way

up to the top of the path and then we cross the road, now so much quieter than it had been earlier in the evening.

'It might be someone staying overnight in the house,' Finn whispers as we make our way slowly towards the front door. 'The person inside might be one of the house's temporary lodgers.'

'Perhaps,' I reply, in an equally hushed tone. 'But I noticed earlier that some of the food was going off in the kitchen. I knew someone would have to visit and replace it soon. That's why I was so keen to keep watch tonight.'

'Ah, I thought you were taking a bit of a chance that some-one might show.'

I turn to Finn and put my fingers to my lips. He nods, and we both approach the front door as quietly as we can.

Like the previous times I've been here, I push the door gently, and as always the door willingly swings open inviting us to enter.

I back turn to Finn, he gives me a quick smile of encouragement, so I take a step into the darkened hallway.

Whoever is in the house has cleverly not put on any lights that would show from the road, but has, as I now recognise, put on a light in the kitchen.

I point to the light, and we begin to creep slowly down the hallway, desperately hoping that none of the old floorboards that we step on are going to creak and give us away.

Just before the kitchen doorway, I pause and look back at Finn.

'Shall I go first?' he mouths silently.

I shake my head. Finding out who was in charge of this house, possibly even who owned it, is my problem, my need. I want to be the one to expose them.

I take a deep breath and step into the light.

'You?' I gasp as I see the owner of the torch standing in front of the fridge, arranging some slabs of butter.

The person spins around, still holding one of the packets, a startled expression on their face.

Finn joins me in the kitchen doorway.

'You?' he asks, looking just as stunned. 'I never expected to see you in here tonight!'

Twenty-One

'Finn,' the owner of the torch says. 'What are you doing here?'

'I should be the one asking you that,' Finn says, stepping into the room. He walks over to the fridge and looks inside. 'Isn't this the butter we use in the hotel kitchen?' He pulls out a slab.

Sarah looks immediately shamefaced.

'And is this our milk too?' Finn pulls a bottle of semi-skimmed milk from the door.

'Yes,' Sarah says, her bulk doing nothing to hide her embarrassment. 'But I can explain, Finn, honestly I can.'

Finn takes the butter from Sarah's hand and puts it back in the fridge with the other supplies, then he closes the door. 'I think you'd better . . . and fast!'

I'm still standing in the doorway, trying to take all this in. Sarah, the cook at the hotel, is the caretaker of the house? Finn had been right all along – it was a female! But she wasn't the owner, was she? Or perhaps she was?

Sarah glances warily at me.

'Ren is a friend of mine, she's grand,' Finn says. 'You can say what you need to in front of her.'

Sarah looks at me again, nods briefly, then she turns back to Finn. 'I've never took things from the hotel kitchen before, I promise you, Finn.' Her eyes are wide with fear as she stares at Finn. I'm surprised to see that Sarah doesn't have to look up to speak to him; Finn always seemed to tower over everyone, including me. But Sarah easily matches him, height wise.

Finn waits for her to continue.

'But I got this letter, see?'

'What letter?' Finn asks, folding his arms across his chest.

I've never seen Finn like this before, all serious and strict; he's usually so relaxed and droll. Right now, I'm finding him more attractive than ever. I shake my head. *Concentrate, Ren. Concentrate. This might be important.*

'I'll get it from my bag, will I?' Sarah gestures to her handbag sitting on the kitchen table.

Finn nods.

While Sarah shuffles over to get her bag, Finn glances at me and gives me a quick reassuring smile, which I happily return.

'Now,' Sarah says, opening up her bag. 'Here it is.'

From her bag she produces a torn, cream-coloured envelope, which she passes to Finn.

Finn glances doubtfully at Sarah before pulling a piece of thick, parchment paper from the envelope. He scans it quickly, then reads it aloud.

'*Dear Sarah, You like me have lived in this area all your life, and*

I know you treasure its history as I do. So that is why The Welcome House is asking for your help.'

Finn looks up from the letter at Sarah.

'I know, imagine how I felt?' she asks looking at Finn and then at me.

Finn continues reading the letter.

'As you know, The Welcome House is always open to those in need of temporary shelter or accommodation, and as such needs to be cared for at all times.

'Sadly however that hospitality is being put under threat by those that would see the end of Ballykiltara's unique and precious legend.'

Finn pauses, but does not look at me this time.

'Until this threat has waned, I feel I have no choice but to take a short break as custodian, to protect my identity and the future of our precious house, hence there is a need for a temporary housekeeper to provide the food and services The Welcome House requires.

'So I am asking you, dear Sarah, if you would, on a temporary basis, step in to care for The Welcome House in my absence.

'I know I can trust in you to keep the legend of The Welcome House alive and well until I can safely return to my post.

'Yours, with eternal gratitude, X.'

Finn looks up from the letter. He turns to me, then to Sarah.

'So this is why you've been stealing food from the hotel?'

Sarah nods.

'And how long has it been going on?'

'This is my first time coming here,' Sarah says. 'And I've banjaxed it already.'

'When did you get the letter?' I ask, entering the kitchen properly.

'Yesterday evening,' she says. 'It was left in my apron pocket, in the hotel kitchen.'

'Someone is getting worried we might find out who the owner is,' I say, not thinking through my words.

'It's you?' Sarah asks. 'You're the one trying to wreck our legend? I should have known it would be the English, trying to take what isn't theirs!'

'No,' Finn interjects. 'Ren isn't trying to take anything; we're simply trying to find out a bit more about the myths that surround the house. Ren is a writer,' he adds, turning his face away from Sarah to wink at me. 'She's doing research, that's all.'

'Yes, that's right,' I back him up. 'It's such an interesting story; I wanted to find out more about it. This letter,' I say, taking it from Finn's hand, 'just proves that there is someone out there looking after the place. I'm simply trying to discover who.'

I look down at the letter; it's written in black ink, in a very ornate style, much like the letter in the visitors' book.

'I'd say you'd be better leaving things alone,' Sarah says meaningfully. She gives me an intimidating look. 'Before you stir up any more trouble.'

'And I'd say *you* would be best keeping your opinions to yourself,' Finn snaps. 'Considering you've just been caught, and admitted to stealing hotel property.'

Sarah flashes her eyes at Finn. But he holds her glare with an equally commanding one of his own.

If this had been taking place a couple of centuries ago, I might have felt myself swoon. Instead I swallow hard and look gratefully at Finn.

'Have it your way,' Sarah eventually concedes. 'But don't say I didn't warn you – there's lots we don't know about this place. Who knows what forces might be awoken if you keep meddling in things you don't understand.' She fires another cautionary look at me.

'You let us worry about that,' Finn insists. 'I . . . we, are quite capable of taking care of ourselves.'

Sarah opens her mouth again, but Finn shakes his head.

'I'll see you in the morning, Sarah,' he says in an authoritative voice. 'And we'll keep this little meeting between the three of us, OK? Dermot and Darcy need never find out . . .'

Sarah's head drops. 'Should I take everything back to the hotel?' she asks quietly. 'The food, I mean?'

'No, leave it here now. It will keep the place going for a few days.'

'I'll be going then, shall I?' she adds.

'I think that's best. Remember now, no one must know what's gone on here tonight.'

'Of course. My lips are sealed.' Sarah gathers up her bag and makes her way over to the kitchen door.

'Thank you, Finn,' she says. She glances at me. 'And Ren.'

Finn gives a brief nod in Sarah's direction before she leaves. Then we hear the front door open and close behind her.

'Well,' Finn says, audibly breathing a sigh of relief now Sarah has gone. 'That was close.'

'Yes, it was. Thanks for defending me – I appreciate that.'

Finn shrugs, 'No worries, I thought you might have been cross – me standing up for you. You're quite the feminist when you want to be.'

'I am – but not so much I can't appreciate a little chivalry from time to time.'

Finn smiles at me.

'You're rather scary when you're cross.' I don't tell him how sexy he is too. 'I'm not surprised Sarah scuttled off with her tail between her legs.'

'Really? I can't see it.'

'Oh yes, you completely went into managerial mode – all commanding and stern.'

'Sorry.'

'No, don't apologise.' I almost tell him how much I liked it, but stop myself. 'It was good to see another side to you.'

Finn smiles, and begins to move towards me again with a similar look to the one he'd had in the car before he spotted Sarah. But instead of responding in the way I want to, I panic and keep talking:

'However, what *is* annoying me is I really thought we were going to discover who the mystery caretaker was. I feel quite cheated.'

Finn stops abruptly halfway across the kitchen; his look of desire rapidly diminishes, and is replaced by his more usual carefree expression.

'I told you,' he says, as if nothing has happened, 'people have tried for years to uncover this mystery, but no one ever gets any closer to unravelling it.'

'Ah,' I say, relieved he doesn't seem to be annoyed by my apparent rejection. 'That's where you're wrong.' I hold up the letter still clutched in my hand. 'We have *this* now. A big clue to who the mystery caretaker is.'

'It is?' Finn looks doubtfully at the letter.

'Yes. This letter, Finn Cassidy, is going to help us solve this mystery once and for all.'

Twenty-Two

'She said what?' Kiki asks as we all sit around a corner table in the hotel bar. It's nearly 2 a.m. and Kiki, Finn, Eddie and I are ruminating over the night's events with an assortment of drinks, both alcoholic and hot, in front of us on the table.

'She warned us not to keep meddling, or who knows what forces we would awaken, didn't she, Finn?'

'She did,' Finn agrees, taking a sip from his mug of tea.

'It sounds like Scooby-Doo!' Kiki exclaims with amusement. 'When the bad guys warn those pesky kids to stop meddling! Did you used to watch that, Eddie?' she asks, looking over at Eddie, who has finished his shift and is enjoying the shot of Irish whiskey that Finn has poured him as a thank you from me for coming out to collect Kiki in her hour of need.

'I did indeed,' Eddie says. 'But Sarah might be right – there's all sorts of stories that surround that house, not all of them good like the ones you've probably heard so far. That's the Ballykiltara publicity machine working overtime. If you consult the Ballykiltara grapevine, you'd probably hear closer to the truth.'

'What do you mean?' I ask, glancing at Finn with a questioning look. Did he know about these alternate stories too?

'Well,' Eddie says, putting his glass purposefully back down on the table, 'let's just say Sarah might have been trying to do you a favour with her warning . . .'

'Come on, Eddie, spill!' Kiki encourages. 'We want to know more, don't we, Ren?'

'Yes please, Eddie. Anything you can tell us might be of help.'

'OK, then. But don't say I didn't warn you.'

Eddie, unusually, is quite enjoying his moment in the spotlight. Normally, he seems to be doing his best to blend seamlessly into the background as he scurries around the hotel completing his daily tasks. But tonight, he's clearly relishing our attention as he sits forward to tell us more.

'There's been tales and myths galore surrounding that old house for years and years,' Eddie says, looking around the table at us. 'Like I said before, most of them are good: a friendly old house that welcomes in strangers – what could be grander than that? It's a visitor-friendly tale for the locals to tell to tourists over a pint of Guinness. But what you don't hear about so readily is the darker stories that surround the place . . .'

'Go on,' I encourage, when Eddie pauses for dramatic effect once more.

'Many folk have tried, like you are, miss,' he says, nodding at me, 'to uncover the secret of The Welcome House. Folk don't always take kindly to things that can't be explained. And most of the time when they can't find answers they give up and move on. But it's the persistent ones that seem to stir up the most trouble.'

'Like?' I ask, wishing he'd get to the point. It's late, and I'm not in the mood for ghost stories, which is what Eddie seems to be building up to.

'They say that if you try too hard to find out the secret of The Welcome House . . .' he looks around the table again, 'the house will swallow you up.'

'Whatever do you mean, "swallow you up"?' I demand, while Kiki looks aghast. 'How can a house do that?'

'It's the cellar, so they say,' Eddie continues, undaunted. 'There have been tales of folk that have gone down there, never to return. When people have gone to look for them, there's no trace – they've disappeared never to be seen again.'

'Whoa!' Kiki whispers. 'No way!'

Eddie nods assuredly. He sits back in his chair, lifts his glass and sips his whiskey.

'Come on, Eddie,' I say, grinning now, 'you don't seriously expect me to believe that nonsense? Surely this is another silly myth that's grown from a lot of tittle-tattle over time?'

'I'm only telling you what I know, miss,' Eddie says without a hint of doubt in his voice.

'And when did you last hear of someone being . . .' I have to gather myself before saying this, 'swallowed up by the house!'

'Well, not recently, no,' Eddie says, considering it. 'But there's evidence of it happening in the past.'

'What evidence?' I ask scornfully. Highly amused by this, I glance over to Finn, who I expect to see sporting a similar expression to mine, but instead his expression is unusually impartial as he listens to Eddie's tale.

'I've never seen them myself,' Eddie says, 'but they say

there's some old books that tell tales of people disappearing in the house.'

'Books? What sort of books?'

'Manuscripts,' Finn says, to my surprise, 'that date back to Viking times.'

'You knew about this?' I ask in astonishment. 'Why didn't you say something before?'

Finn shrugs. 'It didn't seem relevant. Like you said, it's only more tales.'

'But there's actual evidence of this happening? Of people disappearing?'

'Apparently, these manuscripts report it.'

'Have you seen them?'

'*No,*' Finn says, laughing. 'No one has. Not for a long time anyway.'

'So how do you know they exist? More old wives' tales?'

'No – old priests.'

I look at him with a puzzled expression.

'Father Duffy,' he answers for me. 'He says they exist.'

'Father Duffy says books exist that show people disappearing from The Welcome House cellar?' This was getting sillier by the minute.

Finn shrugs again. Suggesting perhaps he doesn't want to believe it either. 'Something like that, yes. Why don't you ask him about it tomorrow night at the quiz?'

'Don't worry, I will.' Anyone would think we were in cloud-cuckoo land right now, not twenty-first-century Ireland. I'm now more determined than ever to get to the bottom of this; not just for Ryan Dempsey, but for my own sanity too. 'I'll also be using my time before then to try and narrow down who sent Sarah's mystery letter.' I tell them.

'Aren't you scared, after what Eddie's told you?' Kiki asks, looking worried. 'What if the house doesn't like what we're doing? We could be swallowed up too!'

'Don't be so silly. How is that ever going to happen?'

Kiki looks anxiously at Eddie.

He simply shrugs with a 'Don't say I didn't warn you' look.

Kiki looks back at me with a terrified expression.

'Look, as long as we don't go down to the cellar, we'll be safe, won't we?' I try, in the hope this will pacify her.

She nods uneasily.

'Oh, that's not the only story,' Eddie pipes up again, to my horror. 'There's lots—'

'Yes, thank you, Eddie.' I glare at him with such force, he visibly reels back against his chair. 'I'm sure that can wait for another time.'

'Yes, I think we've all had enough fun for one evening,' Finn says, standing up. 'I don't know about you, but I'm definitely ready for my bed.'

He collects the glasses and mugs and takes them up to the bar while we gather our things.

Kiki and Eddie walk out into the hotel foyer together to say goodnight, so I'm left slightly awkwardly with Finn.

I feel like I'm sixteen again and on a double-date with my best friend from school. While Jennifer quite happily got off with any of the boys we double-dated together, I was always left feeling awkward and tongue-tied at the end of the date.

'Those two seem to be getting on well,' Finn comments, looking out into the foyer as he walks over to where I stand. 'I'm pleased for them.'

'Yes, Eddie isn't Kiki's usual type of guy. But they're good together.'

'What do you think about holiday romances?' Finn asks casually. 'Do they ever last?'

I'm careful with my answer. 'Sometimes, I guess. But we're not on holiday, are we? This is a business trip.'

'Ah yes, the business – how could I forget?' He looks at me meaningfully.

I'm too tired for this tonight, so I make a quick, and pleasant decision. 'Good night, Finn,' I tell him. 'Thank you for all your help.' And without thinking any further about it, I stand on tiptoe and kiss his cheek, which feels warm as my lips brush against a light covering of stubble.

Without saying anything else, I leave a somewhat surprised Finn in the bar and make my way past an interlocked Kiki and Eddie up to our room, where even after I've cleaned my teeth and got ready for bed, I can still feel the taste of Finn on my lips. And it's a feeling I'm happy to hold on to, as I drift off into a deep and very contented sleep.

Twenty-Three

I'm deep in thought the next day as I take an early morning walk through Ballykiltara out to the park that we'd passed by so many times in the car, but had never had the chance to stop at.

Kiki is still asleep after our escapades last night, so I leave her a note telling her where I've gone, pleased I can have some peace and quiet for once so I can allow my mind to ruminate on everything that's happened so far.

I know we're getting closer by the day to finding the mysterious caretaker of The Welcome House, I can feel it in my bones. I don't think I've ever tried so hard to secure a house for a client in all the time I've been property hunting, but The Welcome House has got under my skin, and now it was as much about solving the mystery that surrounds the house as securing a sale. Everyone else seemed more than happy to accept this peculiar house and its mystery caretaker/owner, so why couldn't I?

Something hadn't sat right with me since I came to Ballykiltara. It isn't just the house, there's something else going on too, and I seem no closer to discovering what that is, than I am to putting a deposit down for Ryan Dempsey.

And now there's this added mystery that Eddie threw into the pot last night: the supposed tales of people going missing in The Welcome House's cellar. That sounds to me even more of a nonsense than a house that magically welcomes guests and provides food and shelter for them.

If I don't find answers to all these puzzles that keep presenting themselves to me on a daily basis, it's going to drive me insane.

I tried to call in on Father Duffy on my way to the park, hoping to get a head start, but he was out. One of his neighbours kindly informed me he was doing his rounds. She made him sound like a doctor, but I guess the local priest has a duty of care to visit his parishioners in their houses if they can't get out to see him, and Father Duffy seems the sort of priest to take his duties very seriously indeed.

I've arrived at the park now, and as I walk through the ornate wrought-iron gates the first thing that catches my eyes is a large map showing the various routes around the park. I'd assumed Ballykiltara Park was a small town park with swings, slides and the like, but apparently not. The vast open expanses of grass, and various options of routes in front of me, suggest this is what I would recognise as a country park back home.

'Do you need any help?' a lady wearing walking attire asks as she approaches me.

'I just wanted to take a stroll around the park,' I tell her. 'I had no idea it was so big.'

She smiles. 'We get that a lot. Most visitors never even make it this far, they're so caught up in the shops buying their fluffy sheep and Guinness memorabilia.'

'Yes, I have noticed a few shops like that,' I say cautiously. Most days, it was all I could do to keep Kiki out of them.

'A few? The high street is full of them! But we can't complain; without the visitors and the tour buses stopping off, we'd have little else to support our economy. It's a shame people can't spend a little longer here, though, so they can appreciate the beautiful surroundings. Are *you* staying long?'

'A few days,' I say carefully. Tonight would be our sixth night here and I still hadn't secured a property for Mr Dempsey. We couldn't stay forever, even though I was pretty sure Kiki would be more than happy to right now.

'That's a good amount of time. You've had time to make it past the shops! Now, what would you like to see in the park and how long do you have?'

'I'm not sure. What is there to see?'

'Well,' she says, gesturing with her hand at the board, 'this is the route I follow most days – it takes me about an hour. It's easy walking on tarmac paths, leading you in a complete circuit of the lake.'

I'm about to say that will do – it would be good to see the lake again – when she continues: 'But this way,' she points to another loop on the map. 'This way will take you past the deer.'

'There are deer?' I ask, suddenly remembering the tale that Jackie had told us on the boat.

'Oh yes, great herds of them roam this area. Would you be wanting to see some?'

'That would be lovely.'

'Well, you've picked the right time; the deer mainly come out in the early morning or early evening. So you shouldn't have

182

any trouble seeing them. But the stags, well, they only come out when they want to see you.'

'So I should take this route?' I point at the map.

'Yes, that's the one. Have fun!'

'Thank you for your help,' I tell her as she marches off swinging her arms. 'You've been very kind.'

The woman waves her hand dismissively. 'Not at all. Us locals are proud of our town; we like to see folk enjoying themselves while they're here. Enjoy your walk.'

She waves again as she walks away at a brisk pace through the park gates. I turn back briefly to the map, debating whether I should take a photo of it, just in case. But it looks a fairly simple route, so I leave my phone in my pocket and head off in the same brisk manner the lady had along one of the tarmac paths.

I've only been walking for about ten minutes, along tree-lined tracks that climb and dip with the undulating countryside, when I spot my first herd of deer. They're quite some way in the distance, but unmistakable with their graceful, yet quick and nervy movements. I stand and watch them for a bit, wishing that they were closer so I might see them in more detail.

Then I continue on my walk, carefully following the marked path my guide had suggested. Occasionally I'm passed by cyclists or joggers, out for their morning exercise, but as I get deeper into the park I find I have the place to myself. It's then that my thoughts begin to turn to The Welcome House once more.

Now we have Sarah's letter, things have changed. The enigmatic caretaker of the house is no longer a myth, some magical entity invisibly entering and leaving the house to deposit provisions and clean sheets. No, we now have proof that an actual person has been doing this, likely someone local too, so all we need to do is find out who that person is, and bingo, we're on a home run.

I smile at my unintentional house pun.

So what do we know about this person? I'm convinced it's a man now Sarah is out of the picture. I haven't seen any more women with Sarah's substantial build since we've been here. According to Eddie, *he* is tall and bulky. This mystery man obviously knows Sarah and, more importantly, trusts her with The Welcome House duties. He's eloquent, too – that letter has been written by someone with an excellent grasp of the English language, and beautiful penmanship. From what he said, our custodian has lived in Ballykiltara for most of his life too.

That has to narrow things down a fair bit, I think to myself as I walk along. Hopefully the quiz night might throw up a few likely suspects. It seems, from what I'd heard about it, that the weekly quiz night is well attended, and the trophy is hotly contested. I have a feeling that our suspect is the sort of person to enjoy putting his grey matter to the test, so I'm hoping he will be there. If I'm lucky, I might be able to spot him from the clues he's given us so far.

The path in front of me takes a sharp turn to the left, so happily I follow it, but as I emerge around the corner suddenly I find myself face to face with a huge stag with antlers almost as tall as its body.

I freeze, and so does the stag, and for what seems like forever we stare at each other, neither of us knowing quite what to do.

'Good boy,' I whisper eventually, as the stag continues to eye me warily. 'I won't hurt you, honestly.'

The stag suddenly bows his head, and as he does I notice a flash of white between his antlers. Then he paws the ground with his hoof, and for one awful moment I think he might be about to charge at me.

Panic-stricken, I hold my hand out. 'No,' I tell him again. 'I'm not here to hurt you. Be on your way.'

The stag looks at me curiously. Then as if he's accepting the situation, he bows his head once more, and trots slowly off the path on to the grass, where he gallops over to join his herd, who I now notice are grazing not far away.

I close my eyes and breathe a huge sigh of relief. When I open them again, I notice another animal galloping towards me, but this time instead of the weight of a pair of giant antlers, it's carrying the weight of a human. As they draw closer, I recognise Finn and Trixie.

'Are you OK?' Finn asks as he pulls Trixie up alongside me and dismounts. 'I saw what happened with the stag.'

'Yes, I'm fine. Would he have hurt me?'

'It's unlikely. Had it been the rutting season, it might have been a different story though.'

'Rutting?'

'Their mating season, you've heard of rutting stags – right?'

'Oh yes, when they lock antlers.'

'That's the one. Any stag attacks on humans are usually documented at that time of the year. Unless you were threatening his harem or him, of course; then he'd probably have cause to get aggressive.'

'I came around the corner and he was just standing in the middle of the path. Gave me quite a scare!'

'He was probably more scared of you than you were of him,' Finn says dismounting. 'What are you doing out here anyway?'

'I wanted to take a walk, clear my head.'

'Yes, I can see that. I mean *all the way* out here. I'd say it was off the beaten track, but there are so many paths around this park it's almost impossible not to be on one. This particular one is a long way from anywhere, that's why I bring Trixie out here.'

I look around me. 'I thought I was on the circular path, the one shown on the board as you come into the park.'

Finn looks up the hill. 'You would be, if you were all the way over there,' he points. 'You must have taken a wrong turn.'

'I didn't think I had, but I have been a bit lost in my thoughts while I've been out here,' I admit.

'Need I ask what your thoughts were about?'

'No, I suspect you can probably guess by now. So, how do I get back on the *right* path?'

'It's a fair way from here,' Finn says, looking around him. 'Unless you want a *really* long walk this morning, that is.'

'I've already been out here over an hour.' I check my watch. 'Golly, make that nearly two hours. I didn't realise it had been that long since I left the hotel. Kiki will be wondering where I've got to. I left her a note, but I said I was only going for a quick stroll to clear my head.'

'Looks like you've one option then,' Finn says matter-of-factly. 'You'd best head back with me.'

'Oh no, I couldn't stop you from finishing your ride,' I pat Trixie's hindquarters. 'Trixie would never forgive me.'

'No, I mean *ride* back with me, on Trixie.'

'But wouldn't that be too much for her?'

Finn shakes his head. 'Look at the size of her. She's one of the horses Mac gives to the *heavy* riders when they come in looking for a horse. She'd take you and me easy. Unless you're a lot heavier than you look?' He raises his eyebrows mischievously and pretends to look me over.

I choose to ignore him. 'But where would I sit?'

'In front of me. Trixie's saddle is massive, and if you don't mind me saying, your bum is not.'

My cheeks pink slightly.

'I'd have to put my arms around you though,' Finn continues. 'To stop you sliding off . . . '

The thought of Finn's arms around my waist is not an entirely unpleasant one . . .

'Right then,' he says, taking off his riding hat and passing it to me. 'You'd better wear this. You'll likely need to adjust it first.'

'But what about you?' I ask, adjusting the inside of the hat when I find it's a bit too big.

Finn knocks on the side of his head with his knuckles. 'I think you'd agree it's pretty thick already! Anyway,' his expression appears to sober, 'I'd rather you wear it. The hotel's insurance policy doesn't cover riding accidents.'

I pause from putting the riding hat on and look at him aghast. Finn appears to be serious, but then he smiles.

'I thought you were serious there for a moment.'

'I am.' Finn winks.

I finish adjusting the riding hat while Finn takes a firm grip of Trixie's reins, pulling her close to us. 'Ready?' he asks.

'I think so.'

'Right then, up you get!'

Hesitantly, I look up at what seems a huge distance between Trixie's saddle and the ground.

'What's wrong?' Finn asks. 'You have ridden a horse before?'

Finn makes it sound like I'm about to ride a bike.

'Not since I was small.' I pretend to readjust the hat on my head. 'Remember, I told you before at the stables?'

'Oh yes . . .' Finn regards me suspiciously. 'So do you mean you *rode* horses as a child, or you've been on the back of one when someone's led you across a field at a garden fete?'

'The latter,' I have to admit.

'Well, it's never too late to start,' Finn says brightly, pulling out one of Trixie's stirrups. 'All you need do is put your left foot in here, hold on to the saddle tightly, then push up and swing your right foot over Trixie's back, OK?'

'Sounds easy enough.'

Finn doesn't comment, he just grips the stirrup firmly, steadying it while I place my foot inside. Then I grab hold of the saddle tightly like he'd said, and I attempt to push myself up.

'Not to worry,' Finn says when I don't make it quite high enough to swing my leg over Trixie's back. 'Have another go.'

So I try a second time, and when that fails I try again.

'Sorry,' I apologise when embarrassingly I don't make it up on the third attempt. 'She's quite high, isn't she?'

'She's a big horse,' Finn agrees, and I'm grateful to him for not laughing at me. 'Would you mind if I gave you a push?'

'A push would be great,' I say, thinking Finn will grab hold of my leg. So when I try for a fourth time and I feel his hand cup itself neatly around my bum, I don't know whether it's the strength of his push that carries me up and over the top of Trixie, or the enormity of my surprise.

'There you are,' he says, without a hint of the embarrassment I'm now feeling. 'Now, hold on tightly, I'm coming up too.'

Finn manages to swing himself up and over Trixie's back

without even using the stirrups. What was he – a circus performer in a previous life? I feel his arms immediately reach around my waist as he takes hold of the reins.

'You hold on to the pommel,' Finn instructs. 'That high bit at the front of the saddle. Yes, that's right, and I'll steady you from behind. Now, give Trixie a good hard kick.'

I gently tap my stirruped heel into Trixie's side.

'Harder than that,' Finn says, 'or we'll never get her to move.'

'Won't it hurt her?' I ask, concerned.

'No, this is how Trixie responds. All horses are different, but they're like dogs, they respond best to good clear commands.'

'OK then ... ' I give Trixie what I consider a relatively hard kick. But she still doesn't move.

'Little bit harder,' Finn says patiently.

I kick again, and to my surprise Trixie begins to walk forward across the grass.

'You OK?' Finn asks. 'Do you feel safe enough?'

'Yes,' I say out loud. 'Absolutely fine.' While inside I'm thinking, *How could I not feel safe when your arms are around me?*

Finn has particularly strong muscular arms that, even though they're not actually holding on to me that tightly, make me feel very secure up here on Trixie.

'Want to go a bit faster?' Finn asks after a bit.

'Should we?'

'Yeah, Trixie will be fine if we trot along slowly. Don't worry, we won't be doing any galloping or I'll be off the back! Give her another kick.'

I do as he says and Trixie begins to move a little faster. I feel Finn's arms tighten around my waist.

'Just making sure I don't fall off,' he explains, leaning forward to whisper in my ear. And suddenly I'm the one who has to hold the saddle that little bit tighter. But when Trixie slows again, and Finn doesn't return to his original position, and remains with his body pressed against mine, I'm not sure he's quite telling me the truth.

The ride back to the stables is over all too quickly. Even though we haven't ridden all that fast, I've enjoyed the feeling of being up on Trixie's back – almost as much as I've enjoyed feeling Finn so close to me. I've heard people talk about the joy and immense sense of freedom they get when riding horses, and even after this short trip I'm beginning to understand what they mean. So when we reach the stable yard and Finn dismounts, then chivalrously helps me climb down from Trixie with some dignity, my face is flushed with exhilaration and pleasure.

'You look like you enjoyed that,' Finn says as he leads Trixie back to her stables to begin her cool-off and post-ride routine.

'I did, very much.'

'Would you like to go for a proper ride sometime?' Finn asks, taking his helmet from me.

'Could you arrange that?'

'It would be my pleasure. We'll get you your own horse to ride next time though, eh?'

'That might be better, yes.' I smile happily up at him.

'You have a very pretty face when you allow it to smile, Ren Parker, do you know that?'

'Is that your way of telling me I don't smile often enough?' I reply jokingly, even though I'm all too aware this is not what Finn means.

'It's my way of telling what I see when I look at you.' He reaches out his hand and gently cups my cheek. 'You're very beautiful when you allow yourself to be.'

As Finn's face moves slowly towards mine I'm not sure what I should do. I know what I want to do, but is that really the best thing for me or for him?

But I don't have to worry because Trixie decides for us, suddenly letting out a loud whinny while stamping her hoof on the ground impatiently.

Finn grins. 'She wants her brush and her food.'

'You can't blame her,' I say, not knowing whether to be annoyed or grateful to Trixie. 'She did do the work of two horses on that ride. Perhaps she should get the rewards of two.'

'You'll get what you're given,' Finn says, turning to Trixie. But he manages to find a treat in his pocket, which Trixie hungrily gobbles from the flat of his hand. 'She's probably right though, I should get her sorted before I head back to my cottage for a shower. Then of course I have work.' He grimaces. 'I wonder what delights and what even more delightful guests will await me today?'

'Nothing you can't handle, I'm sure,' I tell him. 'I'd better be getting back too. I need to do the same – shower, then work.'

'Still ploughing on with the house? Eddie's tales haven't put you off?'

'*No*, why would they? All make believe, isn't it.'

Finn shrugs. 'No smoke without fire.'

'You don't believe all that nonsense, surely?'

'No, but I do trust Father Duffy, and if he says there's truth in these tales, then I think there might be something to them.'

'Well, I'm going to ask him about it tonight at the quiz, and see what he's got to say for himself.'

'Good luck getting anything out of him when he's in competition mode,' Finn smiles. 'I've never met such a competitive priest. When you said you had good general knowledge the

191

other day, his eyes lit up. He's always looking to recruit new members to the quiz team.'

'Even if it is only for one night.'

I notice Finn's amused expression diminish slightly.

'Yeah, shame about that . . . Anyway, if I don't see you before, I'll see you tonight at the quiz, yes?'

'Yes. Have a good day, Finn, and thank you for rescuing me today.'

'No worries. Just think of me as your knight in shining armour!' His eyes twinkle in the bright morning sunshine that has decided to make an appearance at last. 'And don't stress about that house too much, yeah? Everything will sort itself out when it's good and ready. It always does.'

'Perhaps.' I shrug, not quite so convinced. 'I'll see you later.'

Finn leads Trixie away, while I turn and head back to the hotel, allowing the very pleasant thoughts of Finn as a handsome knight on horseback and me as his damsel in distress to fill my mind as I walk.

Twenty-Four

When Kiki and I walk into the same pub we'd visited only a few nights previously, I'm amazed at how different it looks.

Instead of tables set up to receive drinkers, and people looking to have a quick bite to eat, we find everything rearranged in honour of this evening's quiz night. Many of the tables have been spread out on to the open floor where Kiki had danced in front of the band, and instead of an area set up for music with amplifiers and microphones, there is now a long table with three chairs set formally behind it for tonight's quizmaster and scorers.

A few of the tables are occupied by people I don't recognise, but towards the back I spot Father Duffy already set up with a pint of Guinness waiting for the rest of his team to arrive. He waves when he sees me.

'Shall I get the drinks in?' Kiki asks, heading to the bar. 'Usual, Ren?'

'Actually no, I'll have a Guinness, please.'

Kiki turns back, her eyebrows raised. 'Finn really is having an effect on you, isn't he?'

I roll my eyes, determined not to dignify her jibe with a reply. But Kiki just grins and skips up to the bar, where as usual she gets served straight away. A skill I'm always envious of.

I head over towards Father Duffy, weaving my way through the tables to get to him. There are white pieces of card in the centre of most of the tables declaring team names. I read some of them as I pass, and I begin to appreciate how much this quiz night brings the local community together, even if it is in intense rivalry.

'Good evening, young lady,' Father Duffy says, standing up to greet me. 'I'm so pleased you could make it.'

'Good evening, Father. Are you sure it will be all right, me taking part?' I ask anxiously, pulling out a chair. 'Everyone else seems to be local. I'm only a visitor.'

Father Duffy waves away my objection good-naturedly. 'All the teams try to pull in ringers when they can,' he says, looking suspiciously around the other tables. 'It's part of the fun. We're lucky, being a hotel team we often have quite a large pool to choose from.'

'And there was me, thinking I was special,' I say jokily.

'Oh, but you are, Ren,' Father Duffy says solemnly. 'You're special in many ways, and I don't just mean for the quiz team. I knew it the moment we first met.'

I smile hesitantly at Father Duffy. 'I'm sorry, I don't under-stand what you mean?'

'And I wouldn't expect you to, my dear.' He takes a quick drink from his glass. 'You said this was your first visit to Ballykiltara, didn't you?'

'Yes.'

'I thought so. Tell me, have you had any strange feelings since you've been here? Feelings you can't attribute to anything in particular?'

'It's funny you should ask that, because actually I have,' I tell him, surprised by his question.

'Do you feel that you know this place, that it's familiar?'

I think for a moment. 'Yes, I suppose it is a bit like that.'

'Do you feel you've been here before, Ren?' he asks, looking gravely at me.

'Well, like I said, it's familiar, but I'm not sure—'

'Where do you come from, Ren?' Father Duffy asks. 'I mean, where do you hail from originally.'

'Northumberland, not far from Bamburgh.'

'Ah, Northumberland,' Father Duffy says fondly. 'Another area strong in its Celtic roots and traditions. Many a monk travelled from Northumberland to Ireland in the past – some of their own volition, some fled when the Norsemen came calling.'

'Yes, I knew that.'

'Naturally – I'd expect no less of a sharp, enquiring mind like yours, Ren. But I suspect you know facts, not feelings.'

'How do you mean?'

Father Duffy watches me thoughtfully for a moment. 'Have you ever tried letting your feelings guide you, Ren?' he asks. 'Instead of your head.'

'Yes. Of course I have,' I answer quickly.

'And what happened?' Father Duffy asks just as swiftly.

'I got hurt,' I tell him before I have time to think about it.

He nods knowingly. 'I thought so. But you know your heart can tell you so much more than your head ever can.'

I'm annoyed at myself for telling him as much as I have already. 'Perhaps.'

'It can, you know. While you're here, Ren, I think it would be a good idea to let your heart rule your actions occasionally, rather than your head. You may find you discover many, many things you didn't know.'

'Such as?'

Father Duffy smiles enigmatically. 'Why don't you try it and see what happens? I've a feeling you might like what you find.'

I'm about to ask him how using my heart rather than my head to make decisions will help with anything when Finn and Donal arrive at the table.

'Good evening,' Finn says, smiling at me, and then Father Duffy. 'I see you made it then, Ren.'

I smile warmly. 'Yes, I'm looking forward to it.'

'Can I get you both a drink?' he asks.

'I'm grand,' Father Duffy says, holding up his glass.

'I think Kiki is supposed to be getting mine,' I say, looking towards the bar. 'She's been a while though.'

'I think she was on her way over when we arrived,' Finn says. 'But she's been distracted by Eddie.'

I roll my eyes. 'I should have known!'

'Guinness?' Finn asks.

'Yes, please.'

'Orange juice for you, Donal?'

'Oh yes, I never drink alcohol on a quiz night,' Donal says, slipping into one of the chairs positioned around the table.

Finn rolls his eyes behind Donal's back. 'Back in a mo'.'

I watch Finn walk across to the bar, then I turn my attention to the two men sitting at the table with me.

'How's the book research coming along?' Donal asks, fiddling awkwardly with one of the beer mats from the table.

'Er ... yes, quite well, thank you,' I lie, glancing self-consciously at Father Duffy. 'I've made a fair bit of progress recently,' I add, a little more truthfully.

'Good. Good. You know, if you need any help, I'm always here,' Donal offers.

'Donal is quite the font of knowledge on all things local,' Father Duffy says, nodding at him. 'Aren't you, Donal?'

'I like to think I know a fair bit about the area I come from, yes. In fact, I like to think I have quite a broad knowledge of all things. I guess that's why you have me on the team, Father.' Donal folds his hands neatly in his lap while he smiles at his own joke.

'You're on the team because I can't get rid of you,' Father Duffy says, winking at me. 'I've tried, but you keep turning up.'

Donal looks with dismay at Father Duffy.

'I'm kidding, Donal,' the priest replies. 'We are allowed to do that, you know.'

Donal nods hurriedly. 'Of course, Father.'

'The truth is,' Father Duffy explains for my benefit, 'Donal is a walking encyclopaedia – there's no one better for historical facts, that's for sure.'

'Do you all have your own specialist subjects then?' I ask.

Father Duffy thinks about this. 'I suppose we do, to an extent. Donal is our history buff, he also knows a lot about literature. I usually take music and geography. Finn – sports and anything mathematical. Orla is our popular culture expert. Ciaran is very good with food and drink. And you, Ren, will hopefully cover anything we don't know!'

'I'll do my best,' I tell him.

'Drinks!' Finn announces, arriving with three drinks carefully balanced in his two hands. 'Juice for you, Donal, a pint of the black stuff for Ren, and a lemonade for me.' He places our drinks down in front of us, then slips into the seat next to me.

I wonder why Finn isn't drinking again. In fact, come to think of it, I've never seen him take alcohol at all.

'Did you know Ren had never had Guinness before she came here, Father?' Finn says, taking a sip from his glass of lemonade. 'We've corrupted her.'

'I had tasted it, I'd just never enjoyed it before,' I correct him. 'It wasn't the kind of drink I'd usually choose.'

Father Duffy looks between us, and smiles. 'Your head ruling your heart, by any chance?'

'Ha, possibly,' I reply, smiling at him.

Finn looks between the priest and me with a curious expression.

Father Duffy glances at his watch. 'Orla and Ciaran are running a little late, aren't they?' he says, looking up towards the door of the pub.

'Ciaran is at the bar, I just saw him,' Finn says, sounding unconcerned. 'And Orla will make it on time – she usually does.'

'I hope so.' Father Duffy looks concerned. 'We don't want to have to forfeit now we have Ren onside.'

'How many players do you need then?' I ask. 'Six?'

'The rules state a minimum of six, a maximum of eight,' Donal replies. 'Two thirds of whom have to be regular team members.'

'Do you often have hotel guests join in?'

'Not usually,' Finn says. 'Only if we find out they're handy

198

with the old general knowledge.' He winks. 'Usually we make up the team with another member of staff, or someone from the town.'

'I see.' I look around the table. 'So who's running the hotel tonight with you lot here and Eddie at the bar? Won't it fall apart?'

'The joys of delegation!' Finn says, happily lifting his glass. 'Seriously though, everything will be fine back at base. I've got a great team.'

Ciaran comes over to join us. 'Just got a text from Orla,' he says, holding up his phone. 'She won't be able to make it tonight.' He glances nervously at Father Duffy. 'Ladies' problems, apparently,' he whispers.

'No need to hide it from me, Ciaran. I may be a priest, but I do understand how a lady's body works.'

I smile down into my drink.

'However,' Father Duffy continues, 'that does leave us with a slight problem. Who are we going to get to replace her, with . . . ' he looks at his watch, 'minutes to go?'

'Ren, I'm *so* sorry!' I hear Kiki call as she approaches our table with Eddie in tow. 'I got caught up with Eddie and forgot about your drink. Eddie's had your Guinness now – shall I get you another?'

'Kiki,' I say, smiling up at her, 'how's your knowledge of popular culture?'

'My what?' Kiki asks, looking puzzled.

'How much do you know about the inside of *Hello!* and *OK* magazines?' Finn asks, immediately getting where I'm going with this.

'Finn,' Kiki says, wrapping her arms around his broad shoulders. 'That is my surrealist subject!'

'She means specialist,' I quickly inform the others as they stare up at Kiki with puzzled looks. 'Gentlemen, I'd like you to meet your newest team member and expert on popular culture, Miss Kiki Fisher.'

Twenty-Five

Quiz night turns out to be a very enjoyable evening.

After I roped Kiki in as the newest member of the team, Eddie decided he might as well join in too, since that only took our team members to seven.

Apparently this is a real coup because Eddie never joins in with the quizzes, preferring, as he describes it, 'to support from the sidelines' – or as Finn put it, 'from the bar'.

As the evening wears on, I'm amazed at how good everyone's general knowledge is. I'd thought mine was pretty good, but I find myself lacking on many questions that some of the others seem to find easy.

As Father Duffy had said, everyone has their own specialist subjects they excel at. Donal's knowledge of history – Irish history in particular – is outstanding. Not knowing much about sport, I find myself in awe of the way Finn rattles off the answers to that round. It's clear he knows everything there is to know about horse racing.

I'm pleased when I get the chance to keep up with the others and answer some questions myself – there's a round about London, in which to our absolute delight, Kiki and I know every answer.

I've not had much time during the quiz to keep an eye out for our mystery letter writer, but even if I had, the pub is packed this evening with people supporting their teams, drinking and enjoying themselves, so it would be nigh on impossible to spot someone based on the little I know.

'Last round!' our quizmaster calls as we huddle around the table waiting for our next challenge. 'And it's everyone's favourite – Popular Culture!'

There are groans beside me from all but Kiki, who excitedly claps her hands.

'Question one,' Seamus our quizmaster begins. 'Who played the Wicked Witch of the West in the 1939 movie *The Wizard of Oz*?'

We all look at Kiki, who shrugs nervously.

'Does anyone know?' Father Duffy asks. 'I know Judy Garland was Dorothy.'

'It's Margaret Hamilton,' Eddie pipes up. '*What?*' he asks when everyone turns to him in amazement; he's been quiet through the rest of the evening. 'Me mam used to make me watch all them movies when I was a lil'un. Stuff sticks.'

'I think that's right,' I agree. 'She sounds familiar.'

'Well done, Eddie,' Kiki praises, kissing his cheek.

Eddie flushes.

'Question two,' Seamus asks from his table at the front, 'is a two-parter, so one point for each correct answer. In the TV soap *EastEnders*, what is the name firstly of the pub, and secondly of the square in which it stands? I think I'm allowed to give you a little clue here – they're related to each other.'

'Oh lord,' Finn says, rolling his eyes. 'I don't watch Irish soaps, let alone British ones.'

Kiki and I look smugly at each other. Back home, we would quite often have a gossip in the office about any antics in the square the night before. 'I think you'll find the answer is,' I say confidently. 'Kiki?' I hold out my hand.

'The Queen Victoria, and Albert Square,' she says with glee.

Donal, who's been put in charge of recording our answers, hurriedly notes them down on our sheet.

'I'm glad you girls are here,' Father Duffy says, patting my hand. 'I don't think any of us would have known that.'

'Me ma watches it,' Eddie says, 'but I steer well clear when it's on.'

'Question three,' Seamus calls. 'Which popular singer released a live DVD called *Jumpers for Goalposts* and a studio album called *X*.'

'Ooh ooh!' Kiki says, waving her hand in the air. 'Ed Sheeran,' she whispers to Donal. 'He's one of my faves, he is.'

Donal looks around the table. Eddie and I both nod, so he scribbles it down.

'This quiz gets better and better!' Kiki grins happily.

'Question four – our penultimate question tonight. Irish actor Andrew Scott plays Moriarty in the successful TV series *Sherlock*, but can you name the two female characters who regularly appear in the show?'

'I have to admit this is one that has passed me by,' Father Duffy says, looking around the table. 'Anyone know?'

'Mrs Hudson is one,' I say, trying desperately to think of the other. 'Una Stubbs plays her.'

'Molly,' Donal says to my surprise. 'Molly Hooper. I like a bit of *Sherlock* – tests the old grey matter, so it does, trying to figure everything out before he does.'

I watch Donal as he writes our answers down, and I notice for the first time how ornate his handwriting is. Ornate and florid, like his speech . . .

'So, to our final question,' Seamus announces before I have time to think further about this, 'and we go a bit more up to date with our movies this time. In the *Hangover* movies, the Wolfpack had a gangster adversary and sometimes friend who appeared in all three films with them, what was his name?'

'Mr Chow!' Kiki, Finn, Eddie and I all hiss at the same time, while Donal and Father Duffy look blank.

'Looks like we have the definitive answer, Donal,' Father Duffy says, smiling at us. 'Well done, all of you.'

I take another quick glance at Donal's handwriting before he whisks our answers up to the desk to be marked. It's certainly formal, and almost calligraphic in the way he adds flourishes and swirls to his letters. A person who writes like that and speaks like Donal would certainly be able to turn out a letter like the one Sarah received. Could he be our man?

While the others sit and chat about the quiz and the questions we did and didn't answer, I sit thinking about Donal. He's tall – so he fits Eddie's description. I wouldn't call him broad, but maybe he'd been wearing a coat when Eddie saw him. Yes, one of those puffa jackets would make him seem a lot bigger from a distance.

But I can't imagine Donal in anything but a smart mac or trench coat. He's far too traditional for anoraks. I'm beginning to think I'm barking up the wrong tree with this train of thought when Donal says something that immediately changes my mind.

'The question about the Sharpe novels was so annoying. I used to own all of Bernard Cornwell's books before I gave them away to charity. I should have known the answer.'

'Yes, you usually get all the literary questions right, Donal,' Father Duffy says. 'There's not much you haven't read.'

The conversation turns into a chat about books and how no one gets as much time to read as they'd like any more. But I don't join in; I'm still thinking about The Welcome House and the many books I'd seen lined up in the huge bookcase, including a complete set of Sharpe novels by one Bernard Cornwell.

'Not joining in with us, Ren?' Donal asks, looking at me questioningly. 'You being a writer, I'd have thought you'd have much to share on the topic?'

I glance around the table. Other than Ciaran, Donal was the only one who didn't know I wasn't in Ballykiltara to do research for a book. Kiki had told Eddie the truth a couple of days ago, and she said he was cool with it.

'I'm not really a writer,' I announce, deciding to come clean. Also I'm curious to see what Donal's reaction will be. 'I'm a property seeker.'

Ciaran shrugs and takes an indifferent sip from his glass. But Donal looks at me uneasily.

'A what?' He looks at the others to gauge their surprise, but to their credit their expressions remain neutral.

'A property seeker,' I repeat. 'Kiki and I both are. We're here looking for a house for one of our clients.'

'But . . . ' Unusually for him, Donal looks anxious and more than a little unnerved. 'Why would you tell us you were a writer?'

'I didn't want to cause any unease or arouse suspicion. When people hear what you do, especially in close communities such as Ballykiltara, they tend to close ranks. And that can make it more difficult to find properties.'

Donal's reaction is not the one I was hoping for. I'd expected him to clam up and become secretive when put on the spot. Instead he seems upset and hurt that we've lied to him.

'I see,' is all Donal says. 'And have you found anywhere you'd like to buy since you've been here?'

I glance around the table again.

'Ren is interested in The Welcome House,' Father Duffy says openly. 'We've told her about the history and legends that surround the place, but she still feels it's the right house for her client.'

'You can't buy The Welcome House!' Donal explodes, his face reddening. 'It's part of our history, our heritage here in Ballykiltara.'

'I've told her about the bad things that might happen,' Eddie pipes up. 'But it hasn't put her off.'

I look at Father Duffy. He seems puzzled by Eddie's statement.

'Well it should,' Donal says, standing up. 'The Welcome House is not for sale to anyone, let alone an outsider from another country. Who's your client, pray tell – some godawful American celebrity who wants to pretend they have Irish heritage? Or even worse, some Cockney wide boy wheeler-dealer who wants a pad for himself and his bit on the side?'

Hearing Donal say 'bit on the side' in his clipped formal tone should be amusing, but his anger is anything but.

'Donal, sit down!' Finn says, standing up and putting his hand firmly on Donal's shoulder. 'You're creating a scene.'

Donal glares at him.

'I'm guessing you were in on this all the time, Finn? I expect you were putty in her hands from the moment she first fluttered her eyelashes at you!'

'*Donal* . . .' Finn warns, his eyes flashing dangerously. 'I can see you're upset, but I think you've said enough. Now calm down, or if you can't, perhaps you should leave.'

'I'll leave, thank you,' Donal says, pushing his chair back. 'You are a guest in our hotel, miss, and as such I will conduct myself with decorum around you while you continue to stay with us. But you should know how much my opinion of you, and your friend' – he glares at Kiki, who cowers against Eddie, who immediately wraps his arm protectively around her shoulder – 'has plummeted on hearing your true reason for being here in Ballykiltara. And with that I bid you all goodnight.'

Donal exits as quickly as he can through the tables, then he marches out of the pub door.

I look at the others sitting around the table with a mixture of horror, shock and embarrassment on their faces.

'I'm sorry about Donal,' Finn apologises. 'I'll have a word with him in the morning.'

'I'm sure he spoke in haste,' Father Duffy says, tapping my hand. 'He'll come around.'

'Always had too many words to say on too many subjects, that one,' Ciaran agrees good-naturedly.

Eddie doesn't say anything, he just hugs Kiki that little bit tighter, and I get the feeling he's attempting to protect her from me now, as well as Donal.

'Maybe he's right,' I say, looking down at the table. I fiddle with one of the biros that had been supplied to us for making notes throughout the quiz, even though Donal had used his own fountain pen to write our answers. 'Maybe we have pushed things a little too far here. Perhaps it's time to back off?' I can't look at Finn as I stand up. 'I think it's time I went. I hope at least I've been of some use here tonight.' I put the pen down on the table and straighten it before I let it go.

Kiki stands up too.

'No, Kiki, you stay and enjoy yourself with Eddie. I'm going to go back to the hotel and run myself a bath. I need to do some serious thinking about what we do and where we go next . . .'

Twenty-Six

Before they can speak, I turn away from my remaining team-mates and make my way out of the pub, stopping briefly outside to take a few breaths of fresh cool air, then I set off briskly along the street in the direction of the hotel.

This is not how I'd expected tonight to go. I thought I'd spend the evening answering a few questions while I looked out for men who matched my mental picture of our mystery caretaker. I did not expect to have my integrity questioned by Donal in front of my new friends, with half the pub looking on.

Why had Donal suddenly turned on me like that? Was it because he was frightened I might be about to unmask his secret? Or was it because he genuinely felt that strongly about The Welcome House, its history and traditions?

More importantly, why had his words hurt me so much? I'm used to people turning on me when they find out I'm trying to buy a property; it happens a lot when people think you've been sneaky or gone behind their backs – it's a natural human reaction. But for some reason Donal's words had hit home.

I'm so deep in thought as I walk along that I don't hear footsteps coming up quickly behind me until someone calls my name. I spin around, half expecting to see Finn, but it's not his towering figure I find trotting along the street after me, but the much smaller one of Father Duffy.

'Ren, wait!' he calls.

I stop so he can catch up with me. 'What are you doing out here, Father?' I ask when he breathlessly reaches my side.

'I wanted to check you were all right. After what happened in the pub just now.'

I shrug. 'Yeah, I'm OK. A bit shocked maybe, but that's all.'

'Shall we walk?' Father Duffy asks. 'I assume you're heading back to The Stag?'

I nod and we begin to walk along the path together.

'Donal didn't mean to be so blunt, you know,' he says, as we fall into step. 'He's very protective of this area; he's lived here all his life. He was born in a house just along that street, I believe.'

I look down the street of terraced houses that Father Duffy is pointing to.

'That's nice ... You say he's lived here all his life?'

Father Duffy nods.

'Do you think he might be the caretaker of The Welcome House?' I ask frankly.

'Donal?' Father Duffy says, sounding surprised. 'Why would you think that?'

'Apart from the fact he obviously knows a lot about this area and its history, it's his manner – he's eloquent, and he has very ornate handwriting, which would suggest he might be the same person who wrote Sarah's letter.'

'Sarah's letter?' Father Duffy asks, looking puzzled.

I tell him about what happened at the house last night with Finn and Sarah.

'I don't believe Donal is yer man,' Father Duffy says when I've finished.

'Why not? He fits the description Eddie gave, and his style fits the letter.'

'But can you see Donal making up beds and stocking fridges? The other stuff might be his style, but not that. Donal is what you English call a snob. A lovely man, mind, but he knows his place in the system. He is definitely not one for household duties. He spends too much time overseeing the hotel staff to lower himself to taking on their responsibilities in his spare time.'

'You might be right,' I have to agree. 'He didn't react the way I thought he would when I told him I wasn't really a writer. He was shocked, hurt even. If he was the person who wrote that letter, he would have known I wasn't what I was pretending to be. The letter suggested the caretaker was concerned about being unmasked. That's why he asked Sarah to step in.'

We've reached the steps of the hotel entrance, so we pause outside for a moment.

'You know, I don't blame Donal,' I say, looking up at the outside of the hotel. Bright lights are shining through the tall ground-floor windows; it looks cosy and inviting on this dark and now very cool night. 'He might have been a bit blunt, but some would say he was only being honest.'

'Yes, they probably would,' Father Duffy agrees.

'And maybe he's right: maybe I have overstepped the mark with this?' Fearful of what he might say, I don't look at the priest standing next to me. Instead I watch the wooden hotel sign with its dramatic painting of a majestic white stag swinging to and fro in the breeze.

'Do *you* think you have?' I hear Father Duffy ask beside me.

I shrug and turn towards him. 'My head says no. It's telling me I've done what I'm paid to do, I've found the perfect house for my client.'

'I'm sensing a "but".'

'*But* ... my heart is disagreeing with my head. My heart is wondering if I am doing the right thing. It's wondering if I should step back and let this strange house with its even stranger stories be.'

'And which one are you going to listen to?'

'I'll have to get back to you on that one, I'm afraid.'

Father Duffy smiles. 'I think you should. Now, why don't you go upstairs and take your bath, let yourself relax. The answers, I promise, will come to you.'

'You're very wise,' I tell him, smiling now too. 'I expect many have told you that.'

'A few.'

'Thank you.' I go to hug him, then realise that it probably isn't the done thing in Ireland to hug a priest. So I awkwardly reach for his hand instead.

'You can hug me if you want to,' he says, winking at me. 'I won't dissolve in a pool of Holy water.'

I give him a proper hug this time, and I feel Father Duffy's hands gently tap my shoulder blades.

'Now, I'll be on my way,' he says. 'The night is still young and I need to find out where we're going to sit in the league tables after tonight's efforts.'

'I almost forgot about the quiz with everything else going on. I'm so sorry to take you away from it. I expect Finn will have a drink waiting for you when you get back, though.'

'Yes, he's a good lad is that one.' He pats the left side of his chest with the palm of his hand. 'Remember your heart, Ren,' he says, 'not only in dilemmas about the house, but with other things that concern you too. Trust me, there's more going on here than you realise. Come and see me tomorrow,' he adds as a parting comment. 'I think I have some things at the church that might interest you.'

I'm about to ask what sort of things, but he bids me good-night and begins walking back in the direction of the pub.

Looks like I'll find out tomorrow then, I sigh, before I head inside the warm, welcoming and now familiar atmosphere of The Stag Hotel.

I've just run my bath, and I'm about to climb into what looks like heaven in bubble form to my tired body and overwrought mind, when there's a knock on my hotel-room door.

I'd ordered a mug of hot chocolate from room service a few minutes ago, so I'm not too startled; I simply tie the hotel's white bathrobe around me a little tighter and go to the door.

But it's not one of the hotel's many Eddie lookalikes in their smart black-and-white uniform that greets me as I pull open the door without bothering to look through the peephole, it's a worried-looking Finn.

'Sorry,' he apologises on seeing me in my robe. 'Were you about to go to bed?'

'I was about to take a bath actually.'

'I'll go then.' He turns to leave.

'No, it's fine. What did you want?' I ask. 'Is everything all right back at the pub? Is Kiki behaving herself?'

'Oh sure, yes. She hasn't left Eddie's side all night.'

'Sounds familiar.'

'They make a cute couple. Poor Eddie will be heartbroken when you both leave.'

There's an awkward pause, broken by the sound of the lift doors opening down the corridor.

Finn glances to his right to see who's coming. 'Room service,' he says, watching someone walk along the corridor.

'Oh, that might be my hot chocolate,' I say as a young bellboy comes into view carrying a tray. He doesn't look up until he gets level with Finn, so intent is he on not spilling the drink balanced in the middle of his silver tray.

'Oh, Finn – I mean Mr Cassidy,' he says, his tray wobbling so some of the chocolate spills on to the white coaster.

Finn grabs the tray from him to prevent any more spillages. 'I'll take that, Charlie,' he says briskly.

Charlie, his face flushed, glances at me standing in the doorway. His face goes even redder.

'Sorry, miss,' he apologises. 'I was fine until I saw Finn – I mean, Mr Cassidy.'

'I know, he is a bit scary, isn't he?' I wink at Charlie. 'I don't blame you.'

Finn raises his eyebrows at me and I feel my heart beat inside my chest a little faster.

'Should I go get you another?' Charlie asks.

'Yes please, but bring two this time, will you?'

'Of course, miss.' He turns to Finn. 'Should I take that from you?' he asks, holding his hands out for the tray.

'I think you'd better,' Finn says sternly. 'And not a drop spilt next time, you hear?'

'Yes, Mr Cassidy, of course.' Charlie takes the tray and hurries back down the corridor towards the lift.

Finn watches him then turns towards me. 'He's new,' he explains. 'Sorry about that.'

'It's fine. Everyone has to learn, don't they?'

'I guess. So are you feeling thirsty or are you expecting Kiki back very soon? I have to say, by the look of her at the pub, I think that hot chocolate might be stone-cold before she gets to drink it.'

'The hot chocolate isn't for Kiki,' I tell him, stepping back into the room and opening the door a little wider. 'It's for you. Coming in to drink it?'

Twenty-Seven

Finn's stunned expression lessens, but remains on his face as he follows me into the room, closing the door behind him.

'What about your bath?' he asks, looking towards the bathroom door.

'It can wait,' I say, sitting down on the dressing table chair and swinging myself around in his direction.

Finn watches me, and not for the first time I catch him looking at my bare legs as my dressing gown rises up along my thigh.

I gesture towards the bed. 'Take a seat.'

Finn sits himself formally on the end of Kiki's bed because mine is still covered in my abandoned outfit from the quiz night.

'So what do you want?' I ask, trying to pull my robe down to cover my legs without being too obvious.

'I'm sorry?' Finn asks, looking astonished again.

'When you came to my door, what did you want with me?'

'Oh ... yes, that.' Finn's expression changes to one of relief. 'I wanted to check that you were OK – after what Donal said. I was going to come after you when you left the pub, but Father Duffy insisted he would go. Did he catch up with you?'

'He did, yes.'

'And did he have some wise words to impart? He usually does.'

I think about what the priest had said. 'Yes, he did. Very wise.'

'Good. I wouldn't want Donal to have upset you.'

I smile at Finn. 'That's kind of you. It's good to know you care.'

'You're a guest at our hotel. It's my job to care.'

'Oh right.' I look away from Finn towards the generic hotel picture on the wall behind him of a vase of flowers in front of a window.

Finn looks behind him at what I'm suddenly finding so interesting.

'Oh shit,' he says, realising. He runs his hand nervously through his hair. 'I didn't mean it like that. Of course *I* care about you too – that goes without saying, doesn't it? I thought you knew that.'

I can't help smiling. Finn's sexy when he's being all bossy and commanding, but he's even more attractive like this.

'I know,' I tell him quietly. 'It's nice to hear you say it, though.'

To my surprise, Finn grins at me. I'd thought we were having a *moment*. But as always he has to turn it into a joke.

'High maintenance, are you?'

'Sorry?'

'High maintenance – you need a lot of reassurance in a relationship. Someone telling you they love you all the time.'

'No, not at all.'

Finn laughs. 'Yeah, right. I've only known you a matter of days and I figured out you were high maintenance within a few minutes.'

I narrow my eyes at him in annoyance. 'So what are you then, Finn – low maintenance? So low no one wants to bother maintaining you? As far as I can see, there's hardly a queue of women lining up to be by your side.'

The moment the words leave my lips I'm sorry. But not for the first time Finn has irritated me with his offhand remarks, when only moments before he'd seemed genuine in his concern for me. I hadn't meant what I said, but it seemed like the perfect way to counter his jibe. Hopefully, Finn will see it that way too.

But his highly amused expression immediately drops. 'You're probably right,' he says quietly. 'Who would want to maintain me?'

I wait to see if this is one of his jokes, and in a moment he'll grin at me, and likely wink too. So when he doesn't, I get up from my seat, go over and sit next to him on the bed.

'Finn Cassidy,' I say, taking his hand, 'you are the most annoying, secretive, and maddening man I think I've ever had the joy to meet.'

'Thanks,' Finn says, looking with interest at our hands now entwined between us on the bed.

'You're frustrating, exasperating—'

'I think I get the general idea,' Finn interrupts, loosening his grip on my hand.

'Wait, I'm not finished,' I tell him, holding on even tighter.

'You're also one of the kindest, most generous, and loveliest men I've ever met. I'm not sure how you manage to be both at the same time, but you do a damn good job of balancing them.'

Finn's face, close to mine anyway as we sit next to each other on Kiki's bed, becomes even closer as he turns towards me.

'I think ...' he says, a smile flickering at his lips, 'that was meant as a compliment?'

'It was.'

'Then the only way I know to thank you when we're sitting this close is by doing this ...' The tiny gap that was between our two faces disappears as Finn leans forward and kisses me with one of the gentlest kisses I think I've ever had.

Then the gap between our faces widens again as he looks into my eyes, seeking my approval.

I give it to him immediately, by placing my lips back where they'd felt so comfortable on his. This time Finn's kiss becomes firmer and more powerful as his lips begin to explore mine. Willingly I allow them to, enjoying every moment of having Finn this close to me. Our hands are still clasped tightly together between us, so when I feel Finn's free hand reach up and place itself firmly behind my neck, pulling me even closer to him, I don't hesitate in allowing him to.

'Ren?' Finn whispers breathlessly in between kisses.

'Yes,' I ask, doing the same.

'Why did you invite me in here tonight?' His hand leaves my neck and wanders down towards my chest. 'When you were only wearing this?' I feel his fingers run gently along the opening of my robe.

'For hot chocolate,' I murmur, wishing his hand would slip inside the opening.

'Only hot chocolate?' Finn asks, his lips moving down to my neck. 'Or was there another reason maybe?'

So caught up are we in each other we don't hear the door quietly open, and it's not until I hear footsteps crossing the carpeted floor that I'm aware anyone is in the room with us. I snap my eyes open as I feel Finn hastily remove his lips from my neck.

We both turn at exactly the same time to see an elated Kiki. She's standing next to a horrified Charlie, who clutches a silver tray in front of him with two mugs on it this time. 'I'd say get a room,' Kiki says, grinning delightedly, 'but it seems you already have!'

'Er . . .' Finn stutters, looking at Charlie. 'It's not what you think.'

'I'd say it's exactly what we think, eh, Charlie?' Kiki nudges Charlie, and he has to steady his tray. 'Oops, sorry, mate! Do you want to put that down somewhere?'

But Kiki offers a second too late.

Charlie, trembling like a rabbit caught in headlights on a busy motorway, suddenly lets go of the tray, and Kiki has to leap athletically to one side to avoid being covered in two mugfuls of frothy hot chocolate.

Twenty-Eight

So much for an early night, a bath and anything else that might have been on the menu.

After Charlie's accident with the hot chocolate, Finn immediately morphs back from romantic hero to hotel manager. Partly to deal with the large brown patches of liquid chocolate that now cover the carpet and some of the walls of our room, and partly I think to hide his mortification at being caught by one of his staff in a compromising position with me.

'You must change rooms immediately,' he insists, his face red – again, partly from embarrassment and partly from anger at Charlie. 'This will take ages to get out.'

'I'm sorry, Mr Cassidy,' Charlie cries, grabbing a white towel from the bathroom. He then throws himself down on the floor and begins scrubbing furiously at the stain.

'That won't help, will it, you feckin eejit! Get up at once, go downstairs and get whoever is on duty to come up here with buckets of soapy water, sponges and scrubbing brushes. Then ask Sinead on reception to find these ladies another room – no, make that a suite!' he insists. 'Then you come back and help them to move their things, do you hear?'

'Yes, Mr Cassidy.' Charlie almost bows as he backs out of the room. 'And I'm very sorry again, ladies.'

'Oh, don't be too harsh on him, Finn,' I say as Charlie leaves the room. 'It *was* an accident.'

Finn looks at me, then at Kiki. 'Let's get you two packed up and moved,' he says. 'We can deal with *everything else*, later.'

Kiki and I begin to gather our things, throwing items quickly into our suitcases while Finn paces impatiently around in the room, then outside in the corridor, when things aren't happening fast enough.

'I don't want to move rooms,' Kiki whispers when we're in the bathroom, gathering our bits. 'I like this one.'

'Do as he says, Kik,' I whisper back. 'You can see what sort of mood he's in.'

'I bet he's in a mood,' Kiki giggles. 'He's just been prevented from having hot sex with a hot chick!'

'Stop it!' I insist. 'You don't know that was going to happen.'

Kiki stops screwing the lid on to her moisturiser and stands open-mouthed in front of me. 'Are you kidding? The look on your two faces when we came through the door suggested that was exactly what was going to happen.'

My face, already pink after recent events, reddens further.

'Let's not talk about this now – we need to get on with moving to our new room. We can talk later.'

'Oh, that is one hundred per cent what we're going to be doing, lady!' Kiki grins. 'I want all the goss! I'm so glad Eddie had an early shift tomorrow, or I might not have known any-thing about this.'

'Packing, Kiki!'

'Yeah, yeah. One more thing, though: you weren't going to do it on *my* bed, were you? You would have moved to your own when things ... progressed?'

'Enough!' I hiss, hearing Finn coming back into the room. The situation was bad enough without him thinking I was gos-siping about it. The current look on his face suggested this was not something he'd ever dealt with before, and I was secretly quite pleased to know it.

Eventually, we move to a rather lovely suite a little way down the corridor. Our belongings are transported by several members of the night staff, who I suspect haven't dealt with anything so dramatic before either.

I hope, for Finn's sake, that Charlie isn't a gossip. The staff who've come to help us give no sign of knowing what caused Charlie to drop his tray, so either they know nothing or are being super-professional in disguising it.

'Do you have everything you need?' Finn asks, when all the staff have departed, leaving only the three of us in the room. Kiki is investigating the extra rooms we have now we're in a suite, and Finn and I stand by the open door before he follows his staff down the corridor.

'Yes, this is lovely, Finn,' I tell him. 'Thank you for everything.'

'No, thank you for being so understanding. I'm sorry for all the hassle.'

'Don't be silly, it wasn't your fault. Plus we've got a fab new room as a result.' I gesture back inside the suite. 'Will you be OK?' I ask quietly. 'Will Charlie say anything?'

'I think everyone will know he dropped hot chocolate every-where when the cleaners come in tomorrow morning and have a proper go at cleaning it all up.'

'No, I meant about us,' I say quietly, looking up at him.

Finn shakes his head. 'No. Charlie and I have had a quick chat. Let's just say he still has a job, when really he should have been fired for that.'

'Ah, I get it.' I wink at Finn, but he doesn't respond. 'I'm sorry it had to end like that tonight—' I begin to say, but Finn interrupts.

'I'm sorry, Ren, I need to go now. I'll see you tomorrow, yes?'

'Oh yes, sure.'

Finn looks either way down the corridor. Then he plants a quick kiss on my cheek. 'Goodnight.'

'Goodnight,' I whisper as I watch him hurry off down the corridor. He pauses briefly at the lift before deciding to take the stairs, allowing himself one backward glance at me, still standing in the doorway, before he disappears.

I wave, but Finn is gone.

Twenty-Nine

The next morning, I wake up feeling very different.

As I lie in my new bed thinking about the events of last night I can't stop myself from smiling, and neither do I want to; thinking about Finn's kiss and what almost happened is nearly as good as experiencing it the first time.

'What are you grinning about – as if I need to ask?' Kiki pipes up from the next bed.

I roll over on my pillow to face her. 'You're awake early.'

'I know, it's this new room,' she says, looking around. 'I'm not sure about it. It doesn't feel like the old one.'

'It's better than the old one – it's a suite.'

Kiki waves her hand dismissively. 'Enough about the room – let's talk about Finn.' She rolls over in bed and looks expectantly at me.

'What about him?'

'What happens next? Are you going to pick up where you left

off? It looked pretty heated when I entered the room last night. It would be a real crime not to reignite that burning flame . . .'

'I don't know, do I?' I say, rolling over on to my back. 'That depends on him . . .'

'Ah-ha!' Kiki sits up in her bed and pulls the white duvet up around her shoulders. 'So you want to, then?'

As I stare up at the ceiling, a huge, wide grin forms on my face without me giving permission for it to be there.

'That's all the answer I need!' Kiki shrieks. 'Woo-hoo! We've both found love here in the Emerald Isle! What are the chances?'

'Are you in love with Eddie?' I ask, seeing an opportunity to steer the conversation away from me.

'I think I might be.' Kiki pulls her knees up to her chest, and the quilt even tighter around her. 'Eddie is so sweet and kind, I just adore him. Oh, Ren, do we have to go home? Can't we stay here in this hotel in Ballykiltara forever?'

'Sounds good to me,' I joke.

'Seriously?'

'No, of course we can't. We have to go home. We have lives back in London – and, more importantly, jobs!'

'You're carrying on with it then?' Kiki asks. 'The search for the owner of the house? I thought after everything that happened last night, you might have changed your mind.'

'How can I change my mind? That's what we came here for. I can't go home empty-handed, can I?'

'Why not?' Kiki demands, sitting forward now. 'Why can't you just this once tell Ryan Dempsey you couldn't find anything that matches what he was looking for? Why can't you let this go, then we can enjoy some nice relaxed time here – you, me, Finn and Eddie?'

Not for the first time, I give Kiki's proposal serious consideration. I'd given it a lot of thought before I fell asleep last night. Naturally, my thoughts had been focused on Finn, but they'd kept drifting back to The Welcome House too. And I'd thought about Donal's reaction, and Father Duffy's words of advice ... My mind had even wandered back to Jackie and the boat trip. It seemed that no one wanted me to carry on with this search. Even Kiki was keen for me to give up. But giving up simply wasn't in my nature. Then again, my nature seemed to be changing. My brain was fighting it, but my heart ... Like Father Duffy had said, my heart was telling me differently.

There was no denying it would be lovely to spend some quality time here in Ballykiltara instead of running around looking for a person who obviously didn't want to be found. Spending proper time with Finn before we returned home was a very appealing thought. I'd never had a holiday romance; maybe this could be the time to try one ...

'Perhaps everyone is right,' I say eventually. 'Perhaps I should let this one go. I wouldn't want to be known as the person who ruined the legend of The Welcome House, now would I?'

Kiki leaps from her bed straight on to mine. 'Do you mean it?' she asks excitedly. 'Can we really have a little holiday here?'

'A few days' break, maybe – hardly a holiday.'

'Yay!' Kiki claps her hands excitedly. 'I can't wait to tell Eddie! He'll be so pleased we're not here working any more. I think it's really bothered him, us searching for the owner of that house, like he was disturbing me from my work or something.'

I didn't know where Eddie would have got that idea; Kiki's

never needed much of an excuse to take some time off. But I don't say anything.

'When will you tell Finn?' Kiki asks. 'He's gonna be so pleased.'

'When I see him,' I say carefully. 'I'm not sure what his shifts are today.'

'Right!' Kiki leaps off the bed. 'I need to get myself Eddie-ready! He has a day off today, but I told him I couldn't arrange anything until I knew what we were doing.' She grabs her phone from where it's charging on the desk, and begins texting as she heads into the bathroom. 'Back in a bit!'

While Kiki's busy beautifying herself, I lie back in my bed and relive Finn's kiss, hoping I might get to experience it again for real later.

Finn is on duty when we go down for breakfast. He passes us in the lobby of the hotel carrying some files.

'You're looking very smart, Kiki,' he says, smiling at her. 'Special occasion?' He gives me the briefest of glances.

I smile shyly back, worried that if I open my mouth too far the kaleidoscope of butterflies fluttering nervously in my tummy might decide to escape and fly all over the hotel.

'I'm spending the day with Eddie!' Kiki sings happily as she pirouettes her way towards the breakfast room. 'He's taking me for a drive in the mountains.'

Finn smiles at her as she disappears into the restaurant. Then he turns back to me. 'Day off, eh? I didn't think you allowed that.'

'I do sometimes. Look, can we talk later, Finn?' I ask, trying to keep my cool while he's this close to me, when all I really want to do is throw my arms around his neck and kiss him in the same way I had last night.

'Yes, I think we probably should,' Finn says, in a voice so low no one else can hear. 'Are you around at lunchtime?'

Finn whispering like this is doing funny things to me. The sexy Irish lilt in his voice is hard to resist at the best of times, but whispered close to my ear like this, it's doing things to me that oughtn't be done in a public place.

'I can be. Where should I meet you?'

'Come over to the cottage, say around one?'

'Sure.'

'Right, you'd better go and get some breakfast before everything's gone,' Finn says, looking towards the restaurant. 'You're quite late this morning.'

'Yes, I guess we are,' I reply, looking at him. But his gaze doesn't meet mine. Is Finn being a bit offhand with me this morning? It certainly feels that way; his answers are carefully worded and he's barely made eye contact with me. Don't be silly, I quickly reassure myself, it's probably because we might be seen by the staff, and after last night he doesn't want any more rumours spreading. Yes, that must be it.

'See you later then?' I offer, by way of a parting gesture.

Finn simply nods and continues on his way to his office.

After we've had breakfast, Kiki rushes off to spend her day with Eddie, while I walk up the hill to see Father Duffy.

I've no idea what he meant when he said he had 'things to show me'. If they're things to do with The Welcome House, I'm no longer interested now that I've made my decision to step away from it. But I said I'd visit him this morning, and I never go back on my word – especially to a priest!

As I walk up the hill in the bright morning sunshine, I think about that. Wouldn't I be going back on my word by deciding not to pursue The Welcome House for Ryan Dempsey when I'd assured him I would find him his perfect home?

I guess I would be, although it wasn't like I was giving up my search altogether, merely ruling out this one option. Surely I could admit defeat this once if it was for the greater good – and leaving The Welcome House alone had to be in the house's best interests, didn't it?

You're letting your heart rule your head, Ren, I decide when I can find no reason to change my mind. Father Duffy told you to, and now you're following his advice it feels good, doesn't it?

I pass the church as its chimes strike eleven o'clock, arriving at Father Duffy's house as the last note sounds.

'Hello!' he calls, flinging open the door before I've had time to knock. 'I saw you coming up the path.'

'Good morning,' I reply, stepping into his house. 'Lovely day, isn't it?'

'It is that; the sun is shining on our souls as well as our bodies today. Come through, won't you?' he says, leading me to the small sitting room I'd sat in only a few days ago with Finn. 'Take a seat.'

I sit down on the small sofa while Father Duffy makes tea, then he brings through a tray of tea things and sits opposite me on a burgundy red velvet armchair that looks like it's seen better days.

'How are you today?' he asks.

'Good, thank you.'

'You seem different.' He looks at me quizzically. 'Lighter.'

'After the breakfasts we've been eating at The Stag over the last few days, I hardly think so. If anything, I'm a lot heavier!'

Father Duffy smiles. 'No, I mean lighter internally, as if a burden has been lifted.'

230

'Ah, I see. Yes, you're right, it has. I've decided to stop searching for the owner of The Welcome House.'

Father Duffy looks surprised. 'You have? And what made you come to this decision, if you don't mind me asking?'

'I listened to my heart,' I tell him proudly.

'Ah, you did … I'm pleased for you. And is that the only thing you've listened to your heart about since I saw you last?'

My cheeks redden. 'There may have been something else …'

Father Duffy smiles knowingly. 'Well, I'm glad for you, in both respects. But that does put me in a slight quandary …'

'It does?'

'You see, the reason I asked you here today was to show you these.' He gestures to some worn, leather-bound books stacked in the middle of the small coffee table between us.

'What are they?'

'Journals mostly, about The Welcome House.'

I look at the books on the table. 'What sort of journals?'

'They tell tales of the house through the centuries. They tell how people have hidden in the house, died in the house, and travelled from far away in order to stay there.'

'Oh, I've seen one like that – a visitors' book in the hallway of the house.'

Father Duffy shakes his head. 'No, these are not visitors' books. These are journals. They tell the story of the house – and how it came to be.'

I look at the books on the table. 'Really? That's impressive. So, how did it come to be? Didn't you say it was something to do with monks?'

'Indeed I did. In the eighth century, monks were travel-ling the world preaching to those who wanted to learn the stories of the Gospels. But the Norsemen were a constant threat.'

'The Vikings?'

Father Duffy nods. 'So the monks of Tara, as the town was known then, built a hiding place where they and the travelling monks could escape to.'

'The Welcome House?'

'Yes. The house in its current form was built many, many centuries later, but it was built on the site of the monks' original shelter. The place where the magic happened.'

'What magic? Food appearing in cupboards and beds being made?'

Father Duffy shakes his head. 'No, not that magic – the real magic, the stuff of legend.'

I look at him, my curiosity piqued. 'And what is this *legend*?'

'These books' – he taps the cover of the journal on top of the pile – 'tell how the monks would welcome extraordinary people into the house, and then how they would simply disappear.'

'I thought it was people who tried to mess with the house's legend that disappeared?'

Father Duffy waves his hand dismissively. 'That's a myth that has grown up over the years – nothing but tittle-tattle and hearsay. A way to keep outsiders from interfering.' He gives me a knowing look. 'That would be the tale Eddie recounted to you, I expect.'

'So what's the true story?' I ask, ignoring the implication. I had nothing to feel guilty about any more; I was done with the house. My interest now didn't extend beyond curiosity about the house's history.

'The true tale is that the monks would use the house to hide people – usually eminent monks who were recording the stories of the Gospels in picture form. They were concerned that if these monks were killed by the Norsemen, their tales of Christianity would die with them.'

'Are you talking about illuminated manuscripts, Father?' I ask, suddenly understanding. 'Like the Book of Kells?'

'I am indeed, child. Forgive me, I forget you have such a broad range of knowledge. Of course you would know of such a thing.'

'Well, I know a little about it. The Book of Kells is in Trinity Library, Dublin – yes? It's an illuminated account of the four Gospels.'

'It is, absolutely spot on. That's the most famous of the illuminated manuscripts, and the one most people know about. But there are others, some in your home county, I believe?'

'Yes, I think there are. We do have quite a Celtic heritage.'

'Holy Island in particular – that's where some of the monks who hid in The Welcome House originated from.'

'You really think monks came from the Holy Island of Lindisfarne to Ballykiltara?'

'I know they did.' Father Duffy taps the journals again. 'It says so in here.'

I look at the pile of books and feel a strange pull towards them. Resisting it, I return my gaze to the priest sitting opposite me.

'But as I said before, it wasn't called Ballykiltara back then,' Father Duffy explains. 'It was just called Tara.'

'Like the island?'

'Yes. Or to give it its full name, Glentara.'

'Oh, I did know that. Tara is like its nickname.'

'Many of the places around here have Tara in their name – the ones associated with the magic.'

'Do strange things happen on the island, too?'

Father Duffy nods. 'The island has its own tales to tell. I should introduce you to Darcy, one of its owners. She can tell you all about the magic of Tara.'

'I've met Dermot, her husband.'

'Ah, yes, Dermot – a non-believer, if ever I met one. Yet he too has fallen under the Tara spell.'

I look sceptically at Father Duffy. What *is* he talking about – the 'Tara spell'? 'So why did the town of Tara become Ballykiltara?' I ask, hoping to steer this conversation away from magical goings on and back to historical fact. 'It's something to do with your church, isn't it?'

'Possibly. It's believed the name originally meant place of the elevated church, or place of the church on the hill.'

'Yes, you told me that last time we met here.'

'So I did – how well you remember, Ren. "Bally" means "place of" – it's a common prefix for towns in Ireland. "Kil" means church, and the Gaelic word "Tara" or *Teamhair* has come to mean hill – after the hill in County Meath where the high kings of Ireland were crowned, allegedly. But,' Father Duffy says, looking at the books, 'that's the modern explanation, the one that makes sense to folk. There may be another reason, though. According to entries in here' – he lifts the top journal off the pile – 'Tara became Ballykiltara because of The Welcome House.'

'Go on.'

'To begin with, the house was not recognised as being anything to do with the monks. They deliberately kept its existence quiet, in order to ensure its real purpose remained a closely guarded secret.'

'Its real purpose being to hide people away?'

'If the Norsemen realised what it was used for, the priests that were working so hard on the Tara Gospels might have had their work and their lives put in jeopardy. So it was vital that its purpose as a hiding place was kept secret. Hence it was assumed that the name Ballykiltara must be derived from the position of the church at that time, up here on the hill, when in reality the holy place on the hill was the monks' secret house, or what we know today as The Welcome House.'

'That's fascinating,' I say, understanding now. 'It's wonderful to understand some of the history of the town, but I'm still not sure why you're telling *me* all this?'

'Ah, now comes the truly fascinating part. As a Northumbrian, you are no doubt aware that Holy Island and the Lindisfarne Gospels are almost as famous as the Book of Kells. But had you heard of the Tara Gospels, the ones that our monks were secretly working on for so many decades, before I mentioned them to you?'

I shake my head. 'Donal said something about the Annals of Tara, but those were many centuries later than what you're talking about, weren't they?'

'Yes, the Annals of Tara were written after the monks began using the abbey as a learning centre. The Tara Gospels were created much earlier, when the house was still a secret. The only record of them, as far as I'm aware, is here in these books. In fact . . . ' He picks up a book that sits slightly away from the others. It looks different from the rest; it's thinner and less worn. Father Duffy places it on his lap, then he pulls some cotton gloves from the side of his chair and puts them on. With great care he opens the cover, turns some of the pages, then holds the book out so I can see. 'Here, take a look for yourself.'

I lean in for a better view and I'm stunned by what I see.

235

In front of me is a page of intricate script, some of it so small I can barely read it. This on its own would be amazing enough, but surrounding the words are the most beautiful hand-painted Celtic decorations and colourful pictures, some of them inlaid with what appears to be gold leaf.

I have a strong urge to run my fingers over them, to feel if they are real, but I stop myself from doing so. I glance up at Father Duffy for explanation, but he simply turns the page to reveal another beautifully decorated page, and then again to reveal another, and then another.

'There's at least fifty pages like this,' he says, carefully closing the book. 'In this, and other folders like it.'

'But that's amazing! Why don't you do something with them, maybe have them on display? I'm sure people would like to see them.'

'Have you any idea of the value of these pages?' he says, removing his gloves. 'That would require a tremendous amount of security. The church doesn't have that sort of money. Not that they'd be willing to give to me, at any rate.'

'So why show them to me?'

'Because I think there might be more pages like this. The journals suggest that there are.'

'Where?'

'These journals have been kept a closely guarded secret for centuries, passed down from one priest to the next. All I know is what I've been told by my predecessor, and what I can decipher from the pages.'

'It's something to do with the house, isn't it?'

'We know the monks were hidden there while they worked on the pages – that would explain the tales of the monks' disappearance. But as to how they were concealed, your guess

236

is as good as mine. I've tried investigating it myself over the years, but to no avail. As you know all too well, Ren, that house knows how to keep its secrets from the world.'

'I certainly do, Father.' I look up at him. 'But again I have to ask: why are you telling *me* this?'

'Now we come to the *really* interesting part. One of the pages I was able to decipher foretells that one day a visitor will come to Tara from overseas – from Holy Island, to be precise. That visitor will bring turmoil to begin with, but eventually they will bring peace and harmony to the house, and to Tara.'

'And . . . ?' I prompt.

'The journals rarely mention women. In those days, women were not considered important enough to be recorded in important documents. So to see one drawn, and drawn so beautifully, is extremely rare.'

'What does this woman look like?' I ask, still wondering where Father Duffy is going with this story.

Father Duffy smiles. 'She is described as being very beautiful but very fiery. It says she will come from afar, but will be of Celtic origin. And . . . ' he pauses for effect. 'She will have a mane of bright red hair.'

Thirty

'You're having me on!' I reply lightly. 'That's not in those books, is it? You're making it up.'

'Oh it is,' Father Duffy replies, his face serious. 'I've seen it with my own eyes.'

'Let me see,' I demand. I peer at the books on the table. 'Which one is it in?'

'It's not in one of these,' Father Duffy says, straightening the pile. 'It's in one of the ones that are kept in the church.'

'Of course it is . . . ' I raise my eyebrows at him.

'I'm telling you the truth, Ren. I believe you are the woman they talk about on that page.'

I decide to humour him. 'Let's say for one moment that I am this woman. What is it exactly you're expecting me to do?'

'Find the pages, Ren. You've already created the turmoil they spoke about, now it's time for you to create the peace and harmony the house and Ballykiltara deserve.'

'How am I supposed to do that, if no one has been able to find them before?'

'The house will help you, I know it will.'

I close my eyes for a moment, and then I sigh.

'The legend of the house isn't real, Father. You do know that, don't you? The Welcome House is nothing but bricks and mortar.'

'Tell me what you felt the first time you stepped inside it?'

'It's just a house.'

'*Ren*,' Father Duffy says sternly. 'Tell me – use your heart not your head to describe it.'

'OK, OK.' I close my eyes. 'The house felt ...' I cast myself back to when Kiki and I had entered the house for the first time. 'Lost,' I say the first word that springs into my mind.

'And ... ?' Father Duffy prompts.

'Cold.'

'And?'

'Lonely,' I say, surprising myself. The house had felt like this, it had been weird at the time, but now I think about it, this was exactly how it had felt.

'And how did you feel, Ren?' he asks. 'How did you feel in the house?'

'Sad, and frustrated, and ...' I struggle for the last word. 'Unfulfilled?'

Father Duffy nods. 'Now, how did it feel the next time you visited?'

I shrug.

'Ren, please try. Remember, I want to help you.'

'OK ... Better.'

'Better?'

'The house didn't feel as sad.'

'And you?'

'I guess I felt better too – but there could be many reasons for that.'

'You know why, of course,' Father Duffy says, ignoring my last comment as I knew he would.

'No, but I'm sure you're going to tell me.'

'You had taken the first steps on the path to recovery – yours and the house's.'

'Uh-huh . . .' I nod humouring him.

'What you choose to believe is up to you, Ren, of course. But you've come to Ballykiltara for a reason, and the sooner you accept that, the easier your transition will be.'

I hear the church clock strike the hour again, but this time the bell chimes twelve times.

'I'm sorry, but I have to go, Father,' I say, standing up. 'This has all been very . . . enlightening.'

'You're meeting someone,' he states, rather than asks. 'Another, equally important, reason for you being here.'

'Yes, and possibly,' I reply as neutrally as I can. I'm beginning to tire of all this mumbo jumbo, even though I know he means well. 'But I do have to go.'

'Think about what I've said, Ren,' Father Duffy says, getting to his feet. 'Always remember, sometimes bad things have to happen before good things can – the turmoil before the peace, as those pages predict. Everything *will* make sense soon, I promise.'

'Don't make promises you can't keep,' I say, smiling at him.

'I never do, Ren. I never do.'

*

240

I hurry down the hill towards the hotel. My visit with Father Duffy has taken longer than expected, so I'm going to have to rush if I want to get freshened up before I see Finn.

I try not to think too much about what Father Duffy has told me as I race towards the hotel. It all sounded a bit weird, and now that I've decided not to continue my search for the owner of The Welcome House, I'm not sure I want to get involved in hunting for some old manuscripts that may or may not even exist. I'd prefer to spend what little time I have left here in Ballykiltara with Finn, like Kiki is doing with Eddie.

I reach the hotel and dash through reception to take the lift to my room, where I splash some water on my face, squirt deodorant under my arms and perfume on my neck. Then I touch up what little make-up I'm wearing, finishing off with a smear of gloss over my lips.

'Let's hope that gets worn off before lunch!' I smile at myself in the mirror. 'It's been a while since you could say that, Serendipity Parker.' It's the truth; it has been a very long time since I've allowed myself to feel about any man the way I now realise I feel about Finn. I'd made a deliberate decision to avoid becoming involved with men since . . . I swallow, and realise the reflection looking back at me in the mirror has been transformed from one of anticipation and delight to one of sadness and regret. I shake my head. 'No more, do you hear?' I tell myself. 'No more. Finn is different, *things* are different now.' I nod confidently at my reflection, and without allowing myself to engage in further negative thoughts, I head out of the room, through the hotel and out of the back door to follow the path towards Finn's cottage.

I'm not sure why, but I feel nervous as I knock on his door.

No, not nervous, I tell the strange feeling in my tummy, I'm a bit apprehensive, that's all.

On the other side of the door, I hear Fergus barking, then Finn's footsteps walking down the hall. He turns the key on the other side, and the door swings open.

'Hi,' I say, suddenly shy. Goodness, I haven't felt like this for such a long time. It's as if I'm a teenager again, calling on a boy I like.

'Hey,' Finn says, standing back to let me in. 'How are you today?'

'Good, thanks.'

'Come through,' he waves me in with a strangely formal gesture. 'I've prepared some lunch for us in the kitchen.'

'Lovely.' I pat Fergus, and then follow Finn through to the kitchen, where he has laid on quite the lunchtime spread. On the kitchen table, on top of a red gingham cloth, there's a chunky loaf of homemade bread on a breadboard, various meats, cheeses, salad and some fruit in a bowl.

'You didn't need to go to all this trouble,' I say, looking at the table. 'I'm not even that hungry.' Well, only for you, I feel like saying, but I hold my tongue. Finn seems on edge, nervous even. Not like himself at all.

'Neither am I,' he says, focusing on rearranging one of the kitchen chairs that's already perfectly aligned with the table.

I move towards him, assuming he isn't hungry for the same reason I am. But instead of stepping forward to meet me, Finn dodges further around the table.

'OK, what's up?' I ask. 'You're being all … weird.'

'Would you like to sit down?' Finn asks.

'No, I'd like to find out why you're being so odd with me.'

Finn swallows hard. 'OK … about last night,' he begins without looking at me, and I notice Fergus retreat to his bed in the corner of the room.

'I know, it was a bit awkward being caught like that. But if we're careful, no one need see us again.'

'That's just it,' Finn says, looking at me now. 'No one *can* see us again.'

'Yes, that's what I said—'

'No, Ren, you're not listening. What happened last night *can't* and *won't* be happening ever again.'

I stare at him for a moment. 'You're not just talking about us being seen, are you?' I say quietly. My heart, which had been so light and carefree a few moments ago, suddenly feels incredibly heavy in my chest.

Finn shakes his head. 'I'm so sorry, Ren, I can't take the risk. Fraternising with hotel guests is simply not tolerated. If Dermot or Darcy found out, I could lose my job.'

'What if I moved out of the hotel? Found a B&B somewhere – would that make a difference?'

'I can't ask you to do that, Ren.'

'You could if you wanted to,' I reply, seeing exactly where this is going. 'If you were that bothered about me, you would.'

'That's not fair,' Finn says, moving towards me. 'You know I care, it's—'

'Oh really?' I interrupt, backing away angrily. 'You care about me that much you have to make up a bunch of lies to get rid of me?'

'They're not lies. I'm telling the truth … about the hotel.'

Finn does seem genuinely upset, but my usual empathy is blinded by my anger at yet another man letting me down. 'If it is the truth, then why would you encourage Kiki and Eddie to be together, hmm? I never noticed you chastising Eddie for fraternising with hotel guests!'

'Eddie's different.'

'Why is he?'

'He's not the manager, for one thing.' Finn swallows hard and looks down at the tiled kitchen floor. Even he seems to realise this is a feeble excuse.

'Is that the best you can do? Couldn't you at least show me a bit of respect, Finn, and tell me the truth instead of making up silly excuses that insult my intelligence.'

'I'm not making up excuses. The Stag has rules about fraternising with guests – that's the truth. Do you want me to march across to the hotel right now and bring you back the staff manual to prove it?'

Finn is obviously annoyed now, and as I stare at him I feel my bottom lip begin to tremble. I bite hard on it.

'I'm sorry,' he says in a gentler voice. 'I shouldn't have snapped at you.'

I nod, accepting his apology, for this anyway. 'What if, just for one moment, I believe you are telling me the truth?' I ask, now I've steadied myself again, 'and you're not allowed to fraternise with guests—'

Finn opens his mouth, but I hold up my hand to stop him speaking.

'—*If* that is true, what happened to the Finn that doesn't give a toss about rules? The Finn who won't wear a suit and tie when everyone else does, the Finn that shoots off to the stables to see the horses when he's supposed to be working? There are rules about those things too, Finn, yet you break them quite happily on a daily basis.'

Finn's head drops, and I see his mouth open as if he's going to speak, but nothing comes out so he closes it again.

'You see, that's where I have a problem with all this,' I continue when he doesn't. 'You're quite happy to break the rules when it suits you. But you're not happy to break them for me.'

With my heavy heart pounding so hard I think it might burst out of my chest and bounce out of the door in front of me, I turn away from him. Without saying another word, I leave the kitchen, leave the house, and leave the hope that was Finn Cassidy well and truly behind me.

Thirty-One

I reach the bottom of the path that leads from the cottage, and I look both ways. From here I could either go back to the hotel, or in the direction of the stables.

Given the state I'm in, I really don't want to go back to the hotel. Plus, if Finn should decide to come after me, surely that's the way he would choose.

So I run towards the stables; animals have always soothed me in my times of trouble in the past, perhaps the horses will today.

I berate myself as I run: 'Why would Finn even think to come after you, stupid?' I tell myself between breaths. 'He's not interested, is he? The sooner you get used to that, the better.'

By the time I reach the stables, my heart is pounding. Partly from the running, something I never do unless I have to, and partly from the pain that's coursing through it. I walk as calmly as I can into the stable yard; there doesn't seem to be anyone about so I approach one of the stalls. Alfie, the black pony I'd patted a few days ago, hangs his head over the gate.

'I'm sorry I don't have anything for you,' I tell him, reaching out to stroke his nose. 'Will this do?'

Alfie seems quite happy with the compromise, and he nuzzles into my hand as I stroke it rhythmically along the white flash that runs down the centre of his nose.

'Why do I do it, eh, Alfie?' I ask him. 'Why do I even bother opening up my heart, only for it to get trampled on every time?'

Alfie doesn't seem to have an answer for me, but as I'd hoped, simply being this close to an animal, especially one as magnificent as Alfie, is having a soothing effect on me.

'People always let you down,' I continue. 'I should stick with animals. You know where you are with them.'

'You'll be giving this horse a severe case of depression if you carry on like that!'

I jump at the sound of a voice, and then jump again as a head pops up behind Alfie.

'Oh, it's you, Mac,' I say with relief as he pats Alfie and pulls a cover over his back.

'Did you think we had a talking horse here then?' Mac grins. 'I'd be fair minted if I had.'

'No . . . I didn't see you, that's all.' I look down at the ground in embarrassment. Mac must have heard everything I said to Alfie.

'I like to keep my hand in,' Mac says, holding up a grooming brush. He hobbles to the front of the stall, and retrieves his stick. 'And Alfie here has always been one of my favourites.'

He reaches into his pocket and holds out his hand so Alfie

can nuzzle a treat from it. Then he opens the stable door and lets himself out.

'Now what are you doing here today, young lady, pouring out your woes to my horses?'

I shrug. 'Oh, nothing. I fancied a walk, and I find the horses very soothing.'

'They are that,' Mac agrees, patting Alfie. 'Now who is it that's let a fine lady such as yourself down, eh? Shall I go and sort him out for you?' Mac pretends to shadow box, balancing precariously on his good leg.

I have to smile.

'There now, that's better,' he says, putting his stick back down on the ground. 'A face as pretty as yours should always be smiling. Would you like a cup of tea? I'm just going into my office to make one.'

I'm touched by his kindness. 'Yes please, that would be lovely.'

We walk across the stable yard towards Mac's office. It's situated the other side of the tack room, which smells all leathery and warm as we walk past it. The office is a messy, yet cosy room with an old-fashioned feel about it. There's a large wooden desk covered in papers, with mugs holding pencils and pens scattered haphazardly across the top. On one wall there's a large cork board with papers and leaflets pinned to it; the other three walls are covered in framed photos, both old black-and-white prints and colour.

Mac gestures to an antique wooden swivel chair. While I go over and sit down on it, Mac busies himself at a filing cabinet on which his tea-making equipment resides.

'I need to go and refill this kettle,' he says, opening the lid and taking a look inside. 'We get through a lot of tea here. Be right back.'

While Mac is gone, I study the photos on the walls. Practically all of them are horse-related: horses in their stalls, horses being ridden, people standing next to horses ... I'm scanning from one to the next when I spot someone familiar.

I get up to take a closer look. Sure enough, it's a much younger-looking Finn, standing proudly next to a racehorse that looks like it's just finished a race. Finn is holding the horse's bridle with one hand, and in the other he clutches a large silver cup.

'Ah, I see you've spotted the young Mr Cassidy,' Mac says, coming back into the room, his kettle now full. He plugs the kettle in and turns to me. 'That was a proud day, so it was.'

'Does Finn own the horse in the photo?' I ask, still staring at it.

'He did back then. Celtic Cassidy was a fine horse, so she was. Finn won plenty with her.'

'Was he in some sort of syndicate?' I knew owning a race-horse was an expensive pastime, and I didn't think Finn would have had that sort of money to spare.

'Nope, he owned her outright. Doted on that horse, he did, until she had to be put down.'

'Oh no, why?'

'She fell and damaged her hip very badly. The vet said it was the kindest thing to do.'

'Finn must have been devastated.'

'Sure was,' Mac says, turning back to the boiling kettle. He pops a couple of teabags in a brown china teapot then pours boiling water over them. 'I reckon losing that horse was the straw that broke the camel's back.'

'How do you mean?'

'The thing that finally pushed him over the edge.'

I look blankly at Mac.

'Oh, you don't know? There was me thinking he'd have told you, with you two being' – he entwines two fingers – 'like that.'

'I can assure you we are definitely not *like that*,' I tell him, mimicking his fingers. 'Much more like this.' I hold my hands a long way apart. 'Why would you even think that?'

'News spreads fast in that hotel,' he says knowingly. 'And the first place it spreads to is here.'

'Great.'

'So what happened?' Mac decides the tea has stewed long enough and begins pouring it into two mugs. 'Milk, sugar?' he asks.

'A little milk and two sugars, please,' I say. 'And nothing has happened.'

Mac lifts the two mugs from the filing cabinet and passes me one. Then he sits down in the chair behind the desk and takes a sip from his own mug. 'If nothing has happened, why were you pouring your heart out to Alfie?'

I sigh. 'Finn's not interested in me, that's why. I thought he was, but he's not. End of.' I take a drink from my mug, and the hot sweet tea feels soothing as it warms my throat.

'I highly doubt that,' Mac says. 'I could tell he liked you the first time I saw you two together.'

'Well, he doesn't now. He told me so just ...' I check my watch, 'twenty minutes ago.'

'What did he say exactly?'

'Does it matter?'

Mac silently raises his eyebrows, and takes another sip from his mug.

'OK, he said he couldn't risk anyone finding out about us because of his job. Apparently, hotel management are not allowed to fraternise with hotel guests.'

250

'Sounds fair.'

'Fair! How is it fair to lead someone on, only to let them down?'

'No, that's not fair at all,' Mac says calmly. 'But maybe he didn't mean to. Maybe his feelings for you got the better of him, and he allowed himself to slip.'

I think about this.

'Finn is a bit of an enigma around these parts. No one knows too much about him. He keeps himself to himself, and builds a wall around his private life so no one can get in.'

That sounded familiar ...

'He's a grand manager for the hotel, everyone respects him and his decisions, but no one ever knows what's going on in here.' Mac puts his hand to his chest. 'That's the bit he protects the most.'

'But why?'

'Things that happened to him in the past. He doesn't want them to affect what he's doing now.'

'What sort of things? You mentioned before about some sort of breakdown?'

'I didn't quite say that. It's not really for me to say, is it? It should be Finn who tells you, if he wants to.'

I drink some more of my tea. Finn never told me too much before, when I thought he was interested in me, so he's hardly likely to tell me anything now. And why should I care either way, after what happened this morning?

'So, let's talk about something else,' Mac says. 'How's your search for the owner of The Welcome House coming along?'

'You were right about that, Mac. They *really* don't want to be found. I've decided to give up on it.'

'Oh, you surprise me. I thought you had more tenacity than that.'

'But you said yourself, people have tried and failed for years to discover who's looking after the place. Why should I be any different?'

'Because you are, Ren. You *are* different.'

I look at him across the desk. 'You're beginning to sound like Father Duffy,' I say lightly.

Mac places his empty mug firmly down on the desk in front of him. 'I'll take that as a compliment. Father Duffy is a fine priest and an even finer judge of character. What else has he been saying to you?'

I tell Mac what Father Duffy told me this morning, toning down the 'red-haired crusader' part.

'He might be right, you know,' Mac says, not seeming in the slightest bit surprised by talk of magic and monks.

'Right about there being more illuminated pages, or right about me being the one to find them?'

'Both.'

'Why would you say that?'

'Remember when you told me about your boat trip to Rafferty Island? I said to you at the time: if you've taken a boat trip with Jackie, there must be a reason for it.'

'Yes, but—'

'Here's your reason.'

'To find some old manuscripts?'

'It may be as simple as that, or there may be a much wider picture you're not seeing yet.'

'Such as?'

'Life moves in mysterious ways, Ren. No doubt Father Duffy would say God, but I'm not quite the believer he is, not when it comes to one all-seeing, all-knowing being. I'm a horses man and I like to hedge my bets a little.'

I smile at him. 'So you think I should investigate these missing pages?'

'I think you should not only do that, but that you should keep looking for this mystery owner too.'

'Really? But I thought you were against me finding him?'

'Or her,' Mac corrects me. 'No, I'm not against it. I was only warning you that no one had ever been successful. But maybe you, Ren, will succeed where they failed. In fact, I'd bet on it.'

Thirty-Two

I leave the stables feeling like a different person to the one that arrived there a short while ago.

I'd been right about the horses soothing me, but what I hadn't counted on was what a difference Mac's words would make.

I've decided that I will investigate these missing pages. Father Duffy's talk of Celtic connections to Northumberland has stirred up memories of my grandfather. He was a fount of knowledge when it came to Celtic history, and as a child I'd sit spellbound as he told how our family had descended from the Celts, and how we should always be proud of that. He'd actually lived on Holy Island, and when I was little I used to love biking across the causeway at low tide to visit him. Even as an adult, driving over in the car, Holy Island – or Lindisfarne, to give it its proper name – made a deep impression on me. It felt an incredibly peaceful place, especially when all tourists would depart ahead of high tide, anxious not to get cut off by the sea as it surged across the only route on and off the island. My grandfather would have been fascinated by the legend of The Welcome House and those lost illuminated pages, so I felt as if I owed it to him to be of any assistance I could in bringing that secret history to light.

Maybe Father Duffy and Mac were right: maybe I have come here for a reason. I'd thought originally it was to find a house for Ryan Dempsey, but maybe there were other, more compelling reasons. I've felt a strange sense of affinity and familiarity with this place and its history ever since my arrival. At first I couldn't explain those feelings, but the more I think about it, the more I've come to realise it's probably because it reminds me of home.

As I approach the hotel, I debate whether to go inside but decide against it; I can't face bumping into Finn at the moment. Instead, I head straight for the car park, climb into our little hire car and set off in the direction of The Welcome House.

No time like the present.

I don't want to draw any undue attention by parking my car outside the house, so I head for the same dirt track where I'd parked a few nights ago.

Then, when there's a break in the traffic, I run across the road and make my way up to the house, hoping that it isn't playing host to anyone right now.

As before, I push open the unlocked door and step inside. As I do, I remember what Father Duffy had said and stop for a moment, trying to 'feel' the mood of the house.

It does feel oddly welcoming as I stand in the hall with my eyes closed. Not at all like it did the first time when Kiki and

I had stumbled in uninvited. Today, I have to admit, the house feels like it wants me to be there.

I carry out a quick check of the rooms upstairs and down to make sure no one else is residing here at the moment, but everything is in order. The beds are clean and made up, the fridge is stocked with its usual basics, and there's a fresh loaf of bread in the breadbin waiting to be cut.

When I'm done, I let out a sigh of relief. As I'd hoped, I have the house to myself.

To begin with, I walk slowly around all the rooms, examining everything I think might have some meaning, without having the slightest idea what I'm supposed to be looking for. In the sitting room I pull out every book on the bookshelves one by one, and open them up in case a clue should helpfully fall out, like it always does in detective shows on television. But there's nothing except an old receipt that someone once used as a bookmark. I open up the doors to the dresser and discover several cardboard boxes with many more visitors' books like the ones Kiki and I had discovered in the hall. That's odd, I'm sure they weren't there the last time we looked. Perhaps the caretaker who wrote the letter has returned them, worried that someone was getting close to discovering who he or she was. Presumably they wouldn't want to risk leaving evidence hidden around their own home. I glance through a few of the books, but there's nothing new in any of them, just the same style of entries as had been in the original book in the hall.

In the kitchen I go through every cupboard and drawer, but the only documents I find are a couple of menus from take-away restaurants in Ballykiltara, and some instruction manuals for the few appliances in the house. Upstairs is no better;

there's absolutely nothing in any of the drawers, and only clean bedding and towels in the cupboards.

I'm beginning to feel frustrated. Father Duffy and Mac had made it all sound so easy; as if all I had to do was make up my mind I wanted to find the missing pages, and there they'd be. You'd think I'd know by now that nothing in life is ever that easy.

I sit on the edge of the bed in one of the bedrooms, facing a window with the gorgeous view that had first attracted me to the house, and I look out across the lake.

Where would you be hiding? I ask the empty room and the view, but there's no reply. I catch sight of my reflection in the window and shake my head, wondering how I could let my usually sensible self be carried along with all this mystical nonsense – and it's then I hear a noise coming from downstairs.

I jump from my bemoaning, and listen hard. Is someone else in the house? How could anyone have got in? I didn't hear the door open.

But the noise doesn't sound like it's being made by a human. It's more of a tapping and fluttering sort of noise – a bird maybe?

As I head downstairs, the noise becomes louder, but where is it coming from?

I walk around the house like a child playing the hot-and-cold game. Listening hard all the while, moving to rooms where the fluttering is louder, and away from those where it's barely audible. But nowhere can I find whatever is making those sounds. I'm sure it is a bird, because it sounds exactly like one, but is it trapped somewhere in the house? And if so. where?

I go back into the sitting room, because that's where the noise is loudest, and I turn slowly in the middle of the floor, trying to work out where it's coming from. Then I stand very still and close my eyes, desperate to pinpoint which part of the room the noise is loudest in.

It's then I feel it: the strangest of sensations, like I'm being moved across the floor. I open my eyes and the sensation stops, so I close them again, and allow whatever it is to guide me across the room. When I open my eyes again, I'm in front of the bookshelves, and the fluttering and tapping is the loudest I've heard it so far.

'Where are you?' I ask as I begin removing the books one by one. This time, I don't put them back on the shelves; instead, I place them on the floor beside me. And as I clear the bookcase, removing more and more of the books, I realise there's no back to these shelves. What I'd thought was a panel that formed the back of the bookcase is in fact a solid wooden door.

As quickly as I can, I remove the last of the books. Now that the bookcase is completely empty, I can see right through to the other side.

'OK, let's see about moving you out of the way,' I say to the bookcase. It may be empty, but even so it weighs a ton and I have to alternate between dragging and pushing with all my might to shift it. There's no question now that the noise is coming from behind the hidden door, and I'm determined to find out what's in there. Whether it's a bird or some animal making those sounds, it must have got itself trapped and I'm not about to leave it in distress.

I continue to manoeuvre the bookcase along the carpet an inch at a time, until I have enough room to squeeze behind it and open the door. But when I go to turn the large black doorknob I realise that the door is locked, and there's no key in the lock to help me.

'Damn, all that effort for nothing! Where on earth am I going to find a key hidden in this place? I had enough trouble finding the door! I don't know,' I say to the house, exasperated. 'You leave your front door open for any Tom, Dick or Harry to walk in, but you choose to lock this one!'

On a whim, I decide to try the same technique that led me to the door. I step out from behind the shelves, pick my way through the piles of books until I'm standing in the middle of the room, and I close my eyes. At first there's nothing, so I take a few deep breaths and try to clear my mind. Suddenly, an image springs into my head and I snap my eyes open. *Of course!* I dash upstairs to the bedroom I'd been sitting in earlier, only this time instead of looking out of the window at the view, I head straight to the opposite wall and take down the picture that's hanging there.

It's an oil painting of Sheehy Abbey, and it looks as if it might have been painted by someone who once stayed in this house, because the vista in the painting is exactly the same as the one visible from the window. But I don't stop to admire the brushstrokes or the perspective; I'm more interested in the frame. I turn the picture over in my hands and tear as carefully as I can at the brown paper that covers the back, until I've peeled it far enough to find what I'm looking for.

In the gap between the canvas and the paper is a black iron key. I lift it from its hiding place, replace the painting on the wall, and rush downstairs again.

There's a moment of trepidation as I place the key in the lock. What if this isn't the right key? I have nothing else to go on, no other clues, this has to be it. I take a deep breath and start to turn the key.

To my huge relief, there's no resistance; the key turns

smoothly in the locking mechanism, followed by a satisfying click. I reach for the doorknob again, and notice that the fluttering has stopped. In fact, I haven't heard it since I returned downstairs with the key. I hope whatever it is, is OK, I think as I tentatively open the door.

Immediately behind the door are some stone steps that lead down into a pitch-black abyss. Could *this* be the entrance to the mysterious cellar? I wonder. And if it is, do I really want to go down there?

I hesitate at the top of the stairs. It's not that I'm frightened by Eddie's tall tales – Father Duffy had said that the stories about the cellar were nothing more than tittle-tattle and hearsay – but perhaps I should leave some sort of note in case for some reason I can't get back up here. After all, I've no way of knowing what's at the bottom of those steps.

On the other hand, I don't want to alert anyone to the fact I might have found something. This is *my* quest now, *my* mystery to solve; I want to be the one who discovers whatever it is I'm going to find down there – hopefully some illuminated pages to give to Father Duffy, but who knew, there could be a huge cave of gold and treasures waiting for me . . .

OK, stop it now, Ren! I tell myself sternly. You're not in some Indiana Jones film, searching for biblical treasures . . . Well, technically, you are . . .

Stop it! You're starting to sound like Kiki! I tell myself.

Kiki! That's exactly the person I should tell. I pull out my phone and fire off a text:

Some interesting developments here while you've been away, both with Finn and the house. I'm investigating the latter. If

260

there should be any problems when you get back, or you're in any way concerned, go to the house and look behind Miss Marple. Ren x

I read the text twice and edit some of the words. I don't want Kiki to be worried, but at the same time I don't want anyone else who might see the text learning too much from it.

Right: time to go in!

I light up the torch on my phone, and begin to walk gingerly down the stairs, taking each step one at a time. When I get to the bottom, I hold up my phone. I'm surprised and somewhat disappointed to see a large, but very empty cellar.

I hear the flapping again and turn around. In the corner I see a large black bird watching me. At first glance I think it's a crow, but then I realise it's a raven.

'How did you get down here?' I ask. 'Are you hurt?'

The raven shakes himself and walks along his perch – a narrow stone shelf jutting out from the wall.

'Well, you don't appear to be in distress. But how did you get in here?'

I look around the cellar again. There are no windows – but then, there wouldn't be, would there? I must be underground now, surely?

The raven flaps his wings and jumps down to the ground. I start to follow him with my torch as he walks, then I stop and turn my torch back to the spot he's walked over – what's that?

I move closer to the wall to inspect it, and then I run my hands over the rough carving. It's a cross, but it's not just any cross, it's an intricately patterned Celtic cross, and there's another right next to it, and a third. I've seen crosses like this somewhere recently, but where?

261

I think for a moment, the raven watching me all the while. The abbey, that's where, when we went across on the boat trip. There were crosses exactly like this on some of the interior walls there. But I'd seen them somewhere else too …

I think again … Then I remember.

'The books,' I say to the raven. He cocks his head to one side with interest. 'The books that Father Duffy had, some of them had these crosses on too. They must be related, don't you think?'

The raven doesn't appear to have an opinion on the matter; he turns his head and looks up towards the staircase where the light from the sitting room is filtering down.

'I guess we should go back up there,' I say to him. 'I wish I knew how you got down here though.'

I look at the stone carvings again, and in a flash of genius I decide to take a few quick snaps of them for reference. The raven jumps as the flash on my phone camera goes off, and he hops over to the staircase while I finish taking my pictures. Then, after one final look around the cellar, I encourage my feathered friend to follow me as I make my way up the stairs into the safety of The Welcome House once more.

'OK, before I put all these books back, let's get you outside so you can fly home to wherever you came from,' I tell the raven, who's now sitting up on top of the sideboard watching me.

I go to the window and open it wide. Then I gesture to the bird. 'Come on,' I urge him, 'this is your chance.'

The raven merely cocks his head at me.

'Oh, you silly thing, I haven't got time for this. Don't you know I have to put all these books back before I can leave?'

The raven doesn't budge; he carries on watching me, the same fascinated expression on his face.

'Fine. Sit there and watch me then, why don't you?' I say, locking the cellar door and removing the key. With difficulty I push the bookcase back in front of the door, and begin filling it with books again.

When at last I've finished and everything is back to normal, the raven decides to make his move. He takes off from the sideboard, making a strange deep purring sound. It almost sounds like he's saying 'good, good, good' as he flies past my head. Then he lands on the window ledge, takes one last look at me, flaps his huge wings and flies off out of the open window.

How odd, I think as I go over to shut the window. Perhaps ravens are common around here; after all, the pub is named after one. But still, it's strange that it should have got itself trapped down in that cellar, and then hadn't wanted to leave until everything was tidy and back in its rightful place.

'You get stranger by the day, Welcome House,' I tell it, checking to make sure the iron key is still safely in my pocket. It's then I remember a question about ravens we'd had in the quiz last night and what Donal had said about them.

The question was 'Name an Irish proverb that involves ravens, and explain what it means'. Donal had answered: 'To have a raven's knowledge', and we'd all laughed because it was the name of the pub we were sitting in. But he had then explained that it meant to have a seer's supernatural powers, the raven being considered one of the wisest of animals in Celtic mythology, a bird of wisdom and prophecy, often a messenger.

'Yes,' I murmur, looking back at the window the raven had left through. 'Very strange indeed ...'

Thirty-Three

I drive back to the hotel, my mind full of ideas and plans.

I realise I'm going to need some help figuring out this latest mystery, and I think I know just the person to help me.

'Is Donal working today?' I ask Orla at the reception desk.

'It's his afternoon off, I'm afraid, Ren. Is there anything I can help with?'

'Thank you, but no. Donal's the only one that can help me with this particular problem.'

'I know where you might find him, if it's important?' she offers.

'Oh, I wouldn't want to bother him on his day off.'

'Between you and me,' she says, leaning across the desk, 'Donal never really takes a day off from this place – it's his life. I'm sure he wouldn't mind.'

'If you're sure?'

'Donal lives with his mother in one of the cottages on Abbey

Road. You won't miss it; it's the pretty one with all the flowers outside. He'll most likely be home, if you drop by.'

'Thanks, Orla, you've been a great help.'

'Oh, before you go, Ren – I think Finn was looking for you earlier. He asked if I'd seen you return to the hotel.'

'Did he?' I say, hesitating. 'I have to go out again in a minute. Maybe I'll catch up with him later ... '

Orla merely nods in that discreet way receptionists have.

I head up to my room to pick up a few bits and to freshen up. As I brush my hair in front of the mirror, I recall standing in the same spot earlier, full of excitement and anticipation at what my lunch with Finn might bring. Even though my mind is racing with this latest project, my heart still sinks at the thought of what happened earlier.

'Enough of that, Ren!' I tell my reflection sternly. 'Let's go back to old Ren, shall we? The one who thinks with her head and not her heart. That has served you well until now, and you've seen what happens when you try to do otherwise.'

My stomach growls as I look at myself in the mirror, and I realise I haven't eaten since this morning and it's ... I look at my watch – it's almost four o'clock! No wonder I'm hungry. I grab my bag and head down to the bar, hoping I won't bump into Finn. 'Can I grab a sandwich, Danny?' I ask him hopefully. 'I know it's late, but I missed lunch.'

'Of course you can, miss,' Danny says, smiling. 'What would you like?'

I have to wait while the sandwich is being made, all the while feeling on edge and jumpy as I hide in a corner of the bar, hoping Finn won't come in and see me. As soon as Danny brings my sandwich over, I wolf it down as fast as I can, and swig the rest of my Diet Coke in an attempt to exit the bar as quickly as possible.

'You certainly were hungry, miss!' Danny calls as I return my plate and glass to the bar and thank him. 'I think that might be the fastest I've ever seen a guest eat one of Sarah's club sandwiches.'

'Tell her it was delicious!' I call as I leave the bar.

'I will, miss!'

This is ridiculous, I think as I race through the reception and out the door, waving to Orla on the desk as I go. I can't spend the remainder of my time here rushing around or skulking about in corners in the hope I don't see Finn.

My heart sinks at the thought of finding somewhere else to stay; I haven't seen anywhere in Ballykiltara as nice as The Stag. Nevertheless, I resolve to check out the local B&Bs, to see if anyone has a room available. Kiki can stay on here – it wouldn't be fair to make her move when I'm the one who has the problem. A problem caused yet again by a man.

It takes me until I'm almost at Donal's house to realise the answer to my dilemma had been staring me in the face all along, if I'd only been able to step away from my wallowing long enough to see it. The Welcome House, of course! I could stay there. It wouldn't be for long, and it would be the perfect place to work on this mystery I've found myself in the middle of. The house seems to like me now; it'll make me feel welcome, I'm sure of it!

Listen to yourself, Ren! Even you are starting to believe this house has feelings now!

I'm smiling as I arrive at the house that Orla described – a well-kept, pretty terraced cottage, with flower boxes under the windows, planted with colourful geraniums.

'Miss Parker?' The door of the cottage opens and Donal appears in the doorway wearing a blue T-shirt and loose jeans. It takes me a moment to work out what's wrong with this picture, but then I realise I've only ever seen him in his dapper hotel uniform. 'What are you doing here? Are you lost?'

'I've come to see you, Donal. I know we had a little falling out yesterday, but I wondered if we might put all that behind us? Because I think you might just be the person to help me.'

'Oh, I'm afraid I'm not on duty this afternoon,' Donal says, subconsciously tugging at the neck of his T-shirt as if he wants to tighten a tie.

'No, I don't want you for hotel business. I wanted to probe your historical knowledge, if you'll let me?'

'My historical knowledge?' Donal asks proudly. 'On what particular subject?'

'Would it be OK if I came in?' I ask, looking past him into the house.

'Oh, I'm so sorry – where are my manners! Yes, of course. My mother is home – I hope you don't mind?'

'Of course not.'

Donal stands aside to let me pass, and I find myself in a small hallway. He closes the door behind him and leads me through to an old-fashioned sitting room. 'Please, take a seat,' he gestures to a comfortable-looking chintz-covered sofa.

'Donal! Do we have guests?' an elderly female voice calls from another room.

'Yes, Mother, just one.' Donal smiles apologetically at me.

I hear the sound of a chair scraping across a lino floor and then slow steady footsteps coming down the hall.

An elderly lady appears in the sitting room doorway. 'Oh, Donal, do you have a lady friend at last?'

'No, Mother! Miss Parker is a guest at the hotel.'

'Please, call me Ren,' I tell both of them.

'Ren, what sort of name is that?' Donal's mother pushes past him and enters the room; she sits down slowly and with difficulty on a high armchair.

'My full name is Serendipity,' I tell her.

'Ah, much prettier,' she says agreeably. 'You should call yourself that – its suits your pretty face much better than calling yourself after a bird!'

'Thank you.' I smile, amused by her honesty.

'Now, Donal, what are you doing hanging around by that door? We have a visitor, put the kettle on at once and we shall have tea.'

'Yes, Mother,' Donal mutters as he heads down the hall towards the kitchen.

'Now, my dear, what is it we can do for you today? I have to say, I didn't really think you were one of Donal's lady friends – you're far too pretty. Most of them are complete dogs.'

I laugh out loud this time.

'Lovely girls, mind,' she continues. 'But God didn't bless them in the looks department, if you know what I mean?'

'Does Donal have many lady friends then?' I ask, trying to keep a straight face.

'A few. They don't last all that long, though. My Donal is married to that hotel, and as soon as the ladies realise he's not going to be proposing any time soon, they leave pretty quickly. Gold-diggers, the lot of them. I'm minted, you see,' she explains. 'My husband left me very rich when he died – insurance policy scam. He took some and gave me the rest. I was glad to see the back of him, and he … well, let's just say he needed to disappear for a while.' She raises her white eyebrows at me.

I smile hesitantly, not knowing what to say to this.

Donal reappears in the doorway. 'Kettle is on. I do hope Mother isn't telling you any of her tales?' he asks, looking anxiously at his mother. 'She has a tendency to get carried away.'

'No, it's all good,' I say, smiling at him.

'So what is it I can do for you, Miss— I mean, Ren?'

I glance at Donal's mother.

'Don't you worry about me, my dear. I rarely leave the house, do I, Donal? Any secret is safe with me.'

'I wanted to know if you knew anything about these?' I take out my phone and show Donal the photos of the crosses in the cellar.

'They're Celtic crosses, aren't they?' Donal asks. 'They look a lot like high crosses. How big are they?'

I hold my hands about two feet apart.

'Not likely a high cross then, but a Celtic one.'

'What do you know about them, Donal?'

'The Celtic cross is a symbol that combines a cross with a ring surrounding the intersection. It belongs to a wider group of crosses with a nimbus – that's a halo,' he explains. 'The Celtic Christians combined the Christian cross with the nimbus to create high crosses – a free-standing cross made of stone which was often richly decorated with interlaced patterns and insular art.'

'What's insular art?'

'The word insular derives from the word island. Most insular art originates from the Irish monasticism of Celtic Christianity.'

'Oh, stop showing off, Donal!' his mother interrupts. 'The young lady isn't interested in all your waffle.'

'But I am,' I tell her. 'This is exactly what I wanted to hear. Please, go on, Donal.'

Donal looks pleased. 'The insular period began around AD 600 with the combining of Celtic styles and Anglo-Saxon. The finest period of the style was thought to have been completed here in Ireland – you've heard of the Book of Kells?'

'I have, yes.'

'No later Gospels are as heavily or finely illuminated as those created in the eighth century. It's thought the art began to die out when the Viking raids began.'

'That's most interesting . . . ' I say. 'Thank you.'

'What about that tea, Donal?' his mother asks. 'It won't make itself.'

Donal sighs. 'I'll be right back.'

'You're making his day,' the old lady says as we watch Donal leave. 'He would talk about this stuff for hours if he could, but no one wants to listen to him.'

'I do. Donal's knowledge could come in very handy.'

'Could it now? In that case I shall look forward to hearing more over my tea.'

Donal returns shortly with a tray of tea things, by which time his mother has nodded off in her chair. I'd been chatting to her about the hotel when her head began to droop forward and the next thing I knew she was snoring loudly.

'She often takes a nap about this time,' Donal explains, pouring the tea into two of the three china cups on the tray. 'She'll be out for a while now. So what else was it you wanted to ask me?'

'If I tell you this, Donal, you have to promise not to tell anyone else, you understand?'

Donal looks puzzled. 'If this is about the house, then I'm afraid I can't help you. As I—'

'No, it's not about the house . . . well, it is, but not in the way you think – it has nothing to do with my work. You see, Father Duffy has sent me on a mission,' I tell him, thinking the mention of the Catholic priest's name might help things along.

'Father Duffy?' Donal looks impressed. 'In that case, I promise I won't say a word to anyone.'

I tell Donal about my visit to Father Duffy's house – leaving out the part about the red-haired woman. That still seemed too odd to pass on. Then I tell him what Mac had subsequently told me, and then finally what I'd seen in The Welcome House. He listens in silence, a stunned expression on his face.

'Now I need your help to discover the rest,' I tell him. 'There has to be a pattern to all this somewhere – a reason for it?'

'Wait here,' he says, standing up. 'I'll be right back.'

As I wait for him to return, I sit quietly sipping my tea while Donal's mother sleeps peacefully in her chair. I'm glad I came here now. I had wondered if I was doing the right thing; after all, only yesterday I had Donal down as the most likely candidate for the caretaker of The Welcome House. But seeing Donal's response to the stories I'd told him, and his reaction to the crosses, had been more than enough to quash that idea. He seems as excited as I am by the information. This pleases me greatly, as I need someone like Donal onside if I'm to uncover this latest mystery that The Welcome House has thrown at me.

Donal returns to the room with his arms full of books. 'These are all the books I have on Celtic history,' he says, putting them down on the table behind me. 'They might give us some clue as to what we're dealing with.'

'Great. Thanks for this, Donal,' I say, joining him at the table. 'I appreciate your help. I know we haven't always seen eye to eye.'

'Not at all, miss. Now that I know you want to help preserve our history rather than take it away, I'll do everything I can to assist you.'

Gallantly, he pulls out a chair for me, and then when I'm seated he pulls one out for himself and sits down opposite me.

'Right, let's get started!' he says, eagerly opening the first book.

I spend the next few hours with Donal poring over books.

His mother wakes after about an hour, enquires what we're doing and asks for the radio to be put on, and then pretty much leaves us alone as she listens to her favourite programmes.

Dinnertime almost goes unnoticed, we're both so engrossed, but at his mother's insistence Donal goes out for fish and chips. When he returns we take a break from our research to tuck in.

'I think we need to see these books of Father Duffy's,' Donal says, dipping a chip in some ketchup. 'I think we've done everything we can here now.'

He's right, we've looked through all the books, and have moved on to using Donal's old laptop to try and do more research in areas where the books are no help.

'I'm sure I can arrange something,' I say, putting my knife and fork down on my plate. 'When are you free?'

'I'm at work all day tomorrow. Would tomorrow evening be any good?'

'Do you get a lunch break?' I ask. Now that we've made a start, I can't bear the thought of waiting until tomorrow evening to resume it. 'It will depend on when Father Duffy is free, of course, but it would be good if we could give him options.'

'Yes, I'm sure I could leave the hotel for a short while around lunchtime.'

'Good. Oh, and you should know I'm going to be moving out of the hotel into The Welcome House for a while too.'

Both Donal and his mother look surprised.

'But I thought you and young Finn were stepping out together?' Donal's mother asks. 'Why would you want to leave The Stag?'

How did she know that? Not that we were, but still . . .

'I'm not even going to ask where you heard that gossip,' I say lightly. I glance at Donal, who doesn't meet my eyes. 'I can assure you both that we are definitely not *stepping out*. I just think it would be best if I move, that's all.'

'Shame, you'd have made a lovely couple, so you would.'

'Mother,' Donal hisses. 'It's none of our business. If Ren wants to move into the house, that's up to her.'

Donal's mother folds her arms and purses her lips.

'Perhaps I should be going,' I say, standing up. 'Let me help you clear up, then I'll be off.'

'Nonsense, I won't hear of it,' Donal says, jumping up too. 'It's only a few chip papers, we'll be grand.'

'If you're sure?'

'Of course we are, you're a guest.'

'Goodnight, Mrs Ahearn,' I say, turning to the old lady. 'It was lovely to meet you.'

'And you, my dear. You've fair made my Donal's day, you have. There's not many that's interested in listening to him spout his historical facts, is there, Donal?'

Donal pulls a face at me and rolls his eyes.

'And I'm sorry if I said the wrong thing to you about Finn,' she continues unabashed. 'He's a good lad, we just want to see him happy – don't we, Donal?'

Donal nods in agreement.

'OK ... well, I'll be going then.' I edge towards the door.

'Let me see you out,' Donal insists.

'Thank you for tonight,' I tell him, pausing on the threshold. 'I really do appreciate your help with this.'

'Not at all,' Donal waves his hand dismissively. 'Like Mother said, it's been my pleasure. I'll see you tomorrow – yes?'

'Yes. I'll call in the morning to let you know what Father Duffy says. Goodnight.'

I wave goodbye and set off along the street towards the hotel, glancing at my phone as I walk. No texts. Not even from Kiki. She must still be out with Eddie. I'll have to tell her in the morning that I'm moving into The Welcome House – and more importantly, why.

It isn't a conversation I'm looking forward to one bit ...

Thirty-Four

My conversation with Kiki the next morning isn't an easy one.

'But why?' she asks in horror when I tell her I'll be moving out after breakfast.

'It's for the best, that's why. You don't have to come with me – in fact, I think you should stay here.'

'But what about Finn? Won't he be upset if you move out?'

'I expect he'll be quite pleased to see the back of me.'

I explain to Kiki what happened with Finn.

'Ah, so that's why you're moving out – so you can see each other.'

I shake my head. 'No. It's so I can distance myself from him, yet still remain here in Ballykiltara. Finn and I are over, finished – that's if we were ever together in the first place.'

Kiki looks genuinely upset.

'Don't be sad, Kiki. You still have Eddie; one holiday

romance is quite enough for one trip. Plus, I have other fish to fry . . .'

I tell her all about what had happened with Father Duffy, Mac, the house and then Donal.

'Donal!' she shrieks. 'You're working with Donal!'

'Shush, not so loud! And yes, he's being very helpful.'

'Well!' Kiki stands up from where she's been perched on the edge of my bed. 'I'm away for one day, and you've ditched one man, got your hooks into another, played at Indiana Jones, and befriended a bird! That's going some, Ren, even for you.'

I have to smile. 'Yes, I suppose I did do quite a lot yesterday. But I do not have my hooks into Donal! He's helping out, that's all. I mean – as if?' I say, pulling a face.

'I thought I might be pushing it a bit far with that one.' Kiki winks and sit down again.

'Donal is a very nice man – we mustn't make fun of him. He's a bit . . . different, that's all. I'm sure he'll make someone a lovely husband one day. Apparently he's had quite a few ladies in his life—'

'Donal! You're kidding?'

I shake my head.

'Ah, it's always the quiet ones,' she smiles, and then her expression becomes sombre. 'There's no point trying to change your mind about moving out, is there?'

I shake my head again.

'I thought not. So shall I help you pack up and move out to the house?'

'Yes, please.'

'I'll miss you,' Kiki says gloomily.

'I'll only be up the road.'

'I know, but I'll miss you anyway.'

I reach across the bed and give her a hug.

'I'll miss you too, Kiks – more than you know.'

After breakfast, Kiki helps me move my stuff to The Welcome House.

I'm grateful that the only time I see Finn during this process is before it's even begun, as we're on our way back from the breakfast room.

We don't speak. He's behind the reception desk, dealing with a guest, so I hurry extra fast through the foyer, while Kiki follows at a normal pace behind me.

'You'll have to speak to him sometime,' she says when she's caught me up at the lifts.

'Not today, I don't,' I insist. 'Now let's get this move done before anyone notices.'

Considering The Welcome House is quite close to a busy road, it's incredibly quiet. This really would have been the perfect house for Ryan Dempsey, I think as I wait in the sitting room for my guests to arrive.

Enough of that, I tell myself. There are more important things to think about – for the time being, anyway.

Kiki, after helping me unpack my things – and after much encouragement and reassurance from me that I'd be fine here on my own – departed a couple of hours ago. So now I'm waiting for my guests, Father Duffy and Donal, to arrive for our midday meeting.

I glance towards the bookcase. How funny that the entrance to the cellar had been blocked like that, as if someone didn't want its existence to be discovered. But who? Could it be the same person who's been looking after this house?

I'm hoping Donal and Father Duffy might be able to shed some light on these and the many other questions I still don't have answers to.

Father Duffy is the first of my two guests to arrive.

'It's a while since I've been in here,' he says, looking around as he walks into the hall carrying a cardboard box containing some of the bound volumes he'd showed me yesterday. 'The house is looking well. By the way, I've *that* book in here with the others.'

'Which book would that be, Father?' I ask, showing him into the sitting room.

'The one you are featured in.'

Father Duffy places his box on a table and lifts a leather volume from it. Then he pulls his pair of white cotton gloves from his pocket, and puts them on before he touches the pages.

'Here,' he says, sitting down with the book on his lap. 'Come and see.'

I go over to him and glance down at the book.

'You see this figure here,' he says, pointing. 'This is the fiery lady I was telling you about. Look at all her red hair cascading down her back – much like your own.'

I lean forward to peer at the page. In amongst the other faded drawings I can clearly make out a figure, but it's difficult to tell whether the figure is male or female. He or she is wearing a long gown, which might denote a female, but the red hair Father Duffy is pointing to could equally be the fire the figure is surrounded by; it's hard to tell where fire ends and the hair begins.

'I suppose ...' I say hesitantly, not wanting to commit myself.

'It's all here,' Father Duffy says, pointing with his white-gloved finger at the words beneath the picture. 'I spent a long time transcribing this text. It's you, Ren, I'm telling you. You've arrived to save us all! Well, the house at least.' He gently taps the page, 'It says so, right here.'

Father Duffy smiles up at me, and I'm wondering how I'm supposed to respond when I hear Donal hurrying up the path.

'Excuse me a moment,' I say with relief. 'I think that's Donal arriving.'

'My apologies for keeping you both waiting,' Donal says as I lead him into the sitting room. 'I had trouble getting away from the hotel on time. Finn,' he says, looking pointedly at me, 'has been asking questions.'

'Oh, what sort of questions?' I ask casually. 'I've made some sandwiches, Donal – I didn't want you to miss your lunch on account of me. And I've boiled the kettle for tea.'

'That's kind of you, miss – I mean, Ren,' he corrects himself. 'Questions about where you are. Apparently, some of the staff saw you moving your bags out of the hotel this morning and have *gossiped* about it.' Donal is obviously very disappointed that Stag employees would ever do such a thing.

'Has Kiki said anything?' I ask.

'No, I don't believe so. Finn didn't seem to know where you'd gone, only that you'd left.'

'Good.' I glance at Father Duffy, but his expression remains neutral. He simply closes the book on his lap and continues to regard me serenely. 'Right,' I say. 'In that case I'll go and make that tea, then we can get on with our discussions.'

The meeting goes very well. Father Duffy, as requested, has brought along all the books that have a Celtic cross on the front cover. He guides us towards the pages that might have some significance to our search, and I'm relieved when he makes no mention of our previous discussion now that Donal is here.

'This page is obviously part of a map,' he says as he turns the pages of one of the volumes. 'But it's a little vague as to where.'

Donal studies the page. 'You're right, Father – it is a rudimentary map. Is there anything like it in any of the other books?'

While Donal pores over the map, Father Duffy finds another page in a second book that has similar, albeit slightly different markings.

'Ah, it's so difficult to know where this is!' Donal says, squinting at the map. 'It's very cleverly coded. Whoever drew this certainly didn't want just anyone to understand it.'

'Is there anything in any of the other books that can help us break the code, Father?' I ask, hoping he doesn't mention the red-headed woman.

'I don't think so, but you're welcome to take a look.'

Wearing the cotton gloves Father Duffy provided for us, Donal and I carefully thumb through all the books. But other than a lot of tiny ornate script and a few more illustrated pages, there appears to be nothing that can help us.

'These are all the books with the Celtic cross on the front cover?' I double-check.

'They are, Ren,' Father Duffy assures me.

'Then the key to the missing pages *must* be here in the two maps,' Donal says, setting them on the table in front of us. 'We're just not seeing it, that's all.' He glances at his watch. 'Bother, I'm going to have to head back to the hotel – I've gone over my allotted hour. I'll have to leave it with you, I'm afraid.'

'That's fine, Donal. Thank you for coming over.'

'I'm not sure I've been of much use,' Donal says apologetically. 'We're still no further forward, are we?'

'On the contrary, Donal,' Father Duffy says. 'I think we've

made excellent progress. How we proceed from here, though – that is a harder question to resolve, and one I feel only Ren might be able to answer for us.'

'Don't look at me,' I tell them, as they both look hopefully in my direction. 'I have no idea what to do now.'

'But I bet the house does,' Father Duffy says, looking around the room. 'I bet the house knows exactly what's going to happen next.'

After my visitors have left and I've cleared up the lunch things, I'm feeling pretty tired, so I decide to take a nap. Even though it seems to go against the way the house likes to be, I lock the doors before heading upstairs.

I've chosen the bedroom where I'd discovered the key to the cellar. Aside from being the prettiest of all the rooms, it has the gorgeous view that had first attracted me to the house. As I lie on my bed waiting for my drowsy state to turn to sleep, I gaze at the picture on the wall of Rafferty Island and the abbey. The key to the cellar is now safely back in its hiding place between the paper and the canvas.

'You're involved in this somehow,' I think as my eyes grow heavy and I snuggle into the pillow. 'I'm sure you are.'

I wake, I'm not sure how much later, and for a few moments I stare at the ceiling above, not knowing where I am. Then I remember.

I glance at my watch and I'm surprised to see it says ten past four. I've been asleep for nearly two hours! Wow, I must have been more tired than I thought. I'm about to sit up and stretch before heading downstairs to put the kettle on when I hear a noise.

What is it with this room and noises? I sit for a moment, listening. Did I imagine it? A moment later, I hear it again. This time it isn't a strange fluttering and tapping like last time I was in here, but the sound of footsteps.

I sit up straight on the edge of the bed. Someone is downstairs.

I look around, wondering what improvised weapon I can grab to brandish at the intruder. There isn't time to faff around unplugging one of the bedside lamps, and the room holds nothing else that I can use to protect myself.

There's nothing for it but to front it out, go downstairs and hope the footsteps don't belong to a psychopathic axe murderer.

I take a deep breath. Carrying my flip-flops, I creep as quietly as I can to the top of the stairs, and listen. Yes, I can definitely hear footsteps – big ones, by the sound of it, and they're coming from the kitchen. So I begin slowly and carefully to make my way down the stairs one at a time, with the intention of sneaking up on whoever is in there before they can sneak up on me.

I almost make it to the bottom without being discovered, but I forget that one of the lowest stairs lets out an awful creak when you step on it. It's only as I put my foot down that I remember, but by then it's too late. The resulting noise is enough to alert the intruder, and they immediately appear from the kitchen. But they're not brandishing a knife or a gun as I'd dreaded they might be, but an empty dog lead.

'Oh, you're awake,' Finn says, looking at me with concern. 'You haven't seen Fergus, have you?'

Thirty-Five

'Wha … what are you doing here?' I ask, still balancing half on one step, half on the one above. My hand involuntarily runs itself over my dishevelled bed hair.

'Fergus has gone walkabout again,' Finn says, holding up the dog lead as if it were proof. 'We were on a walk around the lake and he suddenly shot off up a path I hadn't come across before. When I followed it, it led here.'

I stare at Finn disbelievingly.

'When I got here, I found the back door open. I assumed Fergus had trotted inside, but when I wandered around the house I found you sleeping upstairs, so I decided to leave you be. You're a deep sleeper, aren't you?'

I can only shrug. I can't believe he has the audacity to walk in here, let alone be chatting away to me like nothing has happened between us.

'I was making quite a noise chasing a bird out of the house

when I first got here,' he continues when I don't speak. 'I thought it would have woken you?'

I shake my head and step down off the stairs. I've been completely thrown off guard by Finn's sudden arrival, and I don't know quite where to begin. Why is he here? And why is he using Fergus as an excuse?

'Why are you here, Finn?' I ask, setting down my flip-flops and slipping my feet into them.

'I told you: I've lost Fergus.'

'Yes, so you said . . . But why, when you found out he wasn't here, did you hang around?' I know I sound hostile, but his story is so implausible it's infuriating.

'I'm not *hanging around*,' Finn says, sounding irritated, 'I was about to leave when I heard you coming down the stairs. Believe me, I didn't want to see you either – after yesterday, I mean,' he adds hastily, his annoyance changing swiftly to discomfort.

'The feeling is mutual,' I say sourly.

There's silence in the hall, broken only by the steady ticking of the old mantelpiece clock in the sitting room.

'I still don't understand how you got in,' I say eventually.

'This is The Welcome House, remember? The doors are always unlocked here!' Finn smiles, but I don't.

'I distinctly remember locking both doors before I went upstairs for my nap.'

'And I'm telling you the back door was open.' Finn's smile rapidly disappears. 'Are you saying I'm a liar?'

'No . . . ' I can't bear this; a few days ago it was such a joy to spend time with him, but now it seems we're incapable of being civil with each other.

'Why don't we go and check the front door too?' Finn says,

stomping down the hall. He grabs the knob, twists it sharply and the door swings open. 'See?' he says accusingly, turning back to me. 'Open.'

'That's impossible,' I say, walking towards him. 'I locked it, I know I did... both of them.'

'Perhaps you thought you had, but because you were tired you didn't quite catch them properly?' Finn suggests in a calmer tone.

I'm sure this wasn't the case, but there's no point going on about it. Finn has proved his point and I'm beginning to believe he's telling the truth.

'So where *is* Fergus?' I ask, changing the subject. 'If he's not here in the house?'

'I don't know,' Finn says, his brow wrinkling with concern. 'Like I said, he ran up the path that leads to the back of this house, and he wouldn't come back when I called, so I had to follow him.'

'And this path led from the lake right to here?'

'Yes.'

'I don't remember seeing it.'

'I hadn't either, it's very odd. But that's what happened, whether you choose to believe me or not.'

'I believe you,' I say quietly. 'And you say there was a bird trapped in the house when you got here?'

'Yes, a crow or a jackdaw or something. Stupid thing wouldn't leave when I tried to open a window for it. It took me ages to persuade it to go.'

'It was a raven,' I say matter-of-factly. 'Something similar happened to me the other day. I wonder if it was the same one?'

Finn looks at me a bit oddly.

'Do you think Fergus chased it up here?' I ask.

'He might have, I guess. He set off fairly purposefully.'

'Hmm . . .'

'Hmm what?'

'Nothing, just thinking, that's all.'

'About?'

'Where Fergus might be,' I say hurriedly. Now was not the time to tell Finn about the cellar and the raven. He'd think I was mad. 'You don't think he's got out the front, do you?' I look at the door. 'Down on to the road? What if it was open – you said it was unlocked?'

Finn quickly pulls open the door and we both rush down the steps of the house towards the road. But there doesn't seem to be anything disturbing the usual stream of passing cars, let alone a big hairy dog wandering amongst them.

'It doesn't look like he's out here,' Finn says with relief.

I continue staring down the road.

'Ren?' he prompts. 'Are you OK?'

I nod.

'I said it doesn't look like he's out here.'

'Yes . . . yes you're right. Such a relief.' I still stare at the passing cars.

'Should we go back up to the house?' Finn asks gently. 'Perhaps we could check the back garden again – if it's OK with you, of course?'

I can only nod, and allow Finn to lead me back up the steps to the house.

'Look, me being here is obviously a bad idea,' Finn says when we're back inside. 'I'll pop outside and have another look for Fergus, then I'll be on my way.'

'No, it's not you,' I say in a weak voice. 'It's . . .' my voice trails off.

'It's what?' Finn asks, sounding concerned.

'Let's look for Fergus, shall we?' I attempt to say brightly. 'You're right, we should try out back.'

I hurry away from Finn down the hall towards the back door. I need air. Fresh air. Not the sort laced with traffic fumes.

Now I know it's there, it's fairly easy to spot the path Finn followed. There are a couple of loose fence panels at the end of the garden; when pushed, they turn into a sort of makeshift gate.

'Wait up!' Finn calls as I'm about to go through the opening. 'Are we sure Fergus isn't in the garden?'

We both take a quick glance round the large but sparse garden of The Welcome House. It's obvious Fergus isn't there; he's too big to remain hidden in a garden with no cover.

'Back to the lake then?' Finn asks. 'Are you sure you're OK doing this, you looked a bit white a few minutes ago.'

'Yes, I'm fine now – it must have been the exhaust fumes from the traffic,' I improvise as I make my way through the gate on to the rough path on the other side.

'Fergus!' I call as I begin to walk down towards the lake. 'Fergus, are you there?'

It takes us only a minute or two to reach the shore of the lake, but we've been calling and whistling Fergus all the way.

'Where is that damn dog!' Finn says, exasperated. 'I swear, when I catch up with him—'

But I'm staring out at the lake. 'Look!' I cry, pointing out to where I've spotted movement in the wide expanse of water. 'What's that?'

Finn follows my hand and immediately sees the same thing I do. In the distance, bobbing about in the water, is a furry head. But instead of looking happy and excited to see us, the furry head looks petrified. A moment later, it disappears under the surface of the lake.

'Fergus!' Finn cries. 'How the hell did he get all the way out there?'

Immediately he begins pulling off his shoes and socks, then he tugs his shirt over his head and yanks at his jeans until all his clothes are in a pile on the ground. I watch as he wades out into the lake wearing only his underpants.

In other circumstances, this might have been a pleasant sight, but I'm suddenly overwhelmed by dread. 'Finn, be careful!' I shout. 'That lake is really deep!' I wonder for a split second how I know this, but I don't have time to try and remember. All I can do is look on in horror as Finn reaches a point where the water is up to his waist, so he plunges in, swimming out towards Fergus with powerful strokes.

There have been a number of times in my life when I've felt helpless, but none of them compare to the way I feel as I stand on the edge of the lake watching Finn try to rescue his dog.

I wonder if I should ring someone, but my phone is back at the house, and even if I did have it on me, who would I call? It's not as if the lake has its own coastguard.

So I can only stand and watch as Finn gets further and further away from me, but closer and closer to Fergus.

At last he reaches his dog, and I see him attempt to wrap his arms around Fergus's body. But Fergus is so terrified that he panics and begins to thrash about, and then they both disappear under the water together.

I clap my hand to my mouth in horror, unable to breathe as I wait for Finn to re-emerge from the dark murky water. When he breaks the surface, I find myself whooping with joy – but it's short-lived.

As he tries desperately to hold on to Fergus, the same thing happens again. There's an agonising wait after they plunge below the surface, and when Finn re-emerges this time I see him trying to calm Fergus down.

He seems to be treading water at the moment with Fergus in his arms, but I know he will soon begin to tire, and he still has to face the long swim back to shore with the frightened dog.

My mind is in turmoil as I frantically try to come up with something I can do to help. Should I run back to the house and call the Gardai? Perhaps there is an emergency service for the lakes, and they could send someone out to help. But then I'd have to leave Finn and Fergus thrashing around out there – what if Finn got dragged under again and didn't come up this time? But if I do stay what good was I going to be if that did happen? I've never been much of a swimmer – even if I could get out that far in time, I doubt I could save someone Kiki's size, let alone Fergus or Finn.

But then something happens that makes my heart surge with relief and joy. I see a small wooden boat travelling across the lake in their direction.

'Help!' I cry from the shore in case the person in the boat hasn't seen them. 'Emergency! Please, HELP!'

The man in the boat continues to row calmly across the lake as if he hasn't heard me, so I jump and wave my arms about at the water's edge, desperately trying to alert him. I'm convinced he's going to row straight past, oblivious to Finn and Fergus, and to all my shouting and waving, but at that moment he expertly turns the boat at a sharp angle and manages to pull up right beside the struggling pair.

I watch as he reaches over the side of the boat and effortlessly lifts a struggling Fergus from Finn, then places him down in the boat beside him. When that's done, he reaches out again and half pulls, half drags an exhausted Finn into the boat beside his dog.

'Thank you,' I whisper upwards. 'Thank you so much.'

To my immense relief, the little boat begins to pull towards shore with Finn and Fergus safely aboard. Only when it draws closer do I recognise the boatman.

'Jackie!' I cry as I wade out into the water to take the rope he's preparing to throw me so I can pull the boat in the final few metres. 'Thank you so much!'

Jackie simply nods as he climbs out into the shallow water. He bends over the boat and lifts out a subdued Fergus then carries him the last few feet to dry ground.

'Fergus,' I cry, ruffling his coat. I wrap my arms around the soaking wet dog, not caring that I'm now almost as wet as he is. Feeling Fergus wriggle in my grip, I let him go. He gives the most almighty shake, wetting me still further, then trots over to a nearby rock and cocks his leg as if nothing has happened.

I look up and see a bedraggled Finn, a blanket wrapped around his shoulders, wading towards me.

'Are you OK?' I ask, rushing over to him.

He nods weakly. Obviously the experience has taken more of a toll on him than Fergus.

'Let's get you back up to the house and get you warmed up,' I tell him. I look for Jackie, but he's already back in his boat.

'Wait!' I call, and Finn turns with me. 'Won't you come up to the house too, Jackie? Let me at least make you a cup of tea to say thank you?'

But I know what he's going to say even before he speaks. 'Thank you, miss, but I won't. Got to get back to my lake . . .' He looks up at The Welcome House as he begins pulling on his oars. 'I see you found the house then? Or did it find you?' he calls as he disappears into the evening mist that is now settling above the lake. 'Take care of them two, won't you?' is the last thing I hear as he is completely engulfed in the soft white cloud. 'And take care of that house ...'

And then he's gone.

I turn back to Finn, who's looking even paler than I had earlier.

'Come on,' I say, resting my hand on his back, 'let's get you into the warm. Come on, Fergus!'

'Wait,' Finn says, speaking for the first time since he left the water. He looks back at the lake. 'Was that who I think it was?'

I nod. 'Yup.'

'And he just rowed me and Fergus back to safety in his boat?'

'Uh-huh.'

Finn nods slowly. 'In that case, I think I might need something a bit stronger than a cup of tea when we get back to the house.'

Thirty-Six

Finn doesn't have anything stronger, even though I find a half-empty bottle of Jameson's in one of the cupboards. He insists that all he wants is a hot mug of tea, so that's what I give him, along with a few biscuits left over from my lunch with Donal and Father Duffy.

Fergus seems to have recovered better than the rest of us after his adventure. He tucks into a tin of corned beef that I find in one of the cupboards, and some of the leftover ham and cheese from lunch. Not an ideal meal for a dog, but Finn and I agree that the circumstances are a little unusual, and now Fergus is fast asleep by the fire that I've managed to make up in the sitting room to ensure that both he and Finn get warmed through.

'So,' Finn says when he's drunk his tea, and a bit more colour has returned to his cheeks. Even though he's now fully dressed, he still has a blanket – a dry one – wrapped around his shoulders as he huddles in an armchair by the fire. 'What's been going on?'

'How do you mean?' I ask innocently from the armchair opposite.

'Well, it's not every day you see a . . . ' He hesitates. 'Let's just call it a strange *phenomenon* perform a heroic rescue from a lake. Yet you seem to be taking it all in your stride. It's almost as if that's not the only strange thing that's been happening to you lately.'

I look at him. It would be so good to talk to someone about all this, but much as I long to confide in him, something is holding me back.

Things feel different between us after what happened down at the lake. They feel comfortable again, the way they had been before. I'm still desperately upset with him for saying the things he said and for the way he'd made me feel, but even so, I really want to talk to him, even if it's only as a friend . . .

So I take a deep breath and tell Finn everything – about the books, and the cellar, and even the raven, and I'm not at all surprised when he reacts as I'd hoped he would: with patience, understanding and a healthy dose of curiosity.

'So you reckon the raven that was in the house earlier is the same one that led you to the cellar?'

'With everything else odd that's going on, it wouldn't surprise me. What have I found myself in the middle of, Finn? I came here to find a house for someone, and now I seem to be embroiled in a search for some ancient documents that may not even exist.'

'You certainly like to mix it up, eh?'

'Er, no. Usually I lead a quiet life, and then I come here to Ireland – a place I'm told is peaceful and relaxing – and suddenly I find myself caught up in a house with an invisible owner, a ghost who runs boat trips, a priest who thinks I'm some sort of divine prophecy, and a raven that might, according to Donal, be an ancient soothsayer!'

'What about the extremely annoying yet loveable hotel manager?' Finn asks, the glint I've been missing so much sparkling in his green eyes.

'Yes, he too is yet another thorn in my side …'

'At least he's made an impression – albeit a prickly one.'

I look down into my now-empty mug, and the awkwardness I'd thought had long since left the room makes an unwelcome reappearance.

'So …' Finn says, determined to dispel it before it has a chance to take hold. 'What an afternoon, eh? I reckon I'm going to have to get one of those extendable leads for Fergus – no more roaming around for you, fella, when we're on a walk.'

Fergus looks up sleepily at Finn, then turns over on to his back and goes back to sleep with his legs in the air.

'Aw, you can't do that to him. Dogs need to be allowed to run free on occasion – so long as they're kept under control and safe.'

'You were pretty worried about him this afternoon,' Finn says, glancing at me.

'I had good reason – for a while there, I thought you were both going to drown!'

'I don't mean then. I'm talking about earlier, when we thought he'd got out on to the road. You turned very pale.'

'Yes … well. You forget I found him running around near a road before, didn't I?'

'And you were angry with me on that occasion too.' Finn's eyes bury deep into mine in a way that makes me desperately want to look away, but I can't. 'What's going on, Ren?' he asks gently. 'What's the story?'

'There isn't one,' I try, managing to look away at last. 'I like dogs, that's all, and I think people should look after them properly.'

'When we first met, I thought you didn't like them. I thought you were scared.'

'No, I'm not scared of dogs.'

'What are you scared of then?' Finn asks with that same penetrating look. 'I know there's something, Ren. Why don't you just tell me?'

'Should I put some more wood on that fire?' I ask, looking at the flames still burning merrily in the grate. 'It might go out.'

'Ren, life's too short to keep things bottled up,' Finn presses on undaunted. 'I should know, I nearly drowned this afternoon.'

'You can talk, Mr Secretive! I've never known anyone so guarded about his past.'

'Well maybe if you tell me your secret, I'll tell you mine … Please, Ren, I've treated you badly, I know that. I want to make it up to you, I want to help.'

I sigh. Maybe he's right – life is too short. And if I was going to tell anyone, I knew Finn would be the person to understand.

'You'll think I'm silly.'

'No, I won't.'

'You might.'

'For the love of God, Ren – tell me.'

'Right … ' I nod and I take a deep breath. 'So … about six years ago I was engaged to a guy who turned out to be a bit of a tool.'

'A common story.'

'Obviously, we planned to get married, so I moved in with him. *We* moved in with him.'

'We?'

'Me and my dog, Harry.' I have to pause for a moment. I haven't said his name aloud in so long. 'I'd had Harry since he was a puppy,' I continue, trying to keep my voice steady. 'A friend of my parents had a dog who had a litter of puppies – no one knew what sort of dogs they were, the mother was a crossbreed and they think the dad was too, so the litter was a right mix.' I smile as I remember going to pick my puppy. 'I didn't choose Harry, he chose me. He rolled out of his bed, trotted straight over to me and climbed up on my lap, and then he sealed the deal by farting.'

Finn laughs.

'But from that moment we were friends forever. I lived on my own and worked mainly from home, so it was just the two of us.'

'What did you do?' Finn asks.

'I was a journalist. I wrote for magazines, it's what I trained to do at uni.'

'Makes sense.'

'I suppose I always have had an enquiring nature.'

'Some might call it nosy . . .' Finn winks at me.

'Anyway, Harry and I spent all our time together, and then I met Jonathan. I'd had boyfriends before, but nothing serious. Jonathan and I seemed to click, we were interested in the same things, had friends in common, you know the sort of thing?'

Finn says nothing, waiting for me to continue. So I do.

'Best of all, Harry seemed to get on with him. He was never jealous or caused any trouble between us, it seemed like the perfect match.'

'But it obviously wasn't.'

'Like I said, we moved in together – to Jonathan's flat in London. Harry and I were used to living near a city, but not in the centre of one. I didn't really like it, it was noisy and there was no air, you know?'

Finn nods.

'But I loved Jonathan, and I was prepared to give it a go, and then one day . . . ' I take a breath. 'I had to go out of town to do some research for an article I was writing. I thought all would be fine: Harry and Jonathan got on, I'd left Harry with him many a time, I saw no problems.'

'But there were?' Finn prompts gently when I pause a bit too long this time.

'Yes . . . ' I say, as the thoughts and feelings that went hand in hand with that dreadful day begin to come rushing back to the surface from the place I kept them buried deep within me. 'I was in the middle of interviewing someone when I got the call – we were talking about something completely banal: Internet shopping, I think? I ignored the phone vibrating in my pocket the first time, I didn't want to seem unprofessional, and the second time it went too, but when it went for a third time, I knew I should pick it up.'

'Had something happened to Jonathan?'

I shake my head. 'No, Jonathan was the one calling. It was Harry; he'd escaped from the house and got out on to the road. He was hit by a van and died immediately,' I hear myself saying in practised form. 'They said he wouldn't have suffered.'

But how did they know? I ask myself for the millionth time since it happened. Had the vet that pronounced him dead been hit by a car, died and then survived to tell the tale? No, I didn't think so. No one knew if Harry had suffered, only Harry, and he was gone.

'I'm not sure how they knew that,' Finn says, reaching across the gap between the two armchairs and squeezing my hand. 'But I hope he didn't.'

I smile at him. Finn understood. I knew he would.

'I've a feeling that isn't the end of your story,' Finn says gently. He releases my hand, but doesn't look like he wants to.

'No, you're right. It only gets worse.'

'Worse than your dog dying?'

'You tell me. Days later, I was still trying to get to the bottom of what happened – you know me; I wouldn't let it rest until I had the full story. We hadn't even got Harry's ashes back yet, but I knew *he* wouldn't be able to rest in peace until *I* was at peace with his death. It was some of the things Jonathan was telling me, they just didn't add up, so I kept pushing and pushing until he broke down and told me the whole story.'

I look at Finn. 'Jonathan was having an affair. The day Harry got out on to the road, Jonathan had his bit on the side in our house – in our bed even – and of course Harry didn't like it. He kept barking and scratching on the bedroom door. So Jonathan put him out in the back yard. Only the gate hadn't been latched properly after he'd sneaked his bitch in, and that's when Harry got out. So not only had my fiancé been having an affair behind my back, but he killed my dog in the process.'

I begin to sob huge wet salty tears that roll down my face and drop into my lap. 'Except Harry was more than my dog,' I say, furiously wiping my face, 'he was my best friend. He knew everything about me, and I knew everything about him. I still miss him, even now.'

Finn doesn't take hold of my hand this time. He gets up and perches on the arm of my chair, wrapping his arms tightly around me. 'Let it out,' he instructs. 'Let it all go, Ren.'

And as I feel myself shudder with each sob that I allow to come to the surface and then be swallowed up by the flames of the roaring fire, it doesn't just feel like Finn is giving me a hug, it feels like the whole of The Welcome House is joining in too.

Later, when my tears have dried, I find myself still cradled safely in Finn's arms as we watch the flames flickering in the grate.

'Better now?' Finn asks, breaking our comfortable silence.

'Yes,' I say, easing myself from his hold so I can see him properly. 'Much better, thank you.'

'Ren, I understand so much more about you now you've told me all that.'

'You do?'

'I get why you're a little mistrusting of people – I'm sure I would be too, if that had happened to me.'

'Is it that obvious?'

'To the casual observer, probably not; but to someone who wants to get to know you better, you definitely hold people at arm's length. I think I understand why you're uncomfortable around animals as well. Is it because you're scared of committing to them too?'

'No. I'm not scared of committing to them, I'm scared of loving them and them leaving me – it hurts too much.' I look down at Fergus, snoring contently by the fire, completely unaware of the drama that's been unfolding above him.

'I understand that.'

'I know *you* do, Finn, that's why I decided to tell you everything. I knew after I watched you risk your own life for your dog, you'd understand how I felt. But most people don't. They don't get how much an animal can touch you, here,' I think about putting my hand on Finn's chest, but I place it on my own instead. 'How you need to mourn them when they're gone, and how losing them can sometimes hurt more than losing a person. I loved Harry with all my heart – a lot more, I now realise, than I loved Jonathan. After it happened, I didn't give a damn about never seeing *him* again, but not seeing Harry was almost too much to bear.'

'Did you go off the rails a bit?' Finn asks.

'No. Quite the opposite, in fact. I became even more driven. I ditched my career as a journalist, I took some time out. Luckily, I had the money we'd saved for the wedding stashed in a bank account, so I withdrew it all and blew it on travelling.'

'Was it a joint account?' Finn asks, a twinkle in his eye.

'It was! And I had a *fabulous* time spending *all* the money!'

'Good girl.'

'But when I returned from travelling,' I say more seriously, 'I was stuck in limbo. I didn't have a job, and I hadn't a clue what I wanted to do. That was when I found my first house. I had some friends who wanted to move, so I offered to help out to give me something to do. And the rest, as they say, is history.'

Finn takes hold of my hand again.

'I'm sorry,' he says placing his other hand over the top of mine. 'I'm sorry you had to go through all that pain, and I'm sorry that while you've been here in Ballykiltara I've only added to your pain, by making you think that all men are total eejits.'

I can't help but smile.

'I'm serious, what I did was unforgivable. I thought at the time it was for the best ... for both of us. My feelings overwhelmed me. I panicked. I did the only thing I thought I could do – push you away. But after today, and seeing how much you care about me, and about Fergus, I'd do anything to make it up to you I'd ...'

'Try.'

'What?' Finn asks, breaking from his impassioned speech.

'Try making it up to me.'

'How?' Finn's woeful expression lifts as he begins to see a chink of light.

'That is up to you.'

'You forgive me?'

'That depends on what you do next. But I do know one thing. Now you know my story, Finn Cassidy, you definitely have to tell me yours ...'

Thirty-Seven

'But why are we meeting here?' I ask Finn the next day as I arrive at the stables at our agreed time of 10 p.m. 'The horses are all in bed.'

Finn smiles. 'Technically they're bedded down for the night, all except two of them, that is.'

Last night, after Finn had said he wanted to redeem himself, I'd tried to get him to tell me what he was planning. But all he would tell me was that he had 'something in mind' and I wasn't to ask him questions about it as it was going to be a surprise. This of course was incredibly hard for me; once I knew he'd thought of something I wanted to know all about it immediately. But I bit my lip and tried to go with the flow for once. Even though I didn't say anything, I was secretly pleased that Finn did want to make amends; his previous behaviour seemed totally out of character for him and I wanted to find out why. So when he'd asked me to meet him at the stables the following evening. I was surprised, intrigued and keen to know more.

Finn now leads me across the stable yard towards Alfie's stall, where I find Mac in the process of saddling Alfie up. 'He's all ready for you!' He smiles at me and winks at Finn. 'I'll go and get Trixie ready.'

'What's going on?' I ask Finn as he leads Alfie out of his stable. 'Are you going for a ride?'

'Nope, *we're* going for a ride – a moonlight one.'

'We are?'

'If you remember, I did promise to take you riding one day. But what I have planned for tonight is going to be so much better.'

'Ah, so that's why you told me not to dress up and to wear jeans. I thought it was odd.'

'I bet you thought more than that. I bet this has been killing you, not knowing what we were going to do.'

'A little.' I try to sound cool and relaxed but I can feel my heart beating in my chest.

Finn looks me up and down. 'You're dressed perfectly – we don't even need to find you boots. But you do need a hat,' he says, 'so pop on over to the tack room and choose one that fits.'

I hurry over to choose my riding hat, excited at the prospect of whatever Finn has planned. Last night we'd sat by the fire and talked and talked until Finn had to go back to the hotel. He hadn't told me much more about himself, but he'd promised he would, as soon as the 'something' he had in mind was arranged. I'd expected him to cook me dinner, or book a table at a restaurant; I never would have dreamt he'd take me on a moonlight ride. I'm eager to hear what Finn is going to tell me too. He was so supportive when I told him my story that I haven't regretted sharing it at all; now I want to give him the same kind of help when he shares the secret that I'm convinced has been burdening him.

It takes a while but I manage to find a hat – actually it looks more like a helmet – that fits, and I fix the strap under my chin. I glance at my reflection in the window of Mac's office as I pass by; I don't exactly resemble one of the elegant show jumpers with their velvet riding hats I've seen on TV. The helmet looks like a large pink egg on my head, but it's there to keep me protected, so I try not to think too much about what I look like as I return to Finn and Mac. Alfie has now been joined by another horse I recognise: Finn's favourite mount – Trixie.

'Will I be riding Alfie?' I ask, looking up at the huge black horse who suddenly seems much bigger now I might be expected to ride him.

'You will indeed,' Finn says, patting him. 'Don't worry, though: Alfie is very calm. He's our best plodder, he won't mess you around. He'll follow whatever Trixie and I do.'

'Oh, OK. Good boy, Alfie.' I stroke his neck and he turns his head towards mine.

'Right, shall we head out?' Finn asks, swinging himself confidently up on to Trixie's back.

'Sure.' I look up hesitantly at Alfie's saddle.

'Do you want a box so you can mount him?' Mac asks. 'It might make it a little easier.'

'No, I'll be fine,' I say, putting my right foot into the stirrup.

'It's your other foot,' Mac whispers. 'Your left one. You swing your right leg up and over.'

'Oh yes, of course.' I glance at Finn, but he's busy controlling Trixie, who is obviously ready to get going as soon as possible. So I change my foot over, and with as much effort as I can muster I try to pull myself high enough to swing my leg over Alfie's back. To my, and I think Finn and Mac's surprise, I manage it first time.

'Well done,' Mac says. 'Now do you know what you're doing up there?'

My hesitation is enough for Mac, who quickly runs through all the basics for controlling Alfie. 'But you'll be fine,' he concludes. 'Finn will look after you, and Alfie will follow Finn.'

'Ready to ride?' Finn asks, pulling on Trixie's reins to guide her out of the stable yard.

'Yes,' I squeak, trying to do the same to Alfie.

'Give him a good tap with your heels,' Mac calls. 'Let him know who's boss.'

I do as he says and Alfie follows Trixie towards the open gate.

But as we ride out of the stable I'm pretty sure that Alfie knows exactly who's in charge right now – and it certainly isn't me.

By the time Finn has led us out through Ballykiltara Park where I'd walked, and then ridden, a couple of days ago, and on into the woods, it's starting to get very dark.

'Where are we going?' I ask Finn, as Alfie decides it would be nice to ride alongside his stable mate rather than behind her.

'Somewhere special,' Finn replies. 'How are you getting on?'

'Good, thanks. It was a bit touch and go to begin with, but Alfie and I seem to have come to an understanding now, and I'm actually starting to enjoy it.'

'Excellent. Not too much further and then we can stop.'

After another ten or so minutes in the saddle we emerge from the woods to suddenly and quite dramatically find ourselves in front of a huge lake, eerily, yet magically lit by a bright and clear full moon.

'Where are we?' I ask Finn.

'This used to be called the secret lake,' Finn says, dismounting from Trixie and guiding her to the edge of the water so she can take a drink. 'Secret because it was so tucked away that hardly anyone knew it was here.'

I try to do the same with Alfie, but my dismount is more of a slide off his back. Luckily Finn doesn't seem to notice, and I take Alfie by his reins and lead him to the water.

'You have to make an extra special effort to visit this lake,' Finn continues, 'not like the others, that you can see whizzing past on a tour bus with fifty other people. That's what makes this one so special: not many people ever see it. I wanted you to be one of those that did.'

I smile at him over the two horses.

'We should tether them,' Finn says. 'I don't think they'd wander too far, but I wouldn't want to be stranded out here without them if they spooked and ran away.'

'Why would they be spooked? It's so calm here.'

'Best if we tether them. I have rope.' Finn reaches into one of the saddlebags that Trixie has been carrying.

'I wondered what you had in there.'

'Oh, I have more than just rope. Give me a minute.' Finn takes hold of Alfie's reins and leads him and Trixie back from the water a little way, then he tethers them loosely so they can wander around under some trees. Before he leaves them, he reaches into the bags and pulls out two picnic blankets, a flask and a small cool bag, and then he walks back to me.

'Supplies!' he says, spreading one of the blankets on the ground. 'Madam?' he gestures for me to sit on the blanket, so

I do, then Finn sits down next to me so we're facing the water. 'Beautiful, isn't it?' he says, unbuckling his riding helmet.

'It certainly is,' I reply, doing the same. 'Thank you for bringing me here.'

'No, thank *you* for giving me another chance, I don't deserve it.'

'I think you do. This is perfect.'

'Not yet, it isn't,' Finn says, lying down on his back.

I look at him, puzzled.

'Come and lie next to me,' he says, patting the blanket.

Hesitantly I do as he says.

'Now look up,' Finn instructs.

The sight that greets my eyes is truly amazing – millions and millions of stars all sparkling brightly, jostling for position in the night sky above us.

'Wow …' I say slowly, trying to take it all in. 'This is incredible.'

'I thought you might like it. Ever since you came up with the dark skies as a ruse to throw Donal off the scent, I've wanted to show you them for real. And the Irish weather, for once, was on my side tonight. That's why we had to ride out so far – you have to be away from any light pollution to get the best experience.'

'It's absolutely spectacular, Finn. Thank you.'

Finn drapes the other blanket on top of us, and silently we lie hand in hand on the blanket staring up at the universe together. It's one of the most special, and most romantic things I've ever done.

Eventually Finn sits up and looks down at me, still lying on the blanket.

'This was only part one of my plan,' he says, 'to amaze and astound you, and hopefully to let you know how special I think

307

you are. This,' he says sighing, 'this was the easy part. Now I need to move on to part two.'

'What's part two?'

'Honesty.'

'Honesty?'

'It's time you knew the full story about me – the stuff I've tried to keep secret from you.'

'Really?' I sit up and pull the top blanket around me. 'Are you sure?'

'But in return you must be honest with me too . . . '

'Of course.' I swallow hard.

'Right then . . . ' Finn is obviously preparing himself. 'The truth of the matter is . . . I'm a failure, Ren. A big fat failure.'

'What? How can you be?'

Finn waggles his finger at me. 'No interruptions. Let me tell my story.'

I nod silently.

'I wasn't always so. For a while, I had everything – a successful multimillion-euro business that I built from scratch. We had restaurants all over the world, and were expanding all the time.'

'Wait, were you behind Cassidy's?' I exclaim, forgetting about my agreement. 'The gourmet burger chain?'

'I was.'

'But that was enormous a few years back – everywhere you went there would be one of those on the high street. I've eaten in them many a time.'

Finn holds his finger to his lips.

'Sorry,' I apologise, 'please continue.'

'Like I said, I had everything I could ever have wanted – a business, the respect of my family . . . ' he hesitates.

I wait this time.

308

'And then I blew it all.'

'How?' I ask when he doesn't immediately continue. I'm finding it hard to believe that the Finn I've come to know could completely wreck his life, as he seemed to think he had, but I wanted to hear everything.

'On a racehorse,' Finn explains.

'Celtic Cassidy!' I exclaim.

'Yes, that's right, but how did *you* know?'

'Something Mac said.' I don't mention the photos in his house. 'But you loved that horse – didn't you?'

'I did. She was my pride and joy, and I ploughed a lot of money into her – too much. And when I didn't have enough I borrowed money from the business. I was convinced she was going places. I had it all planned – the Irish National, the Grand National – I thought she'd earn that money back easily and then some, once she started winning. And she would have done, if she hadn't got injured.' Finn's face clouds over. 'I remember that day as if it was yesterday. It was an early May morning, it had been a miserable spring and it was bitterly cold. It was only a training session, the jumps weren't even that high when she fell, but she landed in an awkward position and suffered a compound fracture . . . ' His voice trails off.

'Couldn't they do anything?'

Finn shakes his head. 'Breaking a leg is an immediate death sentence for a horse. Their bones have evolved differently than ours; they're lighter, they break easily, and they're very, very difficult to mend – almost impossible, in fact, because of the complex healing process required if they're to regain full strength. A dog who breaks his leg will hobble around on three legs, but a horse can't because they spend nearly all their time standing. Believe me, it's been tried, but a horse simply can't keep its weight off the injured leg, and that leads to further, even more complex injuries. So that May morning – May eighth, to be exact – was the last time my beloved Cassidy ran, the last time she took a breath.'

To my surprise, I see a tear rolling down Finn's cheek. He turns away and rubs furiously at his face.

I reach for his hand, but he pulls it away. 'No, let me finish and then you can see if you still want to hold it.' He runs his fingers through his hair and takes a deep breath. 'After my horse had to be put down in front of me, I went a bit off the rails. Understandable at first, I guess ... A few days to get myself back on track, that's what everyone allowed me. They all thought I'd pull myself together, get back to being the old Finn. But I couldn't, I couldn't stop seeing the vision of Cassidy lying there on the cold, frosty ground. But I didn't let it end there, did I? Oh no,' he shakes his head. 'I went off the rails for a year.'

'Go on,' I encourage softly, when he pauses again.

'I frittered what little money I had left on drink – and gambled the rest away in casinos and private poker nights at my supposed friends' houses,' he says bitterly. 'You'd think they would have been looking out for me, trying to steer me back on the right path, but no, they were more than happy to relieve me of what little money I had left. I ended up penniless, and I ran my business into the ground. From a respected and successful multimillionaire businessman, to a pitiful alcoholic who couldn't even keep a roof over his head—'

This must be why I've never seen Finn have an alcoholic drink. I feel even worse about drinking all the Guinness in front of him now.

'What happened then?' I ask quietly.

'I was a burden to my parents for a while – they didn't turn their backs on me, God love 'em. But I knew I had to get back on my feet again somehow, I just didn't know how. Then one day my mam told me she'd signed me up for a self-help group over on Tara. I didn't know what self-help was, let alone how it was going to take place on a remote island. But she insisted I went, even drove me to the boat herself.'

Was that what Finn's mother had been calling him about the other day? I suddenly wonder. Had it been the anniversary of Celtic Cassidy's death, and she was phoning to check he was OK?

'And that's where it happened,' Finn continues, 'where I got my life back.'

'Over on Tara?'

'Yes, I resisted everything at first – the classes, the groups – but one day I was walking around the island on my own when suddenly I felt the wind change, and in that moment I changed too. It sounds completely mad, but it's the truth. After that, I joined in with everything. Instead of putting up a brick wall, I allowed the island to help me – and it did. I still haven't a clue how, but I know I have the island of Tara to thank for it, and Darcy and Dermot too.'

'So you did meet Dermot on the island then?'

'Yes, not exactly in the circumstances I told you I'm afraid, but it was on Tara. They're a good couple, those two – always looking out for the next waif or stray they can help. And I happened to be one of them. By offering me the job at The Stag, Dermot not only gave me a new job, but a whole new life too.'

'That is an amazing story,' I tell him. 'You turned your life around – with a little help, of course, but you did. You're happy now, aren't you?'

'I've been even happier since I met you, Ren. So, what do you think – do you still want to hold my hand after I've told you all that?'

I don't say anything, I just take both his hands in mine, and I kiss them. I'd felt his pain and his anguish as he told his story, and now all I want is to help him mend, like he'd helped me.

I look deep into his eyes, then I gently stroke his cheek, finally I reach my lips up towards his, but something catches my eye in amongst the trees behind us.

'What's that?' I ask, moving my head to the side just as Finn's lips are about to meet mine.

'Well, it was going to be a kiss ... '

'No, I mean behind you, there was something moving in the trees.'

'What sort of something?'

'I don't know. It was light, maybe even white, but it was definitely moving slowly through the trees. It caught my eye as you were leaning towards me.'

Finn turns around to see where I'm staring.

'It's probably nothing,' he says, turning back. 'A reflection off the water. Now where were we?'

Suddenly one of the horses lets out a high-pitched whinny, and we hear them moving around.

'I'd better go check on them,' Finn sighs, pulling himself to his feet. 'Hold that thought and those lips right where they are. I'll be back in a minute.'

While Finn heads back towards where the horses are teth-ered, I peer into the trees where I'd seen the movement. But all I can see are the dim silhouettes of many tall trees in the darkness.

Odd.

'They won't settle,' Finn says, returning to me. 'I think we're going to have to ride back.'

'Oh what a shame, this is such a lovely spot.'

'Then we'll have to come again, won't we?' Finn offers his hand, so I take it. But when he pulls me up, he deliberately pulls me right into his body, and then he takes his kiss.

'I wasn't going to leave here without one,' he says, tucking a stray lock of my hair gently behind my ear.

'I'm so glad you didn't,' I reply, smiling up at him. 'Now let's go home and we'll see if there aren't a few more like that waiting for you when we get there.'

As Finn and I walk hand in hand back towards the horses, I take a quick look behind me. Even though there is no movement now, I can't help feeling that something is hiding in the trees, watching me.

Thirty-Eight

The next morning I wake in a strange bed, but that's not the only thing that makes me jump as I gradually return to consciousness. There's a person in the bed next to me too.

I turn over as quietly as I can, to face Finn.

He's lying on his back, still sleeping, but the bedcovers are only half covering him, so I get another chance to see the well-toned torso that I'd had the enjoyment of seeing again last night when we returned from the stables and headed straight back to The Welcome House after collecting Fergus on the way.

'Are you sure you're all right with him being here?' Finn had asked me. 'Now I know how you feel about dogs, I don't want you to feel awkward.'

'Don't be silly; Fergus is the first dog I've had feelings for in a long time. I love having him here.'

'Should I be jealous?' Finn had asked jokingly.

'I can assure you, as much as I like Fergus, I do not feel the same about him as I feel about you, Finn Cassidy.'

Not long after that, we had scrambled our way up to the bedroom, ripping each other's clothes off on the way.

In fact, I think as I lie in bed gazing at Finn, most of mine are likely still at various points along the staircase.

There's some wriggling at the end of the bed, and Fergus pops his head up.

'Do you want to go out?' I whisper, as he pricks his ears up. 'Come on then.'

I slip on my unused pyjamas from last night, and my flip-flops, and Fergus and I head downstairs. I find the key that opens the door that leads out into the back garden, but as I'd suspected, I don't need it, the door is already unlocked, so I let Fergus out to do his business.

Fergus immediately heads towards the gap in the fence that leads towards the lake.

'Oh no you don't!' I tell him. 'Not after last time!' But it's too late; Fergus has squeezed through the gap and scampered off.

'Wait!' I call to the disappearing dog. 'Fergus, stop!'

I squeeze through after him and sprint along the path in the hope Fergus has stopped to sniff at something interesting and I can catch up with him. But I get further and further along the path and there's no sign of him.

'Fergus, you terror,' I call, starting to get worried. Surely he wouldn't be silly enough to swim out into the lake after what happened yesterday? 'Fergus,' I call a little louder. 'Where are you?'

Suddenly, an animal does appear. It's not the scruffy brown dog I'm hoping to see, but a much bigger animal. It appears as if from nowhere, like its counterpart in Ballykiltara Park, but this time it's not a brown stag I see in front of me, but a pure white one.

We stand for a moment, staring at each other.

I don't know what the stag is thinking, all I know is I'm completely transfixed. It looks like a normal stag, powerful, with large antlers that stand majestically on the top of his head, but this stag is pure white – exactly as Jackie had described it to us on the boat. I look at the eyes staring back into mine; they're dark, not red like an albino animal would have.

'Were you watching me last night?' I ask. I'm not sure what I expect the stag to do by means of a reply, but to my surprise it moves its head up and down.

Oh wow, it understands me! I think joyously. Then a dragonfly buzzes past my ear and I realise the stag was simply shaking an insect from its nose.

The stag turns its head and begins to move away.

'Wait!' I call. 'Don't go.'

But the stag trots slowly away down the path. He pauses for a moment to look back at me.

'You want me to follow you?' I ask, feeling like I'm in a Lassie film, or an Enid Blyton book. The stag doesn't reply; he merely continues on his way down the path towards the lake.

So I follow him.

When we get to the edge of the lake, the stag stops to take a drink. I watch from a short distance as he bows his head gracefully and laps from the cool water.

I'm just thinking to myself how amazing this is to watch, when something even more astounding happens.

In the sky above us a large black bird appears. As I look on, it descends towards the stag, flapping its wings to steer it in the right direction.

I think for one moment the bird might actually be about to land on the stag's antlers as I watch in total amazement this strange scene taking place in front of me. But it doesn't, it simply drops right down in front of the stag's face, and looks deep into its eyes.

Oh my goodness . . . it's a raven again, I realise now that the bird is near enough to see properly. Could it be the same one from the house?

I watch the stag and the raven interact with each other for a few more seconds, and then the stag moves benignly away from its place on the edge of the lake, disappearing into the head-high undergrowth that lines both sides of the path.

The raven now takes the stag's place at the water's edge; he too takes a drink before flapping his wings and soaring majestically up into the morning sky.

I run down the path after him. This can't be a coincidence, surely – to see a rare white stag and then a black raven virtually playing together? But as I reach the water's edge all I see is the raven continuing to fly in a direct line towards Rafferty Island and the ruined abbey.

I watch as he becomes a tiny black dot in the blue sky, and then disappears.

I stand on the edge of the lake and think.

Donal had said the raven was seen as a messenger in Celtic mythology; was this raven trying to send me a message again? Mad as it sounded, I couldn't deny the raven had helped me to find the cellar last time he was close by, and Finn had said the other day there was a black bird that could have been the raven in the house, stubbornly refusing to leave.

This has to be some sort of message, it has to, it's all too weird otherwise. I mean, what are the chances of seeing a white stag, let alone one frolicking with a raven!

I try to recall what Jackie had said about seeing a white stag; I know it had some special significance. He'd said when he saw one he'd been up to no good, poaching. But I wasn't doing anything wrong here on the edge of the lake looking for Fergus . . .

Fergus, I'd forgotten about him!

I look to my left along the edge of the lake, and then to my right, and my heart leaps as I see him sniffing at the edge of the water about twenty metres away.

'Fergus!' I call. 'Fergus, come back here!'

Fergus looks up and sees me, and to my relief comes splashing back along the water's edge.

'Fergus, where have you been?' I ask, ruffling his head. 'You mustn't keep running off like this, it's dangerous. The stag and raven won't rescue you if you get into trouble – you're trespassing on their territory!'

I'm joking when I tell Fergus that, but something I say resonates with me.

Wait . . . trespassing. Now I remember what Jackie said: the Celts believed if you saw a white stag you were transgressing, breaking some taboo. It brought a message from the otherworld . . . but what am I transgressing against and what message can be so important that both a white stag and a raven appear at once?'

I look out to where the raven had flown, out across to the island, and suddenly it hits me.

'Fergus! I have it! Come on, we need to get back to Finn. I might be transgressing, but I believe I'm supposed to do it!'

Thirty-Nine

'OK, tell me again why I'm rowing you across this lake?' Finn asks as we set off with Fergus in a little rowing boat that we'd discovered hidden in the back garden in a wooden shed under a lot of other junk. 'I wish we'd known this was here yesterday,' Finn had said as we'd dragged it down to the lake.

'Because I need to return to the abbey,' I tell him, my eyes constantly trained on the island in the distance. 'I think it might hold the key to all this.'

'Yes, I get that; you told me loudly enough when you woke me up this morning. But why you think that – that's the part I'm not too sure about.'

When Fergus and I had got back to the house this morning, we'd lost no time in waking Finn and telling him what had happened. Finn had listened in his usual calm way, and then insisted that we eat breakfast and get dressed before we did anything too hasty.

I tell Finn in more detail now about the white stag and the raven. I'd felt embarrassed to tell him earlier – it all sounded a bit bizarre, even to me, and I'd seen it with my own eyes.

'I've heard there's white deer around here,' Finn says when I've finished telling him exactly what took place. 'But I've never seen one myself. It's the sort of thing that's only talked about in hushed tones by those in the know. You'll need to keep it quiet, Ren. White deer, especially stags, are worth a fortune to hunters. People will pay a good price to have a white stag's head mounted on their walls.'

'Eww,' I say, wrinkling up my nose. 'Jackie warned us of that too. It's horrible. I don't understand why anyone would ever think that looks good. No animal can ever be as beautiful or as majestic as it is when it's living and breathing.'

'I totally agree. Do you think it was the stag that you saw last night when we were in the woods? That's why I was concerned about the horses taking fright. All the previous sightings I've heard about have taken place around the hidden lake, not on this one.'

'I think it might have been. So you believe me then, about the stag and the raven?'

'Why wouldn't I?' Finn says, looking behind him to check we're heading in the right direction. 'This is Ireland, Ren; there's more strange tales told over pints of Guinness in this country than anywhere else in the world. And I'm not sure what it is about you, but since you've been here in Ballykiltara you've managed to find yourself in the middle of most of them.'

I smile. 'You're not far wrong there.'

I stroke Fergus as we make our way further across the lake. Finn's strong arms flexing underneath his tight T-shirt is almost as pleasant a sight as the misty view across the lake towards the island, and I find my eyes torn between the two magnificent spectacles.

Once we reach the island, Finn steers the boat towards the wooden jetty as expertly as Jackie had done on my previous visit. Fergus leaps on to dry land while I clamber out and pull the boat in a bit tighter with the rope. Finn then helps me to attach the rope to the jetty.

'Right,' Finn says, looking around. 'Now we're here, what are we looking for?'

I lead him up towards the ruined abbey with Fergus bounding out in front of us.

'We're looking for these.' I show him the photo of the stone crosses from the cellar on my phone. 'There's quite a few of them dotted around in the abbey, I saw them last time I was here with Kiki.'

'What about that one?' Finn says, pointing to the large cross that stands in the chapel next to the abbey, where Kiki and I had made our wishes. 'Is that the kind of thing you mean?'

'Yes ... a bit like that, only I think the ones we're looking for will be carved into the stone. However,' I say as I stare at the cross, 'perhaps we should look at this one first.'

I hurry across to the stone and begin examining the designs carved all over it. 'Look at this pattern engraved on the ring and stem of the stonework,' I call, running my hands over it. 'I wonder if it means something?'

The pattern looks similar to many of the other designs I've been looking at over the last couple of days in the books Donal and Father Duffy left me – intricate scrollwork, occasional human figures and rudimentary animals all worked into the design. But although a lot of the patterns had been pretty, they had meant little to me, whereas this one seems familiar.

'Look at these people,' I say to Finn as he catches up with me. 'Do they look like monks to you?'

Finn inspects the stonework. 'Well, they have hoods.'

'But one of them is holding a cross too. Look, follow the pattern around the circle ... the figures are joined by more hooded figures, and then comes this wavy pattern that looks like water, then it goes back to figures, but fewer of them than before. Then there's a sort of building, before the whole thing starts again. There's also this –' I point to an engraving of a bird. 'It looks like a raven.'

Finn pulls a face. 'It might be, I suppose.'

'And this –' I point to a horned animal. 'It could be a stag?'

'Yeah ... ' Finn sounds unconvinced. 'It could well be. But even if they are what you say, what does it all mean?'

I spin excitedly to face him. 'It means, Finn, that the answer to the mystery of The Welcome House could be very close by indeed!'

After I've taken photos of the patterns on the cross, we spend the next hour or so on the island, looking for something that might lead us towards a solution to this mystery.

'Ren, we've looked everywhere now,' Finn says patiently. 'There's nothing either here in the ruins of this abbey, or anywhere else on this tiny island.'

'There has to be,' I say, looking at the photo I've taken of the engravings on the stone cross. 'I just know there is.'

'Look I know you're determined to get to the bottom of all this, but I need to get back. I've told Donal I'll be a bit late in this morning, but it will be afternoon before I get to the hotel at this rate.'

'Yes, I know, and I really appreciate you helping me with

322

this, Finn.' I take another look around me. 'I know you're hiding something!' I call to the island. 'If only you'd help me find what it is!'

I turn to Finn. He's looking all around him too, and he seems worried.

'Have you seen Fergus?' he asks.

'Not for a while. The last time I saw him, we were in the abbey.'

'Me too. Fergus!' Finn calls, walking back towards the abbey ruins. 'Fergus, come on boy!' He lets out a shrill whistle, and then stands still in case he can hear his dog.

'What is it with your dog and running away?' I ask, hurrying along next to him.

'He's independent,' Finn says, scanning the island for a sign of Fergus as we walk.

'That's one word for it.'

We reach the ruined abbey and Finn immediately clambers inside and calls for Fergus once more. I hesitate in the ruined archway, in case he wanders by outside.

It's then that I see it – the raven. He swoops in low above my head so I can't miss him, and then he flies up high above the abbey, fluttering down so he can perch on one of the inner walls.

'Finn! Over here,' I call, rushing as fast as I can over the remains of low walls and through stone archways that would once have been entrances to the abbey's many rooms. 'Where the raven is perching.'

I see Finn's head turn and he hurries towards the bird, but I reach him first.

'What is it?' I ask the bird, who is gazing intently at me. 'Have you got another message?'

The raven turns his head, and jabs with his beak.

'What's it doing?' Finn whispers, as he reaches my side.

'I think it's pointing to something.'

'Don't be daft, Ren! How can it point, it's a bird.'

'Ravens are very intelligent – I looked them up after I found this one the first time.' I watch the raven as it watches us, then it jabs with its beak again. 'They're supposed to be as clever as chimps and dolphins. Sometimes they even mimic human speech.'

'Maybe it can tell us exactly where Fergus is then?' Finn says in a sarcastic tone. 'Where's my dog, Mr Bird, eh? Where's Fergus?'

Not surprisingly the bird doesn't answer; he merely flaps his wings and moves further along the wall. Then he lets out a low croaking sound.

'You see?' Finn says as I follow the bird along the wall. 'No idea.'

'What's this?' I ask, noticing a narrow gap in the wall directly below where the raven perches. 'Look at these Celtic crosses either side of it, they're just like the ones on the front of the books, and the ones I saw in the cellar at The Welcome House. Do you think it might be a passageway?'

Finn comes over as I'm shining the light from my phone's torch into the gap. 'It looks a bit like one. Fergus!' he calls into the gap. 'Fergus, are you in there?'

There's a distant bark.

'It's him!' Finn says, turning to me. 'But how the hell are we going to fit into the gap? It's dog size, but not human size.'

'Fergus!' I call into the narrow passageway, 'Come back up here, good boy!'

But the only response is another distant bark.

'What are we going to do?' Finn asks, looking genuinely frightened. 'He's obviously trapped.'

I turn off the torch on my phone and look at my photos instead.

'Let me try something,' I say, moving Finn to one side. I study my phone, and then I push hard on one of the crosses. Before Finn can say anything, I move to the second cross and do the same, but this time I push twice.

Nothing happens.

'What are you doing?' Finn asks.

'Trying something. OK, let's do it this way.' I repeat the action, but the opposite way round. To my delight, and Finn's amazement, the opening to the tunnel widens slightly.

'What the hell?' Finn says, as I poke my head through the gap, and then manage to slide my body through one shoulder at a time. 'How did you do that?'

'I said there was some sort of code on the cross, and there is. That's what I used to open the tunnel up. What are you doing?'

'I'm coming with you.' Finn has to push hard to make his broad body squeeze through the narrow gap. 'Jeez, those monks must have been tiny to squeeze through here.'

'That's it!' I squeal as Finn manages to get his whole body through the gap. 'This is exactly what that pattern on the cross shows: a secret passageway that the monks must have used to get from the abbey to The Welcome House! Why didn't I think of it before? This must be how they smuggled the travelling monks away from Ballykiltara so they could hide them at the abbey and allow them to complete their illuminated pages in secret.'

'You've got all that from a tunnel?' Even though Finn has

made it through the gap he has to bend his head to fit inside the low passageway.

'No, I got all that from the pattern on the cross – that's what those engravings are all about. They tell the story of how the monks hid their elders. Look –' I show him the phone. 'There's the water in between the two groups of monks, and that explains why there are less of them on the other side. It's not because they've disappeared, but because they've been hidden away.'

Finn looks at me, bewildered. 'And this –' I point to another of the engravings. 'This little pattern told me the order to push those crosses in to make the opening of the tunnel wider. It all makes sense now.'

'Does it?' Finn peers down the tunnel. 'Let's find Fergus, shall we, and then I'll tell you if it makes sense.'

Finn lights up his own phone now and slowly we make our way along the dark and narrow stone tunnel, calling Fergus's name as we go. Eventually we come across him cowering in a narrow alcove that cuts into the side of the main passageway.

'Hey, boy, it's OK,' Finn says, kneeling down next to him. 'We're here now.'

I hold my torch up to the wall next to him. 'It's a dead end,' I say, not trying to hide the disappointment in my voice. 'That's why he didn't go any further.'

'Right, now we've found Fergus, let's get back up to the surface. We don't want that gap to close up and trap us in here.'

'It won't close on its own,' I assure him. 'This isn't magic, you know. The reason the stones widened was because I set in motion some sort of pulley system that the monks must have installed to keep the passageway secret, should anyone come across it.'

'Yes, I knew that,' Finn says, standing up. 'Of course I did.'

'Good, then you won't mind if I press this –' Holding up my phone, I study the next set of repeat engravings from my photos of the high cross, and I press a series of smaller crosses etched on the wall around the alcove that Fergus had been sitting in.

The wall the dog had been cowering against a few moments ago slides open.

'Are you coming?' I ask an astonished Finn.

'Do I have a choice?' he says, as he and Fergus follow me down the next part of the tunnel.

We don't encounter any more dead ends for quite some time, until we suddenly come across a simple, but very solid wooden door blocking our way. There doesn't appear to be a handle or lock like a normal door would have, only a series of black iron bars fastening the wood together, and some wrought-iron decoration.

'What's the code this time?' Finn asks, his eyes searching the wall for crosses that I can press.

'I'm not sure. There don't seem to be any engravings this time.' I look at the photos once more, and then I scroll back to my photos of Father Duffy's books. 'The next symbol on the cross is a sort of scroll – the same one is on the books too. I wonder if that's relevant?'

Finn holds his torch up to the door. 'What about that iron decoration in the middle – is that anything similar to your photo?'

'It is a bit. I wonder . . . ?'

I run my hand over the black metal detailing in the centre of the heavy wooden door, and I find that it moves slightly under my touch. 'It's loose,' I tell Finn, as I move my hand backwards and forwards over the scroll until something begins to shift.

327

'Keep going,' Finn encourages as Fergus barks.

I move my hand in a clockwise direction over the metal, but nothing happens, so I change to an anti-clockwise direction and suddenly I hear a click.

'Let's give the door a push now,' Finn says, moving in behind me. But I don't need Finn's extra strength, because the door is already swinging open.

I hurry into what at first appears to be a cave, but as I hold up my torch, and Finn does the same with his, I realise we've arrived in the cellar of The Welcome House.

Wondering how I hadn't noticed the door the last time I was in the cellar, I close it to and hold my phone up to study the back of the door. It's covered in stone so it blends in with the rest of the cellar. There are two Celtic crosses etched into the wall either side of the doorway.

'We're back in The Welcome House,' I tell Finn eagerly. 'I was right: this *is* the secret tunnel that leads from the original house out to the abbey. This must be why that rumour started that if you came down to the cellar you didn't come back. You didn't disappear, like people thought; you just came out the other side in the abbey. I can't believe we've discovered the monks' secret. How exciting is that?'

'Very,' Finn says, in a much calmer-sounding voice than mine. 'I'm assuming that those steps over there lead back up to the house?'

'Yes, they come out in the sitting room, behind the bookcase.'

'And I'm assuming that when you came down here last time you locked the cellar door behind you?'

'Yes I— Oh . . .' I say, as I realise where Finn is going with this.

'I can only surmise from your tone that you didn't happen to bring the key with you on this little trip?'

I shake my head.

'So other than going all the way back through that tunnel, how are we supposed to get into the house?'

Forty

'How long do you think Kiki will take to get here?' Finn asks as we sit on the floor of the cellar waiting for her to arrive.

'Not too long. But she doesn't have the car, so she'll probably have to walk up here.'

'She might ask Eddie?' Finn says hopefully.

'No, I told her to come alone. The less people that know about this, the better.'

Luckily, Finn was able to get a phone signal when we went all the way to the top of the cellar steps and held his phone aloft. So he'd rung Kiki and I'd told her where we were, and what she needed to do to find us. After that, all we could do was sit back and wait.

'Yes, you're probably right,' Finn agrees. 'So, you've found the secret passageway that the monks used to hide people away on Rafferty Island, but you've not found any more of the elusive illuminated pages.'

'I know. There was nothing in the tunnel that could have been used to hide them, was there?'

Finn shakes his head. 'Nope. If there was, I didn't see it.'

I sigh. 'Maybe it was just wishful thinking on Father Duffy's part?'

'Perhaps. Or maybe someone got to them first.'

'How do you mean?'

'Think about it, Ren,' Finn says, stroking Fergus's head, which is resting on his knee. 'If *you* could find this passage, why couldn't someone else know it was here too?'

He's right. I'd been congratulating myself as if I was some kind of genius for figuring out the secret passageway, but it hadn't been that hard.

'My guess is whoever looks after this house knows all its ins, outs *and* secret tunnels.'

'You think they might have got to the pages first?'

'It's possible.'

'But why? What would they do with them? They can't have sold them or donated them to a museum, otherwise we'd know about them. I did some research before I started this search and there's no record of any pages ever being found from the Book of Tara, but Father Duffy insists there are several missing.'

'Looks like you're back to square one. Find the caretaker of The Welcome House and you might find the missing pages too.'

Suddenly we hear noises coming from the top of the staircase. It sounds like things being thrown to the ground.

'It's Kiki! She's moving all the books from the shelves.'

I dash to the top of the stone steps. 'Kiki, is that you? We're right here, behind the door.'

'Yes, Ren, it's me!' Kiki sounds out of breath. 'Give me a minute!'

The sound of books being thrown to the ground stops and then we hear a dragging noise.

'She's moving the bookcase,' I tell Finn, who's waiting at the bottom of the steps with Fergus. 'It might take her a while. It's really heavy.'

But far sooner than I'd expected, I hear a key being put into the door and turned, and then the staircase is flooded with light as the door swings open.

'Ren!' Kiki flings her arms around me. 'How did you get here?'

Fergus bounds up the stairs behind me and through the door, and I hear Finn following on.

'Let's get everyone out and then I'll explain,' I tell her, moving forward into the sitting room. 'Oh, Eddie,' I say, surprised to see him there. 'I didn't know you were with Kiki.'

'Just as well I was,' Eddie says. 'That bookcase weighs a ton.'

'Eddie was passing by on his motorbike and saw me walking up here,' Kiki explains. 'He insisted on bringing me the rest of the way.'

Finn looks at his watch. 'Aren't you supposed to be working, Eddie? If we weren't so grateful for being let out of that cellar, I'd tell you off for being with Kiki on the hotel's time.'

'So where does the tunnel lead to?' Eddie asks, looking with interest through the cellar door.

'Long story,' Finn says, looking at me. 'Shall I pop the kettle on and then we can tell you all about it.'

'No, let me,' Eddie says. 'You two look like you need a sit down after all your adventures.'

I let Finn tell the lion's share of the story to Kiki and Eddie, while we sit drinking tea in the dishevelled sitting room.

Something was bugging me, and I wasn't sure what, so I was happy for Finn to do most of the talking.

'Just as well we were here to help,' Eddie says, smiling at Kiki. 'How's your tea?' he asks me. 'You're a bit quiet, if you don't mind me saying, miss?'

I stare down into my half-drunk mug of tea.

'Where did you get this from, Eddie?' I ask, looking up from my mug at him. 'The tea, I mean.'

Eddie looks puzzled. 'The kitchen, where else, miss?'

'But Finn said we were out of tea this morning. He said he'd used the last teabag at breakfast, and we'd need to get some more.'

Eddie shrugs. 'I don't know, do I?' he says, looking at Finn and then Kiki. 'There was tea in the kitchen when I got there.'

'Maybe Eddie found some that you'd missed?' Kiki suggests. 'Why does it matter so much, Ren?'

I look suspiciously at Eddie, who doesn't return my stare. He looks down into his own empty mug now, no doubt wishing there was something left for him to drink.

'Eddie, when we came up from the cellar, you asked where the tunnel led to. How did you know there was a tunnel that led from the cellar? I never told Kiki when I spoke to her on the phone. I only gave her directions where to find us.'

'I must have guessed.' Eddie looks distinctly uncomfortable as he fidgets in his chair.

'It's funny you should say that, Ren,' Kiki says, looking at Eddie, 'because I was going to ask how you knew where the key for the cellar door was.'

'You told me, that's how,' Eddie says, his face reddening.

'No, I didn't. I told you I was going up to The Welcome House because Ren and Finn were stuck in the cellar, and as soon as we got here you rushed upstairs to get the key while I was busy pulling books from the shelves. I didn't have time to ask you how you knew where it was.'

'Eddie?' Finn asks, looking at him. 'How *did* you know?'

'Maybe I should be getting back to work,' Eddie says hurriedly, standing up. 'Donal will be wondering where I am.'

'Donal will be wondering where I am too. But I'm in charge and I say you stay here for now.'

'Wait there a moment,' I say, standing up. 'I'll be right back.' I dash upstairs to the bedroom where Finn and I had slept last night and I pause at the door.

I thought so.

I walk calmly back downstairs and enter the sitting room, but I don't sit down.

'Finn,' I ask, 'did you make the bed before we left this morning?'

'What?' Finn asks, looking at me like I've flipped.

'Did you make the bed we slept in last night?'

Kiki gasps in delight.

'No, sorry,' Finn says, mystified now. 'We were in a bit of a hurry.'

'I didn't make it either, and yet it's been made. How do you explain that, Eddie?'

Eddie doesn't speak. He just looks down into his lap.

'Eddie, are you the caretaker of The Welcome House? Has it been you all along?'

Forty-One

We all stare at Eddie.

'Don't be silly, Ren,' Kiki says. 'How could it be Eddie? He'd have told us ages ago if it was, wouldn't you, Eddie?'

Eddie looks at Kiki, 'I'm sorry, Kiki,' he says quietly. 'I never wanted to hide it from anyone, especially you.'

'It is you then?' I say gently, as Kiki looks like she might burst into tears. 'You're the one behind everything?'

'Not everything,' Eddie says, looking at me now. 'I only look after the house, I'm not a thief or anything.'

'We never said you were.' I turn to Finn; he looks as shocked as I am. 'Perhaps you'd better tell us the whole story, Eddie?'

'I will, but you must all promise this goes no further than these four walls, OK?'

We all nod. 'Of course,' I promise. 'You have our word.'

'Right then.' Eddie takes a deep breath. 'The protection of this house has been entrusted to my family for as long as anyone can remember. I didn't know anything about it until me da, on his deathbed, told me that it was him who looked after the place. My face looked much like yours all do now when he told me.'

Eddie pauses for a moment to remember.

'I had no idea me da was the mystery caretaker everyone talked about. He wasn't the type of fella I expected would look after a house. Me da was a bricklayer by trade, straight as a die, and a man of few words. Me mam would never have believed he came here to clean and change beds!' Eddie smiles for a moment. 'But da said it was an O'Grady tradition for the eldest male of the family to care for this place. He didn't know when the custom began, though he thought it might have been when the monks abandoned the abbey. They'd have wanted to leave the house with someone they trusted to protect it and its secrets. All I know is, generations of O'Gradys have taken on the role without questioning why. Me granddad had passed it on to me da when he could no longer do it, and now it's my turn. Me da made me promise I wouldn't tell no one, not even Orla. He said when the time came I was to pass the job on to my own son, if I had one, but in the meantime I was to keep it a secret. So I've been doing it ever since.' Eddie shrugs. 'That's it. That's the whole story.'

We sit in silence for a moment, trying to take this in.

'Is that why you said the person you saw early one morning was tall and broad, so it would deflect suspicion from you?' I ask, looking at Eddie's slight frame sitting in the chair.

Eddie nods.

'And why you tried to scare me off with tales of bad things happening in the cellar?'

'Sort of. I made that sound a lot worse than it was. There are

336

tales of people disappearing down there – I just embellished them a little. I thought it might scare you off from investigating the house any further. But it didn't, did it?' Eddie says ruefully. 'You kept pushing and pushing to find the truth.'

'Sorry about that,' I say, meaning it. 'I was prepared to give up the search for the owner after Donal gave me grief at the quiz. He made me think hard about why I was doing this and whether I should carry on with it.'

'Why did you then?' Eddie asks. 'I tried everything to put you off.'

'It was Father Duffy. He told me all about the illuminated manuscripts the monks left behind, and how pages of them were missing. Much like your family secret, these manuscripts have been passed down from priest to priest. As each new priest took over Ballykiltara church, they were shown the manuscripts and told the tale of how the books were originally created over on Rafferty Island while the monks hid from the Vikings. I wanted to help him find the missing pages, to give something back to the Celtic monks who worked so hard to complete these beautiful books.' I hesitate. 'You see, even though I'm English, I've been told I might be distantly related to one of the monks who came to Tara from Lindisfarne.'

'I told you, I knew you had Celtic blood when I first met you,' Finn says, smiling at me. 'It's partly your hair, but mostly your attitude.'

'Thanks!'

But instead of making fun like Finn, Eddie frowns. 'What sort of pages are you looking for?'

'Illuminated pages – intricate drawings and paintings on old paper.'

'Like biblical stuff?'

'Yes exactly that, why?'

'Because I think I know where they are.'

He jumps up, but then hesitates. 'If I find them for you, do you promise not to tell anyone what I've told you about today – about me and my family?'

'Eddie, we've already told you we won't say anything,' I assure him.

'Not even to Father Duffy? If this *is* what you're looking for, he'll wonder where they came from.'

'I think he'll just be pleased to have them back. He won't worry too much about the source.'

'OK then,' Eddie says, and we all watch in silence as he goes to the back of the bookcase. I think he's going to disappear down into the cellar, to follow the tunnel that Finn and I came through, but he doesn't; he crouches down behind the empty bookcase and begins to feel underneath it.

'Here,' he says, pulling something free. 'I think this might be what you want.'

Eddie hands me a flat brown paper package. I look at him in astonishment, before I begin to prise it open gently, in case this is what Eddie seems to think it might be.

Wrapped inside several sheets of brown paper is a battered leather folder held together with leather cord. With the others watching my every move, I manage to untie the cord. Then using the cotton gloves Father Duffy left behind, I open up the folder. Inside I find a sheet of parchment that looks very much like the pages in Father Duffy's books; it's covered in tiny, ornate script, and one of the letters at the beginning of the page has been illustrated with brightly coloured inks that don't seem to have faded at all. I gingerly lift the first page, and find another piece of parchment, and underneath that one another, all covered with script and illuminated illustrations.

'There must be about a dozen pages here,' I say excitedly. 'This is it! These are the missing pages!'

'How did you know they were under there, Eddie?' Finn asks.

'Because I put them there,' Eddie says. 'I was told about the passageway that you two went down when I was told about the O'Gradys looking after the house. Part of our job in protecting the house over the years has been to protect those documents too – until their rightful owner would come along to collect them, me da said. They used to be kept in the passageway, tucked in a little alcove. But I was worried that water might seep into that passage and ruin them, so I moved them into the house. I had to hide them somewhere, so I thought why not hide pages underneath pages.'

I have to smile. It's so obvious.

'I didn't know Father Duffy was looking for them though, or I'd have given them to him.'

'No, you did the right thing,' I tell him. 'You were told to protect the house and these pages, and that's exactly what you did do – admirably. And protecting the house is what you will continue to do in the future – won't he?' I turn to Finn and an unusually quiet Kiki.

'Of course,' Finn says. 'It's good to know the house is in safe hands.'

'Kiki?'

'Yes, I'm sure you'll continue to do a great job,' Kiki says flatly.

'Kiki, I'm sorry I couldn't tell you,' Eddie says, going over to where Kiki sits. He kneels down next to her chair. 'But you understand why, don't you?'

'I guess. I don't like being lied to, that's all.'

'I didn't lie to you, ever.' Eddie insists. 'I just didn't tell you the truth. I wanted to, if it makes any difference, but I couldn't break my family's vow.'

'He's right, Kiki,' I say. 'Much as I wanted to know who the caretaker was of this place, I wouldn't have wanted Eddie to come out and tell me – it wouldn't have been right. Even though we know now, we're the only ones that do, and we're going to keep this a secret, aren't we?'

Kiki looks at me and nods. Then she gazes down at Eddie.

'No more secrets OK?' she insists, to Eddie's obvious delight. 'Next time I won't be so forgiving. And I can assure you, you don't want Kiki Fisher as an enemy.'

Eddie takes Kiki's hand and kisses the back of it, then he looks into her eyes with such tenderness and love that I'm quite taken aback.

I knew Kiki and Eddie were fond of each other, but I hadn't realised how much until I see the look that passes between them.

'Well, I think this calls for a celebration!' Finn says. 'Let's all recover from this morning's events, and tonight we'll re-group and have a little get-together at The Stag – my treat.'

We all give a cheer.

'Right, Eddie. We'd better be getting back to work – Donal will be having kittens, puppies and who knows what else if we're gone for much longer.'

'Yes, boss!' Eddie salutes.

'Are you girls going to stay here?' Finn asks.

340

'Yes, I'm going to be needing Kiki's help for a while,' I say, looking at Kiki.

Kiki groans. 'Are we back to work again?'

'Not just yet. No, this afternoon I'm going to need your help packing. It's time I left this house for someone that really needs it. I'm moving back to the hotel.'

I turn to Finn, who looks as pleased as I feel at the thought of me returning to The Stag.

After all, without a stag, a raven, and a mischievous dog we wouldn't be where we are now...

Forty-Two

A few hours later, my things are all packed up and ready to go back to the hotel. The time has come to say a grateful goodbye and thank you to The Welcome House.

'Thank you,' I whisper, standing alone in the middle of the hall, while Kiki takes the last of my bags down to the car. 'You've helped me more than you could ever know.'

The house is silent, but as I leave and close the front door behind me, I'm sure I hear it say, 'You're welcome.' With a shake of my head, I put it down to the strong wind that's blowing through the trees at the bottom of the path.

On our arrival at the hotel we're welcomed by Donal, who rushes over to greet me.

'Did you find them?' he asks.

'I did,' I tell him gleefully.

Donal claps his hands together in delight. 'How?'

'Let's just say we were right about the symbols,' I say. 'The clues were right in front of us all along, and the map was correct. Would you like to see the pages before I give them to Father Duffy?'

'Oh, yes, I would like that very much,' Donal says in a hushed voice.

'Let me get unpacked first, and I'll bring them down before I go over to see Father Duffy before dinner.'

When I arrive at Father Duffy's house and present the pages to him, I'm still thinking about the sheer pleasure and enjoyment Donal had derived from seeing them. It prompts me to make a suggestion: now that Father Duffy has the full set, maybe the time has come to bring the Book of Tara out of hiding.

'I think you could be right, Ren,' he says, nodding slowly. 'The monks made these books to keep the stories of the Gospels alive. They only hid them away in order to preserve them. Now that the threat of the Norsemen has gone and it's safe to bring the Book of Tara into the open, I'm sure the monks would want as many people as possible to see it.' He smiles. 'It looks as if they were right: our red-headed saviour did come to save the day.'

'I don't know about that, Father Duffy,' I say, blushing. 'But I'm pleased the pages are back where they belong.'

'So did you solve the mystery of The Welcome House too?'

I shake my head. 'Not fully, no. I think that particular legend is best left alone now we have the pages back, don't you?'

Father Duffy smiles an enigmatic smile. 'I couldn't agree more. We must let the house continue to work its magic for generations to come, just as it has done for you, my dear . . .'

*

343

I'm on my way back from Father Duffy's house, heading towards the hotel, when the wind, which has been gusting since I left The Welcome House, suddenly becomes even stronger.

Goodness, I'll be blown away if you get any stormier, I think as I lean into the wind. But suddenly the wind changes direction and pushes me hard from behind. The gust is so strong, and I'm so taken by surprise, that it pushes me out into the road.

A Land Rover has to brake hard to avoid hitting me.

'Are you OK?' A head appears from the driver's window as I gather myself and hop back on to the pavement.

'Yes, I'm so sorry,' I call back. 'The wind changed direction and blew me out into the road.'

'It's Ren, isn't it?' the driver says, and as I look properly at him I realise it's Dermot, the owner of the hotel.

'Yes, it is. Hello.'

Dermot pulls into the kerb to allow traffic to pass, then he gets out and comes over to me.

'Are you sure you're OK? Would you like a lift to the hotel? We're on our way there ourselves.'

I look back at the vehicle and see a dark-haired woman sitting in the passenger seat.

'That's my wife, Darcy,' Dermot explains. 'We're just popping into The Stag to see how Megan is getting on.'

'She's doing very well, from what I've seen. Yes, if it's no trouble, I'd be grateful for a lift. This wind is so strong, it's an effort to stay on the pavement.'

Dermot ushers me to the Land Rover and opens the door for me.

'Hello,' I say to Darcy as I climb into the back seat.

'Hi,' she says, turning and smiling at me. 'I saw what happened – did the wind suddenly change?'

'It sure did,' I say as Dermot gets into the driver's seat beside her. 'I've never felt such a strong shift in wind direction.'

Darcy looks purposefully at Dermot, who shrugs in reply before pulling out into the traffic.

'Ren, that's your name, isn't it?' Darcy asks, turning to look at me again.

'Yes.'

'Ren, what I'm about to ask you may sound odd ... but has anything *strange* happened to you since you've been here in Ballykiltara?'

It's a short journey, but by the time we arrive at the hotel, Darcy and I have managed to cover a lot of ground.

Dermot pulls up just to the side of the hotel steps and then he too turns to face me. 'When I first came to live on Tara, I wasn't a believer in this so-called magic that seems to operate around here.'

'Dermot, it's not "so-called",' Darcy corrects him. 'You've seen it happen yourself, many a time.'

'Doesn't mean I have to fully believe it, eh, Ren?' he winks. Darcy growls.

'If you remember rightly, Darcy, you didn't believe either when you first came to the island!' he reminds her.

'That's true, I didn't. But I allowed the magic to change me, and change me for the better. You have to accept the change first, and when you do, life suddenly becomes a lot clearer. Whatever Dermot says, he accepted the change, and so did our lovely Finn – who I believe you know well?'

'Er ... yes, sort of,' I reply, unsure how much they know.

Gossip seems to spread pretty quickly at the hotel, but could it have spread to the owners too?

'There is something very unusual about anything associated with Tara,' Darcy continues. 'I don't know why or how, but there is, and if you feel the wind change, Ren, like you did today – and so strongly too – then it's time for you to change. My advice to you is, don't fight it.'

'And there ends the sermon,' Dermot says, grinning at me. 'I must apologise for my wife, she's passionate about helping people and there's no stopping her when she finds someone she considers to be in need. Today, Ren, I'm afraid that was you.'

'No need to apologise,' I smile. 'There is something a bit odd and a bit magical about this place, I have to agree. But how it's going to change me, I'm not quite sure.'

'You'll know soon enough,' Darcy says. 'Be sure to let me know if you need any help. I was like you once, Ren ... lost. The spirit of Tara helped me find happiness, just as I know it's going to help you.'

'Right, let's leave young Ren alone now,' Dermot says. 'I need to park this thing, otherwise they'll all know we're here – if they don't already. Then they'll all start making a fuss. I hate fuss.'

'Thanks for the lift,' I say, climbing out of the car. 'I really appreciate it, and all your advice too.'

'My pleasure,' Darcy says, smiling.

'One more thing,' I say, as something occurs to me. 'I've heard all about the two of you from various different people here at the hotel. I think your story of how you set up your island is fascinating. Has anyone ever written about it?'

'We've had a few articles written, why?'

'Oh nothing, just a thought, that's all.'

'Come on, Darcy,' Dermot calls. 'One of the porters is coming out.'

'Hold on to that thought!' Darcy calls as Dermot begins to pull away. 'See you soon, Ren!' and she waves from the window as Dermot heads towards the guest car park.

'There you are, Ren,' Eddie says as he comes hurrying down the steps towards me. 'How did your visit with Father Duffy go?'

'Very well,' I reply vaguely, my thoughts preoccupied with my trip back to the hotel. 'Don't worry, Eddie, Father Duffy doesn't know anything. He's delighted to finally have his pages back, though.'

'Good. Good.' Eddie's gaze follows the large black Land Rover disappearing into the car park. 'By the way, was that Dermot O'Connell I just saw driving into the guest car park?'

Finn has reserved us a corner table in the bar tonight, which is fine with me. I'm not in the mood for anything elaborate. All I want is a nice cosy evening with my friends, not worrying about anything or anybody.

Kiki is getting ready in the bathroom, and I have a while before our agreed meet-up time, so I decide to take a stroll down to the stables.

As always, the horses have a calming effect on me as I wander through the stable yard, stopping occasionally to stroke any long furry noses that pop over the stable doors.

'How happy you are here,' I tell Alfie as I stop to stroke his black nose. 'This is your perfect home, isn't it, here in this stable. I can't blame you, I always feel happy here too.'

How strange it is that I spend all my time looking for other people's perfect homes, but I've yet to find my own. Not somewhere I can be truly happy anyway.

I think about this as I continue to stroke Alfie's nose. The stable isn't the only place where I feel happy in Ballykiltara, though, is it? I always feel calm here, but I've felt happy most of the time I've been in this little Irish town, probably happier than I've ever felt in my whole life.

I think about what Darcy had said in the car earlier, about how I should allow the change to come, and it's while I'm here, surrounded by animals, that it hits me like a bolt of lightning. Suddenly I know exactly what that change must be.

Our celebratory evening in the bar is a great success. It's everything I'd hoped it would be: chilled, relaxed and filled with laughter. It's such a joy to spend time with Finn, Kiki and Eddie now the weight of The Welcome House isn't on our shoulders.

'I know I shouldn't bring this topic up tonight,' Kiki says after we've eaten and are relaxing with our drinks, Finn and I snuggled into one side of the corner booth, Kiki and Eddie on the other. 'But what are you going to do about Ryan Dempsey? Now we know the secret behind The Welcome House, we know it's never going to be for sale. And you haven't found him an alternative property.'

'You're right, you shouldn't have brought that up tonight,' I tell her. 'This is supposed to be a work-free evening. But, since you have, I'll let you in on what I've decided: I'm going to let this one go.'

Kiki looks stunned, 'No way!'

'Yep. I'm going to have to disappoint Mr Dempsey.'

'Why is that so hard to believe, Kiki?' Finn asks. 'Surely

there have been times when Ren hasn't been able to find a property?'

'Not on my watch,' Kiki says, taking a long sip from her glass. 'No, siree-bob!'

'Perhaps things have changed?' Finn says, squeezing my hand.

'They have indeed,' I say, gazing back at him. 'They've changed quite a lot in fact. It's knowing that I can let the hunt for the perfect property go that has made my next decision so much easier.'

'Ooh, what decision?' Kiki asks. 'It's all coming out tonight!'

'I'm giving up property hunting.'

'What!' she shrieks, so loudly that almost everyone in the bar turns to see what's wrong. 'Sorry,' she whispers. 'What?'

'I'm going to sell my business and give up looking for the perfect home for other people, because I think I've found *my* perfect home. Right here in Ballykiltara.'

'No way!' Kiki says again. 'When did you decide this?'

'Earlier this evening, when I was at the stables. I realised I've been happy since I've been here. I've spent so long searching for other people's perfect homes; I'd neglected to look for one for myself. I knew something felt different about being here almost as soon as I arrived – what, I didn't realise – it was because I'd come somewhere that felt like home.'

'I can't believe you're going to sell your business,' Finn says, looking astonished. 'I thought it meant the world to you?'

'It did. Until I came here, my business was everything to me. Now I realise that was part of my problem; I needed other things in my life to make me truly happy, but I had no idea what those things were until I came to Ballykiltara. I shouldn't have trouble selling the business,' I continue while everyone stares at me in amazement. 'I've had plenty of generous offers in the past, but I've always turned them down because I couldn't see a reason to sell. Now I can.'

'But what will you do here?' Eddie asks. 'If you're not hunting for houses?'

'Once I've found somewhere to live and to work, I'm going to go back to writing.'

'I didn't know you wrote? I mean, I know that's what you told everyone to throw them off the scent, but I didn't know it was the truth.'

'I used to, a long time ago.' I turn to Finn; his astonishment has now waned slightly and he gives me a reassuring nod. 'It was a very special animal who took me away from writing many years ago, and now several special animals have played their part in giving me a reason to go back to it. Finn, I include your Fergus in that.'

'I'm delighted to hear it. Fergus will enjoy having you around.'

'Will *you*?' I whisper.

'You bet I will.' Finn leans in to kiss me, but there's a loud *ahem* from Kiki.

We turn towards her.

'This is all lovely and romantic and everything, and I'm thrilled you're happy, Ren. Really I am. But what about me? If you're going to give up property hunting, you won't need me any more, will you?'

This is the bit I've been dreading – telling Kiki.

'I'm sorry, Kiki; I didn't want to break the news like this. I'd planned to tell you tomorrow, when we were on our own, but—'

Kiki holds up her hand to stop me.

'It's fine,' she says calmly. 'Honestly. As a matter of fact, I have some news that I'd been dreading telling *you* ... ' She looks at Eddie. He nods his encouragement.

'I've decided to stay on in Ballykiltara too – to be with Eddie. But, unlike you, Ren, I'm not sure what I'm going to do here.'

I stare at Kiki – amazed, pleased and excited all at the same time.

'You'll find something,' Eddie says, gazing at her. 'We'll look for it together.'

Kiki nods and squeezes his hand. Beaming happily, she turns back to me. 'I knew this place was magical the minute we arrived here. I told you so, didn't I, Ren?'

'You did indeed,' I have to agree.

'I can probably find you something here at the hotel to tide you over,' Finn says. 'I can't promise it will be as glamorous as being Ren's assistant, but we don't pay too badly, and I hear the boss is quite reasonable.'

Kiki leaps up and flings herself at Finn. 'Finn, you are amazing!' she cries, hugging him. 'Isn't he amazing?' she asks Eddie, turning back to him.

'Cheers, Finn.' Eddie nods gratefully. He wraps his arm tightly around Kiki's shoulders as she returns to him, pulling her even closer.

'What sort of writing are you thinking of doing?' Finn asks, putting his arm around me.

'Anything I can get paid for, to begin with. The sale of the business should support me for a bit while I get started. But I've a couple of ideas I want to pursue in the long term. I'm hoping that *they* will let me write about them,' I say, nodding in the direction of Darcy and Dermot, who have just come into the bar with Megan.

They wave when they see us sitting in the corner, and Eddie practically jumps up and salutes.

'At ease, Eddie,' Finn says. 'You're not on duty.' Finn waves casually at Dermot and Darcy, and Eddie returns to his adoration of Kiki.

'Do you think they'll let you?' Finn asks, continuing our conversation.

'I hope so. I'd love to tell the story of how they came to live on Tara. 'And,' I say, taking a deep breath, because this is the idea closest to my heart, 'I'd like to write a series of children's books – about animals. I mean, I don't know if they'll be published or any—'

Finn stops me by placing his finger on my lips. 'It's a wonderful idea,' he whispers. 'Absolutely perfect for you.'

I smile at him, then I lift my drink from the table and take a reassuring sip. My announcement had taken place a lot quicker than I'd planned, but it had also gone a lot better than I thought it might, and I was over the moon that Kiki would continue to be close by. I'd have missed her terribly if we'd been parted.

'Oh – talking of writing,' I say, suddenly remembering. 'I'm not the only one sitting around this table with a talent for the written word. Am I, Eddie?'

Eddie, hearing his name, tears himself away from Kiki with a puzzled expression on his face.

'That letter you wrote was very eloquent, Eddie. I hope you don't mind me saying I was quite surprised when I realised it was you.'

'What letter?' Eddie asks, looking blankly at me.

'The letter you sent to Sarah asking her to take over as

caretaker for a while. The one you sent when you were scared I'd discover who you were.'

'I didn't send any letter,' Eddie says. 'I thought it was odd when you got that, but I couldn't say anything at the time or I'd have blown my cover.'

'But if you didn't send it, who did? The sender was so concerned for the future of the house, I thought it had to be the caretaker.'

'Have you still got it, Ren?' Finn asks.

'Yes, it should be here in my bag.' I reach into the pocket of my bag where I'd tucked the letter away, and I unfold the stiff parchment paper the letter had been written on.

But nearly all the words, so carefully inscribed in black calligraphy ink, have disappeared; instead they've been replaced by just two words:

Fáilte.

Welcome.

As the others examine the letter in amazement, I sit quietly smiling.

Those two words tell me exactly who sent that original note. Now in its own unique and magical way, the house is telling me that I'm going to be as welcome here in Ballykiltara as it has always been, and I always will be.